Bet Me

Also by Jennifer Crusie

Faking It

Fast Women

Welcome to Temptation

Crazy for You

Tell Me Lies

Jennifer Crusie

Bet Me

St. Martin's Press
New York

www.stmartins.com

Library of Congress Cataloging-in-Publication Data

Crusie, Jennifer.
    Bet me / Jennifer Crusie.—1st U.S. ed.
      p.   cm.
    ISBN 0-312-30346-7
    1. Wagers—Fiction.   I. Title.

PS3553.R7858B48 2004
813'.54—dc22

                    2003058182

10 9 8 7 6 5 4

For
Monica Pradhan McLean

Because her price is above rubies
Which she knows how to invest,
And because every book she writes
is a diamond

 *Acknowledgments*

My Thanks To

Meg Ruley
for selling this book against my better judgment
and for being right again,

Jen Enderlin
for buying this book against my better judgment
and for being right again,

St. Martin's Press
especially John Sargent, Sally Richardson, Matthew Shear,
Kim Cardascia, John Karle, and John Murphy,
for being supportive beyond the call of publishing
(and a big kiss to Sally for matchmaking the movie option),

Mollie Smith
for improving my Web site, organizing my business records,
critiquing my book, and illuminating my life,

Val Taylor
for working with me again
even though I promised her I'd never rewrite this one,

The Ladies of XRom
especially Jo Beverley for coming up with the pumpkin couch,

The Cherries
for critiquing the first scene, researching recipes,
putting up with my moaning, and being Cherries,

and
**The Nantucket Beach Patrol,
Police Department, Fire Department, and
Cottage Hospital Emergency Room Staff,**
whose speed and skill ensured that
this wasn't a posthumous book.
(If you're going to have an asthma attack in the surf,
I strongly recommend you do so in Nantucket.)

Women's total instinct for gambling
is satisfied by marriage.

—Gloria Steinem

Bet
Me

Chapter One

Once upon a time, Minerva Dobbs thought as she stood in the middle of a loud yuppie bar, *the world was full of good men*. She looked into the handsome face of the man she'd planned on taking to her sister's wedding and thought, *Those days are gone*.

"This relationship is not working for me," David said.

I could shove this swizzle stick through his heart, Min thought. She wouldn't do it, of course. The stick was plastic and not nearly pointed enough on the end. Also, people didn't do things like that in southern Ohio. A sawed-off shotgun, that was the ticket.

"And we both know why," David went on.

He probably didn't even know he was mad; he probably thought he was being calm and adult. *At least I know I'm furious*, Min thought. She let her anger settle around her, and it made her warm all over, which was more than David had ever done.

Across the room, somebody at the big roulette wheel–shaped bar rang a bell. Another point against David: He was dumping her in a theme bar. The Long Shot. The name alone should have tipped her off.

"I'm sorry, Min," David said, clearly not.

Min crossed her arms over her gray-checked suit jacket so she couldn't smack him. "This is because I won't go home with you tonight? It's Wednesday. I have to work tomorrow. You have to work tomorrow. I paid for my own drink."

"It's not that." David looked noble and wounded as only the tall, dark, and self-righteous could. "You're not making any effort to make our relationship work, which means . . ."

Which means we've been dating for two months and I still won't sleep with you. Min tuned him out and looked around at the babbling crowd. *If I had an untraceable poison, I could drop it in his drink now and not one of these suits would notice.*

". . . and I do think, if we have any future, that you should contribute, too," David said.

Oh, I don't, Min thought, which meant that David had a point. Still, lack of sex was no excuse for dumping her three weeks before she had to wear a maid-of-honor dress that made her look like a fat, demented shepherdess. "Of course we have a future, David," she said, trying to put her anger on ice. "We have *plans*. Diana is getting married in three weeks. You're invited to the wedding. To the rehearsal dinner. To the *bachelor party*. You're going to miss the *stripper*, David."

"Is that all you think of me?" David's voice went up. "I'm just a date to your sister's wedding?"

"Of course not," Min said. "Just as I'm sure I'm more to you than somebody to sleep with."

David opened his mouth and closed it again. "Well, of course. I don't want you to think this is a reflection on you. You're intelligent, you're successful, you're mature. . . ."

Min listened, knowing that *You're beautiful, you're thin* were not coming. If only he'd have a heart attack. Only four percent of heart attacks in men happened before forty, but it could happen. And if he died, not even her mother could expect her to bring him to the wedding.

". . . and you'd make a wonderful mother," David finished up.

"Thank you," Min said. "That's so not romantic."

"I thought we were going places, Min," David said.

"Yeah," Min said, looking around the gaudy bar. "Like here."

David sighed and took her hand. "I wish you the best, Min. Let's keep in touch."

Min took her hand back. "You're not feeling any pain in your left arm, are you?"

"No," David said, frowning at her.

"Pity," Min said, and went back to her friends, who were watching them from the far end of the room.

"He was looking even more uptight than usual," Liza said, looking even taller and hotter than usual as she leaned on the jukebox, her hair flaming under the lights.

David wouldn't have treated Liza so callously. He'd have been afraid to; she'd have dismembered him. *Gotta be more like Liza,* Min thought and started to flip through the song cards on the box.

"Are you upset with him?" Bonnie said from Min's other side, her blond head tilted up in concern. David wouldn't have left Bonnie, either. Nobody was mean to sweet, little Bonnie.

"Yes. He dumped me." Min stopped flipping. Wonder of wonders, the box had Elvis. Immediately, the bar seemed a better place. She fed in coins and then punched the keys for "Hound Dog." Too bad Elvis had never recorded one called "Dickhead."

"I knew I didn't like him," Bonnie said.

Min went over to the roulette bar and smiled tightly at the slender bartender dressed like a croupier. She had beautiful long, soft, kinky brown hair, and Min thought, *That's another reason I couldn't have slept with David.* Her hair always frizzed when she let it down, and he was the type who would have noticed.

"Rum and Coke, please," she told the bartender.

Maybe that was why Liza and Bonnie never had man trouble: great hair. She looked at Liza, racehorse-thin in purple zippered leather, shaking her head at David with naked contempt. Okay, it wasn't just the hair. If she jammed herself into Liza's dress, she'd look like Barney's slut cousin. "*Diet* Coke," she told the bartender.

"He wasn't the one," Bonnie said from below Min's shoulder, her hands on her tiny hips.

"Diet rum, too," Min told the bartender, who smiled at her and went to get her drink.

Liza frowned. "Why were you dating him anyway?"

"Because I thought he might be the one," Min said, exasperated. "He was intelligent and successful and very nice at first. He seemed like a sensible choice. And then all of sudden he went snotty on me."

Bonnie patted Min's arm. "It's a good thing he broke up with you because now you're free for when the right man finds you. Your prince is on his way."

"Right," Min said. "I'm sure he was on his way but a truck hit him."

"That's not how it works." Bonnie leaned on the bar, looking like an R-rated pixie. "If it's meant to be, he'll make it. No matter how many things go wrong, he'll come to you and you'll be together forever."

"What is this?" Liza said, looking at her in disbelief. "Barbie's Field of Dreams?"

"That's sweet, Bonnie," Min said. "But as far as I'm concerned, the last good man died when Elvis went."

"Maybe we should rethink keeping Bon as our broker," Liza said to Min. "We could be major stockholders in the Magic Kingdom by now."

Min tapped her fingers on the bar, trying to vent some tension. "I should have known David was a mistake when I couldn't bring myself to sleep with him. We were on our third date, and the waiter brought the dessert menu, and David said, 'No, thank you, we're on a diet,' and of course, he isn't because there's not an ounce of fat on him, and I thought, 'I'm not taking off my clothes with you' and I paid my half of the check and went home early. And after that, whenever he made his move, I thought of the waiter and crossed my legs."

"He wasn't the one," Bonnie said with conviction.

"You *think?*" Min said, and Bonnie looked wounded. Min closed her eyes. "Sorry. Sorry. *Really* sorry. It's just not a good time for that stuff, Bon. I'm mad. I want to savage somebody, not look to the horizon for the next jerk who's coming my way."

"Sure," Bonnie said. "I understand."

Liza shook her head at Min. "Look, you didn't care about David, so you haven't lost anything except a date to Di's wedding. And I vote we skip the wedding. It has 'disaster' written all over it, even without the fact that she's marrying her best friend's boyfriend."

"Her best friend's *ex*-boyfriend. And I *can't* skip it. I'm the maid of honor." Min gritted her teeth. "It's going to be hell. It's not just that I'm dateless, which fulfills every prophecy my mother has ever made, it's that she's crazy about David."

"We *know*," Bonnie said.

"She tells everybody about David," Min said, thinking of her mother's avid little face. "Dating David is the only thing I've done that she's liked about me since I got the flu freshman year and lost ten pounds. And now I have no David." She took her diet rum from the bartender, said, "Thank you," and tipped her lavishly. There wasn't enough gratitude in the world for a server who kept the drinks coming at a time like this. "Most of the time it doesn't matter what my mother thinks of me because I can avoid her, but for the wedding? No."

"So you'll find another date," Bonnie said.

"No, she won't," Liza said.

"Oh, *thank you*," Min said, turning away from the over-designed bar. The roulette pattern was making her dizzy. Or maybe that was the rage.

"Well, it's your own fault," Liza said. "If you'd quit assigning statistical probability to the fate of a union with every guy you meet and just go out with somebody who turns you on, you might have a good time now and then."

"I'd be a puddle of damaged ego," Min said. "There's nothing wrong with dating sensibly. That's how I found David." Too late, she realized that wasn't evidence in her favor and knocked back some of her drink to ward off comments.

Liza wasn't listening. "We'll have to find a guy for you." She began to scan the bar, which was only fair since most of the bar had been scanning her. "Not him. Not him. Not him. Nope. Nope. Nope. All these guys would try to sell you mutual funds." Then she straightened. "Hello. We have a winner."

Bonnie followed her eyes. "Who? Where?"

"The dark-haired guy in the navy blue suit. In the middle on the landing up by the door."

"Middle?" Min squinted at the raised landing at the entry to the bar. It was wide enough for a row of faux poker tables, and four men were at one talking to a brunette in red. One of the four was David, now surveying his domain over the dice-studded wrought-iron rail. The landing was only about five feet higher than the rest of the room, but David contrived to make it look like a balcony. It was probably requiring all his self-control to keep from doing the Queen Elizabeth Wave. "That's David," Min said, turning away. "And some brunette. Good Lord, he's dating somebody else already." *Get out now,* she told the brunette silently.

"Forget the brunette," Liza said. "Look at the guy in the middle. Wait a minute, he'll turn back this way again. He doesn't seem to be finding David that interesting."

Min squinted back at the entry again. The navy suit was taller than David, and his hair was darker and thicker, but otherwise, from behind, he was pretty much David II. "I did that movie," Min said, and then he turned.

Dark eyes, strong cheekbones, classic chin, broad shoulders, chiseled everything, and all of it at ease as he stared out over the bar, ignoring David, who suddenly looked a little inbred.

Min sucked in her breath as every cell she had came alive and whispered, *This one.*

Then she turned away before anybody caught her slack-jawed with admiration. He was not the one, that was her DNA talking, looking for a high-class sperm donor. Every woman in the room with a working ovary probably looked at him and thought, *This one.* Well, biology was not destiny. The amount of damage somebody that beautiful could do to a woman like her was too much to contemplate. She took another drink to cushion the thought, and said, "He's pretty."

"No," Liza said. "That's the point. He's *not* pretty. David is pretty. That guy looks like an adult."

"Okay, he's full of testosterone," Min said.

"No, that's the guy on his right," Liza said. "The one with the head like a bullet. I bet that one talks sports and slaps people on the back. The navy suit looks civilized with edge. Tell her, Bonnie."

"I don't think so," Bonnie said, her pixie face looking grim. "I know him."

"In the biblical sense?" Liza said.

"No. He dated my cousin Wendy. But—"

"Then he's fair game," Liza said.

"—he's a hit and run player," Bonnie finished. "From what Wendy said, he dazzles whoever he's with for a couple of months and then drops her and moves on. And she never sees it coming."

"The beast," Liza said without heat. "You know, men are allowed to leave women they're dating."

"Well, he makes them love him and then he leaves them," Bonnie said. "That is beastly."

"Like David," Min said, her instinctive distrust of the navy suit confirmed.

Liza snorted. "Oh, like you ever loved David."

"*I was trying to,*" Min snapped.

Liza shook her head. "Okay, none of this matters. All you want is a date to the wedding. If it takes the beast a couple of months to dump you, you're covered. So just go over there—"

"No." Min turned her back on everybody to concentrate on the black and white posters over the bar: Paul Newman shooting pool in *The Hustler*, Marlon Brando throwing dice in *Guys and Dolls*, W. C. Fields scowling over his cards in *My Little Chickadee*. Where were all the women gamblers? It wasn't as if being a woman wasn't a huge risk all by itself. Twenty-eight percent of female homicide victims were killed by husbands or lovers.

Which, come to think of it, was probably why there weren't any women gamblers. Living with men was enough of a gamble. She fought the urge to turn around and look at the beast on the landing again. Really, the smart thing to do was stop dating and get a cat.

"You know she won't go talk to him," Bonnie was saying to Liza. "Statistically speaking, the probable outcome is not favorable."

"Screw that." Liza nudged Min and sloshed the Coke in her glass. "Imagine your mother if you brought that to the wedding. She might even let you eat carbs." She looked at Bonnie. "What's his name?"

"Calvin Morrisey," Bonnie said. "Wendy was buying wedding magazines when he left her. She was writing 'Wendy Sue Morrisey' on scrap paper."

Liza looked appalled. "That's probably why he left."

"Calvin Morrisey." Against her better judgment, Min turned back to watch him again.

"Go over there," Liza said, prodding her with one long fingernail, "and tell David you hope his rash clears up soon. Then introduce yourself to the beast, smile, and don't talk statistics."

"That would be shallow," Min said. "I'm thirty-three. I'm mature. I don't care if I have a date to my sister's wedding. I'm a better person than that." She thought about her mother's face when she got the news that David was history. *No, I'm not.*

"No, you're not," Liza said. "You're just too chicken to cross the room."

"I suppose it might work." Bonnie frowned across the room. "And you can dump him after the wedding and give him a taste of his own medicine."

"Yeah, that's the ticket." Liza rolled her eyes. "Do it for Wendy and the rest of the girls."

He was in profile now, talking to David. *The man should be on coins,* Min thought. Of course, looking that beautiful, he probably never dated the terminally chubby. At least, not without sneering. And she'd been sneered at enough for one night.

"No," Min said and turned back to the bar. Really, a cat was a good idea.

"Look, Stats," Liza said, exasperated, "I know you're conservative, but you're damn near solidifying lately. Dating David must have been like dating concrete. And then there's your apartment. Even your furniture is stagnant."

"My furniture is my grandmother's," Min said stiffly.

"Exactly. Your butt's been on it since you were born. You need a change. And if you don't make that change on your own, *I will have to help you.*"

Min's blood ran cold. "*No.*"

"Don't threaten her," Bonnie said to Liza. "She'll change, she'll grow. Won't you, Min?"

Min looked back at the landing, and suddenly going over there seemed like a good idea. She could stand under that ugly wrought-iron railing and eavesdrop, and then if Calvin Morrisey sounded even remotely nice—ha, what were the chances?—she could go up and say something sweet to David and get an intro, and Liza would not have movers come in while she was at work and throw out her furniture.

"Don't make me do this for you," Liza said.

Standing at a roulette wheel bar sulking wasn't doing anything for her. And with all she knew ahead of time, it wasn't likely that he could inflict much damage. Min squared her shoulders and took a deep breath. "I'm going in, coach."

"Do not say 'percent' at any time for the rest of the night," Liza said, and Min straightened her gray-checked jacket and said a short prayer that she'd think of a great pick-up line before she got to the landing and made a fool of herself. In which case, she'd just spit on the beast, push David over the railing, and go get that cat.

"Just so there's a plan," she said to herself and started across the floor.

Up on the landing, Cal Morrisey was thinking seriously about pushing David Fisk over the railing. *I should have moved faster when I saw them coming*, he thought. It was Tony's fault.

"You know, that redhead has great legs," Tony had said. "See her? At the bar, in the purple with the zippers? You suppose she likes football players?"

"You haven't played football in fifteen years." Cal had sipped his drink, easing into an alcohol-tinged peace that was broken only slightly when somebody with no taste in music played "Hound Dog." As far as he was concerned the only two drawbacks to the place were the stupid décor and the fact that Elvis Presley was on the jukebox.

"All right, it's been a while since I played, but she doesn't know that." Tony looked back at the redhead. "I got ten bucks says she'll leave with me. I'll use my chaos theory line."

"No bet," Cal said. "Although that is a terrible line, so that would shorten the odds." He squinted across the room to the roulette wheel bar. The redhead was flashy, which meant she was Tony's type. There was a little blonde there, too, the perky kind, their friend Roger's dream date. Behind the bar, Shanna saw him watching and waved, but she didn't smile, and Cal wondered what was up as he nodded to her.

Tony put his arm around Cal. "Help me out here, she's in a group. You go over and pick up her chubby friend in the gray-checked suit, and Roger can hit on the short blonde. I'd give you the short blonde, but you know Roger and midget women."

Roger jerked to attention at Cal's elbow. "What? What short blonde?" He peered across the room at the bar. "Oh. *Oh.*"

"Suit?" Cal looked back at the bar.

"The one in gray." Tony nodded toward the bar. "Between the redhead and the mini-blonde. She's hard to see because the redhead sort of dazzles you. I bet you—"

"Oh." Cal squinted to see the medium-height woman between the redhead and the blonde. She was dressed in a dull, boxy, gray-checked suit, and her round face scowled under brown hair yanked back into a knot on the top of her head. "Nope," he said and took another drink.

Tony smacked him on the back and made him choke. "Come on, live a little. Don't tell me you're still pining for Cynthie."

"I never pined for Cynthie." Cal glanced around the crowd. "Keep an eye out for her, will you? She's in that red thing she wears when she's trying to get something."

"She can get it from me," Tony said.

"Great." Cal's voice was fervent. "I'll even go pick up that suit if you'll marry Cyn."

Tony choked on his drink. "Marry?"

"Yes," Cal said. "She wants to get married. Surprised the hell out of me." He thought for a moment of Cynthie, a sweetheart with a spine of steel. "I don't know where she got the idea we were that close."

"There she is." Roger was looking over Cal's shoulder. "She's coming up the stairs now."

Cal got up and tried to move past Tony to the door. "Out of my way."

Tony stayed in his chair. "You can't leave, I want the redhead."

"So go get her," Cal said, trying to get around him.

"Cynthie's got David with her," Roger said, and there was great sympathy in his voice.

"Cal!" David's voice grated over Cal's shoulder. "Just who we were looking for." He sounded mad as hell, but when Cal turned, David was smiling.

Trouble, Cal thought and smiled back with equal insincerity. "David. Cynthie. Great to see you."

"Hello, Cal." Cynthie smiled up at him, her heart-shaped face lethally lovely. "How've you been?"

"Great. Couldn't be better. You, too, looking great." Cal looked past her to David, and thought, *Take her, please.* "You're a lucky man, David."

"I am?"

"Dating Cynthie," Cal said, putting all the encouragement he could into his voice.

Cynthie took David's arm. "We just ran into each other." She turned her shoulder to Cal and glowed up at David. "But it is nice seeing him again." Her eyes slid back to Cal's face, and he smiled past her ear again, radiating no jealousy at all as hard as he could.

David looked down into her beautiful face and blinked, and Cal felt a stab of sympathy for him. Cynthie was enchanting up close. And from far away. From everywhere, really, which was how he'd ended up saying yes to her all the time. Cal glanced at her impeccably tight little body in her impeccably tight little red dress and then took a step back as he jerked his eyes away, reminding himself of how peaceful life was without her. Distance, that was the key. Maybe a cross and some garlic, too.

"Of course," David was saying. "Maybe we can do dinner later." He glanced at Cal, looking triumphant.

"Well, don't let us keep you." Cal took another step back and bumped into the railing.

Cynthie let go of David's arm, her glow diminished. "I'll just freshen up before we go." Tony and David watched as her perfect rear end swung away from them, while Roger ignored her to peer across the room at the pixie blonde, and Cal took another healthy swallow of his drink and wished he were somewhere else. Anywhere else. Dinner, for example. Maybe he'd stop by Emilio's and eat in the kitchen. There were no women in Emilio's kitchen.

"So, David," Tony was saying. "How'd our seminar work out for you?"

"It was terrific," David said. "I didn't think anybody could teach some of those morons that new program, but everybody at the firm is now up to speed. We've even . . ."

He went on and Cal nodded, thinking that one of the many reasons he didn't like David was his tendency to refer to his employees as morons. Still, David paid his bills on time and gave credit where it was due; there were much worse clients. And if he took over Cynthie, Cal was prepared to feel downright warm toward him.

David wound down on whatever it was he'd been saying and looked toward the stairs. "About Cynthie. I thought that you and she—"

"No." Cal shook his head with enthusiasm. "She left me a couple of months ago."

"Isn't it usually the other way around?"

David arched an eyebrow and looked ridiculous. And still women went out with him. Life was a mystery. So were women.

"Aren't you supposed to be the guy who never strikes out?" David said.

"No," Cal said.

"He's losing his edge," Tony said. "I found an easy pickup for him, and he said no."

"Which one?" David said.

"The gray-checked suit at the bar." Tony motioned with his glass, and David looked at the bar and then turned back to Cal, smooth as ever.

"Maybe you *are* losing it." David smiled at him. "She shouldn't be that hard to get. It's not like she's a Cynthie."

"She's all right," Cal said, cautiously.

David leaned in. "After all, nobody says no to you, right?"

"What?" Cal said.

"I'm willing to bet you that you can't get her," David said. "A hundred bucks says you can't nail her."

Cal pulled back. "*What?*"

David laughed, but there was an edge to his voice when he spoke. "It's just a bet, Cal. You guys love risk, I've seen you bet on damn near everything. This isn't even that big a bet. We should make it two hundred."

That was when Cal had contemplated giving David a healthy push. Tony turned his back to David and mouthed, *Humor him*, and Cal sighed. There must be something he could ask for that would make David back down. "That baseball in your office," he said. "The one in the case."

"My Pete Rose baseball?" David's voice went up an octave.

"Yeah, that one. That's my price." Cal slugged back the rest of his scotch and looked around for a waitress.

David shook his head. "Not a chance. My dad caught that pop-up for me in seventy-five. But I like your style, upping the stakes like that." He leaned in closer. "Tell you what. The last refresher seminar you ran for us set me back ten grand. I'll bet you ten thousand in cash against a free seminar—"

Cal forced a smile. "David, I was kidding—"

"But for ten thou, you have to get her into bed. I'll play fair. I'll give you a month to get her out of that gray-checked suit."

"Piece of cake," Tony said.

Cal glared at Tony. "David, this isn't my kind of bet."

"It's *my* kind," David said, drawing his brows together, and Cal thought, *Hell, he's going to push this, and we need his business.*

Okay, clearly booze had shut down David's brain. But once it was back up and working again, David would back down on the ten thousand, that was insane, and David was never insane about money. So all he had to do was stall until David sobered up and then pretend the whole thing never happened. He stole a glance across the room to the bar and was delighted to see that the gray suit had disappeared some time during their conversation.

Cal turned back to David and said, "Well, I would, David, but she's gone." *And God bless you, gray suit, for leaving,* he thought and picked up his drink again.

Things were finally going his way.

Min had walked across the room, telling herself that it was a real toss-up as to which would be worse, trying to talk to this guy or enduring

Di's wedding unescorted. When she neared the landing, she edged her way under the rail, catching faint snatches of conversations as she went, not stopping until she heard David's voice faintly above her, saying, "But for ten, though, you have to get her into bed."

What? Min thought. It was noisy up there by the door, maybe she hadn't heard him—

"I'll play fair," David went on. "I'll give you a month to get her out of that gray-checked suit."

Min looked down at her gray-checked suit.

"Piece of cake," somebody said to David, and Min thought, *Son of a bitch, the world is full of sex-crazed bastards*, and forced herself to move on before she climbed the railing and killed them both.

She headed back to Liza and Bonnie, fuming. She knew exactly what David was up to. He assumed she wouldn't sleep with anybody because she'd turned him down. She'd warned him about that, about the rash assumptions he made, but instead of taking her advice, he'd kept asking her out.

Because he thought I was a sure thing, she realized. Because he'd looked at her and thought, *Overweight smart woman who'll never cheat on me and will be grateful I sleep with her.* "Bastard," she said out loud. She should have sex with Calvin Morrisey just to pay David back. But then she'd have no way of getting even with Calvin Morrisey. God, she was dumb. Fat and dumb, there was a winning combo.

"What's wrong?" Liza said when she was back at the bar. "Did you ask him?"

"No. As soon as you finish your drinks, I'm ready to go." Min turned back to the balcony and caught sight of them, just as they caught sight of her.

David's face was smug, but Calvin Morrisey clutched his drink and looked like he'd just seen Death.

"There she is," David crowed. "I told you she'd be back. Go get her, champ."

"Uh, David," Cal began, consigning the gray-checked suit to the lowest circle of hell.

"A bet's a bet."

Cal put his empty glass down on the rail and thought fast. The suit did not look happy, so the odds weren't impossible that she'd go for a chance to get out of the bar if he offered dinner. "Look, David, sex is not in the cards. I'm cheap, but I'm not slimy. You want to bet ten bucks on a pickup, fine, but that's it. Nothing with a future."

David shook his head. "Oh, no, I'll bet on the pickup, too, ten bucks if you leave with her. But the ten thousand is still on. If you *lose* . . ." He smiled at Cal, drawing out the 'lose,' "you do a seminar for me for free."

"David, I can't make that bet," Cal said, trying another tack. "I have two partners who—"

"I'm good for it," Tony said. "Cal never misses."

Cal glared at him. "Well, *Roger* isn't good for it."

"Hey, Roger, you in?" Tony said, and Roger said, "Sure," without looking away from the blonde at the bar.

"*Roger,*" Cal said.

"She's the prettiest little thing I've ever seen," Roger said.

"Roger, you just bet that I could get a woman into bed," Cal said with great patience. "Now tell David you don't want to bet a ten-thousand-dollar refresher seminar on sex."

"What?" Roger said, finally looking away from the blonde.

"I said—" Cal began.

"Why would you bet on something like that?" Roger said.

"That's not the question," Tony said. "The question is, can he do it?"

"Sure," Roger said. "But—"

"Then we have a bet," David said.

"No, we do not," Cal said.

"You don't think you can do it," David said. "You're losing it."

"This is not about me," Cal said, and then Cynthie slid back into the group and put her hand on his arm. She leaned into him, and he felt his blood heat right on cue.

"She's over there waiting for you," David said, an edge in his voice.

"She?" Cynthie's glow dimmed. "Are you seeing somebody?"

Oh, hell, Cal thought.

"Cal?" David said.

"Cal?" Cynthie said.

"I *love* this," Tony said.

"What?" Roger said.

Cal sighed. It was the suit or Cynthie, the rock or the soft place who wanted to get married. He detached her hand from his arm. "Yes, I'm seeing somebody. Excuse me."

He pushed past Cynthie and David and headed for the bar, wishing them both the worst fate he could think of, that they'd end up together.

Min watched Calvin Morrisey move toward the stairs. The beast. He thought that he could get her in a month, that she was so pathetic she'd just—

Her brain caught up with her train of thought, and she straightened.

"Will you tell us what's wrong?" Liza said.

"A month," Min said.

He walked down the steps and made his way through the crowd, ignoring the come-hither looks of the women he passed.

He was coming to pick her up.

Suppose she let him.

Suppose for the next three weeks she made him pay by stringing him along and then took him to Di's wedding. He wouldn't leave her; he had to stick for a month to win his damn bet. All she had to do was say no to sex for three weeks, drag him to her sister's wedding, and then leave his ass cold.

Min settled back against the bar and examined the idea from all sides. He more than deserved to be tortured for three weeks. And in that three weeks she could figure out a way to make David suffer, too. And her mother would have somebody beautiful to point out to people at the wedding as her date. It was a plan, and as far as she could see, it was all good.

The bartender came back and Min said, "Rum and Diet Coke, please. A double."

"That's your third," Liza said. "And fourth. The aspartame alone will make you insane. What are you doing?"

"Was he mean to you?" Bonnie said. "What happened?"

"I didn't talk to him." Min waved them away. "Move down the bar a couple of feet will you. I'm about to get hit on and you're cramping my style."

"We missed something," Liza said to Bonnie.

"Move," Bonnie said, and pushed Liza down the bar.

Min turned away when the bartender brought her drink, so when The Beast spoke from beside her, she jerked her head up and caught the full force of him unprepared: hot dark eyes, perfect cheekbones, and a mouth a woman would betray her moral fiber to bite into. Her heart kicked up into her throat, and she swallowed hard to get it back where it belonged.

"I have a problem," he said, and his voice was low and smooth, warm enough to be charming, rich enough to clog arteries.

Dark chocolate, Min thought and looked at him blankly, keeping her breathing slow. "Problem?"

"Well, usually my line is 'Can I buy you a drink?' but you have one." He smiled at her, radiating testosterone through his expensive suit.

"Well, that is a problem." She started to turn away.

"So what I thought," he said, his voice dropping even lower as he leaned closer to her and made her heart pound, "was that we could go somewhere else, and I could buy you dinner."

The closer he got, the better he looked. He was the used car salesman of seducers, Min decided, trying to get her distance back. You could never get a good deal from a used car salesman; they sold cars all the time and you only bought a couple in a lifetime so they always won. Statistically speaking, you were toast before you walked on the lot. She could only imagine how many women this guy had mutilated in his lifetime. The mind boggled.

His smile had disappeared while he waited for her answer, and he looked vulnerable now, taking a chance on asking her out. He faked vulnerable very well. *Remember,* she told herself, *the son of a bitch is doing this for ten bucks.* Actually, he was trying to do *her* for ten bucks.

Cheapskate. Suddenly, breathing normally was not a problem.

"Dinner?" she said.

"Yes." He bent still closer. "Somewhere quiet where we can talk. You look like someone with interesting things to say. And I'm somebody who'd like to hear them."

Min smiled at him. "That's a terrible line. Does it usually work for you?"

He froze for a second, and then he segued from sincere to boyish again. "Well, it has up till now."

"It must be your voice," Min said. "You deliver it beautifully."

"Thank you." He straightened. "Let's try this again." He held out his hand. "I'm Calvin Morrisey, but my friends call me Cal."

"Min Dobbs." She shook his hand and dropped it before it could feel warm in her grasp. "And my friends would call me foolhardy if I left this bar with a stranger."

"Wait." He got out his wallet and pulled out a twenty. "This is cab fare. If I get fresh, you get a cab."

Liza would take the twenty and then dump him. There was a plan, but Liza didn't need a wedding date. What else would Liza do? Min plucked the twenty from his fingers. "If you get fresh, I'll break your nose." She folded the twenty, unbuttoned her top two blouse buttons, and tucked the bill into the V of her sensible cotton bra so that only a thin green edge showed. That was one good thing about packing extra pounds, you got cleavage to burn.

She looked up and caught his eyes looking down, and she waited for him to make some comment, but he smiled again. "Fair enough," he said, "let's go eat," and she reminded herself to ignore what a beautiful mouth he had since it was full of forked tongue.

"First, promise me no more lame lines," she said, and watched his jaw clench.

"Anything you want," he said.

Min shook her head. "Another line. I suppose you can't help it. And free food is always good." She picked up her purse from the bar. "Let's go."

She walked away before he could say anything else, and he followed her, past a dumbfounded Liza and a delighted Bonnie, across the floor and up onto the landing by the door, and the last thing she saw as they left was David looking outraged.

The evening was turning out *much* better than she'd expected.

Chapter Two

Liza scowled at the empty doorway. This was not good. When Calvin Morrisey came back in and spoke to David for a moment, it didn't get better.

"Do you suppose it was the booze?" Bonnie asked.

Liza thought fast. "I don't know what it was, but I don't like it. Why was he hitting on her?"

Bonnie frowned. "It's not like you to be jealous."

"I'm not jealous." Liza transferred her scowl to Bonnie. "Think about it. Min sends out no signals, he's never talked to her so he can't know how great she is, and she's dressed like a nun with an MBA. But he crosses a crowded bar to pick her up—"

"It's possible," Bonnie said.

"—right after he's talked to David," Liza finished, nodding to the landing where a red-faced David was now moving in on the brunette.

"Oh." Bonnie looked stricken. "Oh, no."

"There's only one thing we can do." Liza squared her shoulders. "We've got to find out what Calvin the Beast is up to."

"How—"

Liza nodded at the mezzanine. "He was with those two guys. Which one do you want, the big dumb-looking blond or the bullet head?"

Bonnie followed her eyes to the landing and sighed. "The blond. He looks harmless. The bullet head looks like all hands, and I'm not up to that tonight."

"Well, I am." Liza put her drink on the bar and leaned back. The bullet head was looking right at her. "The last time I saw a brow that low I was watching slides in anthropology class." She met his stare dead on for a full five seconds. Then she turned back to the bar. "Two minutes."

"It's a crowded room, Lize," Bonnie said. "Give him three."

David had watched Cal open the street door for Min and felt a flare of jealous rage. It wasn't that he wanted to kick Cal. He always wanted to kick Cal. The guy never broke a sweat, never made a bad business move, never lost a bet, and never hit on a woman and missed. *Your therapist warned you about this*, he told himself, but he knew it wasn't just his need to be first in everything. This time the jealousy had an extra twist.

This time Cal had taken Min. Min who was good, solid wife material except for that stubborn streak which he could have worn down, she'd have come back eventually. But now—

He stiffened as Cal came back through the door and motioned him over.

"We're going to dinner," Cal said, holding out his hand. "Ten bucks."

He sounded mad, which made David feel better as he took out his wallet and handed Cal the ten.

"Smart move not tipping me that she hates men," Cal said.

Then he was gone, and David went back to the railing and said, "I think I just made a mistake."

"You, too?" Cynthie said, her voice sad over her martini glass.

David glanced at the door. "So it wasn't your idea to break up with Cal?"

"No." Cynthie stared at the door. "I thought it was time to get married, so I said, 'Now or never.'" She smiled tightly up at David. "And he said, 'Sorry.'" She drew in a deep breath and David tried not to be distracted by the fact that she was braless under her red jersey dress.

"That's lousy." David leaned against the rail so he couldn't look down her dress since that would be crass, something Cal Morrisey would do. "Cal must be a moron."

"Thank you." Cynthie turned back to watch the bar as Tony got up from the next table and walked down the stairs with Roger following. Her hair moved like TV hair, a dark silky fall that brushed her shoulders. "I'd love to know how Cal met that woman. I could have sworn he wasn't dating anybody."

David considered telling her that Cal had picked up Min because of the bet and then thought, *No.* The bet had not been his finest hour. In fact, for the life of him, he couldn't think why he'd done it, it was as if some malignant force had whispered in his ear. No, it was Cal's fault, that's what it was, and it was a disaster because if Min ever found out he'd made that bet . . .

"Do you know her?" Cynthie said.

"She's my ex-girlfriend."

"Oh." Cynthie put her drink down. "Well, I hope Cal's sorry he picked her up. I hope he realizes what he's lost once he gets her back to his place."

"They're not going back to his place," David said. "She won't." Cynthie waited, and he added, "She doesn't like sex."

Cynthie smiled.

David shrugged. "At least, she wouldn't try it in the two months we were together. So I ended it."

Cynthie shook her head, still smiling. "You didn't give the relationship enough time. What does she do for a living?"

David stiffened at the criticism. "She's an actuary. And it strikes me that *two months*—"

"David," Cynthie said, "if you wanted sex in the first five minutes, you should have dated a stripper. If she's an actuary, she's a cautious person, her career is figuring out how to minimize risk, and in your case, she was right."

David began to dislike Cynthie. "How was she right?"

"You left her over sex." Cynthie leaned forward, and David pretended not to watch her breasts under the jersey. "David, this is *my* specialty. If you loved her, you wouldn't have given her an ultimatum over sex."

"What is it you do?" David said, coldly.

"I'm a psychologist." Cynthie picked up her drink, and David remembered some of the gossip he'd heard.

"You're the dating guru," he said, warming to her again. She was practically a celebrity. "You've been on TV."

"I do guest spots," Cynthie said. "My research on relationships has been very popular. And all of it tells me you do not give an ultimatum over sex."

"You gave Cal one."

"Not over sex," Cynthie said. "I'd never deny him sex. And it wasn't an ultimatum, it was strategy. We'd been together nine months, we were past infatuation and into attachment, and I knew that all he needed was a physiological cue to make him aware of his true feelings."

"That makes no sense at all," David said.

Cynthie smiled at him without warmth. "My studies have shown that the process of falling into mature love happens in four steps." She held up one finger. "When you meet a woman, you subconsciously look for cues that she's the kind of person you should be with. That's assumption." She held up a second finger. "If she passes the assumption test, you begin to get to know her to find out if she's appropriate for you. If she is, you're attracted." She held up a third finger. "If, as you get to know her, the attraction is reinforced with joy or pain or both, you'll fall into infatuation. And . . ." She held up her fourth finger. "If you manage to make a connection and attach to each other during infatuation, you'll move into mature, unconditional love."

"That seems a little clinical," David said, faking interest. After all, she was almost a celebrity.

"That doesn't mean it's wrong," Cynthie said. "Take assumption. Your subconscious mind scans women and picks out those that meet your assumptions about the kind of woman you're attracted to."

"I like to think I'm not close-minded," David said.

"Which is why I'm surprised Cal picked up your Min." Cynthie sipped her drink. "One of his assumptions is that his women will be beautiful."

"I always thought Cal was shallow," David said, and thought, *He picked her up for the bet, the bastard.*

"He's not shallow at all," Cynthie said. "Since they've passed assumption, they'll now subconsciously gauge attraction. For example, if they fell into step when they left the bar, that could be a strong psychological hint that they're compatible." She frowned. "I wish we could watch them at dinner."

"And see what?" David said, picking up his drink again. "Them eating in unison?"

"No," Cynthie said. "If they mirror each other in action, both crossing their legs the same way, for example. If she accepts his touch with pleasure. If they exchange a copulatory gaze."

David choked on his drink.

"It's a look that's held a few seconds too long," Cynthie said. "It's a clear sexual signal. All species do it."

David nodded and reminded himself not to stare in the future.

"If their conversation picks up a rhythm with no long silences, that will be attractive. If they develop enough of a relationship to use nicknames."

"Min hates nicknames," David said, remembering a disastrous "honey bun" incident.

"If they have the same tastes in music or film. If they establish shared secrets or private jokes. If they value the same things. Is Min self-employed?"

"No," David said. "She works for Alliance Insurance. Her father is a vice president there."

Cynthie's smile curved across her beautiful face. "Excellent. Cal likes to gamble, so he admires people who take risks. That's why he refused to go into his father's business and started his own company instead. He's not going to be impressed by somebody who's riding her father's coattails. He'll think she's dull."

"That's good," David said. *The superficial bastard.*

Cynthie nodded over her glass. "Even her attitude will make a difference. Someone who likes you and likes being with you is attractive." She looked woebegone for a moment. "And of course your Min will be delighted to be with him."

"No, she isn't," David said, feeling better. "She's mad at all men right now because I broke things off with her. And she's got a sharp tongue."

Cynthie brightened. "So he'll combine her bad temper with his analysis of her as someone who's too conservative. This is sounding very good, David. Will she let him pay for dinner?"

David shook his head. "Min insists on going Dutch. She's a very fair woman."

"Every species has a dinner date as part of courting ritual," Cynthie said. "A woman who won't let you pay for dinner is rejecting your courtship. She may think she's playing fair, or that she's being a feminist, but at a very deep level, she knows that she's crossing you off her list of possibilities."

"She won't let him pay," David said, rethinking his stance on that. When Min came back, he was going to pay for dinner.

"So they'll fight over the check. That's wonderful." She sat back, her face relaxed for the first time. "From what you've told me about her, Cal is already regretting asking her to leave with him."

"That's good," David said, cheering up at the thought.

Cynthie's smile wavered. "So did you want to go to dinner, or did you ask me out just to make Cal mad?"

Dinner. If he took Cynthie to dinner, Tony and Roger would tell Cal he and Cynthie had hooked up. That would serve Cal right. He could walk off with the hot brunette who'd dumped the legendary Calvin Morrisey. He'd win.

He put his drink down. "I asked because I wanted to have dinner with you."

Cynthie smiled and he was dazzled. Cal was a fool for letting this woman go.

"And you can tell me more about Min," Cynthie said.

"Of course," David said.

All about Min. Nothing about the bet.

Min had waited outside while the beast went back in to retrieve whatever he'd forgotten—his morals, maybe—and the cool air of the June night cleared her head and her anger a little. The bar was on one of her favorite streets, full of funky little shops and restaurants and a great revival theater, and a gentle breeze blew through the skinny trees that struggled to grow in their iron cages along the street edge. For a moment, Min watched the trees and thought, *I know just how you feel.* Well, she didn't know the skinny part. But the trapped? Yep.

Because she was stuck, no doubt about it. Stuck dateless in a stupid bridesmaid's dress for her sister's wedding to a dweeb with her mother sighing at her. Because the truth was, she wasn't going to be able to play somebody like Cal Morrisey for three weeks. It had been a dumb, dumb idea, fueled by rum and rage. For a moment, she wished that she was back in her attic apartment, curled up on her grandmother's old pumpkin-colored sofa, listening to Elvis's *Moody Blue* album. Maybe she wasn't the type to date, maybe she should just give in to her well-upholstered genes and become a kindly maiden aunt to Diana's inevitable offspring. It wasn't as if she wanted kids of her own. And what other purpose did men serve? Well, sex, but look how they acted about that. Honestly—

A cell phone rang behind her, and she started. When she turned, it was Calvin Morrisey, back again. He reached in his jacket and took out his phone, the kind that had more bells and whistles than any human being needed, and it confirmed her decision: There was no way in hell she was going to spend three weeks with a soulless yuppie just to get a date to Diana's wedding. She'd go Dutch on dinner and then say goodbye forever; *that* was a plan.

She crossed her arms and waited for him to impress her with a business call, but he turned the phone off.

Min raised her eyebrows. "What if it's important?"

"The only person I want to talk to is here," he said, smiling that *GQ* smile at her.

"Oh, for crying out loud," Min said. "Can you turn that off, too?"

"Excuse me?" he said, his smile fading.

"The constant line." Min began to walk again. "You've got me for dinner. You can relax now."

"I'm always relaxed." He caught up to her in one stride. "Where are we going?"

Min stopped, and he walked a step past her before he caught himself.

"The new restaurant that everybody's talking about is this way. Serafino's. Somebody I used to know says the chef is making a statement with his cuisine." She thought of David and looked at Cal. Two of a kind. "I assumed that'd be your style. Did you have someplace else in mind?"

"Yes." He put one finger on her shoulder and gave her a gentle push to turn her around, and Min shrugged off his touch as she turned. "My restaurant's that way," he said. "Never go any place the chef is trying to talk with food. Unless you want Ser—"

"Nope." Min turned around and began to walk again. "I want to check out your taste in restaurants. I'm assuming it'll be like your taste in cell phones: very *trendy*."

"I like gadgets," he said, catching up again. "I don't think it's a comment on the real me."

"I've always wanted to do a study on cell phones and personality," Min lied as they passed the Gryphon theater. "All those fancy styles and different covers, and then some people refuse to carry them at all. You'd think—"

"Yours is black," he said. "Very practical. Look out for the glass." He reached to take her arm to steer her around a broken beer bottle, but she detoured on her own, rotating away from him.

He looked at her feet and stopped, probably faking concern, and she stopped, too. "What?"

"Nice shoes," he said, and she looked down at her frosted-plastic open-toed heels tied with floppy black bows.

"Thank you," she said, taken aback that he'd noticed.

"You're welcome." He put his hands in his pockets and started walking again, lengthening his stride.

"But you're wrong." Min took a larger step to catch up. "My cell phone is not black. It's green and it's covered in big white daisies."

"No, it's not." He was walking ahead of her now, not even pretending to keep pace with her, and she broke into a trot until she was even with him. "It's black or silver with a minimum of functions, which is a shame because you never know when you're going to get stuck somewhere and need a good poker game."

When she glanced up at him, he looked so good that she stopped again to make him break stride. The key was to keep him off balance, not gape at his face, especially when he was being so annoyingly right about her black cell phone. "I beg your pardon," she said stiffly, folding her arms again. "I know what my cell phone looks like. It has daisies on it. And I know I'm wearing a suit, but that doesn't mean I'm boring. I'm wearing scarlet underwear."

"No, you aren't." His hands were still in his pockets, and he looked big and broad and cocky as all hell.

"Well, with that kind of attitude, you'll never find out," Min said and walked on until she realized he wasn't following her. She turned back and saw him watching her. "Uh, dinner?"

He ambled toward her while she waited for him, and when he was beside her again, he leaned down and said, "I will bet you ten dollars that your cell phone does not have daisies on it."

"I don't gamble," Min said, trying not to back up a step.

"Double or nothing you're wearing a plain white bra."

"If you think I'm that boring, what are you doing with me?"

"I saw the bra when you put the twenty in it. And you have conservative taste, so there's no way you have a phone with daisies on it. The only exciting thing about you is your shoes."

Ouch. Min scowled. "Hey—"

"And what I'm doing with you," he said, clearly at the end of his patience, "is trying to take you to a great restaurant, which is just up ahead, so if we could call a truce until we're there—"

Min started to walk again.

"No bet?" he said from behind her.

"No bet." Min walked faster, but he caught up with her anyway, with no visible effort. *Long legs*, she thought and then kicked herself for thinking about any part of his body. Or the fact that he'd noticed how great her shoes were. Which was *just* the kind of thing his kind of guy would do. *Think about the bet*, she told herself. *He's a beast and a gambler.*

The beast and gambler stopped in front of a dimly lit storefront window that was covered with red velvet café curtains. Above the curtains, EMILIO'S was written in gold script.

"This is the restaurant?" Min said, surprised he hadn't picked something flashier.

"Yep." He reached for the door.

"Wait." Min squinted at the card on the door. "It closes at ten on weekdays. It must be close to that now. Maybe we should—"

"I'm Emilio's favorite customer," he said, pulling the door open. "At least until he meets you."

"Another line?" Min said, exasperated.

"No," he said with great and visible patience. "Keep busting my chops all the way through dinner, and Emilio will give you a free dessert."

"I thought you were his favorite customer," Min said.

"I am," he said. "Doesn't mean he won't appreciate the show. You coming in or not?"

"Yes," Min said and walked past him into the restaurant.

It was a minute and a half by Liza's watch before the bullethead tapped her on the shoulder. "Excuse me," he said, "but I believe you were staring at me."

Liza blinked at him. "That was disbelief. I couldn't believe you were so slow."

"Slow?" He looked insulted. "Nobody could have gotten through that crowd faster than me. I didn't even have blockers."

Liza shook her head. "You spotted me a good hour ago. What did you do, sit down and think about it?"

He rolled his eyes. "I heard redheads were hard to handle." He leaned on the bar. "I'm Tony. And you owe me."

Okay, here we go, Liza thought, and leaned on the bar, too, mirroring him. "I owe you?"

"Yes." He grinned at her. "Because of chaos theory."

Liza shook her head. "Chaos theory."

He moved closer to her. "Chaos theory says that complex dynamical systems become unstable because of disturbances in their environments after which a strange attractor draws the trajectory of the stress."

Liza looked at him, incredulous. "This is your line?"

"I am a complex dynamical system," Tony said.

"Not that complex," Liza said.

"And I was stable until you caused a disturbance in my environment."

"Not that stable," Liza said.

Tony grinned. "And since you're the strangest attractor in the room, I followed the trajectory of my stress right to you."

"That's not what you followed to me." Liza turned so that her back was against the bar, her shoulder blocking him. "Give me something better than that, or I'll find somebody else to amuse myself with."

From the corner of her eye, she saw the other guy, the vacant-looking blond, lean down to Bonnie. "Is she always like this?" he said to Bonnie, and Liza turned to size him up. Big. Husky. Boring.

"Well, your friend isn't exactly Prince Charming," Bonnie said, giving him her best fluttery smile.

He beamed back down at her. "Neither am I. Is that okay?"

Oh, come on, Liza thought, and caught Tony-the-bullethead's eye.

"He means it," Tony said. "Roger has no line."

"After the chaos theory debacle, that's a plus," Liza said.

"Poor baby," Bonnie was saying as she put her hand on Roger's sleeve. "Of course, that's okay. I'm Bonnie."

Roger looked down at her with naked adoration. "I'm Roger, and you are the most beautiful woman I've ever seen in my life."

Bonnie's smile widened, and she moved closer to him.

"Which doesn't mean he's bad with women," Tony said, sounding bemused.

"I begin to see his appeal." Liza turned back to Tony. "What's yours?"

"I'm great in bed," Tony said.

"Right," Liza said. "You're hopeless, but you can buy me a drink and tell me all about yourself. And your friends."

"Anything you want," Tony said, and waved to the curly-headed bartender. When she came down the bar, he said, "Hey, Shanna, you playing on my side of the street yet?"

The bartender shook her head. "No, but when I do, you'll be the last to know."

"Just so I'm somewhere on the list," Tony said. "Shanna, this is Liza. We need refills all around here."

"You know him?" Liza said to Shanna.

"He hangs out with my next-door neighbor," Shanna said. "I get him by default because of Cal."

"Cal?" Liza said, and thought, *Damn, I could have just asked the bartender about him without picking up this yahoo. Well, later for her.*

"You don't want to know about Cal," Tony was saying. "He's no good. Women should stay far away from him."

Shanna rolled her eyes and moved away.

"That's interesting," Liza said, smiling at him. "Tell me all about Cal and why he's no good."

"I lied. He's great," Tony said. "We met in summer school—"

"You went to high school together?" Liza said, taken aback.

"We went to third grade together," Tony said. "Although why you think this is interesting—"

"I want to know everything about you, sugar," Liza said. "I find you fascinating."

Tony nodded, accepting this as fact. "I was born—"

"You and *your friends*," Liza said. "So you and Roger and *Cal*—"

Tony began to talk, while behind her, she heard Bonnie say, "You know my mama would like you," and Roger answer, "I'd love to meet your mother."

Liza jerked her head toward Roger. "Does he say that to every woman?"

"What?" Tony said, startled out of his story about being a football star in the third grade.

"Never mind," Liza said. "Let's fast forward to puberty. You and Roger and *Cal . . .*"

Cal watched the shock on Min's face as she caught the full force of Emilio's for the first time, seeing his favorite restaurant in all its funky glory, the wrought-iron chandeliers with the amber flame bulbs, the old black and white photos on the walls, the red and white checked table-cloths on the square tables, the candles in the beat-up Chianti bottles, the hand-lettered menus and mismatched silver. He waited for her lip to curl and then realized it couldn't because her mouth had fallen open. Well, she deserved it for being such a pain in the—

"This is *great*," she said, and started to laugh. "My God, how did somebody like you ever find this place?"

"What do you mean, somebody like me?" Cal said.

She walked over to look at the photos of Emilio's family for the past eighty years. "Where did they get this stuff?" She smiled, her soft lips parted and her dark eyes alight, and then Emilio came up behind him.

"Ah, Mr. Morrisey," Emilio said, and Cal turned to meet his old roommate's glare. "How excellent to see you again."

"Emilio," Cal said. "This is Min Dobbs." He turned back to Min. "Emilio makes the best bread in town."

"I'm sure you make the best everything, Emilio," Min said, offering him her hand. She looked up at him from under her lashes, and her wide smile quirked wickedly.

Emilio cheered up, and Cal thought, *Hey, why didn't I get that?*

Emilio clasped her hand. "For you, my bread is poetry. I will bring my bread as a gift to your beauty, a poem to your lovely smile." He kissed the back of her hand, and Min beamed at him and did not pull her hand away.

"Emilio, Min is my date," Cal said. "Enough kissing already."

Min shook her head at him, with no beam whatsoever. "I'm not anybody's date. We don't even like each other." She turned back to Emilio, smiling again. "Separate checks, please, Emilio."

"Not separate checks, Emilio," Cal said, exasperated beyond politeness. "But a *table* would be good."

"For you, anything," Emilio said to Min and kissed her hand again.

Unbelievable, Cal thought, and kicked Emilio on the ankle when Min turned to look at the restaurant again. The guy was married, for Christ's sake.

"Right this way," Emilio said, wincing. He showed them to the best table by the window, slid Min into a bentwood chair, and then stopped by Cal long enough to say under his breath, "I sent the servers home half an hour ago, you bastard."

"You're welcome," Cal said loudly, nodding to him.

Emilio gave up and went back to the kitchen, while Cal watched Min examine the room in detail.

"It's like an Italian restaurant in the movies," she told Cal. "Except not. I love it. I love Emilio, too."

"I noticed," he said. "You're the first woman I ever brought here who was on a kissing basis with him before we sat down."

"Well, he's going to feed me." She picked up her napkin. "That's always a good sign in a man." She spread the napkin in her lap, and then her smile faded and she looked tense again. "Except . . ."

Cal braced himself for her next shot.

She leaned forward. "I can't eat the bread or pasta, but I don't want to hurt his feelings. Can you order something else?"

"Sure," Cal said, surprised. "Salad. Chicken marsala, there's no pasta with that."

"Thank you." Min smiled at him. "I wouldn't want to ruin his evening."

"I think you just made his evening," Cal said. Her lips were full and soft, and when she smiled her gratitude at him, her face changed from grim prison warden to warm baby doll, but the wicked glint she'd had in her eyes when she'd flirted with Emilio was gone, which was a real shame.

Emilio brought the bread, and Min leaned forward to see it. "Oh, that smells good. I missed lunch so this is wonderful."

"It is good," Cal said. "Emilio, we'll have the house salad to start and then the chicken marsala."

"Excellent choice, Mr. Morrisey," Emilio said, and Cal knew it was because everything was simple to make. "And a nice red wine to accompany?"

"Excellent," Cal said, knowing they were going to get whatever Emilio had left over and open in the kitchen.

"Ice water for me," Min said with a sigh, still looking at the bread.

When Emilio was gone, Cal said, "The bread's excellent. He makes it here."

"Carbs," Min said, her scowl back in place, and Cal had heard enough about carbs in his nine months with Cynthie so he let it drop.

"So," he said, picking up one of the small loaves. "What do you do for a living?" He broke the bread open and the yeasty warmth rose and filled his senses.

"I'm an actuary," Min said, the edge back in her voice.

An actuary. He was on a dinner date with a cranky, starving, risk-averse statistician. This was a new low, even for him.

"That's . . . interesting," he said, but she was watching the bread and didn't notice. He held half the small loaf out to her. "Eat."

"I *can't*," she said. "I have this dress I have to fit into three weeks from now."

"One piece of bread won't make that much difference." He waved it, knowing that the smell of Emilio's bread had driven stronger Atkins people to their knees.

"No." She closed her eyes and her lips tight, which was useless because it wasn't looking at the bread that was going to bring her down, it was smelling it.

"This might be your only chance to eat Emilio's bread," he said, and she took a deep breath.

"Oh, hell." She opened her eyes and took the bread from him. "You really are a beast."

"Who, me?" Cal said, and watched her tear off a piece of the bread and bite into it.

"Oh," she breathed, and then she chewed it with her eyes shut, pleasure flooding her face.

Look at me like that, he thought, and felt something nudge his shoulder. He looked up to see Emilio standing with a half bottle of wine, staring at Min. He nodded at Cal and whispered, "Keeper."

Min opened her eyes and said, "Emilio, you are a genius."

"The pleasure is all mine," Emilio said.

Cal took the wine from him. "Thank you, Emilio," he said pointedly and Emilio shook his head and went back to the kitchen for the salads.

When he'd brought them and was gone again, Cal said, "So you're an actuary."

She looked at him with contempt again. "Please. You don't care what I do. Take the night off, Charm Boy."

"Hey." He picked up his bread. "I don't do this nightly. It's been a while since I picked up anybody."

Min looked at her watch as she chewed. She swallowed and said, "It's been twenty-eight minutes."

"Besides you. My last relationship ended a couple of months ago, and I've been enjoying the peace and quiet." She rolled her eyes and he added, "So of course, when I decide to start dating again, I pick up somebody who hates me. What's all the hostility about?"

"Hostility? What hostility?" Min stabbed her fork into her salad and tasted it. "*God*, this is good."

She chewed blissfully, and Cal watched her, trying to figure out what he was doing wrong. She should be *liking* him. He was charming, damn it. "So what are your interests in life besides great shoes?"

"Oh, please," Min said, when she'd swallowed. "You talk. I know why I picked you out, tell me why you picked me."

He stopped with his glass halfway to his mouth. "You picked me up?"

Min shook her head. "I picked you *out*. I saw you on the landing. Well, my friend Liza saw you first, but she gave you to me."

"Thoughtful of her," Cal said. "So you were expecting me when I showed up?"

"Pretty much." Min shoved the bread toward him. "Take this bread basket away from me, I'm making a fool of myself."

He pulled the basket toward his plate. "Then why did you give me such a hard time?"

Min snorted. "You think that was a hard time? You must not get much grief from women."

"Well, not in the first five minutes," Cal said. "They save that for the future."

"Yes, but we don't have a future," she said, looking longingly at the bread. "I had to be proactive."

Cal pushed the basket back to her. "Why don't we have a future?" he said, even though he'd come to the same conclusion about thirty seconds after he'd said hello in the bar.

"Because I'm not interested in sex." Min tore off another piece of bread and bit into it, and Cal watched while the pleasure spread across her face.

You lie, Cal thought.

"And that means you're not interested in me," Min said when she'd finished chewing.

"Hey," he said, insulted. "What makes you think I'm only interested in sex?"

"Because you're a guy." She picked up the bread again. "Statistics show that men are interested in three things: careers, sports, and sex. That's why they love professional cheerleaders."

Cal put his fork down. "Well, that's sexist."

Min licked a crumb off her lip, and his irritation evaporated. She was fun to look at when she wasn't scowling: smooth milky skin, wide-set dark eyes, a blob of a nose, and that lush, soft, full, rosy mouth. . . .

"Yes, I know," she said. "But it's true, isn't it?"

"What?" Cal tried to find his place in the conversation. "Oh, the sports and sex thing? Not at all. This is the twenty-first century. We've learned how to be sensitive."

"You have?"

"Sure," Cal said. "Otherwise we wouldn't get laid."

She rolled her eyes, and he picked up the bottle and filled her wineglass.

"I can't," she said. "I had too much to drink at the bar."

He slid her glass closer. "I'll make sure you get home okay."

"And who'll make sure I get away from you okay?" she said and he put the bottle down.

"Okay, *that* was below the belt," he said, more sharply than he'd intended.

She met his eyes, and he thought, *Oh, hell, here we go again*. Then she nodded and said, "You're right. You've done nothing to deserve that. I apologize." She frowned, as if thinking about something. "In fact, I apologize for the whole night. My boyfriend dumped me about half an hour before you picked me up—"

"Ah *ha*," Cal said.

"—and it made me insane with rage. And then I realized that I'm not even sure I *liked* him anymore, and that the person I'm really mad at is me for being so stupid about the whole thing."

"You're not stupid," Cal said. "Making mistakes isn't stupid, it's the way you learn."

She squinted at him, looking confused. "Thank you. Anyway, this evening is not your fault. I mean, you have your faults, but you shouldn't pay for his. Sorry."

"That's okay," he said, confused, too. *What faults?* "Now drink your wine. It's good."

She picked up her glass and sipped. "You're right. This is excellent."

"Good, we'll come here often," he said, and then kicked himself because they weren't going anywhere again.

"Another line," Min said, without venom. "We're not going anywhere again and you know it. What is it with you? You see a woman and automatically go into wolf mode?"

Cal sat back. "Okay, was that because of the ex-boyfriend, too? Because I'm usually not paranoid, but you are definitely out to get me."

"Don't be a wimp," Min said as she tore the bread. "You've got that gorgeous face, and a body that makes women go weak at the knees, and then you whine."

Cal grinned at her. "Do I make you go weak at the knees?"

Min bit into her bread and chewed. "You did until you whined," she said when she'd swallowed. "Now I know. The magic is gone."

Cal watched her lick her full lower lip, and two months of celibacy plus a lifetime of habit kicked in. "Give me a chance," he said. "I bet I can get the magic back."

She stopped with the tip of her tongue on her lip, and her eyes met his for a long, dark, hot moment, and this time that glint was there, and sound faded to silence, and every nerve he had came alive and said, *This one.*

Then her tongue disappeared, and he shook his head to clear it and thought, *Not in a million years.*

"I never bet," Min said. "Gambling is a statistically impractical form of generating income."

"It's not a method of generating income," Cal said. "It's a way of life."

"Could we be any more incompatible?" Min said.

"Can't see how," Cal said, but then her eyes went past him and he watched while she drew in her breath.

Cal turned and saw Emilio, this time with a fragrant platter of chicken marsala, golden-brown filets and huge braised mushrooms floating in luminous dark wine sauce.

"*Oh, my Lord,*" Min said.

Emilio beamed at her as he served. "It's a pleasure to serve someone who appreciates food. Taste it."

Min cut into the chicken and put a forkful in her mouth. She looked startled and then she closed her eyes and began to chew, her face flushed with pleasure. When she'd swallowed, she looked up at Emilio, her eyes shining. "This is *incredible*," she said, and Cal thought, *Me, look at me like that.*

"Try the mushrooms," Emilio said, happy as a half-Italian clam.

"Go away," Cal told him, but Emilio stayed until Min had bitten into one of the huge mushrooms and told him with heartfelt passion that he was a genius.

"Can I get some credit for bringing you here?" Cal said when Emilio was gone.

"Yes," Min said. "You are a genius at restaurants. Now be quiet so I can concentrate on this."

Cal sighed and gave up on the conversation for the rest of the meal. There was a skirmish at the end when Min tried to insist on separate checks, but Cal said, "I invited you, I pay. Back off, woman." She looked as though she were going to argue for a moment, and then she nodded. "Thank you very much," she told him. "You've given me a lovely meal and a new favorite restaurant," and he felt appreciated for the first time that night.

When they left, she kissed Emilio on the cheek. "Your bread is the greatest, Emilio, but the chicken is a work of art." Then she kissed him on the other cheek.

"Hey," Cal said. "I'm right here. I *paid* for the chicken."

"Don't beg," Min told him and went out the door.

"Morrisey, I think you just met your match," Emilio said.

"Not even close," Cal said, grateful to be without her for a moment. "This was our first, last, and only date."

"Nope," Emilio said. "I saw the way you looked at each other."

"That was fear and loathing," Cal said, opening the door.

"God, you're dumb," Emilio said, and Cal ignored him and went out into the dark to find Min.

Chapter Three

"Infatuation is the fun part of falling in love," Cynthie said to David when they were ensconced in Serafino's and the waiter had brought their very expensive filets and departed.

David smiled at her and thought, *I bet Min isn't talking psychology with Cal.* God knew what Min was doing with Cal. Whatever it was, he was going to have to find a way to stop it.

"Infatuation triggers a chemical in the brain called PEA," Cynthie said. "Your heart races, and you get breathless and dizzy, you tremble, and you can't think. It's what most people think of when they think of falling in love, and everybody goes through it." She smiled a lovely, far-away smile. "Our infatuation was wonderful. We couldn't resist each other."

"Hmm." David picked up his blue-frosted margarita glass. "Tell me again how it's not working out for them."

"Well," Cynthie said, "about now, he should be realizing it's time to cut his losses. He'll take her to her car to make sure she's safe, and then he'll shake her hand and say, 'Have a nice life,' and that'll be it."

"What if he was attracted to her?"

"I told you, he wasn't," Cynthie said, but her smile faded. "But if he was, which he wasn't, then he'd ask her out again and look for more cues, more evidence that she's somebody he should love. Like whether his family and friends like her. But she's not Roger's type, he likes giggly little blondes, and I doubt Tony even saw her since he's pretty much a breast-butt-legs man, so it wasn't his friends who prompted him to pick her up."

"Hard to tell what made him do that," David said, trying to sound innocent.

"And she's not going to meet his family, but even if she did, his mother would hate her, his mother disapproves of everything, so that wouldn't be a cue, since Cal needs his family to approve of him."

"So you're saying that's all it would take for them to reject each other?" David said. "Friends and family disapproving?"

"Unless she doesn't like her family or wants to rebel against them. Then their disapproval would push her into his arms, but it doesn't sound like that's the case."

"No," David said, thinking of two dinners with Min's parents in the past two months. "They're very close."

"Then family and friends are very powerful," Cynthie said. "Which is why I've been nice to Tony for nine months. But, David, it's not going to happen. Cal is in the mature love and attachment stage with me, which means he won't be attracted to Min."

"Mature love. That would be the, uh, fourth stage," David said, trying to show he'd been listening.

"Right," Cynthie said. "Infatuation doesn't last because it's conditional and conditions change, but if it's real love, it turns into mature, unconditional love, and new chemicals are released in the brain, endorphins that make you feel warm and peaceful and satisfied and content whenever you're with the one you love." She took a deep breath. "And miserable when you're without him because if he's not there, the brain won't produce the chemicals."

"Oh," David said, understanding now. "So you're going through endorphin withdrawal."

"Temporarily," Cynthie said, her chin up. "He'll be back. He's going without sex, which is pain, a physiological cue to deepen his attachment to me."

"Pain," David said, thinking anything that hurt Cal was a good idea.

Cynthie nodded. "In order to move from infatuation to attachment, Cal will have to feel joy or pain when he's with Min. The joy could be great conversation or great sex, the pain could be jealousy, frustration, fear, almost anything that adds stress. The pain cue is the reason there are so many wartime romances. And office romances."

"Right," David said, remembering an intern from his earlier years.

"But I don't think that's going to happen tonight. I think he's going to be bored. I must say that it's a great comfort to know that your Min is dull and frigid."

"I didn't say she was dull and frigid," David said. "I wouldn't date somebody who was dull and frigid."

"Then you should have stuck it out," Cynthie said. "Infatuation lasts anywhere from six months to three years, and you can't know you've found the right person until you've worked your way through it. You quit at two months so you couldn't have reached attachment and neither could she." She shrugged. "Mistake."

"Six months to *three years?*" David said. "And you pushed Cal after nine months?" He shrugged. "Mistake."

Cynthie put down her fork. "Not a mistake. I know Cal, I have written articles on Cal, and he is in the attachment stage, we both are."

David stopped eating, appalled. "You wrote about your lover?"

"Well, I didn't call him by his real name," Cynthie said. "And I didn't say he was *my* lover."

"Isn't that unethical?"

"No." Cynthie pushed her plate away, most of her dinner untouched. "That's how we met. I'd heard about him through a couple of my clients. He had quite a reputation."

"I know," David said, thinking vicious thoughts about Cal Morrisey, God's Gift to Women. "Totally undeserved."

"Are you kidding?" Cynthie said. "I was *studying* him, and he got me." Her mouth curved again. "Nature gave him that face and body, and his parents gave him conditional affection as a child. He's been trained to please people to get approval, and the people he likes to please most are women, who are more than willing to be pleased by him because he looks the way he does. So his looks guarantee assumption and his charm guarantees attraction. He's one of the most elegant adaptive solutions I've ever observed. The papers I wrote on him got *a lot* of attention."

David tried to picture Cal Morrisey as a child, trying to earn affection. All he could come up with was a good-looking dark-haired kid in a tuxedo, leaning on a swing set and smiling confidently at little girls. "Did he know you wrote papers on him?"

"No," Cynthie said. "He still doesn't. He never will. I finished that work, it's over. I'm writing a book now, already under contract. It's almost done." She smiled, a satisfied feline smile. "The point is, I'm not some silly woman moaning, 'But I thought he loved me,' I have clinical proof he does love me. And he'll come back to me soon, as long as your Min doesn't distract him."

"So," David said, leaning closer. "If we wanted to make sure they didn't get to—what was it? Attraction?—what would we do?"

Cynthie's eyes widened. "Do?" She put her wineglass down and thought about it. "Well, I suppose we could talk to their friends and families, poison the well, so to speak. And we could offer them joy in different forms to counteract whatever happens between them. But that wouldn't be . . . David, we don't have to do anything. Cal loves me."

"Right," David said, sitting back. *Family*, he thought. *I have an in with the family.*

Cynthie smiled at him. "I'm tired of talking about them," she said. "What is it that you do for a living?"

David thought, *It's about time we got to me.* He said, "I'm in software development," and watched her eyes glaze over.

Outside Emilio's, Min took a deep breath of summer night air and thought, *I'm happy.* Evidently great food was an antidote to rage and humiliation. Good to know for the future.

Then Cal came out and said, "Where's your car?" and broke her mood.

"No car," Min said. "I can walk it." She held out her hand. "Thank you for a lovely evening. Sort of. Good-bye."

"No," Cal said, ignoring her hand. "Which way is your place?"

"Look," Min said, exasperated. "*I can walk*—"

"In the city alone at night? No, you can't. I was raised better than that. I'm walking you home, and there's nothing you can do about it, so which way are we going?"

Min thought about arguing with him, but there wasn't much point. Even one short evening with Calvin Morrisey had taught her that he got what he wanted. "Okay. Fine. Thank you very much. It's this way."

She started off down the street, listening to the breeze in the trees and the muted street noises, and Cal fell into step beside her, the sound of his footfalls matching the click of her heels in a nice rhythm.

"So what is it you do for a living?" she asked.

"I run a business seminar group with two partners."

"You're a teacher?" Min said, surprised.

"Yes," he said. "So you're an actuary. I have a great deal of respect for your profession. You do it for money. I do it for recreation."

"Do what?"

"Figure out whether something's a good bet or not." He looked down at her. "You're a gambler. You do it with millions of dollars of an insurance company's money. I do it with ten-dollar bills."

"Yeah, but I don't lose any of my own money," Min said.

"Neither do I," Cal said.

"You win *every* bet?" Min said, disbelief making her voice flat.

"Pretty much," Cal said.

"Hell of a guy," Min said. "Is that why you went into business for yourself? So you could control the risk?"

"No, I just didn't want to work for anybody else," Cal said. "That didn't leave me any other options."

"We turn here," Min said, slowing as they came to the corner. "Look, I can—"

"Keep walking," Cal said, and Min did.

"So what's the name of this company?"

"Morrisey, Packard, Capa."

"Packard and Capa being the other two guys on the landing with you," Min said. "The big blond and the bull—uh, the jock-looking one."

"Yeah." Cal grinned. "Bull?"

"One of my friends mentioned his head looked like a bullet," Min said, wincing. "She meant it as a compliment."

"Bet she did," Cal said. "That would be the redhead, right?"

"You noticed her," Min said, and felt a twinge.

"No, the bullet-head noticed her," Cal said.

"Don't tell him she said that," Min said. "She wouldn't want to hurt his feelings."

"It takes a lot to bring Tony down," Cal said. "But I won't mention it."

"Thank you."

The farther they got from the busier streets, the darker it became, even with the streetlights, and Min began to feel grateful he was there. "So why do people hire you to teach? I mean, you specifically. Instead of somebody else."

"We tailor the programs," Cal said. "In any instructional situation, a certain percentage of the student population will fail to master the material. We guarantee one hundred percent and we stay until it's achieved."

"That sounds like promotional literature."

"It's also the truth."

"And you do this how?" Min said. "Charming them?"

"What have you got against charming?" Cal said.

"It so rarely goes hand in hand with 'honest,' " Min said.

Cal sighed. "People shut down because of fear. The first thing we do is analyze the students to find out who's afraid and how they're coping with it. Some of them freeze up, so we put them with Roger. Very gentle guy, Roger. He can reassure anybody into learning anything."

"That's a little creepy," Min said, trying to picture Roger as one of those slick self-help gurus.

"You are a very suspicious woman," Cal said. "Then some people hide their fear in wisecracks, disrupting class. Tony takes them. They joke around together until everybody's relaxed."

"And who do you get?" Min said.

"I get the angry ones," Cal said. "The ones who are mad that they're scared."

"And you charm them out of it," Min said.

"Well, I wouldn't put it that way, but yes, I suppose that's one interpretation."

The angry ones. They walked on in silence, their footsteps echoing together.

Min looked up at him. "You must have felt right at home with me tonight."

"Nope," Cal said. "You're not mad because you're scared. I doubt that much scares you. You're mad because somebody was lousy to you. And there's not enough charm in the world to get you out of that until you've resolved the deeper issue."

"And yet you kept on trying," Min said.

"No, I didn't," Cal said. "Once you'd told me you'd been dumped, I backed off."

Min thought about it. "I guess you did. Pretty much."

"Now aren't you sorry you were such a grump all night?" Cal said.

"No," Min said. "Because you were pouring on the charm before that which means you were trying to get something from me, God knows what—" *Sex to win a bet, you beast.* "—and you deserved to be called on that."

A few steps later Cal said, "Fair enough."

Min smiled to herself in the darkness and thought, *Well, he does have an honest bone in his body. Too bad it's just one.* They walked on in silence until they reached the steps to her house. "This is it. Thank you very much—"

"Where?" Cal said, looking around. "I don't see a house."

"Up there," Min said, pointing up the hill. "The steps are right there. So we can—"

Cal peered up the hill into the darkness. "Christ, woman, that looks like Everest. How many steps are there?"

"Thirty-two," Min said, "and another twenty-six after that to get up to my apartment in the attic." She held out her hand. "So we'll say goodnight here. Thank you for the walk home. Best of luck in the future."

He ignored her to look up the hill again. "Nope. I'm not leaving you to climb up there in the dark."

"It's okay," Min said. "Seventy-eight percent of women who are attacked are attacked by men they know."

"Is that another shot at me?" Cal said.

"No. I don't know any men who would climb thirty-two steps to attack me, so I'm safe. You can go home with a clear conscience."

"No," he said patiently. "I can't. Get moving. I'll be right behind you."

Behind her? Thirty-two steps with him looking at her butt? "No, you won't."

"Look, it's late, I'm tired, can we just—"

"It'll be a cold day in hell when you follow me up those steps. You want to go up, you go first."

"*Why?*" he said, mystified.

"You're not looking at my rear end all the way up that hill."

He shook his head. "You know, Dobbs, you look like a sane person, and then you open your mouth—"

"Start climbing or go home," Min said.

Cal sighed and took the first step. "Wait a minute. Now you'll be looking at my butt all the way up the steps."

"Yes, but you probably have a great butt," Min said. "It's an entirely different dynamic."

"I can't even see yours," Cal said. "It's dark and your jacket is too long."

"Climb or leave," Min said, and Cal started up the steps.

When they got to the top, he hesitated, and she saw the mid-century stone and stucco house through his eyes, dark and shabby and overgrown with climbing rosebushes that were so ancient they'd degenerated into thornbushes. "It's nice," she said, on the defensive.

"It's probably great in the daytime," he said, politely.

"Right." Min pushed past him to climb the stone steps to the front porch. She unlocked the door. "There, see? You can go now."

"This is not your door," he said. "You said you live twenty-six steps up."

"Fine, climb all the way to the attic." She waved him in front of her into the square hall of the house. With him there, the faded blue wallpaper and dull oak woodwork looked shabby instead of comfortable, and that irritated her. "Up," she said, pointing to the narrow stairway along one wall, looking even narrower now that he was at the bottom with what looked like several yards of shoulder blocking her way, and he climbed two more flights of stairs to the narrow landing with her following.

He had a great butt.

And that's all that's nice about him, Min told herself. *Be sensible, keep your head here. You're never going to see him again.*

"Well, at least you know anybody who walks you home twice is serious about you," he said, as he reached the top.

He turned as he said it, and Min, still two steps down scoping out his rear end, walked into his elbow and clipped herself hard over the eye, knocking herself enough off balance that she tripped back, grabbed the railing, and sat down on the step.

"Oh, *Christ,*" he said. "I'm sorry." He bent over her and she warded him off.

"No, no," she said. "My fault. Following too close." *Ouch,* she thought, gingerly feeling the place he'd smacked her. *That's what you get for being shallow and objectifying the beast.*

"Just let me see it," he said, trying to look into her eyes. He put his hand gently on the side of her face to tip her chin up.

"No." She brushed his hand away as her skin started to tingle. "I'm fine. Aside from being part of the seventy-eight percent of women who are attacked by—"

"Oh, cut me a break," he said, straightening. "Are you all right?"

"Yes." She stood up again and detoured around him to unlock her door. "You can go now."

"Right." He picked up her hand and shook it once. "Great to meet you, Dobbs. Sorry about the elbow to the head. Have a nice life."

"Oh, I'm going to," Min said. "I'm giving up men and getting a cat." She slipped inside and shut the door in his face before he could say anything else. *Have a nice life. Who is he kidding?*

She turned on her grandmother's china lamp by the door, and her living room sprang into shabby but comforting view. The light on her machine was blinking, and she went over and pressed the button, and then rubbed her temple while she listened.

"Min," her sister's voice said. "Just wanted to make sure you didn't forget the fitting tomorrow. It'll be nice to see you." Diana sounded a little woebegone, which was not like her, and Min replayed the message to hear her again. Something was wrong.

"The Dobbs girls cannot win," she said, and thought about Calvin Morrisey. She went over to her battered mantel and looked over the snow globes lined up there into the tarnished mirror that had once hung in her grandmother's hall. A plain round face, plain brown hair, that's what Cal Morrisey had looked at all night. And now it had a nice bruise. She sighed and picked up the snow globe Bonnie had given her for Christmas, Cinderella and her prince on the steps of their blue castle, doves flying overhead. Cal Morrisey would look right at home on those steps. She, on the other hand, would be asked to try the servant's entrance. "Just not the fairy tale type," she said and put the globe down to go turn on her stereo, hitting the up button until Elvis started to sing "The Devil in Disguise."

"And let's not forget that's what Calvin Morrisey is, Dobbs," she told herself, and went to put arnica on her bruise and take a hot bath to wash the memory of the evening away. At least the part with David in it. There were some moments after David that weren't entirely horrible.

But she definitely wasn't going to see Calvin Morrisey again.

When Cal got to work the next morning, the sun was shining through the tall windows in the loft office, the smell of coffee permeated the room, Roger waved to him from his desk by the window, and Elvis Costello was singing "The Angels Wanna Wear My Red Shoes" on the

CD player. *All right*, Cal thought. He dropped a folder on the frosted glass desktop, poured himself a cup of coffee, and pulled out his Aeron chair, ready to make the world a better place for people trapped in business training seminars.

Tony came through the door and slapped him on the back. "Nice going last night. Tell me you won."

"What are you talking about?" Cal said.

"The bet with David," Tony said. "The one about the gray-checked suit. Tell me you won it."

"Sure." Cal dropped into his desk chair. "You saw me leave with her."

"You're right, you're right, I should have had faith. You want to tell David or should I?"

"Tell him what?" Cal turned on his Mac and hit the GET MESSAGE button for his e-mail.

"That you had sex with the suit," Tony said.

"What?" Cal said, squinting at the screen while Elvis sang backup to his morning. "Of course I didn't."

"Oh." Tony nodded. "Well, you've still got a month."

"Tony," Cal said as the list of messages showed up in the window. "I don't know what you're talking about, but I'm positive it's wasting my time."

"David bet you that you could get the suit into bed in a month," Tony was saying with obvious patience. "I could use the money, too, so if you'd—"

"No," Cal said. "I did not make that bet."

"David thinks you made the bet," Tony said.

"No, he doesn't," Cal said. "Now that he's sober he does not think that he bet me ten thousand dollars I could get a strange woman into bed. Now could we get some work done? There's money in it for you. They pay us to do this stuff."

He slid the folder on his desk across to Tony, who picked it up and leafed through it. "Piece of cake," he said, and began to move away. "Oh, just so you know, Cynthie left with David last night."

"Good for them." Cal turned back to his e-mail.

"This doesn't bother you?" Tony said.

"Why are you harassing me this morning?" Cal said, putting an edge on his voice.

"I just want to make sure you're not going back to her," Tony said. "My future is on the line here."

"How?" Cal said.

"Well, you'll get married first," Tony said, coming back to sit on the corner of Cal's desk. "You always do everything first. And then Roger will get married and you'll both move to the suburbs. And Roger is going to marry somebody as uptight as he is, which means I'll have to live with you, and since Cynthie never did like me, she'd be a problem to convince on that."

"So would I," Cal said. "Get off my desk."

"It wouldn't be *with* you, not in the house," Tony said. "I figure a nice apartment over the garage. It'd be convenient for you. You could come over and watch the game and get drunk and not have to drive home. And I could baby-sit the kids when you and the wife wanted to go out."

"First," Cal said, "I'm not getting married, so forget the wife. Second, if I was insane enough to get married, I wouldn't have kids. Third, if I was insane enough to get married and have kids, it would be a cold day in hell I'd let you baby-sit."

"Well, we'll both have matured by then," Tony said. "I wouldn't let me baby-sit now, either."

"I'm getting married first," Roger said.

They both turned to him, and he smiled back, big, blond, and placid in the sunlight from the big loft windows.

"I'm going to marry Bonnie," Roger said.

Cal frowned at him. "Who's Bonnie?"

"The mini-blonde he met last night," Tony said, disgust in his voice.

"Her name is Bonnie," Roger said, his voice like ice, and both Cal and Tony straightened.

"He's serious," Cal said to Tony. "What happened?"

"The redhead wanted me," Tony said. "So I went over. And Roger followed and hooked up with the mini . . . with Bonnie. And sometime between then and now he lost his mind." He shook his head at Roger.

"This is a woman you've known less than twelve hours. It took you a year to pick out a couch, but you're seriously—"

"Yes," Roger said. "She's the one."

"Maybe," Cal said, thinking, *The hell she is.* "You didn't tell her that, though. Right?"

"No," Roger said. "I thought it was too soon."

"You *think?*" Tony said. "Jesus."

"I'm going to marry her," Roger said, "so stop yelling and get used to it. She's perfect."

"No woman is perfect," Tony said. "Which is why we must keep looking. You going to see her tonight?"

"No," Roger said. "They have some Thursday night thing they do every other week. Bonnie called it their 'If Dinner.' "

"They?" Tony said.

Roger nodded. "Bonnie, Liza, and Min."

"Who's Min?" Tony said, lost again.

"The one I'm not going to sleep with," Cal said. If Bonnie was anything like Min, Roger was in big trouble.

"You seeing Bonnie on Friday?" Tony said to Roger, sticking to the basics.

Roger nodded. "She said they'll be at The Long Shot. It's not their regular hangout, but she said she'd look for me there. And she's coming to the game Saturday. And we might go to dinner Saturday night."

"She's coming to watch you coach a kid's baseball game?" Cal said. "She must love you a lot."

"Not yet," Roger said. "But she will."

"Friday," Tony said, ignoring them. "That's good. I can hit on Liza, and Cal can move on the suit."

"No," Cal said.

Roger looked sympathetic. "What happened?"

Cal went back to his computer. "She's a conservative, antigambling actuary who spent dinner bitching at me. Then I took her home, climbed fifty-eight steps to her apartment to make sure she didn't get mugged, and elbowed her in the eye. It was the worst date of my life, and I'm sure it was in her bottom five."

"You hit her?" Tony said.

"By accident," Cal said. "I'd send flowers to apologize, but she's anticharm, too. It's over. Move on."

"So you're going to give up on another one," Tony said, shaking his head.

Cal looked up at him, annoyed. "Now tell me about your deep and lasting relationships."

"Yes, but that's me," Tony said. "I'm shallow."

"Bonnie lives on the first floor of that house," Roger said, as if they hadn't spoken, "so I just had to make the first thirty-two steps. And then she felt bad for me, so she invited me in for coffee. I can get used to the steps."

"Does that mean Liza lives on the second floor?" Tony said.

"No, Liza lives over on Pennington," Roger said. "She moves every year to a new place, about the time she changes jobs. Bonnie says Liza likes change."

Cal looked at Tony. "You didn't walk her home?"

"She ditched me while I was in the john," Tony said. "I think she's playing hard to get."

"Sounds like Min," Cal said, going back to the computer. "Except I don't think she's playing."

"Bonnie and I walked Liza home," Roger said. "It was nice. It gave me more time with Bonnie."

"Jesus, man, pull yourself together," Tony said.

"You're serious about this?" Cal said, turning back to Roger.

"Yes."

Cal saw determination on his face. "Congratulations," he said, deciding to check Bonnie out. "Wait a month to propose. You don't want to scare her."

"That's what I thought," Roger said.

"You're both nuts," Tony said.

"We're all going to be unemployed if we don't get to work," Cal said. "Start with the Batchelder refresher."

"Bonnie says Min is great," Roger said. "She looked nice."

"Min is not nice," Cal said. "Min is mad at the world and taking it out on whatever guy is standing next to her. Now about the Batchelder refresher—"

"Are you sure David knows there's no bet?" Tony said.

"Positive," Cal said. "I'm never seeing that woman again. Now about the *Batchelder refresher* . . ."

At half past four that afternoon, Min walked into the ivory moiré–draped fitting room of the city's best bridal emporium, well aware she was late and not caring much. Her mother was probably so absorbed in harassing Diana and the fitter that—

"You're late," Nanette Dobbs said. "The appointment was for four."

"I work." Min crossed the thick gold carpet and detoured around the dark-haired bundle of exasperation that had given birth to her, dropping her jacket on an ivory-upholstered chair. "That means the insurance company gets first dibs on my time. If you want me here on the dot, schedule this for after work."

"That's ridiculous," Nanette said. "Your dress is in the second dressing room. The fitter is with Diana and the other girls. Give me your blouse, you'll just drop it on the floor in there." She held out one imperious, French-manicured hand, and Min sighed and took off her blouse.

"Oh, *Min*," her mother said, her voice heavy with unsurprised contempt. "Wherever did you get that bra?"

Min looked down at her underwear. Plain cotton, but perfectly respectable. "I have no idea. Why?"

"White cotton," Nanette said. "Honestly, Min, plain cotton is like plain vanilla—"

"I like plain vanilla."

"—there's no excitement there at all."

Min blinked. "I was at work. There's never any excitement."

"I'm talking about men," Nanette said. "You're thirty-three. Your prime years are past you, and you're wearing white cotton."

"I was at *work*," Min said, losing patience.

"It doesn't matter." Her mother shook out Min's blouse, checked the label, saw it was silk, and looked partly mollified. "If you're wearing white cotton lingerie, you'll feel like white cotton, and you'll act like white cotton, and white cotton cannot get a man, nor can it keep one. Always wear lace."

"You'd make a nice pimp," Min said, and headed for the dressing room.

"*Minerva,*" her mother said.

"Well, I'm sorry." Min stopped and turned around. "But honestly, Mother, this conversation is getting old. I'm not even sure I want to get married, and you're critiquing my underwear because it's not good enough bait. Can't you—"

Nanette lifted her chin, and her jawline became even more taut. "This is the kind of attitude that's going to lose David."

Min took a deep breath. "About David . . ."

"What?" Her mother's body tensed beneath her size four Dana Buchman suit. "What about David?"

Min smiled cheerfully. "We're no longer seeing each other."

"Oh, *Min,*" Nanette wailed, clutching Min's blouse to her bosom, the picture of despair in the middle of a lot of expensive gold and ivory décor.

"He wasn't right for me, Mother," Min said.

"Yes," Nanette said, "but couldn't you have kept him until after the wedding?"

"Evidently not," Min said. "Let's cut to the chase. What do I have to do to keep you from mentioning his name ever again?"

"Wear lace."

"That will get you off my back?"

"For a while."

Min grinned at her and headed for the dressing room door. "You are a piece of work."

"So are you, darling," Nanette said, surveying her eldest. "I'm very proud of you, you know. You have a blotch of makeup over your eye. What is that?"

"Oh, for crying out loud." Min closed the door behind her. She unzipped her skirt, let it fall to the gold carpet, and studied herself in the gold-framed mirror. "You're not that bad," she told herself, not convinced. "You just have to find a man who likes very healthy women."

She unclipped the long lavender skirt from the gold hanger and stepped into it, being careful not to rip the knife-pleated chiffon ruffle at the bottom, and sucked in her stomach to get it buttoned. Then she shrugged on the lavender chiffon blouse and buttoned the tiny buttons, stretching the fabric tightly across her bust so that her white bra showed at the corners of the low, squared bodice. She shook out the sleeves, and the chiffon fell over her hands in wide double ruffles that she would drag through everything at the reception. The blouse also erupted around her hips in more ruffles at the side. "Oh, yes," she said. "More width at the hip. Can't ever get enough of that."

Then she picked up the corset, a blue and lavender watercolor moiré tied with lavender ribbons. The fabric had been so beautiful when Diana had chosen it six months before that Min had hired the seamstress to make a comforter for her bed with it, and she looked at the narrow corset now and thought, *I'm going to have to wear the comforter. This is never going to fit.* She took a deep breath and wrapped the corset around her. It shoved her breasts up to a dizzying height and then failed to meet in the middle by almost two inches. *Carbs.* She thought vicious thoughts about Cal Morrisey and Emilio's bread. Then she tried to smooth out the extra foundation without showing the bruise and went out into the dressing room to face her mother.

Instead, she found Diana, standing on the fitting platform in front of the huge, gold-framed mirror, flanked by her two lovely bridesmaids, the women Liza called Wet and Worse, while the Dixie Chicks played on Diana's portable CD player.

" 'Ready to Run,' " Min said to Diana. "And so not appropriate."

"Hmmm?" Diana said, staring into the mirror. "No, it's *Runaway Bride.*"

"Right," Min said, remembering that Diana had decided to score her wedding to music from Julia Roberts's movies. Well, at least it was a plan.

"I loved that movie," Susie said. She looked blond, bilious, miserable, and, well, wet in corseted green chiffon, the loser in the bridesmaid dress lottery.

"I thought it was ridiculous," dark-haired Karen, a.k.a. Worse, said, looking sophisticated and superior in corseted blue chiffon.

Min waved her hand at Worse. "Scoot over so I can see my sister."

Worse moved, and Min got her first look at Diana. "Wow."

Diana looked like a fairy tale come to life in ivory chiffon and satin. Her dark curling hair fell from an artfully messy knot into pearl-strewn tendrils around her pale oval face and her neck rose gracefully above the perfect expanse of skin revealed by a very low, square-necked bodice identical to the one flashing Min's white bra. Her neckline had chiffon ruffles cascading over the beaded ivory corset that cinched her slim waist, and more ruffles fell from her wrists and flowed out from under the corset, parting to reveal a straight skirt flounced with more ruffles along the side like panniers and ending in a knife-pleated border that touched the toes of her satin buckled pumps. She turned on the platform to look into the mirror and Min saw the bustle of gathered chiffon at the base of her spine that erupted in more and more ruffles and pleats until the back of the dress took on a life of its own, quivering when Diana moved.

"What do you think?" Diana said, no expression at all on her face.

I think you look like a sex-crazed princess on heroin, Min thought, but she said, "I think you look beautiful," because that was true, too.

"You look gorgeous," Worse said, straightening Di's skirt, which didn't need straightening.

"Uh huh," Wet said. Min wanted to feel sorry for her—it couldn't be easy watching your best friend marry your ex-boyfriend, especially when you looked like hell in green—but Wet was so spineless that it was hard to sympathize.

"It wouldn't do for a morning wedding," Diana said, touching the ribbon bow at her breasts. "It wouldn't work for evening, either. But my wedding is at dusk. That's magic time. It changes everything."

"You look like magic," Min said, hearing the same strain in Diana's voice that she'd heard on her answering machine the night before. "Are you all right?"

Diana turned back to the mirror. "You wouldn't be caught dead in this, would you?"

"If I looked like you, I might."

Worse surveyed Min from head to toe, taking in the bursting corset and white bra along the way. "It's not Min's style."

"You think?" Min said. "Because I was going to wear the corset to the office when this whole deal was done. Could I talk to my sister alone for a minute, please?"

Worse raised her eyebrows, but Wet escaped into the dressing rooms gladly, and when Min folded her arms and stared, Worse gave up and left, too.

"What's going on?" Min asked Diana, as the Dixie Chicks finished and Martina McBride began to sing the impossibly chipper "I Love You."

"Nothing," Diana said, watching herself in the mirror. "Well, the cake, we're having problems with the cake, but everything else is perfect."

"Is it Greg?" Min said, thinking, *I wouldn't want to marry a wimp no matter how cute and rich he was.* If she ever got married, it'd be to somebody with edge, somebody who'd be tricky and fast and interesting forever—

"Greg is perfect," Diana said, fluffing the ruffles that somehow made her hips looks slimmer.

"Oh, good," Min said. "What about the cake?"

"The cake . . ." Diana cleared her throat. "The cake didn't get ordered in time."

"I thought Greg knew this great baker," Min said.

"He does," Diana said. "But he . . . forgot, and now it's too late, so I have to find a new baker."

"Who can do a huge art cake for three weeks from now?"

"It's not Greg's fault," Diana said. "You know men. They're not dependable on stuff like that. It was my fault for not checking."

"Not all men are undependable," Min said. "I met a real beast last night, but he'd have gotten that cake."

"Well, Greg isn't a beast," Diana said. "I'd rather have a good man who forgets cakes than a beast who remembers them."

"Good point," Min said. "Look, I'll find you a cake. It's the least I can do to make up for my screwups."

Diana gave up on her ruffles and turned around. "What's wrong? You're not a screwup. What's the matter?"

"I lost David, and I'm too fat for this corset thing," Min said, holding up the ribbon ends.

"You're not fat," Diana said, but she stepped down off the platform. "They probably sent the wrong size. Let me see."

Min untied the corset and handed it over and then watched as Diana flipped it inside out with expert hands.

"What happened with David?" Diana said as she frowned at the tag.

"I wouldn't sleep with him so he left."

"What a dumbass." Diana looked up, mystified. "You know, this is an eight, it should fit."

"In what universe?" Min said, outraged. "I wasn't an eight at birth. Who ordered this thing?"

"I did," Nanette said from behind her. "I assumed you'd be losing weight for your sister's wedding. You're still on your diet, aren't you?"

"Yes," Min said, biting the word off as she turned to face her mother. "But let's be realistic here. You bought a blouse that fit." She looked down to where the tiny buttons stood at attention as they crossed her bustline. "Sort of. Why not—"

"You've had a year," her mother said, clutching a lot of lace from the lingerie department. "I thought the corset could cinch you in if you missed your target by a few pounds, but you've had plenty of time to lose that weight."

Min took a deep breath and popped the button on her skirt. "Look, Mother, I am never going to be thin. I'm Norwegian. If you wanted a thin daughter, you should not have married a man whose female ancestors carried cows home from the pasture."

"You're half Norwegian," Nanette said, "which is no excuse at all because there are plenty of slim Nordic beauties. You're just eating to rebel against me."

"Mother, sometimes it's not about you," Min snapped as she held her skirt together. "*Sometimes it's genetics.*"

"Not your loud voice, dear," her mother said, and turned to Diana as she held up the corset. "We'll just have to tie it tighter."

"Good idea," Min said. "Then when I pass out at the altar, you can point out how slim and Nordic I am."

"Minerva, this is your *sister's wedding*," Nanette said. "You can sacrifice a little."

"It's okay, it's okay," Diana said, holding out her hands. "There's time to have one made in Min's size. Everything will be fine."

"Oh, good." Min stepped up on the platform to look at herself in the trifold mirror. She looked like the blowsy barmaid who worked in the inn behind the castle, the one who'd trash-picked one of the princess's castoffs. "This is so not me."

"It's a great color for you, Min," Diana said softly as she came to stand behind her on the platform, and Min leaned back so their shoulders touched.

"You're going to be the most amazing bride," she told Diana. "People are going to gasp when they see you."

"You, too," Diana said, and squeezed Min's shoulder.

Yeah, when my corset explodes and my breasts hit the minister.

"What happened to your eye?" Diana said in Min's ear, low enough so that Nanette couldn't hear.

"The beast hit me last night," Min said, and then when Diana straightened she added, "I walked into his elbow. Not his fault."

"That's the wrong bra for that dress," Nanette said from behind them.

"You're not by any chance my stepmother are you?" Min said to her mother's reflection. "Because that would explain so much."

"Here, darling," Nanette said and handed her five different colored lace bras. "Go in there and put one of these on and bring me that cotton thing. I'm going to burn it."

"What cotton thing?" Diana said.

"I'm wearing a plain white bra," Min told her as she stepped off the platform, her hands full of lace.

Diana widened her eyes and looked prim. "Well, you're going to hell."

"*Diana,*" Nanette said.

"I know," Min said as she headed for the dressing room. "That's where all the best men are."

"*Minerva,*" Nanette said. "Where are you going?"

"It's Thursday," Min said, over her shoulder. "I'm meeting Liza and Bonnie for dinner, and I don't want to talk about my underwear anymore." She stopped in the doorway to the dressing room. "Order the bigger corset—*much bigger, Mother*—and we'll try this again when it comes in."

"No carbs," her mother called after her as she went into the dressing room. "*And no butter.*"

"I know you stole me from my real parents," Min called back. "They'd let me eat butter." Then she shut the door behind her before Nanette could tell her to avoid sugar, too.

Chapter Four

W hen Cal got home from work, he flipped on the white overhead light, kicked off his shoes, and went into the white galley kitchen behind the white breakfast bar to pour himself a Glenlivet. Even as he poured, Elvis Costello blared out in the next apartment, reverberating "She" through the wall.

"Oh, Christ," Cal said, and put his glass on his forehead. Shanna's rocky romance must have crashed. He tossed back the drink and went to pound on her door.

When Shanna opened the door, her pretty face was tear-stained under her tangled mop of soft kinky hair. "Hi, Cal," she said and sniffed. "Come on in."

He followed her into the Technicolor version of his apartment, wincing until she'd turned Elvis down to a reasonable volume. "Tell me about it."

"It was awful," she said, going to her bright red bookcase and moving aside a madly colored tiki god doll to get the bottle of Glenlivet she kept for him.

"I just had one," he said, warding her off.

"I thought this was it." Shanna put the tiki back and changed course to the big old couch she'd covered with a purple Indian bedspread. "I thought it was forever."

"You always think it's forever." Cal sat down beside her and put his arm around her. "Who was it this time? I lost track."

"Megan," Shanna said, her face crumpling again.

"Right." Cal put his feet on the ancient trunk she used for a coffee table. "Megan the bitch. You know, maybe you should try dating for fun instead. Or take a break, that's what I—"

"Megan was fun," Shanna said.

"Megan was a humorless pain in the ass," Cal said. "Why you always fall for women who make you feel guilty is beyond me. That kind makes me run."

Shanna looked at him with watery contempt. "All kinds make you run."

"This is not about me," Cal said as Elvis finished with a last big, "She!" and began again; Shanna had put him on replay. "You have to get a new breakup song."

"I love this song," Shanna said.

"I used to like it," Cal said. "But that was many months ago before you bashed me over the head with it every time your latest disaster left. You're ruining Elvis Costello."

"Nobody can ruin Elvis. Elvis is a god," Shanna said.

"Isn't Megan the one who hated Elvis?" Cal said.

"No, that was Anne," Shanna said. "Although Megan wasn't a fan, either."

"Well, there it is," Cal said. "Play Elvis on the first date, and if she doesn't like him, get rid of her before you get attached."

"Is that what you do?" Shanna let her head fall back on his arm. "Is that how you go through all those women unscathed?"

"This is not about me," Cal said. "This is about you. Stop dating people you think you should like and spend time with somebody who's fun to be with."

"There are people like that?" Shanna said.

"They all are in the beginning," Cal said, and then remembered Min. "Well, except for the woman I had dinner with last night. She was pretty much a pain in the butt from the start."

"Of course you picked up a woman last night." Shanna rolled her head to look at him. "They could drop you in the middle of a guy's locker room and you'd come out with a woman. How do you do it?"

Cal grinned at her. "My natural charm." He could almost see the actuary rolling her eyes as he said it.

Shanna rolled her head away. "And the sad thing is, that's true. I have no natural charm."

"Yes, you do," Cal said. "You just don't use it."

Shanna looked back at him. "I do?"

"When you're not worried about impressing some snobby twit, you're great," Cal said. "You're smart and funny and a good time."

"I am?"

"I hang out with you, don't I?"

"Well, yeah, but you're just being nice."

"I'm not nice," Cal said. "I'm selfish as all hell. And since you've made it clear you'll never sleep with me, I must be spending time with you because you're fun, right? Not counting these wet Elvis nights."

"Right," Shanna said, brightening some.

"Well, my standards of fun are very high," Cal said. "So you must be great. You just date the biggest bitches I've ever met in my life."

"Oh, and the women you date are all sweethearts." Shanna got up and moved away from him.

"This is not about me," Cal said. "The reason you keep crashing and burning is that you have no confidence and you keep picking women who like that about you."

"I know." Shanna sat down on the red barstool next to her breakfast bar and shoved back the yellow curtain she'd draped in the opening to reach for her Betty Boop cookie jar.

"So you should pick somebody who makes you feel good."

Shanna opened the cookie jar and took out an Oreo. "I know."

"How many times have we had this talk?"

"A thousand." Shanna bit savagely into her cookie.

"And every time, you abuse Elvis. That was a good song and you ran it into the ground. Sooner or later, you're going to pay for that."

"I know," Shanna said around her Oreo.

"Pick something that has some fight to it," Cal said. "There must be a pissed-off breakup song."

"I've always liked 'I Will Survive,' " Shanna said, cheering up a little.

"Oh, Christ." Cal stood up. Behind him, Elvis began to sing "She" again. "Set him free, will you?"

Shanna crossed to the bookcase and turned Elvis off. "They're not mean when I meet them, you know."

"Remember your first date with Megan?" Cal said. "You introduced us in the hall?" Shanna nodded. "She apologized for your clothes. I would have bitch-slapped her then but she looked like she could take me."

"She had very high standards."

"She was a bitter, controlling snob," Cal said. "You should have cut your losses after the first date."

"Is that what you did last night?" Shanna said.

"Hell, yes," Cal said.

"Well, I can't do that," Shanna said, going back to her cookie jar. "I'm not like you. I have to give it a fair shot."

Cal sighed. "All right. Why did she leave?"

Shanna's face crumpled again. "She said I was too much of a doormat."

"Well, she wiped her feet on you often enough to know," Cal said. Shanna burst into tears, and he went to her and put his arms around her. "Get mad at her, Shan. She was not a nice person."

"But I loved her!" Shanna wailed into his chest, spitting Oreo crumbs on his shirt.

"No, you didn't," Cal said, holding her tighter. "You wanted to love her. It's not the same thing. You only knew her a couple of weeks."

"It can happen like that." Shanna looked up into his face. "You can just know."

"No," Cal said. "You do not look at somebody, hear Elvis Costello singing 'She' on the soundtrack in your head, and fall in love. It takes time."

"Like you'd know." Shanna pulled away and picked up her cookie jar. "Have you ever stayed with anybody long enough to love her?"

"Hey," Cal said, insulted.

"That's no answer," Shanna said, retreating to her couch with her cookies. "Is that why you keep walking away so fast? Because at least I *try*."

"This is not about me," Cal said.

"I know, I know," Shanna said, fishing out another Oreo. "God, I'm a mess. Want a cookie?"

"No," Cal said. "Get your act together and try again tomorrow. If you swing by the office, I'll take you to lunch before you go to work."

"That would be nice," Shanna said. "You're a good person, Cal. Sometimes I wish you were a woman—"

"Thank you," Cal said doubtfully.

"—and then I remember you have that commitment phobia and I'm glad you're a guy. I have enough problems."

"This is true." Cal put his hand on the doorknob. "Can I go home now?"

"Sure," Shanna said. "Take me someplace expensive tomorrow."

"I'll take you to Emilio's," Cal said. "He needs the business and you like the pesto."

While Cal was trying to prop up Shanna, Min stopped by Emilio's to pick up salad and bread.

"Ah, the lovely Min!" he said when she tracked him down in his kitchen.

"Emilio, my darling," Min said. "I need salad and bread for three right now and a kickass wedding cake for two hundred three weeks from Sunday."

"Oh." Emilio leaned against the counter. "My grandmother makes wedding cakes. They taste like . . ." He shut his eyes. ". . . heaven. Light as a feather." He opened his eyes. "But they're good, old-fashioned cakes, they don't have marzipan birds or fondant icing."

"Could she make a cake and decorate it with fresh flowers?" Min said. "I can get some real pearls. Maybe if the cake is covered with real things instead of sugar imitations, people will be impressed."

"I don't know," Emilio said. "But what matters is how it tastes, and it will taste—"

"Emilio, that's sweet," Min said, imagining Nanette's reaction to that one. "Unfortunately, in this case, what matters is how it looks."

"How about this," Emilio said. "I'll see if she'll do the cake. If she says yes, she'll ice it plain, and you can put the flowers and the pearls on it."

"Me," Min said doubtfully. "Well, not me, but Bonnie can do it, she has fabulous taste. It's a deal. Call your grandma."

Emilio picked up the phone. "So you taking Cal to this wedding?"

"I'm never seeing Cal again," Min said.

"God, you guys are dumb," Emilio said as he punched the numbers into the phone. In a moment, his face brightened. "Nonna?" he said and began to talk in Italian. The only word Min recognized was "Cal" which was worrying, but when Emilio hung up, he was smiling.

"It's all set," he said. "I told her you were Cal's girlfriend. She loves Cal."

"All women do." Min kissed him on the cheek. "You are my hero."

"That's the food," Emilio said, and packed up bread and salad for three for her. Then she went home and walked up thirty-two steps to Bonnie's apartment on the first floor.

"So," Liza said when she answered Bonnie's door. "You want to explain last night?"

"Can I come in first?" Min said, and slid past Liza into Bonnie's bright, warm apartment.

Bonnie had set her mission table with her Royal Doulton Tennyson china and a cut glass vase of grocery roses. It looked so pretty that Min thought, *Okay, my apartment will never look this good, but I could set a better table. I could even cook. I could get my grandmother's kitchen things out of the basement.* It would be nice to do kitchen stuff like her grandmother had. Maybe bake cookies.

That she couldn't eat.

Min sighed and put the Styrofoam boxes down on Bonnie's table.

"What's that?" Bonnie said, poking at the Styrofoam.

"The best salad you'll ever eat, and even better bread," Min said, and Bonnie went to get serving bowls.

"Bread?" Liza said to Min. "You're going to eat bread?"

"No," Min said. "I ate bread last night and then paid for it today. You're going to eat bread, and I'm going to live vicariously."

Liza made a face as she pulled out one of Bonnie's tall dining room chairs. "Like dessert. Stats, you—"

"What did you bring?" Min said, dreading the answer.

"Raspberry Swirl Dove Bars," Liza said, as she sat down.

"Rot in hell," Min said, pulling out her own chair. "Why can't you ever bring fruit?"

"Because fruit is not dessert," Liza said. "Now explain to us why you left the bar with Calvin Morrisey last night."

Min shoved the bread box Liza's way. "David bet him ten bucks he couldn't get me into bed in a month." She watched them freeze in place, Bonnie with a platter of chicken and vegetables in her hands, Liza opening the bread.

"You are *kidding me*," Liza said, her face dangerous with anger.

"I let him pick me up because I had a plan to get a date to the wedding, and then I realized I couldn't put up with that smarmy charm for three weeks, so I ate an excellent dinner and left."

Bonnie's face crumpled. "Oh, honey, that's awful."

"No," Min said. "Let's forget Cal Morrisey and eat. I want to talk about Diana. She's not happy."

"Wet and Worse." Liza gave Min a look that said they'd be talking about Cal again soon. "They'd bring anybody down."

Min closed her eyes. "Do not call them that. I almost called Susie Wet this afternoon at the fitting. She looked like she was about to sob through the whole thing."

"Well, that's understandable," Bonnie said, sympathy in her voice. She put the platter in the middle of the table and sat down, too.

Liza dumped the bread into a bowl. "Maybe Di shouldn't have asked Wet to be a bridesmaid. That's almost cruel."

"It would be worse not to be asked," Bonnie said. "Is that why she's upset, Min?"

"I think it's Greg," Min said, starting on her salad, "but she won't admit it. He's the one who forgot to order the wedding cake."

"Whoa," Liza said. "This is a man who's resisting his own wedding. And let's face it, your mother and Diana railroaded him into it."

"He proposed on his own," Bonnie said.

"I think he wanted a longer engagement," Min said. "But he said yes when they set the date. He's not incapable of speech. He could have said 'No.'"

"To Nanette and Diana?" Liza said as she started on her salad. "Fat chance. Worse will do a kind deed before Greg will grow a spine. Now you talk about Calvin Morrisey and this damn bet. We want to know *everything*."

Half an hour later, the salad was gone, the leftover chicken was in the refrigerator, and Bonnie was unwrapping a Dove Bar as Min finished her recap of the evening.

"At least he walked you home," Bonnie said. "That was nice." She sounded doubtful.

"Yes. And then he hit me in the head, said, 'Have a nice life,' and left me," Min said. "I didn't like him, you guys don't like him, and he didn't like me. I think that's a perfect score."

"I think that whole good-bye thing is a trick," Liza said around a mouthful of Dove Bar. "I think he's putting you off guard, and he'll be back. If you're not careful, he'll charm you into bed and break your heart."

Min frowned at her in exasperation. "How naïve do I look? I know about the bet. Anyway, I have a new plan."

"Oh, good," Liza said. "Because you don't have enough plans."

Min ignored her. "I was listening to Elvis singing 'Love Me Tender' last night, and it occurred to me that if he'd been reincarnated, he'd be about twenty-seven now, and I'm open to younger men. Statistically, the most successful marriages are those in which the woman is eight years older than the man. So I've decided to wait for Elvis to find me."

"You'd only be six years older," Bonnie said.

"Yes, but it would be Elvis, so I'd try harder," Min said.

"Why Elvis?" Liza said.

"Because he always tells the truth when he sings. Elvis is the only man in my life I can trust."

"So let me get this straight," Lisa said, pointing with her half-eaten Dove Bar. "Bonnie is waiting for a fairy tale character to make her life complete, and you're holding out for the reincarnation of a guy who ate fried banana sandwiches."

"Yep," Min said, and Liza shook her head.

"I might have found my prince," Bonnie said. "Roger's good."

"Roger?" Min asked, trying not to watch Liza consume her Dove Bar.

"We picked up the beast's friends last night," Liza said around her ice cream. "Bonnie got the one that walks upright."

"Roger is a sweetheart," Bonnie said. "I'm thinking of breaking my date Saturday night and going out with him instead. I'll wait and see how Friday night with him works out."

"He asked you out?" Min said, relieved to be off the subject of Cal. "Tell all."

"He asked her out for every night for the rest of her life," Liza said. "He's blind for her."

"That's nice." Min picked a last salad leaf out of her bowl to compensate for her lack of sugar. "So he has potential, Bon?"

"Maybe." Bonnie came as close to frowning as she ever did. "I think if I keep seeing him for a couple of weeks and it's working, I'll take him home to Mama and let her scope him out."

Min raised her eyebrows. "You think he'll cross three states to meet your mother after two weeks?"

"He would cross the Andes to get her a toothpick," Liza said. "It's pathetic."

"No, it's not." Bonnie frowned over her ice cream stick. "It's sweet. And he thinks Cal is great, which is confusing."

"So Bonnie met a good one," Min said to Liza, ignoring the Cal reference. "Who'd you get?"

"The village idiot," Liza said. "He also thinks Cal is the man. They're like the Three Stooges. Only not funny."

"The Three Stooges aren't funny," Bonnie said.

"Too true," Min said. "Are you seeing the idiot again?"

"Yes." Liza licked the last of her ice cream off the stick. "I think your beast is coming back, and my idiot babbles nicely when I ask him questions. Plus, there is a bartender who lives next door to the beast with whom I must bond."

"Well, don't ask questions for me," Min said. "Calvin Morrisey is not part of my future."

"He will be tomorrow night," Bonnie said. "He'll be at The Long Shot with Roger and Tony."

Min shook her head. "Then I'll stay home."

"No," Bonnie said, stricken. "We don't have to go there. We'll go somewhere else so you can come, too."

"And make you miss Roger?" Min reconsidered. "No. Not even I am selfish enough to cross True Love. I'll go. I want to see this Roger up close anyway."

"Are you sure Cal made that bet?" Bonnie said.

"I was standing right there," Min said. "I heard it. With my own ears. He said, 'Piece of cake.'" That rankled more than anything.

"Because Roger thinks the world of him," Bonnie said. "He told me all about him, about the three of them. It's kind of sad. They met in summer school when they were in the third grade. Roger said he was a slow thinker, and Tony didn't care about school, and Cal was dyslexic, so everybody thought they were dumb."

"Cal's dyslexic?" Min said, surprised.

"Tony *is* dumb," Liza said at the same time.

"No," Bonnie said, with the heavy patience that meant "back off." "Tony is not dumb. When he cares, he's very smart. And Roger isn't dumb, either, he's just very methodical, you can't hurry him. He's like my uncle Julian."

"Oh, God," Liza said to the ceiling. "He's like family. I will bet you anything that Roger is her If this week."

"I don't bet," Min said. "Bonnie? What's your If?"

Bonnie stuck her chin out. "If Roger turns out to be as sweet as I think he is, I'm going to marry him."

"Oh, good grief," Liza said.

"Leave her alone," Min said to Liza. "She gets whatever If she wants. What's yours?"

Liza straightened. "If my job doesn't get any more interesting, I'm quitting next week."

"Get the calendar," Min said to Bonnie.

"I don't have to," Bonnie said. "It was August when she quit the last time because she said nobody should work in a heat wave."

"Ten months," Min said. "That's not good. Her attention span is getting shorter."

"It's an If," Liza said to Min. "I'm keeping an eye on my options. I think I might want to waitress again if I can find someplace fun. What's your If?"

Min thought of Cal Morrisey, and her head began to throb. "If I can find the reincarnation of Elvis, I'll date again. Until then, I'm taking a break from inter-gender socialization. It's just too painful."

"I am the only sane woman in this room," Liza said.

"Sanity is overrated," Min said, and went home to get an aspirin.

The next night, Cal was back at The Long Shot, as far away from the landing as possible to give himself a wide escape path. Roger was ten feet away, looking at Bonnie as if she were the center of the universe. Bonnie was looking at Roger as if he were a very nice man she didn't know very well. Cal shook his head. Watching Roger date was like watching a toddler in traffic.

Tony sat down beside Cal and slid his Scotch over. "I think you should go for it," he said, nodding toward the bar.

"What?" Cal looked past Bonnie, to see a tall, slender redhead. Tony's Liza. Then she shifted and he saw Min standing behind her, draped in a loose red sweater. It had some kind of hood hanging down the back, and Roger tugged on it and said something that made her smile. "Great." Now he'd have to put up with Min slanging at him for another evening.

"It's not like you to stare and not do anything about it," Tony said. "You are losing it."

"I was watching Roger and Bonnie," Cal said.

"Oh." Tony looked over at Roger and shrugged. "Yep, he's a goner. Well, we all gotta die sometime."

"Yeah, you're the guy I want watching my back," Cal said.

"Well, what are you gonna do?" Tony looked past him and straightened. "What the hell? Where do they think they're going?"

Cal turned back to see the four of them commandeer a poker table on the other side of the bar. "Not here," he said, cheering up. Evidently Min had had as bad a time as he'd had. Which was her own fault because she was impossible to please. God knew he'd tried. Well, except for clipping her there at the end.

She sat down beside Liza, and he watched her as she leaned back and stretched out her black-clad legs. Her legs were pretty good, strong full calves, sturdy, like Min in general.

"She'll be over here in five minutes," Tony said.

"Ten bucks says she won't," Cal said, turning back to his Glenlivet.

"You're on," Tony said. "She wants me."

"You?" Cal said, startled. "Oh, you mean Liza." He looked back at the redhead who was laughing with Min and giving no evidence whatsoever that she knew Tony existed. "Nope, she won't, either."

"Oh, you were talking about the chub?" Tony said.

"Don't call her that," Cal said. "Her name is Min. She's a good woman, apart from her rage." He watched her as she leaned sideways in her chair to say something to Bonnie. "She's not chubby. She's just got a really round body. Everywhere."

"Nice rack," Tony said, trying to be fair. "So you struck out, huh?"

"No," Cal said, turning his back on them again. "I asked her to dinner and she went. Then I walked her home and said good-bye. I did not strike out."

"Finally, a woman you can't get," Tony said, satisfaction in his voice. "That's kind of depressing because it's like an era is passing—"

"I didn't *try*," Cal said.

"—but it's good to know you put on your pants one leg at a time like the rest of us."

"I've never understood that," Cal said. "How else would you put on your pants?"

Tony leaned over. "Ten bucks says you can't get Min to go out with you tomorrow night."

"I don't want to go out with her tomorrow night," Cal said.

"Take her to the movies," Tony said. "You won't have to talk to her."

"Tony . . ."

"Ten bucks, hotshot. I don't think you can do it."

Cal looked over his shoulder at Min. All the laughing aside, she didn't look any more relaxed than she'd been Wednesday night. And she was ignoring him. He shook his head at Tony. "She won't go. No bet."

"This is hard to believe," Tony said. "You chickening out."

"Tony, she hates men right now. She just broke up with somebody."

"Well, there you go. She's on the rebound," Tony said. "That gives you an edge. You could get her into bed."

"I don't want her in bed," Cal said. "She'll probably ice pick the next guy she sleeps with to get even with the guy who dumped her. Trust me, this is not a woman you close your eyes around."

"Wuss," Tony said. "I'll make it easy. Lunch. Ten bucks says you can't get her to lunch."

Cal looked over at Min again. What would get her to lunch? She was sitting back in her chair now, smiling at Roger, as if she were sizing him up. Protective of her friend. She could relax about Roger. If Bonnie got him, she'd be a lucky woman.

Of course, Min didn't know that.

"You in?" Tony said.

So if he went over and said—

"Cynthie just came in," Tony said.

"*Hell.*" Cal sat up but didn't look toward the door. "She hates this bar. Why—"

"She's stalking you," Tony said. "She must really want to get married. And she's headed this way."

"Right." Cal stood up. "Come on."

"Where?" Tony said, not rising.

"Over there so you can harass your redhead while I get a lunch date and duck Cyn. You're on."

"You just lost ten bucks, old buddy," Tony said, practically chortling. "I saw Min's face when you came in, and she was not happy to see you." He stood up, too. "I can't believe you went for that. You hit her in the head, you dork. Why would she go anywhere with you?"

"Ten bucks first," Cal said, holding out his hand.

"You have to get the date first," Tony said. "Which ain't happening."

"No, this is for the redhead who did not come to get you in five minutes," Cal said, and Tony sighed and got out his wallet.

Min was ignoring Cal and checking out Roger, when Liza pulled up the chair to her right and sat down.

"So," Liza said, sliding over a Diet Coke and rum. "What's new with Di?"

"I called her today," Min said, picking up her drink. "I asked her if everything was okay with Wet—" She closed her eyes. "—with *Susie*, and she said, yes, Susie's dating a very nice man and she's fine with the wedding. And Worse . . . and *Karen* has talked to Susie and has assured Diana that Susie's fine with it."

"Is she delusional?" Liza said, as somebody pulled up a chair to Min's left.

"Who? Wet, Worse, or Diana?" Min said.

"All of them," Liza said.

"My guess is that Wet's being brave, Worse is being a bully, and Diana's in denial," Min said, turning to see who was on her left. "Oh," she said, when she saw Cal sitting there with two glasses in front of him. He was as beautiful as he'd been two nights before, and her DNA went wild again.

"Hello, little girl," he said and flipped the hood on her sweater.

Liza snorted and turned to talk to Bonnie on her other side.

"Oh, that's good," Min said. "You're definitely the first person to make a Red Riding Hood crack to me tonight. I'm never wearing this sweater again."

"Hostility," Cal said. "It's déjà vu all over again. How's your head?"

"The pain comes and goes," Min said. "And then there are the voices."

"Good. Now you have someone to talk to. Who are Wet, Worse, and Diana, and how did they get those terrible names?"

"Nobody you want to know." Min picked up her drink. "What are you up to?"

"Let me guess," Cal said, his voice heavy with scorn. "That's a rum and Diet Coke. The breakfast of dieters."

"Don't you have somewhere else to be?"

"No, Buffy. Fate sent me over here to teach you to drink with dignity." He took her rum away from her and slid one of his glasses over to her. "Glenlivet. Drink it slowly."

Min frowned at him. "This is your idea of charm?"

"No," Cal said. "I don't waste charm on you. I'm trying to help you grow. Real women do not screw up good booze with diet soda."

"Peer pressure," Min said. "It never stops."

"Try it," Cal said. "One sip. You hate it, I'll give you this slop back."

Min shrugged. "Okay." She picked it up and took a drink and then choked as the Scotch seared her throat.

"I said, *sip*, Dobbs," Cal said over her gasping. "You're supposed to savor it, not guzzle it."

"Thank you," Min said when she had her breath back. "You can go now."

"No, I can't." He leaned closer, and Min started to feel too warm in her sweater. "I have a deal for you."

Min picked up the Scotch again and sipped it. It was nice when you sipped it.

Cal leaned closer until he was almost whispering in her ear. "I want to know about Bonnie."

His breath was warm on her neck, and Min blinked at him. "Bonnie? I think Roger's got dibs on Bonnie."

"I know. That's why I want to know about her. Roger is . . ." Cal looked across the table. ". . . not adept with women. I want to know about your friend."

"Well," Min said, prepared to give Bonnie a perfect report card.

"Not here," Cal said, still too close. "I think they'll notice. I'll meet you for lunch tomorrow. You know where Cherry Hill Park is?"

"I've heard of it," Min said. "I don't have the bank account to go up there and hang around."

"There's a picnic area on the north side," Cal said. "I'll meet you at the first table tomorrow at noon."

"Why do I feel like there should be a code word?" Min said, finally pulling away from him. "I'll say 'pretentious' and you say 'snob.'"

"You want to know about Roger or not?" Cal said.

Min looked back at Bonnie. If you didn't know her, she looked detached, but Min knew her. Bonnie was glowing. "Yes."

"Good," Cal said. "Let me see your shoes."

"What?" Min said, and Cal looked under the table. She pulled her foot out, and he looked down at her open-toed high-heeled mules, laced across her instep with black leather thongs that contrasted with her pale skin and bright red toenail polish. "Liza calls them 'Toes in Bondage,'" she said helpfully.

"Does she?" Cal sat very still, looking at her toes for a long moment. "Well, that's made my evening. See you tomorrow at noon." He pushed back his chair and left, taking his Scotch and her rum and Diet Coke with him.

"Okay, I couldn't hear the part at the end," Liza said, leaning over to her. "What was he asking you?"

"I'm going to lunch tomorrow," Min said, not sure how she felt about that. If he whispered in her ear again, she was going to have to smack him, that was all there was to it.

"Where?"

"Cherry Hill Park."

"Jeez," Liza said. "Softball of the Rich and Famous. What time?"

"Noon."

Liza nodded. Then she raised her voice and called, "Tony."

Min looked around for him and saw him at the roulette bar, handing Cal a ten-dollar bill. "I don't *believe* it," she said, straightening in outrage. The sonofabitch had bet on lunch and she'd fallen for it.

Tony looked up, and Liza crooked her finger. He walked over and said, "You know, I'm not the kind of guy you can do that to."

"You and I are having lunch at noon tomorrow in Cherry Hill Park," Liza said.

"Okay," Tony said. "But only because I've gotta coach a softball game there in the morning anyway."

"Good," Liza said. "You can go now."

Tony shook his head at her and went back to the bar and Cal.

"Well, at least he's obedient," Min said.

"Don't get any ideas about saying yes at lunch," Liza said.

"It's *lunch*," Min said. "In broad daylight. In a public park."

"You said you weren't going to see him, and he still got you to lunch."

"I had a reason for that," Min said, casting a bitter glance at the bar. Cal was still there, but now the brunette from Wednesday was there, too, moving closer to him in a blue halter top. That figured. Beast. "I'll be fine, believe me, I know what he is." She cast another look at the bar where Cal appeared to be sliding away from the halter top. Playing hard to get, the jerk.

"Yeah, well, I'm watching your back just the same," Liza said. "And if it hits the grass, Calvin's going to lose a body part."

"Boy, you really don't like him, do you?" Min said.

"I think he bet Tony he could get that lunch date," Liza said.

"I think so, too," Min said.

"See if you can do something horrible to him tomorrow," Liza said.

"Already planning it," Min said.

After another excruciating Saturday morning forcing fourteen eight-year-olds to play baseball against their better judgments, Cal was not in the mood to put up with Min, but he grabbed his cooler from the car, stopped by the charity hot dog stand for the main course, and went to meet her at the picnic table he'd told her about. She wasn't there, so he threw an old blanket across the massive teak table—Cherry Hill did not stint on the amenities—put the basket on it, and then sat on top of the table, feeling cheerful about being stood up. It was a beautiful day, the park was thick with shade trees, the kids were gone, and nobody was bitching at him.

Then Min came into the park through the trees, following the curving crushed gravel path. She was wearing her long red sweater again, but this time she had on a red-and-black-checked skirt that floated when the breeze blew. Her hair was still wound in a knot on the top of her head, but her stride was long and loose as she came toward him, and the sun picked up glints of gold in her hair, and she smiled at him as she drew closer, and it suddenly seemed better not to have been stood up. And when he offered her his hand to help her up on the table, she hesitated and then took it, and her fingers were pleasantly, solidly warm as she boosted herself up beside him on the table.

"Hi," she said and he grinned at her.

"Hi," he said. "Thank you for coming."

"Thank you for inviting me." Min dropped her bag on the bench below them. "Give me ten bucks."

Cal blinked. "What?"

Min smiled at him, cheerful as the sun. "I was going to make your lunch a living hell, but it's such a beautiful day, I've decided to enjoy it. You bet Tony ten bucks you could get me to lunch."

"No, I didn't," Cal said.

Min's smile disappeared.

"Tony bet me ten bucks I could get you to lunch."

Min rolled her eyes. "Whatever. Give me ten bucks or I'm leaving you cold and you'll have to give Tony his ten bucks back plus ten more because you've lost."

"I think I won when you said, 'Yes,'" Cal said, suddenly a lot more interested in Min.

"Try explaining that to Tony," Min said.

"Okay," Cal said. "How about we split it?"

Min held out her hand and wiggled her fingers. "Ten bucks, Charm Boy."

Cal sighed and dug out his wallet, trying not to grin at her. She took the ten, picked up her bag, stuffed the bill in it and then pulled out a twenty and handed it to him.

"What's this?" Cal said.

"That's the twenty you gave me for cab fare on Wednesday," Min said. "I forgot to give it back to you."

"So now I'm up ten bucks," Cal said.

"No, now you've broken even. It was your twenty to begin with. I had no right to it since you didn't get fresh."

Cal looked up at the sun. "The day's young."

"I don't see you making your move on a picnic table," Min said. "In fact, I don't see you moving on me at all, so tuck that away and tell me everything you know about Roger."

"I'm glad to see you, too," he said, and her smile widened.

"Sorry. I forgot your lust for small talk. And how have you been in the fourteen hours since we last spoke, eight of which you were sleeping?"

"Fine. And you?"

"Wonderful. How much of this before we get to Roger and Bonnie?"

"You're a very practical woman," Cal said, and then Min pulled her legs up to tuck them under her and he caught sight of her shoes, ridiculous sandals made mostly of ribbons with a single bright red flower over the instep. "Except for your shoes."

"Don't make fun of my shoes." Min wiggled red-tipped toes under the flowers. "I love these shoes. Liza gave them to me for Christmas." She untied the ribbons and pulled them off and put them on the table behind her, patting the flowers before she turned back to him.

"I can see why you love them," Cal said, distracted by her toes, and then she pulled her skirt over them and he added, "They're very Elvis."

She raised her eyebrows. "*You* are an Elvis fan?"

"Best there is," Cal said. "You, too?"

"Oh, absolutely." Min looked perplexed and then said, "Well, I guess it does makes sense. You are the devil in disguise."

"What?" Cal said, and then it hit him. "Elvis *Presley*?"

"Well, of course, Elvis Presley," Min said. "What other . . . *oh*. The angels want to wear my red shoes. Elvis Costello." She shrugged. "He's good, too."

Cal shook his head in disbelief. "Yes, he is."

"Good thing this isn't a date," Min said cheerfully. "Or there'd be a really awkward silence while we tried to come back from that one."

Cal grinned at her. "Have you ever had an awkward silence in your life, Dobbs?"

"Not many," Min said. "You?"

"Nope." Cal dumped the bag of wrapped hot dogs out on the blanket. "Okay. Roger and Bonnie. Have a hot dog while we talk."

"A hot dog?" Min said, in the same tone of voice she'd have used to say "Cocaine?" "Those aren't good for you."

"They're protein," Cal said, exasperated. "You can have them. Just lose the bun."

"Fat," Min said.

"I thought fat was okay on no-carb diets," Cal said, remembering Cynthie chowing down on buttered shrimp.

"It is, but I'm on a no-fat Atkins," Min said.

Cal looked at her, incredulous. "Which leaves you *what* to eat?"

"Not much," Min said, looking at the hot dogs with patent longing.

"They're brats," Cal said.

"Oh, just hell," Min said.

"It's Saturday," Cal said. "Live a little."

"That's what you said Wednesday at Emilio's. I've already sinned this week."

"Saturday is the first day of the new week. Sin again."

Min bit her lip, and the breeze picked up again, rustling the trees and lifting the edge of skirt, floating it closer to him.

"I brought you Diet Coke to compensate," he said, opening the cooler. "Also, this conversation is boring."

"Right. Sorry." She took the can he handed her and popped it open. "Really sorry. There's nothing more boring than talking about food."

"No," Cal said. "Talking about food is great. Talking about not having food is boring." He picked up one of the wax-paper-wrapped sandwiches and handed it to her. "Eat."

Min looked at the hot dog, sighed, and unwrapped it. "You are a beast."

"Because I'm feeding you?" Cal said. "How is that bad? We're Americans. We're supposed to eat well. It's the American Way."

"Hot dogs are the American Way?" Min said, and then stopped. "Oh. I guess they are, aren't they? Right up there with baseball and apple pie."

"Baseball you can have," Cal said and bit into his hot dog.

Min squinted at his team shirt. "Isn't that shirt sort of baseball-ish?"

"Yes," Cal said. "For my sins, I teach children to run around bases on Saturday mornings. Someday, your husband will be doing this, too, while you sit in the bleachers and cheer on little whosis. It's the price you pay for liberty."

"I'm not having kids," Min said, and bit into her hot dog.

"You're not?" Cal said, and then was distracted by the look of bliss on her face while she chewed. The brats were good, but they weren't that good.

She swallowed and sighed. "This is wonderful. My dad used to sneak us out for brats every time there was a festival anyplace within driving distance. My mother would have killed him if she'd known. Do you know how long it's been since I tasted one of these? It's heaven."

"It looks like heaven," he said, and then she leaned over to take another bite, keeping the sandwich over the waxed paper to catch the drippings, and he looked down the v-neck of her loose red sweater and saw a lot of lush round flesh in tight red lace. *Tony would have a heart attack*, he thought and then realized he was a little lightheaded himself. The breeze blew again and wafted her skirt against the hand he had braced on the table, and it tickled, soft and light.

"So," he said, moving his hand. "All right. Why don't you want to be part of the American Way?"

She chewed with her eyes closed, and he looked down her sweater again and had impure thoughts. Then she swallowed and said, "I have to give birth to be a good American? No. There are more than four million babies born in this country every year. The American Way is covered. If it worries you, you can have extra to make up for mine."

"Me?" Cal sat back away from distraction. "I don't want kids. I'm just surprised that you don't. You'd make a great mom."

"Why?" Min stopped with the sandwich halfway to her mouth.

Because she looked soft all over. Because she looked like she'd age into the kind of mother he'd have killed for. "Because you look comfortable."

"Oh, God, *yes*," Min said, glaring at him. "That's *exactly* the compliment every woman longs for."

She leaned forward to bite into her sandwich, and he watched transfixed as her breasts pressed against the lace again.

"It's a very sexy comfortable if that makes it better," he said.

"Marginally better," she said, following his eyes down. "You're looking down my sweater."

"You're leaning over. There's all that red lace right there."

"Lace is good, huh?" Min said.

"Oh, yeah."

"My mother wins again," Min said and bit into her hot dog.

Cal picked up his hot dog. "How'd your mother get into this?"

"She's pervasive." Min swallowed, frowning. "So if you don't like kids, how'd you end up coaching?"

"I didn't say I didn't like kids," Cal said, trying to think of something beside Min's red lace. "I said I didn't want kids. There's a difference."

"Good point. And yet I ask, why coach?"

"I got shanghaied," Cal said. "We both did. Harry hates baseball as much as I hate coaching."

"Who's Harry?"

"My nephew."

"Why don't the two of you go AWOL?"

"Turns out there are other kids on the team besides Harry," Cal said. "Who knew?"

"Funny. So you're out here every Saturday morning?" Min shook her head. "That must have been some shanghai."

"I got hit by the best." He picked up a pickle and bit into it. "It's not that bad. Roger and Tony do most of the work. They like it."

"Roger," Min said. "Ah yes, Roger. I have some questions about Roger."

"Not Tony?" Cal said.

"Tony is seeing Liza," Min said. "If Tony turns out to be a rat, Liza will exterminate him."

"Tony's hard to put down," Cal said, "but I get your drift. So Bonnie's not like that?"

"Bonnie is no pushover," Min said. "She's smart and she's tough but she has this one blind spot. She believes in the fairy tale, that there's one man in the world for her. And she thinks your friend Roger is her prince on very little evidence. So tell me about Roger."

"Roger's the best guy I know," Cal said. "And he's crazy about Bonnie. He's going to get banged up if she walks away. Tell me about Bonnie."

Min shifted on the blanket as she reached for her Coke can, and Cal watched her, aware of every move she made, of the smooth curve of her neck as her sweater slipped toward her shoulder, the ease in her round body as she leaned back and smiled at him, the swell of her calf under her checked skirt as it blew toward him again. "Bonnie," she said, bringing him back to the subject at hand, "spent a year and a half looking at couches. Couches are very important, they're right up there with beds in hierarchy of furniture, but even I thought a year and a half was a long time looking for a couch."

"Yes," Cal said, trying to think of Roger instead of curves. "But—"

"Then one night we were on the way to the movies and she stopped in front of a furniture store window and said, 'Wait a minute,' and went in and bought this horribly expensive couch in about five minutes." Min leaned forward again, and Cal looked down her sweater again and thought, *Don't do that, I'm getting a headache from the blood rush.* "She had to put it on two different credit cards," Min went on, "and it took her two years to pay it off, but it's a great couch and she's never regretted it, and when she had it reupholstered, the upholsterer said it would last forever."

"Great," Cal said, still looking down her sweater. She was breathing softly, just enough for the rise and fall to—

"*Hello,*" she said and he jerked his head up. "Not that I'm not flattered, but I'm making a point here. Roger is Bonnie's new couch. She's always been sure that some day her prince would show up, and she's done a lot of dating looking for him, and now she's taken one look at Roger and she's sure he's the one, and she's going to buy him in about a minute. So if he isn't a good guy, I want to know now so I can break it to her. Tell me he's not a rat."

"Roger took a year to buy a couch, too," Cal said, regrouping.

"What kind of couch?" Min said.

"Sort of a La-Z-Boy with a thyroid problem," Cal said. "I think it's brown."

Min nodded. "Bonnie bought a reproduction mission settle with cushions upholstered in a celadon William Morris print."

"I think I know what 'mission' is," Cal said. "Everything else, you were speaking Chinese."

"Roger's couch is toast," Min said. "Will he mind?"

"She can chop it into kindling in front of him and he won't blink," Cal said.

"Can he take care of her?" Min said. "She probably won't need it, but in a crunch—"

"He will throw his body in front of her if necessary. You have nothing to worry about with Roger. He's the best guy I know. If I had a sister, I would let Roger marry her. It's Bonnie I'm worried about it. She's got that efficient look that usually means she likes to boss people around. And since she's so little, there's probably a Napoleon complex—"

"Nope," Min said. "She's solid. Roger's a lucky guy." She finished the last of her hot dog and then licked a smear of ketchup off her thumb, and Cal lost his train of thought. "So they're okay and we don't have to worry," she said when she'd wiped her hands on a napkin.

"Yep," Cal said. "How about dessert?"

"I don't eat dessert," Min said.

"Really?" Cal said. "What a surprise."

"Oh, bite me," Min said. "I told you there's this bridesmaid's dress—"

Cal pulled a waxed paper bag from the cooler. "Doughnuts," he said, but before he could go on, a too-familiar piping voice came from behind him.

"Can I have one?"

He sighed and turned around to see his skinny, grubby, dark-haired nephew standing at the end of the picnic table. "Shouldn't you be home by now?"

"They forgot again," Harry said, putting a lot of pathetic in his voice. It helped that he wore glasses and was small for his age. He peered around Cal. "Hello," he said cautiously to Min.

"Min," Cal said, glaring at Harry. "This is my nephew, Harry Morrisey. He was just leaving. Harry, this is Min Dobbs."

"Hi, Harry," Min said cheerfully. "You can have all the doughnuts."

Harry brightened.

"No, you can't." Cal took out his cell phone. "You'd just throw them up again."

"Maybe not." Harry sidled closer to the doughnut bag.

"You do remember the cupcake disaster, right?" Cal said as he punched in his sister-in-law's number.

"Can't he have *one*?" Min smiled at Harry as he drew closer, her face soft and kind, and Cal and Harry both blinked at her for a moment because she was so pretty.

Then while Cal listened to the phone ring, Harry looked at Min's skirt and poked it with his finger.

"*Harry,*" Cal said, and Min pulled out one of her sandals.

"Here," she told Harry, and he poked at the flower.

"Those are *shoes*," Harry said, as if he were observing an anomaly.

"Yep," Min said, watching him, her head tilted.

Harry poked the flower again. "That's not real."

"No," Min said. "It's just for fun."

Harry nodded as if this were a new idea, which, Cal realized, it probably was. Not a lot of floppy flowers on red toes in Harry's world.

Min reached in the bag and handed him a doughnut.

"Thank you, Min," Harry said, still channeling abused orphans.

"Don't buy his act," Cal said to Min.

"I'm not." Min grinned at Harry. "You look like you're doing fine, kid."

"I had to play baseball," Harry said bitterly. "Are those hot dogs?"

"No," Cal said. "You know you're not allowed to have processed meat. Go over there on that bench and eat your doughnut."

"He can eat it here," Min said, putting her arm around him protectively.

Harry, no dummy, leaned into Min's hip.

Bet that's soft, Cal thought, and then realized he was close to being jealous of his eight-year-old nephew. "Harry," he said warningly, but then his sister-in-law answered her phone. "Bink? You forgot to pick up your kid."

"Reynolds," Bink said in her perfectly modulated tones. "It was his turn."

"He's not here," Cal said.

Bink sighed. "Poor Harry. I'll be right there. Thank you, Cal."

"Anything for you, babe." Cal shut off his phone and looked over at Harry. "Your mother is coming. Look on the bright side, you get a doughnut and your mother, instead of nothing and your father."

"Two doughnuts," Harry said.

"Harry, you barf," Cal said. "You can't have two doughnuts. Now go away. This is a date. Seven years from now, you will understand what that means."

"This isn't a date," Min said. "He can stay."

Harry nodded at her sadly. "It's okay."

"Oh, come off it, Harrison," Cal said, knowing Harry was milking the situation. "You have a doughnut. Go over on that bench and eat it."

"All right." Harry trailed disconsolately across the grass to a nearby Lutyen bench, his doughnut clutched in his grubby little hand.

"He's so cute," Min said, laughing softly. "Who's Bink?"

"My sister-in-law," Cal said, watching Harry, who still looked skinny, grubby, and bitter to him. "I don't see the cute part. But he's not a bad kid."

"Bink," Min said, as if trying to get her head around the name.

"It's short for Elizabeth," Cal said. "Elizabeth Margaret Remington-Pastor Morrisey."

"Bink," Min said. "Okay."

Cal picked up a doughnut. "Your turn, Dobbs."

Min leaned back. "Oh no. No, no, no."

He leaned forward to wave it under her nose. "Come on, sin a little."

"I hate you," Min said, her eyes on the doughnut. "You are a beast and a vile seducer."

Cal lifted an eyebrow. "All that for one doughnut? Come on. One won't kill you."

"I am not eating a doughnut," Min said, tearing her eyes away from it. "Are you crazy? There are twelve grams of fat in one of those. I have three weeks to lose twenty pounds. Get away from me."

"This is not just a doughnut," Cal said, tearing it in two pieces under Min's eyes, the chocolate icing and glaze breaking like frost, the tender pastry pulling apart in shreds. "This is a chocolate-iced Krispy Kreme glazed. This is the caviar of doughnuts, the Dom Perignon of dough-nuts, the Mercedes-Benz of doughnuts."

Min licked her lips. "I had no idea you were a pastry freak," she said, trying to pull back farther, but the wind blew her skirt over to Cal again, and this time he moved his knee to pin it down.

He broke a bite-size piece from one of the halves. "Taste it," he said, leaning still closer to hold the piece under her nose. "Come on."

"No." Min clamped her lips shut, and then shut her eyes, too, screw-ing up her face as she did.

"Oh, that's adult." He reached out and pinched her nose shut, and when she opened her mouth to protest, he popped the doughnut in.

"Oh, God," she said, and her face relaxed as the pastry melted in her mouth, her smile curling across her face.

Cal relaxed, too, and thought, *Feeding this woman is like getting her drunk.*

Then she swallowed and opened her eyes, and he held out another piece so he could see that expression again. "Come here, Dobbs."

"No," Min said, pulling back. "No, no, *no.*"

"You say that a lot," Cal said. "But the look in your eyes says you want it."

"What I want and what I can have are two different things." Min leaned back farther, stretching her skirt, but her eyes were on the doughnut. "Get that thing away from me."

"Okay." Cal sat back and bit into it while she watched, the sugar rush distracting him for a moment until Min bit her lip, her strong white teeth denting the softness there. His heart picked up speed, and she shook her head at him.

"*Bastard,*" she said.

He bit into the doughnut again, and she said, "That's enough, I'm out of here," and leaned forward to pull her skirt out from under him. "Would you get off—" she began, and he popped another piece of doughnut in her mouth and watched as her lips closed over the sweetness. Her face was beautifully blissful, her mouth soft and pouted, her full lower lip glazed with icing, and as she teased the last of the chocolate from her lip, Cal heard a rushing in his ears. The rush became a whisper—*THIS one*—and he breathed deeper, and before she could open her eyes, he leaned in and kissed her, tasting the chocolate and the heat of her mouth, and she froze for a moment and then kissed him back, sweet and insistent, blanking out all coherent thought. He let the taste and the scent and the warmth of her wash over him, drowning in her, and when she finally pulled back, he almost fell into her lap.

She sat across from him, her sweater rising and falling under quick breaths, her dark eyes flashing, wide awake, her lush lips parted, open for him, and then she spoke.

"*More,*" she breathed and he looked into her eyes and went for her.

Chapter Five

Cal's eyes were as dark as chocolate, and Min panicked as he leaned close again. She put her hand on his chest, and said, "No, wait," and he looked down and said, "Right," and picked up another piece of doughnut. She opened her mouth to say, "No," and he slipped the piece in and the heat of her mouth dissolved the icing as she closed her eyes, and the tang went everywhere, melting into pleasure. And when she opened her eyes, he was there.

He leaned forward and kissed her softly, his mouth fitting hers so perfectly that she trembled. She tasted the heat of him and licked the chocolate off his lip and felt his tongue against hers, hot and devastating, and when he broke the kiss, she was breathless and dizzy and aching for more. He held her eyes, looking as dazed as she felt, but she wasn't deceived at all, she knew what he was.

She just didn't care.

"More," she said, and he reached for the pastry, but she said, "No, *you*," and grabbed his shirt to pull him closer, and he kissed her hard this time, his hand on the back of her head, and she fell into him, as glitter exploded behind her eyelids. She felt his hand on her waist, sliding hot under her sweater, and her blood surged, and the rush in her head said, *THIS one.*

Then he jerked forward and smacked into her.

"Ouch?" she said, and he looked behind him, still clutching her with both hands.

"What the *hell?*" Cal said.

"I said," Liza said, holding up her leather purse, "what are you doing?"

"What does it look like I'm doing?"

"I cut my mouth," Min said, touching her finger to her lip.

Cal turned back to her and pulled her finger away, his face flushed and concerned, and he was so close to her that she leaned forward as her heart pounded, and he did, too, his eyes half closed again, and she thought, *Oh, God, yes.* Then Liza jerked at Min's arm and almost pulled her off the table.

"Get *down* from there, Stats," Liza said as Min's head reeled.

"Tony," Cal said through his teeth.

"Sorry, pal," Tony said. "She's uncontrollable."

"We were just having dessert." Min scooted back as far as she could with Cal still sitting on her skirt. *I know that was dumb,* she thought, trying not to look at him, *but I want that again.*

"Dessert?" Liza looked down at the table. "You're eating *doughnuts?*"

"Oh," Min said, guilt clearing some of her daze.

"What are you?" Cal glared at Liza. "The calorie police? Go away."

"No," Liza said. "I think she should eat all the doughnuts she wants. I just don't want you feeding them to her."

"Why?" Cal said savagely.

"Because you are Hit-and-Run Morrisey, and she's my best friend." Liza tugged on Min's arm again. "Come on. Bonnie's waiting."

"I'm *what?*"

Min tried to scoot back a little more, but Cal was still on her skirt. *Which is all right, really.*

"Bonnie's over there on a park bench talking to Roger," Tony said to Liza. "She could care less."

"Couldn't care less," Liza said. "And she could." She fixed Min with a stare. "We've talked about this. Get off that table."

Right, Min thought. *I don't want to.*

Across from her, Cal looked even more gorgeous than usual, enraged in the sunlight, but as her daze lifted, she remembered why she wasn't supposed to be there. "Could I have my skirt back, please?" she said, faintly, and he rolled back enough that she could pull the fabric free. "Thank you very much. For lunch. I had a wonderful time."

"Stay," he said, and she looked into his eyes and thought, *Oh, yes.*

"No," Liza said and pulled Min off the table so that she stumbled onto the grass.

"She can make up her own mind," Cal said.

"Yeah?" Liza took a step closer to him. "Tell me you know her. Tell me you care about her. Tell me you're going to love her until the end of time."

"*Liza,*" Min said, tugging on her arm.

"I just met her three days ago," Cal said.

"Then *what are you doing kissing her like that?*" Liza turned her back on him. "Come on, Min."

"Thank you for lunch," Min said as Liza tightened her grip. She reached back for her sandals on the table and caught the ribbons, and then Liza dragged her away through the trees.

When they were gone, Cal turned to Tony and said, "I can't decide whether to have you killed or do it myself."

"Not me, Liza," Tony said. "And she did call Min's name and poke you in the side a couple of times before she whacked you in the back of the head with her purse." His eyes went to the table. "Hey, hot dogs." He sat on the table and reached for a sandwich.

"That woman is insane," Cal said, rubbing the back of his head. The heat was subsiding now that Min was gone, but it wasn't making him any happier. "That was assault."

"She's insane?" Tony said, as he unwrapped a brat. "How about you?"

"It wasn't that big a deal." *Ten minutes more and we would have been naked.* That *would have been a big deal.*

"Tell that to Harry," Tony said. "That was probably more than he needed to know about what Uncle Cal does with his free time."

"Harry?" Cal said and looked over to where Harry had been sitting. He was still there, only now there was a thin blonde with him. Bink. Cal closed his eyes and the memory of Min's heat vanished. "Tell me Bink wasn't watching us, too."

"Don't know. She wasn't there when we got here so she may just have caught the big finish. What the hell am I sitting on?" He pulled a red-flowered shoe out from under the blanket.

"Min's," Cal said, getting a nice flashback to her toes. "Give it to Liza when you get the chance. Down her throat, if possible."

"Yeah, like I'll remember," Tony said and tossed it in the cooler.

Cal dug it out again before the ice could get the flower wet and tried to get his mind off Min. "It turns out that Bonnie's a good deal, so Roger's okay." He turned Min's sandal around in his hand. It was a ridiculous thing with a little stacked heel that probably sank into the ground when she walked across the grass and that dopey flower that would get screwed up if she wore them in the rain, and that was a turn-on, too.

"Roger's not okay," Tony said around a mouthful of brat. "He's going to get married."

"It's not death," Cal said, trying to imagine why anybody as practical as Min would wear a shoe like that. But then Min clearly had an impractical streak or she wouldn't have frenched him on a picnic table. The rush he got from that blanked out sound for a moment. "What?" he said.

"I said, yes, that's why you're running like a rabbit from Cynthie," Tony said.

"Well, marriage is not for me, but it's probably for Roger," Cal said, dropping the shoe on the table. "He's never been big on excitement."

"True," Tony said. "And if Bonnie is a nice woman, maybe I'll live over their garage after all."

"More good news for me," Cal said, and thought of Min again, full and hot under his hands— *No.* He didn't need any more hostility in his life. If he wanted great sex, he could always go back to Cynthie, who at least was never bitchy. He tried to call up Cynthie's memory to blot out Min's, but she seemed gray and white next to Min's lush, exasperating, heat-inducing, open-toed Technicolor.

"What?" Tony said.

"Are there any hot dogs left?" Cal said. "That you haven't sat on?"

Tony found one under a fold in the blanket and passed it over, and Cal unwrapped it and bit into it, determined to concentrate on a sense that wasn't permeated with Min. Then he remembered her face when she'd tasted the brat, and imagined her face like that with her body moving under his, hot and lush, her lips wet—

Oh, hell, he thought.

"So what are you going to tell Harry?" Tony said.

"About what?"

"About you doing Min on a picnic table," Tony said. "You guys looked pretty hot."

"I'm going to tell him I'll explain it when he's older," Cal said, and thought, *We were hot. And now we're done.* "Much older," he said, and went back to the cooler for a beer.

"Okay, *why* did we have to leave?" Bonnie said when they were in Liza's convertible and Min was banished to the backseat.

"Because Min was swapping tongues with a doughnut pusher." Liza looked back over the seat at Min the sinner and shook her head.

Bonnie turned so she could see over the seat, too. "You ate doughnuts?"

"Yes," Min said, still trying to fight her way back from dazed. "Big deal."

Bonnie nodded as Liza started the car. "Was he a good kisser?"

"Yes," Min said. "Pretty good. Very good. World class. Phenomenal. Woke me right up. Plus there were the doughnuts, which were *amazing*." She thought about Cal again, all that heat and urgency, and as Liza started down the curving drive to the street, Min lay down on the back seat before she fell over from residual dizziness. It felt good to lie down but it was such a shame she was alone.

"Have you lost your mind?" Liza said, over the seat.

"Just for that minute or two," Min said from the seat, watching the treetops move by overhead. "I kind of enjoyed it." *A lot.*

"You know," Bonnie said to Liza, "he might be legit. He looked really happy with her. Roger even said so."

"Oh, well if *Roger* says so," Liza said.

"Don't make fun of Roger," Bonnie said, warning in her voice.

"Okay," Min said, sitting up again as her world steadied. "I'm fine now. Very practical." She picked up her shoe to untangle the ribbons. "So how was Tony?"

"Mildly amusing," Liza said. "Stop changing the subject. What are you going to do about Cal?"

"Not see him again," Min said, looking for her second sandal. "Oh, for heaven's sake. I left a shoe behind. We have to go back."

"No," Liza said and kept driving.

"They're my favorite shoes," Min said, trying to sound sincere.

"All your shoes are your favorite shoes," Liza said. "We're not going back there."

"Are you okay, honey?" Bonnie said to Min.

"I'm great," Min said, nodding like a maniac. "Cal told me all about Roger. You have my blessing."

"Based on Calvin the Beast's say-so," Liza said.

"I have ways of telling," Min said. "I know how to handle him."

"Yeah, I saw you handling him," Liza said. "You're weak."

"Oh, come on," Min said, guilt making her exasperated. "I heard the bet. I know what's going on. I'm not seeing him again. Especially since you yelled at him and called him names." She thought about Cal leaning close, how hard his chest had been against her hand, how hot his mouth had been on hers, how good his hand had felt on her breast. "I found out how he gets all those women, though," she said brightly. "Turns out it's not just the charm."

"Maybe you should see him again," Bonnie said, sounding thoughtful. "I think sometimes you just have to believe."

That might be good, Min thought.

"*Bonnie,*" Liza said. "Do you *want* her to get mutilated by the same guy who broke your cousin's heart and made that bet with David?"

That would be bad, Min thought.

"No," Bonnie said, doubt in her voice.

"Then no more pep talks about believing in toads," Liza said.

"Don't they turn into princes when you kiss them?" Bonnie said.

"That's frogs," Liza said. "Entirely different species."

"Right," Min said, trying to shove Cal out of her mind. "Toad not frog. Beast. Absolutely." Then she sighed and said, "But he really had great doughnuts," and lay back down on the seat again to recover her good sense.

David was settling down in front of the television on Sunday afternoon when the phone rang. He picked it up and heard Cynthie's voice.

"Cal and Min were in the park today," she said. "He kissed her. That's joy, it's a physiological cue, that could push them into—"

"*Wait*," David said, and took a deep breath. It was that damn bet. Cal would do anything to win that bet.

"He fed her doughnuts," Cynthie said. "He took her on a picnic and—"

"Min ate doughnuts?" David went cold at the thought. "Min doesn't eat doughnuts. Min doesn't eat carbs. She never ate carbs with me."

"And every time he fed her a piece, he kissed her."

"Sonofabitch," David said, viciously. "What do we do?"

"We have to work on their attraction triggers, create joy, make them remember why they wanted *us*," Cynthie said. "Take her to lunch tomorrow. Make it perfect. Make her feel special and loved, give her joy, and *get her back*."

"I don't know," David said, remembering Min's face when he'd dumped her. The idea was for her to come crawling back to him, not for him to go to her.

"I'll have lunch with Cal," Cynthie said as if he hadn't spoken. "I've been lying low, hoping he'd come back on his own, but there's no time for that now. I'll have him in bed before dessert, and that should finish the whole thing."

"Min's mad at me," David said. "I think it's too soon for a lunch."

"Oh, that's very aggressive." There was a long silence and then

Cynthie said, "Her family. Did you say she needs them to approve of her lovers?"

"Yes," David said. "Her mother was crazy about me."

"There you go," Cynthie said. "Call her mother and tell her the truth about Cal and women."

"No," David said, remembering Nanette's lack of focus on anything not involving calories or fashion. "Her sister's fiancé. Greg. I'll call him tonight."

"How will that help?"

"He'll tell Diana right away," David said. "He sees her every night. And she lives with her parents, so she'll tell her mother and father. Her father is very protective."

"That's good," Cynthie said.

"He fed her doughnuts?" David said, wincing at the thought.

"One piece at a time," Cynthie said.

Bastard. He was doing it for that damn bet. After all that big talk about being cheap but not slimy, he was going to seduce Min with doughnuts and then come back to collect his ten thousand bucks. The great Calvin Morrisey wins again.

Not if I have anything to do about it.

"David?" Cynthie said.

"Trust me," David said, grimly. "Min just ate her last doughnut."

On Monday, Roger came in late to work. *Bonnie,* Cal thought, which made him think of Min, which was ridiculous.

"What is this?" Tony said. "I'm the last one in to work. It's tradition."

"Bonnie." Roger yawned as he sat down at his desk. "We talked pretty late last night."

"Talked," Tony said, sitting on the edge of the work table. "The least you could do is get laid."

Roger narrowed his eyes.

"Okay, now that we're all here—" Cal said.

"I'm going to marry Bonnie," Roger told Tony. "You don't talk like that about the woman you marry."

"Sorry," Tony said. "I'm never getting married so I wouldn't know."

"—we need to block out the Winston seminar—"

"You'll know when you find the right woman," Roger said.

"No such animal," Tony said.

"—and get *the packets done*," Cal said, raising his voice.

"She has a perfect kiss," Roger said, looking out the window, probably in what he thought was Bonnie's direction. "Did you ever kiss like that, where everything was exactly right and it just blew the top of your head off?"

"No," Tony said, looking revolted.

"Yes," Cal said, Min coming back to him in all her hot and yielding glory. They both turned to look at him, and he said, "Can we go to work now? Because we're about a minute away from breaking out the ice cream and talking about our feelings, and I don't think we can come back from that."

"I'll get on the invoices," Roger said and went to his desk.

Cal leaned back in his desk chair, opened a computer file, and thought about Min. He'd had no intentions of kissing her and then he'd jumped her, some insane impulse shoving him into her lap. And she'd been no help. She should have slapped him silly and instead there she was, saying "More," egging him on—

The phone rang and Tony picked it up. "Morrisey, Packard, Capa," he said and then rolled his eyes at Cal. "Hey, Cynthie."

Cal shook his head.

"He's not here," Tony said. "I think he's gone for the morning." He scowled at Cal, who sighed and leaned back in his chair to look at the ceiling.

"Lunch?" Tony said. "Sorry, he's got a lunch date. At Emilio's. With his new girlfriend."

Cal sat up so fast his feet that hit the floor hard. *No*, he mouthed at Tony and made a slicing motion across his throat with his hand.

"So you don't have to worry about him being depressed over losing you," Tony said. "He got right back on the horse."

Cal stood up, rage in his eyes, and Tony said. "Gotta go," and hung up.

"*Are you insane?*" Cal said.

"Hey, it got rid of her, didn't it?" Tony said. "I did you a favor." He frowned. "I think. The whole thing sort of came to me in a flash." He looked at Roger. "Was that a bad move?"

"I'm not sure," Roger said. "You might want to stay away from flashes in the future."

"I don't want to see Min again," Cal said, and thought about seeing Min again.

"So? Cynthie doesn't need to know that," Tony said.

"So now I have to take Min to Emilio's because Cynthie will check," Cal said.

"I don't see why," Roger said. "If Cynthie asks, you can say you went someplace else."

"I try to tell as few lies as possible." Cal sat down again, trying to feel exasperated about the whole mess. He picked up the phone and dialed Min's company, tracking her down through the switchboard operator, but her phone was busy and voice mail was not an option. Nobody ever talked anybody into lunch on voice mail.

He hung up the phone and saw Roger and Tony watching him. "What?"

"Nothing," Roger said.

"Nothing," Tony said.

"Good," Cal said and ignored them to go back to his computer screen.

When her office phone rang, Min thought *Cal*, and then kicked herself. The beast must have the power to cloud women's minds if she was thinking about him at 9 A.M. on a Monday morning in the middle of a prelim report.

"Minerva Dobbs," she said into the phone, tapping her red pen on the frosted glass top of her desk.

"Tell me about this man you're dating," her mother said.

"Oh, for crying out loud." Min leaned back in her Aeron chair, exasperated.

"Greg says he has a horrible reputation with women," Nanette said. "Greg says he uses them and leaves them. Greg says—"

"Mother, I don't care what Greg says," Min said over her mother's panic. "And I'm not dating him. We went to dinner and had a picnic in the park and that's it." She wrote Cal's name in block letters on the cover sheet of her report and then drew a heavy red line through it. Gone, gone, gone.

"Greg says—"

"Mother."

"—that he's a heartbreaker. He's worried for you."

Min started to say, *Oh, please,* and stopped. Greg probably was worried about her. Greg worried about everything.

Why was Greg worried about her?

"How does Greg even know this guy exists?" Min said as she wrote "Greg" in red block letters and drew two heavy lines through it. Then she wrote "Dweeb" below that and "Snitch" below that.

"*I'm* worried for you," her mother was saying. "I know you're being brave about losing David, but I just hate it. I can't stand it if you're hurt."

Min felt her throat close. "Who are you and what did you do with my mother?"

"I just don't want you hurt," Nanette said, and Min thought she heard her voice shake. "I want you married to a good man who will appreciate you for how wonderful you are and not leave you because you're overweight."

Min shook her head. "You had me right up to the last line." She wrote "Mother" in block letters, drew a heart around it, and then, while Nanette talked on, she drew four heavy lines across it.

"Marriage is hard, Min," Nanette was saying. "There are a million reasons for them to cheat and leave, so you have to work at it all the time. You have to look good all the time. Men are very visual. If they see something better—"

"Mom?" Min said. "I don't think—"

"No matter how hard you work, there's always somebody younger, somebody better," Nanette said, her voice trembling. "Even for Diana, for everybody. You can't start with a handicap, you can't—"

"What's going on?" Min said. "Is Greg cheating on Diana?"

"No," her mother said, sounding taken aback. "Of course not."

Min tried to imagine Greg betraying Diana, but it was ridiculous. Greg didn't have the gumption to cheat. Plus, he loved Diana.

"Why would you say that?" her mother said. "That's a horrible thing to say."

"You were the one who brought up cheating," Min said. So if not Greg, then who? *Dad?* Min rejected that thought, too. Her father had three interests in life: insurance, statistics, and golf. "The only thing Dad would leave you for is the perfect four iron, so that's not it. What's going on?"

"I want you married and happy and this Cabot isn't—"

"Calvin," Min said.

"Bring him to dinner Saturday," Nanette said. "Wear something black so you'll look thinner."

"I'm not seeing him, Mother," Min said. "That's going to make it doubtful that he'll want to meet my parents."

"Just be careful," her mother said. "I don't know how you find these men."

"He looked down my sweater and saw that red lace bra," Min said. "It's all your fault."

She spent a few more minutes reassuring Nanette, and then she hung up and went back to editing for another five minutes until the phone rang again. "Oh, great," she said and answered it, prepared to argue with her mother again. "Minerva Dobbs."

"Min, it's Di," her sister said.

"Hi, honey," Min said. "If this is about Greg ratting out my picnic date, it's okay, it's over, I'm never going to see him again." She drew another line through Greg's name. As far as she was concerned, there couldn't be too many lines through Greg's name.

"Greg says David says he's awful," Diana said.

Min sat up a little straighter. "David said that, did he?" The rat fink didn't even play fair on his bets. She wrote "David" in big block letters and then stabbed her pen into it.

"He told Greg not to tell me he'd told him," Diana said.

"Right," Min said, not bothering to follow that.

"He just doesn't sound like part of your plan," Di said.

Min stopped stabbing. "My plan? What plan?"

"You always have a plan," Di said. "Like me. I've planned my wedding and my marriage very carefully and Greg fits perfectly. He's perfect for me. We're going to have a perfect life."

"Right," Min said, and drew another line through Greg's name.

"So I know you must have a plan and this wolf—"

"Beast," Min said.

"—frog, whatever, can't fit your plan."

"He's not a frog," Min said. "I kissed him and he did not turn into a prince." *He turned into a god. No, he didn't.* "Look, I'm never going to see him again, so everybody can relax."

"Good," Di said. "I'll tell Mom you're being sensible as usual and she won't worry anymore."

"Oh, good," Min said. "Sensible as usual. Nobody mentioned this to Dad, did they?"

"Mom might have," Diana said.

"Oh, hell, Di, why didn't you stop her?" A vision of her overprotective father rose up before her like a big blond bear. "You know how he is."

"I know," Di said. "I'm still not sure he likes Greg."

Are you sure you like Greg? Min wanted to say, but there wasn't any point since Diana would insist it was True Love to the death. "Well, good news, I got you a cake—"

"You did?" Di's voice went up a notch. "Oh, Min, thank you—"

"—but it won't be decorated so Bonnie and I are going to do that with Mom's pearls and a lot of fresh flowers." Min began to draw a wedding cake.

"You're going to decorate my cake?" Di said, her voice flat.

"People are going to love it when they taste it," Min said, adding some doves to the top.

"Taste?" Di said. "What about when they look at it?"

"Are you kidding? Fresh flowers and real pearls? It'll be a sensation." Min drew in some pearls. They were easier than doves, and she was experiencing enough difficulty with her morning.

"What does Mom say?"

"Why don't we ask her at the wedding?" Min said, keeping her voice chirpy.

"Okay," Di said, taking a deep breath into the phone. "I really am grateful. And it's good that it'll taste good, too. For the cake boxes and everything."

"Cake boxes?" Min said.

"The little boxes of cake that the guests take home for souvenirs," Diana said. "To dream on."

"Cake boxes," Min said and began to draw little squares. "Two hundred. You bet."

"You didn't get cake boxes?"

"Yes," Min said, drawing boxes faster. "I got cake boxes. Will you relax? You sound like you're strung up on wires. How are you doing?"

"I'm *fine*," Diana said, with too much emphasis.

"No trouble with Wet and Worse?" Min said and then winced. "I mean Susie and Karen?"

Diana laughed. "I can't believe you said that."

"I'm sorry," Min said. "It's . . ."

"Min, we know about it. Karen overheard Liza say it back when we were in high school. She calls Bonnie and Liza Sweet and Tart."

Min laughed in spite of herself.

"Don't tell them," Diana said. "I'll go on pretending you don't call Susie and Karen Wet and Worse if you'll go on pretending we don't call Bonnie and Liza Sweet and Tart."

"Deal," Min said. "God, we're horrible people."

"Not us," Diana said cheerfully. "It's our friends who make this stuff up. We're those nice Dobbs girls."

"I think that depends on who you ask," Min said, thinking of Cal. She had to remember to be nicer to him. Except she wasn't going to see him again so it didn't matter. Also, when she was nice to him in the park, it went badly. "I've been really bitchy lately. . . ." Her voice trailed off as her father loomed in the doorway, looking like an anxious Viking. "Hi, Daddy."

"Oh, no," Diana said.

"I'll talk to you later," Min said to Diana and hung up. "So, what brings you down here?" she said to her dad. "Air get too thin on the fortieth floor?"

"About this man you're seeing," George Dobbs said, glowering at his daughter as he came into her office.

"Don't even try it," Min said. "I know you have junior account executives for breakfast, but that doesn't work with me. I'm not seeing Cal anymore, but if I were, it would be my choice. Come on, Dad." She smiled at him, but his face stayed worried. "Two and a half million people get married every year in this country. Why not me?"

"Marriage isn't for everybody, Min," he said.

"Daddy?" Min said, taken aback.

"This man is not a good man," George said.

"Now wait just a minute," Min said. "You don't even know him. He was a perfect gentleman both times we went out—" *Well, there were hands in the park.* "—and since we've decided not to see each other again, it's pretty much not a problem."

"Good." Her father's face cleared. "Good for you. That's smart. Why take chances with a man you know isn't a good risk?"

"I'm not selling him insurance," Min said.

"I know, Min," he said. "But it's the same principle. You're not a gambler. You're too sensible for that."

He smiled at her, patted her hand, and left, and Min sat at her desk and felt dull, frumpy, and boring. Not a gambler. Sensible as usual. She let herself think about kissing Cal in the park, his mouth hot on hers, his hands hard on her, and she felt the heat rise all over again. That hadn't been sensible, that hadn't been a plan. And now she was never going to see him again.

She looked down at her report and realized she'd perforated it. She must have been stabbing it, the Norman Bates of statistical analysis. "Great," she said, and tried to pull the pages apart. The top sheet ripped, and her phone rang, and she picked it up and snarled, "Minerva Dobbs," ready to perforate the caller this time.

"Good morning, Minerva," Cal said, and all the air rushed out of Min's lungs. "How did you get that godawful name?"

Breathe. Deep breaths. Very deep breaths.

"Oh," she said. "This is good. Grief about my name from a guy named Calvin." *I do not care that he called. I am totally unaffected by this.* Her heart was pounding so loudly she was convinced he could hear it over the phone.

"I was named after my rich uncle Robert," Cal said, "which turned out to be a total waste when he left everything to the whales. What's your excuse?"

"My mother wanted a goddess," Min said faintly.

"Well, she got one," Cal said. "I take it back, it's the perfect name for you."

"And my father's mother was named Minnie," Min said, trying to get back to offhand and unfazed. "It was a compromise. Why isn't your name Robert?"

"I got his last name," Cal said. "Which is good. I don't see myself as a Bob."

"Bob Morrisey." Min leaned back in her chair, pretending to be cool. "That weird guy in the shipping department."

"The insurance agent you can trust," Cal said.

"The used car salesman you can't," Min said.

"Whereas Calvin Morrisey is the old fart who started the company in 1864," Cal said. "Or in this case, the guy who has your shoe."

"Shoe?"

"Red ribbons, funky heel, big dopey flower."

"My *shoe*." Min sat up, delighted. "I didn't think I'd ever see it again."

"Well, you won't unless you come to lunch with me," Cal said. "I'm holding it for ransom. There's a gun to its heel right now."

"I have lunch at my desk," Min began, and thought, *Oh, for crying out loud, could I be any more pathetic?*

"Emilio is experimenting with a lunch menu. He needs you. I need you."

"I can't," Min said while every fiber in her being said, *Yes, yes, anything.* Thank God her fiber couldn't talk.

"You can't let Emilio down," Cal went on. "He loves you. We'll have chicken marsala. Come on, live a little. A very little."

A very little. Even Cal knew she was a sensible, non-gambling, plan-ridden loser. "Yes," Min said, her heart starting to pound again. "I would love to get my shoe back and have chicken marsala for lunch."

"Keep in mind, you have to eat it with me," Cal said. "You're not seeing that shoe until you eat."

"I can stand that," Min said, and felt lighter all over. Then she hung up and looked at her report.

She'd been drawing hearts on it, tiny ones, dozens of them.

"Oh, my Lord," Min said and put her head on her desk.

When Min got to Emilio's, a dark-haired teenage boy at the door said, "You looking for Cal?" and when she nodded, said, "He's at your table," and jerked his head into the restaurant.

"I have a table?" Min said, but then she saw Cal sitting by the window at the table they'd had Wednesday night, and she lost her breath for a minute. *I keep forgetting how beautiful he is*, she thought, and watched as he sat relaxed in his chair, his dark eyes fixed on the street outside, his profile perfect. He was tapping his fingers on the table, and his hands looked strong, and Min remembered how good they'd felt on her and thought, *Get out of here*. Then he saw her and straightened and smiled, his eyes lighting as if he were glad to see her, and she smiled back and went to meet him. *Charm Boy*, she thought, and slowed down again, but he already had her chair pulled out for her.

"Thanks for coming," he said, and she slid into the chair thinking, *He's up to something, be careful*. Then she noticed him looking at the floor and said, "What?" her voice cracking with nerves.

"Shoes," he said. "What are you wearing?"

"You sound like an obscene phone call," she said, trying to keep her treacherous voice steady, but she stuck her foot out so he could see her blue reptile slides, open-toed to show off the matching blue nail polish.

He shook his head. "You can do better. The toes are nice, though."

"These are work shoes," she said, annoyance clearing up her nerves. "Also, you have my red shoe so I couldn't wear those. Can I have my shoe back?"

"Not until after lunch," he said, sitting down across from her. "It's my only leverage."

"Have you had this foot fetish long?" she said, as he passed her the bread basket.

"Just since I met you," he said. "Suddenly, there's a whole new world out there."

"Glad to know I've made an impact," she said, and was appalled to realize that she really was. It was enough to make her nerves come back. *He doesn't matter.* She shoved the bread basket back to him, determined to be virtuous in consumption if not in thought, and said, "So who's the charmer at the door? He needs lessons from you."

"Emilio's nephew." Cal picked up a piece of bread and broke it. "His tableside manner could use some work."

"Doesn't Emilio have somebody else to put up front?" Min picked up her napkin to keep her hands off the bread. "He can't be good for business."

"Brian's the socially adept one in the family," Cal said. "His brothers are back in the kitchen where they won't hurt anybody. Fortunately, they can cook. I already ordered. Salad, chicken marsala, no pasta."

"Oh, good," Min said, "because I'm starving. Did you know that forty percent of all pasta sold is spaghetti?" *Geek*, she thought, and tried to suppress her statistical instinct while she smiled at him. "I think that shows a huge lack of imag—"

Brian slung a salad in front of her and another in front of Cal. "Your chicken's up in about fifteen," he told Cal. "You want wine with that?"

"Yes, please," Cal said to him. "I thought you were working on your finesse."

"Not with you," Brian said. "I know it's chicken, but for you, red wine, right?"

"Right," Cal said. "Now ask me what kind of red."

"Whatever Emilio puts in the glass," Brian said, and left.

"Just a little ray of sunshine," Min said. "But enough about him. Give me the ten bucks."

"Ten bucks?" Cal looked beautifully blank and then shook his head. "There wasn't a bet. Stop harassing me for cash."

"You asked me out without a bet?" Min said.

"No money will change hands," Cal said. "Except for me paying the tab."

"We can go Dutch," Min offered.

"No, we can't."

"Why not? I can afford it. We're not dating. Why—"

"I invited you, I pay," Cal said, his face beginning to set into that stubborn look that exasperated her.

"That means if I invite you, I pay," Min said.

"No, I pay then, too," Cal said. "So tell me who Diana, Wet, and Worse are."

"That's why you invited me to lunch?" Min said, infusing her voice with as much skepticism as possible.

"No." Cal put his head in his hands. "Could we just for once meet like regular people? Smile at each other, make small talk, pretend you don't hate me?"

"I don't hate you," Min said, shocked. "I like you. I mean, you have flaws—"

"*What* flaws?" Cal said. "Of course I have them, but I've been on my best behavior with you. Except for hitting you in the eye and attacking you on a picnic table. How are you?"

"I'm fine," Min said, putting as much chipper as she could into her voice. "I'm turning over a new leaf. Taking risks. Like having lunch with a wolf."

"I'm a wolf?" Cal said.

"Oh, please," Min said. "You picked me up on Friday with 'Hello, little girl.' Who did you think you were channeling, the prince?"

Emilio appeared with wine before Cal could say anything, and Min beamed at him, grateful for the rescue. "Emilio, my darling. I forgot to mention cake boxes. Two hundred cake boxes."

"Already on it," Emilio said. "Nonna said you'd need them. She said to get four-inch-square boxes for three-inch-square cakes."

"I'm getting the boxes," Min said, nodding. "Sure. Great. Fine. Your grandmother is an angel and you are my hero. And of course, a genius with food."

"And you are my favorite customer." Emilio kissed her cheek and disappeared back into the kitchen.

"I *love* him," she told Cal.

"I noticed," Cal said. "Been seeing him behind my back, have you?"

"Yes," Min said. "We've been having conversations about cake."

"Whoa," Cal said. "For you, that's talking dirty."

"Funny." Min stabbed her salad again and bit into the crisp greens. Emilio's dressing was tangy and light, a miracle all by itself. "God, I *love* Emilio. This salad is fabulous. Which is not a word I usually use with 'salad.'"

"Tell me about the cake," Cal said, starting on his own salad.

"My sister Diana is getting married in three weeks," Min said, glad to be on a topic that wasn't dangerous. "Her fiancé said he knew this great baker and that he would order the cake as a surprise. And then the surprise turned out to be that he hadn't ordered the cake."

"And the wedding's still on?" Cal said.

"Yes. My sister says it's her fault for not reminding him."

"Your sister does not sound like you," Cal said.

"My sister is my exact opposite," Min said. "She's a darling."

Cal frowned. "Which makes you what?"

"Me?" Min stopped eating, surprised. "I'm okay."

Cal shook his head as Emilio appeared with a steaming platter of chicken marsala. When he and Min had assured each other of their undying devotion, he left, and Cal served chicken and mushrooms. "So how do Wet and Worse figure in this cake story?"

"They don't," Min said. "Except that they're my sister's bridesmaids. But do *not* tell anybody I called them that." She ate her first bite of chicken, savoring it, and then teased an errant drop of sauce from her lower lip. "Do you think—"

"Don't do that," Cal said, his voice flat.

"What?" Min blinked at him. "Ask questions?"

"Lick your lip. What were you going to ask me?"

"Why? Bad manners?" Min said, dangerously.

"No," Cal said. "It distracts me. You have a great mouth. I know. I was there once. What were you going to ask me?"

Min met his eyes, and he stared back, unblinking. *Oh*, she thought and tried to remember what they'd been talking about, but it was hard because all she could think about was how he'd been there once, and how good he'd felt, and how hot his eyes were on her now, and how much she—

"You guys okay?" Brian said.

"What?" Cal said, jerking his head up.

"Is there something wrong with the chicken?" Brian frowned at them both. "You guys looked strange."

"No," Min said, picking up her fork again. "The chicken is wonderful."

"Okay," Brian said. "You need anything else?"

"A waiter with some class?" Cal said.

"Yeah, right, like I'd waste that on you," Brian said, and wandered off.

"So anyway," Min said, scrambling for a safer topic, "when Diana told me about the cake, I turned to Emilio in my hour of need, and he called his grandmother. So he's my hero."

"Wait'll you taste the cake," Cal said. "She only makes it for weddings and it's like nothing else in this world."

"When did you eat wedding cake?" Min said.

"When Emilio got married," Cal said. "When my brother got married. When everybody I've ever known got married. Tony, Roger, and I are the last hold-outs, so there have been a lot of weddings. And now Roger's going down for the count."

"Well, at least you and Tony will have each other," Min said brightly. "So you have a brother. Younger or older?"

"Older. Reynolds."

Min stopped eating. "Reynolds? Reynolds Morrisey?"

"Yes," Cal said. "Husband to Bink, father to Harry."

"Isn't there a fancy law firm called Reynolds Morrisey?"

"Yes," Cal said. "My father, his partner John Reynolds, and my brother." He didn't sound too thrilled about any of them.

"Cozy," Min said. "So how is Harry?"

"Permanently scarred from watching us on a picnic table."

Min winced. "Really?"

"Hard to say. I haven't seen him since. Bink probably has him in therapy by now. So what's your take on Bonnie and Roger?"

"They'll be engaged before fall," Min said, and they began to discuss Bonnie and Roger and other safe topics for the rest of the meal. When they were finished and Cal had signed the charge slip, he said, "So lunch with me is risky. Does that mean you need an apology for our last lunch?"

"No." Min smiled and tried to look unfazed. "I've been working on the theory that if we don't talk about it, it didn't happen. Although a lot of people seem to know about it. Greg, for example. He ratted us out, and now my mother wants you to come to dinner." Cal looked taken aback for a minute, and she said, "I told her you were a complete stranger so dinner was unlikely." Then out of the blue, she blurted, "So what was that on Saturday?"

"Well." Cal took a deep breath. "That was chemistry. And it was phenomenal. I'd be more than interested in doing that again, especially naked and horizontal, but—"

Min's pulse picked up, but she slapped herself in the forehead to forestall him and her own treacherous imagination.

"What?" he said.

"I'm remembering why you never ask guys to tell you the truth," she said. "Because sometimes they do."

"My point is," Cal said, "that Liza was right, I had no business kissing you like that because I don't want anything that serious. I just got out of a relationship that was a lot more intense than I'd realized and—"

Min frowned. "How could it have been more intense than you'd realized?"

"I thought we were just having a good time," Cal said. "She thought we were getting married. It ended okay, there are no hard feelings—"

Min looked at him in amazement. "She wanted to get married, you didn't, but there are no hard feelings."

"She said if I wasn't ready to commit, she'd have to move on," Cal said. "It was pretty cut and dried."

"And you're the guy who's supposed to be a wizard at understanding women. It was not cut and dried. She either hates you, or she thinks you're coming back."

Cal shook his head. "Cynthie's very practical. She knows it's over.

And so are we because, even though it was great, this is not something either one of us wants to pursue."

"Right," Min said, understanding completely if not happily. "It would be different if we were at all compatible. I'm not averse to commitment especially if it'd be that much fun, but the last thing I need is to fall for somebody I already know is no good for me just because he kisses like a god. Also, I'm waiting for the reincarnation of Elvis and you are not him. But—"

She stopped because Cal had a strange look on his face.

"What?" she said. "I was kidding about Elvis."

"I'm no good for you," he said, "but I kiss like a god?"

Min considered it. "Pretty much. Why? Did you have a different take on it?"

Cal opened his mouth and then stopped and shrugged. "I guess not. I don't think you'd be bad for me, I just can't take the hassle. You're not a restful woman."

"This is true," Min said. "But you ask for it. You're such a wolf."

"I'm retired," Cal said. "All I want now is some peace and quiet. I just need a break."

"That's my plan," Min said. "I'm taking a break from dating."

"Until Elvis shows up," Cal said.

"Right. As far as I can see, there's no downside to this at all."

"No sex," Cal said.

"I can stand that," Min said.

"Yeah, you're good at denying yourself things."

"Hey," Min said, insulted. "We were doing just fine there and then you had to take a shot at me."

"Sorry," Cal said.

They got up to go, Min kissed Emilio good-bye, and they went out into the street.

"Okay, it's broad daylight and my office is only six blocks away," Min said. "You don't have to walk me."

"Fair enough." Cal held out his hand. "We'll probably meet again at Roger and Bonnie's wedding. In case we don't, have a nice life."

Min shook his hand and dropped it. "Likewise. Best of luck in the future."

She turned to go and he said, "Wait a minute," and made her heart lurch. But when she turned around, he was holding her shoe, the red ribbons fluttering in the light breeze.

"Right," she said, taking it. "Thank you very much."

He held on to it for a moment, looking into her eyes, and then he shook his head and said, "You're welcome" and let go, and she set off down the street without looking back, full of excellent food but not nearly as happy as she should have been.

Charm Boy, she thought, and put him out of her mind.

On Tuesday, Min looked at the salad on her desk at lunch and thought, *There has to be more to life than this.* It was Cal's fault; she'd had real food in the middle of the day and it had tainted her. Until Cal, she'd never thought about food except as something she couldn't have. Even before she'd started dieting for the bridesmaid's dress, there'd been no butter in her life. *There should be butter,* she thought, and then realized the folly of that.

But there could be chicken marsala.

Min shoved her salad to one side, logged onto the net, and did a search for "chicken marsala" because doing a search for "Cal Morrisey" would not have been helpful to her damn plan.

"Very popular dish," she said when she got 48,300 matches. Even allowing for the weird randomness that more than 48,000 of them would demonstrate if she ever got that far, that was still a lot of recipes. There was one with artichokes, that was insane. One had lemon juice, which couldn't be right, another peppers, another onions. It was amazing how many ways people had found to garbage up a plain recipe. She printed off two that sounded right and went to log off the net, but instead, on a random impulse, Googled for "dyslexia" instead. An hour later, she logged off with a new respect for what Calvin Morrisey had accomplished.

When she got off work, she stopped by the grocery. There was something about having a plan for dinner, a recipe in hand, that made her feel much less hostile about food. Of course, she was going to have to adapt the recipe. It called for the chicken to be breaded in flour, which was just extra calories, and carb calories no less. Skip the breading. Salt and pepper she already had, and parsley had no calories, so she picked up a jar of that. Skinless, boneless chicken breasts she was familiar with, no problem there, but butter and olive oil? "It is to laugh," she said and got spray olive oil in a can. Mushrooms were mostly water, so she could have those, and then there was the marsala. She found it in the cooking wine section. Resolutely passing by the bread section, she checked out feeling triumphant, went home and changed into her sweats, cranked up the CD player, and sang her head off to her *Elvis 30* album as she cooked.

An hour later, Elvis was starting all over again and she was staring at the mess in her only frying pan trying to figure out what had gone wrong. She'd browned the chicken in the non-stick skillet and then followed all the other directions but it looked funny and tasted like hell. She tapped her spatula on the edge of the stove for a few moments and thought, *Okay, I'm not a cook. I still deserve great food,* and dropped the spatula to pick up the phone.

"Emilio?" she said when he answered. "Do you deliver?"

The Parker seminar was turning into the worst mess Morrisey, Packard, Capa had ever seen, mostly because the idiot who was in charge of training kept changing the seminar information. "I'm faxing some information over," she'd say when she called. "Just slot it in somewhere."

"That bitch must die," Tony said when she called at ten till five on Tuesday. "I've got a date with Liza tonight."

"I'll stay for the fax," Roger said. "Bonnie will understand."

"You go, I'll stay," Cal said. "I'm dateless and too tired to move anyway."

Tony and Roger left, both heading for warm women, and Cal read the fax and tightened the seminar packet one more time, trying to feel grateful that there wasn't any place he had to be, no woman demanding his time and attention. At seven, he turned off the computer with relief and realized he was starving.

Emilio's seemed like an excellent idea.

"Don't tell me," Emilio said when Cal came through the swinging doors into the kitchen. "Chicken marsala."

"I've had enough chicken marsala for a while," Cal said as the phone rang. Emilio turned to get it and Cal added, "Something simple. Tomato and basil on spaghetti—" No. Forty percent of all pasta sold was spaghetti. No imagination. "Make that fettuccine—"

He stopped when Emilio held up his hand and said, "Emilio's," into the phone. Emilio listened and then looked back over his shoulder at Cal and said, "We usually don't, but for such a special customer, we'll make an exception. Chicken marsala, right? No, no, no trouble at all. You can overtip the delivery boy."

He hung up and smiled at Cal. "That was Min. She wants chicken marsala. You can deliver it to her."

"What?" Cal said, dumbfounded.

"You know the way. It's probably on your way home."

"It's not on my way home, it's not on anybody's way home except God's, the damn place is vertical. What gave you the idea I'd do this?"

Emilio shrugged. "I don't know. She called, you were here, you two are great together, it seemed like a good idea. Did you have a fight?"

"No, we didn't have a fight," Cal said. "We're not seeing each other because I'm all wrong for her and she's waiting for Elvis. Call her back and tell her your delivery boy died."

"Then she won't have anything for dinner," Emilio said. "And you know Min. She's one of those women who eats."

Cal thought about the look on Min's face when she ate chicken marsala. It was almost as good as the look on her face when she ate doughnuts. Which wasn't anywhere near as good as the look on her face when he'd kissed her, that had been—

Emilio shrugged. "Fine. Brian can take it to her."

"No," Cal said. "I'll take it to her. Hurry up, will you? I'm hungry."

Chapter
Six

Forty-five minutes later, Cal was climbing the steps to Min's place when something small and orange streaked past him and almost knocked him down the hill. He finished the climb cautiously, but when he looked around at the top, nothing was there. He rang the doorbell, and Bonnie came to let him in.

"Hi," he said. "Min ordered takeout." He held up the bag, feeling stupid, his least favorite feeling in the world.

"And you're delivering?" Bonnie said as she stepped back.

"Well, you can never have enough extra cash," Cal said and hit the stairs, knowing she was watching him. When he got to the top, he heard Elvis Presley singing "Heartbreak Hotel" through Min's door and sighed.

Min looked surprised when she opened the door at his knock, and he felt pretty stunned himself: as far as he could see, all she was wearing was a very long, very old blue sweatshirt and lumpy sweatsocks. Her hair was down in frizzy waves, and she was wearing no makeup, so the only color on her face was the fading yellow bruise from where he'd clocked her.

"What the hell?" she said. "How did you get in the front door?"

"This is how you open the door to delivery guys?" Cal said, staring at the good strong legs he'd scoped out in the bar on Friday.

"No, this is how I open the door to Bonnie," Min said. "Stop ogling. I have shorts on under this." She pulled up the edge of her shirt and he saw baggy plaid boxers that were only marginally less ugly than her shirt and socks. "*Why* did you get in the front door?"

Then something orange streaked past both their legs and into the apartment.

"What is *that?*" Min said, and Cal came in, leaving the door open behind him.

"I don't know." Cal put Emilio's bag down on an old cast iron sewing machine table beside a couch that looked like a moth-eaten, overstuffed pumpkin. "It ran past me on the steps—"

"Oh, *Lord,*" Min said and Cal turned to look where she was looking.

The mangiest-looking animal he'd ever seen was glaring at them from the end of the couch, its left eye closed and sinister. It was mottled all over in browns and oranges so that, in general, it matched the couch.

"What *is* that?" Min said.

"I think it's a cat," Cal said.

"What kind?" Min said, an awful fascination in her voice.

"Not a good kind," Cal said. "Although you did say you wanted one."

"No, I didn't," Min said.

"When I brought you home last week," Cal said. "You said you were going to get a cat."

"That was a *joke,*" Min said, keeping an eye on the cat. "That's what every woman in her thirties who's been screwed over by men says. 'I'm going to give up the bastards and get a cat.' It's *a cliché.*"

"You know," Cal said, watching the cat, too, "if you're going to talk in code, you have to warn me."

The cat didn't seem to be moving, so Cal looked around the rest of her apartment. It appeared to be the entire attic, its crazy angles punctuated by dormers, and it was furnished in ancient pieces, none of them antiques. He frowned and thought, *This doesn't look like her.*

Min tilted her head at the cat, nonplussed. "Why is its eye shut?"

"My guess is, that one's missing," Cal said.

"Hard life, huh, cat?" Min sighed. "I have extra chicken. I tried the marsala and screwed it up. Maybe the cat will be desperate enough to eat it."

"If you feed it, it'll stay forever," Cal said. "Yo, cat, the door's open. Leave."

The cat curled up on the back of the couch and stared at him haughtily.

"It looks very Cheshire," Min said. "Like it could disappear a little bit at a time."

"And it's already started with the eye," Cal said. "Min, this cat probably has every disease in the Cat's Book of Death."

"I can at least feed it," Min said and went to get some chicken.

"It does go with the couch." Cal closed the door and moved Emilio's bag from the sewing machine table to a battered old round oak table behind the couch. The cat watched his every move while pretending not to care.

Min brought some chicken slivers on a paper towel. She put it under the cat's nose and then stepped back. It sniffed at the chicken and then looked at her. "I know," she said, despair in her voice. "It's awful. You don't have to eat it."

The cat lifted its nose and then nibbled at the closest piece.

"That's a very brave cat," Min told Cal and went to the mantel to get her purse. "Let me pay you or Emilio or whoever."

"No," Cal said, still looking around. The furniture was all comfortable, but none of it was interesting or attractive, nothing like Min. It was almost as if it were somebody else's apartment. "Are you subletting?"

"No," Min said, fishing in her purse. "How much do I owe you?"

"Nothing." There were snow globes on the mantel, lined up on both sides of a kitschy old clock made from fake books, and he went over beside her to look at them, saying, "You didn't pick out this furniture."

"It was my grandmother's," Min said. "Look, you're not going to pay for my dinner. You did me a favor by bringing it, so—"

"You collect these?" Cal said, picking up Rocky and Bullwinkle.

"Cal," Min said.

"There's enough food there for an army," he said. "If you want company, I'm staying and eating half of it. If you don't, I'll take half with me, although I am reluctant to leave you alone with that animal." Cal put Rocky down and looked at the next one. Chip and Dale. "Where did you get these?"

"Friends," Min said. "Family. Flea markets." She paused. "You can stay." She looked at the cat which, having wolfed down the chicken, now seemed to be considering sleep. "You I don't know about," she said, and it regarded her gravely, its right eye closed. "Wasn't the other eye closed before?" Min said to Cal. "The left one?"

"I can't remember," Cal said. "I wouldn't be surprised. It's a very shifty cat. You know, this furniture is not you, that clock is not you, and you don't seem like the snow globe type."

"I know it's not me," Min said, looking around at it. "But it's good furniture, so it doesn't make sense to buy new. Besides, it reminds me of my grandmother. And the snow globe thing started by accident." She turned back to him. "At least let me pay for half of dinner."

"No." Cal picked up a massive piece that had a globe with Lady and the Tramp sitting on top of a detailed Italian restaurant. "What kind of accident?"

"My Grandma Min had a Mickey and Minnie Mouse snow globe. They were dancing and Minnie was wearing a long pink dress and Mickey was dipping her." Min's voice softened as she spoke. "My grandpa gave it to her for a wedding anniversary, but I loved it so much that she gave it to me when I was twelve."

Cal scanned the mantel. Christine and the Phantom, Jessica and Roger Rabbit, Blondie and Dagwood, Sleeping Beauty and the Prince, Cinderella and her prince in front of a castle with white doves suspended in air, even Donald and Daisy were there, but no Mickey and Minnie. "Where is it?"

"I lost it," Min said. "In one of the moves when I was in college. You know how it is, you move every year and stuff disappears. I was upset about it so people started giving me other ones on my birthday and for

Christmas to make up for it. I tried to tell them I didn't want any more, you know, 'Thank you, it's lovely, but you shouldn't have,' but by then it had taken on a life of its own." She looked at the mantel and sighed. "I have boxes of them in the basement. These are just my favorites. Never collect anything. People never let you quit."

Cal looked over the assortment again. There was one big, dark one at the end of the mantel that looked like monsters. "What's this?" he said, picking it up.

"Disney villains," Min said. "Liza and Bonnie each got me one for Christmas two years ago."

"Liza got you that one," Cal said, putting it back.

"How do you know it wasn't Bonnie?" Min said.

"Because that's not Bonnie." He pointed to the Cinderella globe with the doves. "She got you that one."

"Yes," Min said. "I still don't see—"

"Bonnie wants the fairy tale," Cal said. "Liza's a realist, she sees the bad guys. Also Bonnie wouldn't have missed the important part. She got you a couple."

"A couple of what?" Min said.

"A couple," Cal said. "Twosome. These are all couples. Look. Lady and the Tramp, Christine and the Phantom, Jessica Rabbit and Roger . . . except for Liza's, they're all couples."

"I wouldn't call Rocky and Bullwinkle a couple exactly," Min said, looking at them doubtfully. "And Chip and Dale. I mean, I know there have been rumors, but—"

"C'mon, Minnie," Cal said. "You started with a couple."

"Don't call me Minnie," Min said, her eyes flashing at him.

"You can call me Mickey," Cal said, grinning at her, wanting that flash again.

"I'm going to call you a cab if you don't stop annoying me," Min said. "Can we just eat?"

Cal gave up and went back to the table to unpack Emilio's bag, detouring around the cat in case it decided to go rogue and start on him. "That guy really did a number on you."

"What guy?"

"The one who dumped you the night I picked you up. You must have loved him a lot."

"Oh." Min blinked. "Him? No. Not at all."

Good, Cal thought, even though it didn't make any difference. "Do you have plates?"

She went around the table and into an alcove that anybody else would call a closet, but that her landlord evidently thought was a kitchen.

"Get wineglasses, too," Cal said as he opened the box with the bread in it.

"What?" Min said, leaning out of the alcove.

"Glasses," Cal said. "For the wine."

Min came out of the alcove with two wineglasses and set the table while he pulled the cork from the wine and poured, trying not to look at her sweats. It was nice of her to dress so badly. If she'd been wearing that red sweater again, he might have had a problem. Then she opened the carton with the salad in it, and tried to plate it using a tablespoon. "Damn," she said, as the dressing spilled onto the table.

"You don't cook, do you, Minerva?" Cal said.

"Oh, and you do?" Min said.

"Sure." He took the spoon from her. "I worked in a restaurant while I was in college. You need a big spoon, Minnie. This one is for eating."

"Or I could just jab you with it," Min said.

He shook his head and went around her into the kitchenette to look for a larger spoon and instead found a frying pan with something horrible in it.

"What is this?" he said when she came in for a paper towel.

"None of your business," Min said. He raised his eyebrows at her and she said, "I thought I could make it on my own. I got the recipe. But it didn't—"

Light dawned. "This is chicken marsala?"

"No," Min said. "That is a mess, which is why I called Emilio's."

"What did you do?" Cal said.

"Why?" Min said. "So you can make snarky comments?"

"Do you want to know how to make chicken marsala or not?" Cal said, exasperated. She was such a pain in the ass.

She scowled up at him. "Yes."

"What's the first thing you did?" Cal said.

"Sprayed the pan with olive oil," Min said.

"Sprayed?" Cal said. "No. Pour. A couple of tablespoons."

"Too much fat," Min said.

"It's good fat," Cal said. "Olive oil is good for you."

"Not for my waistline," Min said.

"You're going to have to pour, Minnie," Cal said. "It's part of the flavor."

"Okay," Min said, but she looked mutinous. "Then I browned the chicken."

"Too fast," Cal said. "Pound the chicken breasts first. Use a can if you don't have a mallet, put them in a plastic bag, and pound them thin. Then dredge them in flour mixed with ground black pepper and kosher salt."

"You're kidding," Min said. "Flour just adds calories."

"And seals the chicken," Cal said. "So it doesn't get . . ." He picked up a fork, jabbed one of the petrified slabs in the pan, and held it up. ". . . dry. Then what did you do?"

Min folded her arms. "When they were browned, I put the mushrooms in and poured the wine over and let it reduce."

"No butter?"

"No butter," Min said. "Are you insane?"

"No," Cal said, dropping the chicken back in the pan. "But anybody who makes chicken marsala without olive oil, butter, or flour may be. If you wanted broiled chicken, you should have made broiled chicken." He dipped his finger in the sauce and tasted it. It was so vile he lost his breath, and Min ran him a glass of water and handed it to him.

"I don't know why that part didn't work," she said.

"What marsala did you use?" Cal said when he'd gotten the taste out of his mouth, and she handed him a bottle of cooking wine. "No, no, no," he said and then relented when she winced. "Look, honey, when you make wine sauce, you're cooking the wine down, concentrating it. You have to use good wine or it'll taste like . . . He looked down at the pan. ". . . this. It's a wonder the cat's not dead."

"Ouch," Min said. "Could you write that down for me?"

"No," Cal said, and then they heard a crash from another room. He looked around. "Your cat's gone, Minnie. You leave a window open anywhere?"

"I have one of those cheapo sliding screens in the bedroom," Min said and went through a doorway beside the mantel to look. "Oh, this is good," she said when she was inside, and Cal followed her in.

Her sliding screen was gone from the dormer window, which was now open to the night air. Cal went over and looked out. The screen was halfway down the roof, and the cat was sitting in a tree branch that tapped the shingles, washing its paws. Its left eye was closed.

"It does switch eyes," Cal said, pulling his head back in. "Maybe it's conserving . . . " His voice trailed off as he saw Min's bedroom.

Most of it was filled with the most elaborate brass bed he'd ever seen, a huge thing covered with a watery lavender-blue satin comforter and lavender satin pillows that were piled against a headboard that curved and twined, erupting in brass rosettes and finials, until he grew dizzy just looking at it. "How do you keep from falling out of bed?"

"I just hold on and try not to look at the headboard," Min said. "I love it. I bought it last month even though it was completely impractical. . . ."

She went on, but Cal had stopped listening when she said, "I just hold on," imagining her lying back on the soft blue satin comforter, her soft gold-tipped curls spread out on the pillows, her soft lips open as she smiled at him, her soft hands gripping the headboard, her soft body—

"Cal?" Min said.

"It smells good in here," Cal said, trying to find a thought that didn't have "soft" in it. Or "hard," for that matter.

"Lavender pillows," Min said. "My grandmother always put lavender in her pillowcases. Or maybe it's the cinnamon candles."

Cal cleared his throat. "Well, it's . . . nice. It's the first thing I've seen in this apartment that looks like you." The thought of tipping her onto that blue comforter was entirely too plausible, so he said, "We should go eat. Now."

"Okay," Min said and started for the door.

"You want the window closed?" Cal said.

"Then how will the cat get back in?" Min said.

"Good point," Cal said, thinking, *Oh, Christ, I gave her a feral cat*, and followed her out.

When they were eating Emilio's salad, Min said, "So chicken marsala is not heart smart or weight friendly."

"Heart smart?" Cal said, picking up his tumbler of wine. "Does that mean good for your heart? Because it is. I told you, olive oil is good for you. And a little bit of flour and butter won't kill you."

"Tell that to my mother." Min tasted her salad again. "This is so good. You know, the lesson here is, I shouldn't be cooking."

"Why?" Cal said. "It was the first time you tried. Everybody makes mistakes." He picked up the chicken carton and filled the two plates, managing it so that nothing spilled.

"Except you," Min said, watching him. "You do *everything* well."

"Okay," Cal said, putting the carton down. "You just got dumped, I get that, but you didn't care about the guy, so why are you still so mad and taking it out on me?"

Min cut into her chicken. "He was sort of the last straw." She put the chicken in her mouth and chewed, and got the same blissful look she always got when eating good food.

"You should never diet." Cal picked up his fork and began to eat. "So what did he do that you can't get over?"

"Well." Min stabbed a mushroom with more antagonism than it deserved. "It was mostly my weight."

"He criticized your weight?" Cal shook his head. "This guy has the brains of a brick."

"He didn't criticize, exactly," Min said. "He just suggested that I should go on a diet. And then he left because I wouldn't sleep with him."

"He told you to go on a diet and then asked you to bed?" Cal said. "I take it back. Bricks are smarter than this dipwad."

"Yes, but he has a point," Min said. "I mean, about my weight." She looked at him, defiant. "Right?"

"There is no way I can answer that without getting all that rage put back on me," Cal said. "Keep it on the loser who dumped you. I'm the good guy."

Min stabbed another mushroom, and then put the fork down. "Okay, I'll give you a free pass on this one. No matter what you say, I won't get mad."

Cal looked at her stormy face and laughed. "How are you going to work that?"

Min nodded. "Okay, I'll get mad, but I'll play fair. The thing is, you're the only man I trust enough to tell me the truth."

"You trust me?" Cal said, surprised and flattered. "I thought I was a beast."

"You are," Min said. "But you do tend to tell me the truth. On most things."

Cal stopped eating. "On all things. I've never lied to you."

"Yeah," Min said dismissively. "So what am I supposed to do about my weight?"

Cal put his fork down. "All right. Here's the truth. You're never going to be thin. You're a round woman. You have wide hips and a round stomach and full breasts. You're . . ."

"Healthy," Min said bitterly.

"Lush," Cal said, watching the gentle rise and fall of her breasts under her sweatshirt.

"Generous," Min snarled.

"Opulent," Cal said, remembering the soft curve of her under his hand.

"Zaftig," Min said.

"Soft and round and hot, and I'm turning myself on," Cal said, starting to feel dizzy. "Do you have anything on under that sweatshirt?"

"Of course," Min said, taken aback.

"Oh," Cal said, ditching that fantasy. "Good. We should be eating. What were we talking about?"

"My weight?" Min said.

"Right," Cal said, picking up his fork again. "The reason you can't lose weight is that you're not supposed to lose weight, you're not built that way, and if you did manage through some stupid diet to take the weight off, you'd be like that chicken mess you just made. Some things are supposed to made with butter. You're one of them."

"So I'm doomed," Min said.

"Another problem is that you don't *listen*. You want to be sexy, be sexy. You have assets that skinny women will never have, and you should be enjoying them and dressing like you enjoy them. Or at least dressing so that others can enjoy them. That suit you were wearing the night I picked you up made you look like a prison warden." He remembered looking down the front of her red sweater and added, "Your underwear's good, though."

"There are no clothes that look good on me," Min said.

"Of course there are," Cal said, still making his way through dinner. "Although you're the kind of woman who looks better naked than dressed." His treacherous mind tried to imagine that and he blocked it. "I'm assuming. Eat, please. Hunger makes you cranky."

"I look better naked?" Min said, picking up her fork again. "No. Listen—"

"You asked, I told you," Cal said. "You just don't want to hear it. The truth is, most guys would rather go to bed with you than with a clothes hanger, you're a lot more fun to touch, but most women don't believe that. You keep trying to lose weight for each other."

Min rolled her eyes. "So I've been sexy all these years? Why hasn't anybody noticed?"

"Because you dress like you hate your body," Cal said. "Sexy is in your head and you don't feel sexy so you don't look it."

"Then how do you know I am?" Min said, exasperated.

"Because I've looked down your sweater," Cal said, flashing back to that. "And I've kissed you, and I have to tell you, your mouth is a miracle. Now *eat something*."

Min looked at her plate for a moment and then dug in. "God, this is good," she said a few minutes later.

"Nothing better than good food," Cal said. "Well, except for—"

"There's got to be a way to make this heart smart," Min said.

Cal shook his head. "Good to know I've been talking to myself here. Did you hear anything I said?"

"Yes," Min said. "So I looked like a prison warden when you picked me up, huh?"

"No," Cal said. "You had great shoes on. You do let yourself go on shoes." *Nice toes, too.*

"So the reason you crossed the bar to pick me up even though I looked like a prison warden was because of my shoes?"

The question sounded pointed, so he tried to remember why he had picked her up. The dinner bet. He winced. That stupid dinner bet with David. "Oh, hell."

"There was a bet, wasn't there?" Min said, sounding disgusted.

Cal took out his wallet and put a ten on the table. "There you go, it's all yours. Can I finish dinner before you throw me out?"

"Sure," Min said. "You know, you're taking losing that bet pretty well."

"I didn't lose," Cal said, stabbing another mushroom. "I don't lose."

"You collected on that bet?" Min said, sounding outraged.

Cal frowned at her. "You walked out the door with me. I won."

"And everybody just *assumes* . . ."

"Assumes what?" Cal said, exasperated. "Somebody bet me ten bucks I could get you to leave with me. You left with me. I got the ten bucks. Now you've got the ten bucks. Can we move on?"

"So the bet's over," Min said, disbelief palpable in her voice.

"Yes," Cal said, moving beyond exasperation. "Okay, it wasn't the best start to a relationship, but we don't have a relationship, what with you waiting for Elvis and both of us with our non-dating plans. Plus I'm feeding you. Again. Why are you mad?"

"No reason at all," Min said, flatly, and went back to her chicken.

"I'm missing something big here, aren't I?" Cal said.

"Yep," Min said. "Keep eating."

Cal offered to help with the dishes, but Min shoved him out the door, fed up with him because of the bet and with herself for caring. She put the leftovers from Emilio in the fridge and dumped the mess she'd made into the trash, and then she went into her bedroom and crawled under the satin comforter. Cal had said the bed was the only thing that looked like her. In an apartment full of plain lumpy furniture, he'd picked out the one beautiful, rich, sexy thing and said, "That's you." The bastard.

The cat jumped up on the bed and padded across to her. "Hey," she said as it curled up by her side. She petted it, feeling its skinny little body under its fur, and it opened both eyes. They were different colors, one of them stained with a blotch that matched the blotch of its fur. "Patchwork cat," she said, and it snuggled next to her, incredibly comforting. She turned on her bedside stereo and listened to Elvis sing about how lousy life had been since his baby left him. The cat pricked up its ears for about a verse, and then relaxed into the comforter again. "Moving into Heartbreak Hotel, are you?" Min said to it, and scratched it behind the ears. It lifted its head to press closer to her fingers, and she looked at its weird little face, screwed up in ecstasy with both eyes shut, and felt a rush of affection for it. It began to purr, and the sound was more comforting that she could have imagined. "It would not be sensible to keep you," she told it, and it opened its eyes slowly and then closed them again, and she kept petting it as it curled close, warm and peaceful and comforting. No wonder all those single women kept cats. They certainly beat charming, lying, compulsive gamblers who kissed like gods and had hands like— "Oh, I'm so lonely, baby," Elvis sang, and Min reached over and punched the UP button. The cat picked up its head, but it seemed to like "Don't Be Cruel" as well as "Heartbreak Hotel" and curled up again, warm against her stomach. "You can stay," she told it, and they lay together in companionable silence, listening to Elvis, until they both fell asleep.

"There's a real babe waiting in your office," David's assistant said when David came in on Wednesday. "Very nice."

Min, David thought and then realized with disappointment that it couldn't be. Nobody described Min as a babe.

When he opened the door, Cynthie was sitting across from his desk, looking phenomenal in a red suit.

"There you are," she said, standing up.

"That's a great suit," he said, closing the door behind him. He walked around her, impressed by the way the skirt curved under her tight little butt without hugging it.

"David," Cynthia said. "Forget the suit. Why is Cal still dating the woman you love?"

"Dating?" David lost interest in Cynthie's suit and sat down behind his desk.

"He took her to lunch on Monday which meant he couldn't go with me. He took her dinner last night at her place." Cynthie leaned closer, her lovely little face tense. "I thought you were going to call Greg. Why is he still with her?"

"I did call Greg." David moved some papers around while he thought fast. "I don't know why it didn't work. Maybe Cal had a good time when he was with her." *Maybe he wants to win ten thousand dollars.*

"But no sex," Cynthie said.

"No," David said, praying Min was still frigid. "They will not be having sex."

"I think you're right." Cynthie began to pace. "She doesn't sound like a woman who would do it that fast, and he wouldn't push it. He has great instincts."

"Well, hooray for him," David said. "Is there anything else you wanted?"

Cynthie leaned over the desk. "I want you to call Min. Ask her to lunch, ask her to dinner, pay for it, and *get her back.*"

David looked down the neckline of her suit and revisited her cleavage. "You do this on purpose, don't you?"

Cynthie took a deep breath, her jaw rigid. "David, I am a dating expert who is losing the man she loves. This isn't just about my private life, this is about my public life, it's about my *whole* life. I have a potential bestseller on my hands, my editor wants to put our wedding picture on the back cover, everything is riding on this, and I am not going to see it go down the drain because *you're too spineless to get your girlfriend back.*" She leaned closer. "I'll go away when you promise me you'll call her for lunch, and you tell me who her best friends are. I saw two in the bar on Friday. A little blonde and a tall redhead. Are they close to her?"

Her perfume wafted toward him, very faint, a whisper of a scent that made him dizzy. "What perfume are you wearing?" he said, trying to ignore the "spineless" crack.

"It's a special blend made just for me," Cynthie said, her voice lower now. "It's made of the scents that most strongly activate a man's libido. I put it on for you, David. Who's her best friend?"

David shook his head to clear it and slid his chair back, away from her. "What's in that stuff?"

"Lavender and pumpkin pie." Cynthie straightened. "I need to know her best friend. I'm helping you, David. You want the actuary back, right?"

She stood in front of him, lithe and lean in red wool crepe, smelling like lavender and cinnamon, and it took him a minute to remember who the actuary was.

"I don't even *like* you," he told her. "Why am I so turned on?"

She rolled her eyes. "Because you're male. Who's her friend?"

"Why do you want to know?"

Cynthie exhaled through her teeth. "I told you this. Attraction. If I can tell her best friend about Cal's pathology with women, I can ensure that the friend finds out enough to worry, and then she will tell Min she dislikes him. And that will help to ward off the infatuation stage. It's all science, David. Nobody is going to get mugged in an alley."

"Okay," David said, still fixated on her breasts. "Are you wearing anything under that jacket?"

"If I show you, will you give me a name?" Cynthie said.

"Yes," David said, knowing he was low and weak and not caring.

Cynthie popped the two buttons on her jacket and opened it. Her red silk bra matched the lining of the suit, and her breasts were perfect B cups, high and taut and, from where he sat, real.

"Oh, God," David said, freezing in his seat.

"Damn right," Cynthie said, buttoning back up again. "Now give me the name."

"The redhead," David said. "Liza Tyler. She thinks all men are bastards anyway."

"She's right," Cynthie said. "Call Min for lunch."

Then she left and David watched her go, the afterimage of her perfect breasts imprinted on his retinas, trying to tell himself that he'd done the right thing because somebody had to stop Cal Morrisey. And save Min, that was important, too.

"Very hot," his assistant said from the doorway. He sniffed the air. "Wow. Is that her perfume?"

"Yes," David said, picking up his phone. "It's brimstone. Don't let her in here again."

At eight that night, Liza was sitting with Tony and Roger in The Long Shot waiting for Bonnie and Min to come back from the bathroom when Tony said, "Uh oh," and turned away from the bar.

"What?" Roger followed his gaze. "Oh." He shrugged. "She's clear across the room."

"She who?" Liza squinted through the dim light. A brunette lounged at the bar, looking expensive, lean, and bored while the guy next to her made his pitch. "Old girlfriend?"

"Nope," Tony said as Bonnie came back from the bathroom. "I don't date the insane. Well, not until you."

"Do you date the insane?" Bonnie said to Roger with interest as she sat down.

"No, no, Cal, not me," Roger said, almost falling off his chair. "I hardly ever date."

"It's all right, baby." Bonnie patted his knee. "You're allowed to date."

"I don't want to date," Roger said and Tony rolled his eyes.

"So that's Cal's old girlfriend." Liza stood. "I'll be right back."

"Wait a minute," Tony said and caught her arm. "Why do you care about Cal's love life?"

"He's dating my best friend," Liza said, trying to sound innocent. "I'm curious."

"What I meant by the not-dating thing," Roger said to Bonnie, "was not dating anybody but you."

"I really don't expect monogamy on the third date," Bonnie said.

"Okay," Roger said. "But it's here anyway."

"Am I going to have to put a chain on you?" Tony said to Liza. He stopped to contemplate that for a moment and then shook his head. "Forget the chains. Stay away from Cynthie. She has psychology on the brain. Probably because she's a psychologist, but still, she comes up with some very whacko stuff."

"Analyzed you, did she?" Liza said, looking back across the bar.

"The not-dating-other-people is just for me, of course," Roger said to Bonnie. "You don't have to just date me. Unless you want to."

Tony shook his head. "She has this insane four-steps-to-love theory that she thinks explains all relationships."

"Oh," Liza said, taken aback.

"Which is dumb because chaos theory explains relationships," Tony said, tugging her back into her seat.

"What?" Liza said, trying to pull her arm away.

"Human relationships, like the weather, cannot be predicted," Tony said, holding on, and Liza sat down again to relieve the pressure on her arm. "Take, for example, Min and Cal. Cal's a complex dynamical system who's trying to maintain stability by not dating."

"He's not dating?" Liza said.

"No," Tony said. "Can you believe it? That alone is making him unstable. The man is not good at celibacy. Then he meets Min, a disturbance in his environment. He begins to move at random because of the disturbance, trying to find stability, but he's caught in the field of her attraction, and starts bouncing off the sides of that field at random, never repeating himself but still caught in her pattern. She's the strange attractor."

"Uh huh," Liza said. "And what good is all of this?"

Tony leaned closer. "Cynthie thinks relationships follow a pattern and that you can predict them. But how can you? People are complex, the disturbances in their lives are complex, and the attractors in their lives are complex. People in love are pure chaos theory."

"Okay," Liza said, still confused.

"That's why Cynthie is crazy," Tony said, letting go of her. "She thinks love can be analyzed and explained. It can't."

Liza sat back and considered Tony for the first time. Somehow he didn't look dumb anymore, and it wasn't because of whatever the hell chaos theory was. It was because he was interested in what he was saying. When he cared, he was smart.

"What?" Tony said.

"Have you ever been in love?" Liza said.

"No," Tony said. "I don't think it's going to happen." He grinned at her. "It would cause too much disturbance in my environment."

Liza frowned. "So why don't you like Cynthie?"

"She tried to pin Cal down. She analyzed him and thought she knew him. He deserves better than that. He should be with somebody who's willing to face the chaos. No rules, no conditions, no theories, no safety nets. The way Bonnie is with Roger."

Liza looked over at Bonnie, laughing with Roger. "You're right. We all deserve that."

"Good," Tony said. "Then you don't have to talk to Cynthie."

Roger said something, and Tony turned away to answer him, and Liza got up and went to meet Cynthie.

When Liza slid into a seat and said, "Hi, I'm Liza," Cynthie looked up and did a double take.

"Hi," she said, sounding surprised, almost as if she recognized her. "I'm Cynthie. Do we know each other?"

"No," Liza said. "But your ex is dating a friend of mine. Tell me everything you know about Calvin Morrisey."

Fifteen minutes later, Liza sat back and thought, *Chaos theory, my ass, Calvin Morrisey has a pattern.* "I knew it," she said to Cynthie. "I knew he was going to break her heart. How many times has he done this?"

Cynthie shrugged. "I was at a party one night after we broke up, and I started talking to a woman who had dated him, too. Then somebody else drifted over. By the end of the night there were four of us, all the same story. A couple of months, life is good, you think 'he's the one' and then he kisses you on the cheek, says 'Have a nice life,' and he's gone."

"You're kidding," Liza said. "And nobody's hunted him down with a tire iron?"

"You can't," Cynthie said. "What are you going to say, 'You dated me for two months, how dare you leave me?' You'd sound demented." She sipped her drink. "And he doesn't do it on purpose," she added, for what must have been the thousandth time.

"You know, I don't care," Liza said. "I just don't want him hurting Min."

"Maybe they're not that serious," Cynthie said. "Do they have anything in common?"

"Not that I can tell," Liza said.

"Are they relaxed together?"

"No," Liza said. "Mostly they fight."

"Do they have shared secrets? In-jokes?"

Liza shook her head. "They don't know each other that well."

Cynthie drew her fingertip around her glass. "Do you like him? I mean, have you told Min you don't like him?"

"Hell, yes," Liza said. "Bonnie and I have both warned her."

"Hmmm." Cynthie smiled at Liza. "Does he have a nickname for her yet?"

"A nickname?" Liza tried to remember. "He calls her by her last name sometimes. Never anything like 'pookie' or 'baby doll.'"

"How about her?" Cynthie said. "Does she have a nickname for him?"

"The beast," Liza said. "I don't think it's affectionate."

Cynthie laughed. "Then why is she dating him?"

"I'm not sure she is," Liza said. "But I think she's going to. I think she's falling for him even though she doesn't want to."

Cynthie stopped laughing.

"And that worries me," Liza said. "She's a terrific person, she doesn't deserve to be dallied with. Can you give me some pointers on how he works?"

Cynthie straightened and nodded. "Sure. Has he given her anything yet?"

"He's only known her a week," Liza said. "I don't . . ." She stopped when Cynthie shook her head.

"If he's serious at all about her, he'll give her something. He'll find out what she wants most, and he'll make sure she gets it. He has to, it's this pattern he's fallen into because of his mother."

"His mother?" Liza said.

"She's withholding," Cynthie said. "He only knows conditional love. So he acts out the same pattern with every woman he meets, trying to win her love. And then when he gets it, the pattern breaks because if she loves him, she's not a stand-in for his mother, and he moves on, to make somebody else love him."

"He's got an Oedipus complex?" Liza said, appalled.

"No," Cynthie said. "She just set up the pattern. He's not in love with her."

"So that means the more Min rejects him . . ." Liza said.

"The more he'll chase her," Cynthie said, all traces of amusement gone. "He can't help it. He doesn't even know he does it. Does she collect anything?"

"Snow globes," Liza said, and then when Cynthie tried to hide her contempt, added, "It's not her fault. It was a family thing that got out of hand."

"He'll buy her a snow globe," Cynthie said. "And it'll be the perfect one, the one she's been missing or always wanted or maybe didn't even know she wanted until he gives it to her. And when he does, you get her out fast, or it'll be all over but the weeping."

"Snow globe," Liza said, looking back at the table where Cal had joined the group after working late.

"He's not a bad person," Cynthie said again. "He'd never hurt anyone on purpose. He's just got this . . ."

"Pathology where he mutilates women because of his mother," Liza said. "I think that was Norman Bates's story, too."

"He'd *never* hurt her physically," Cynthie said, shocked.

"Well, he's not going to hurt her emotionally either," Liza said. "Thank you very much, I appreciate this."

"My pleasure," Cynthie said. Liza thought, *Your pleasure?*, and she must have looked at her oddly, because Cynthie added, "To help. Out. Your friend." She looked down at her drink. "I don't want her to get hurt."

"Me, either," Liza said, and headed back to the others.

When she got back to the table, Tony was saying to Min, "I don't believe it."

"Believe it," Min said. "There are ways you can tell."

"Tell what?" Liza said, sitting down beside Tony but keeping an eye on Cal.

"If a guy is worth dating early in the game," Min said. "We were talking about the old dating tests we used in college."

"Tests," Cal said, leaning his head back and closing his eyes. "I *hate tests*."

"Like what?" Tony asked Liza.

Liza shrugged. "Like you ask him over to watch a video."

"This is good," Tony said. "Videos are good."

"And you show him *Say Anything*," Bonnie said.

"Chick flick," Tony said.

"You flunked this test before it started," Liza said.

Bonnie went on. "And then you wait until he's watching the scene where John Cusack brushes the broken glass out of Ione Skye's path."

Liza watched Cal grin at Min, and Min shake her head at Cal. *Secrets*, she thought, and straightened a little in her chair.

"And then what?" Tony said.

"And if you say . . ." Bonnie deepened her voice. " '*What the hell? She's wearing shoes, ain't she?*' you're gone."

"Well, she was," Tony said, exasperated.

"But they were open-toed," Roger said.

"You get extra points for noticing they were open-toed," Bonnie told him.

"Great," Tony said. "The guy with the foot fetish gets extra points."

"Okay, Minnie," Cal said to Min, "the guy says that and then what happens?"

Minnie? Liza thought and waited for Min to savage him.

"I become ill with something communicable," Min said, trying not to smile.

"How ill?" Cal said, grinning at her.

Damn it, Liza thought.

"There will be retching," Min said, and grinned back.

"And in your case, I will throw up on your shoes," Liza said to Tony, needing to yell at somebody.

"What happens to me?" Roger asked Bonnie.

"Wonderful things," Bonnie said, slipping her arm into his.

"I hate you," Tony said to Roger. "You keep fucking up the curve."

Min laughed, and Cal watched her laugh, and Liza thought, *Oh, no. He looked like a man with a goal, and she knew what it was. I catch you with a snow globe, buddy,* she thought, *and you are dead meat.*

Cal glanced over at her and froze. "What?" he said.

"Nothing," Liza said and smiled at him with intent. "Nothing at all."

"Who's the lucky woman tonight?" Shanna said when Cal went to the bar for refills.

"No woman," Cal said. "I'm resting. How's Elvis? Still singing 'She' on permanent rotation?"

"Don't knock Elvis. If he was a girl, I'd marry him." She craned her head to look around Cal. "I see the Goon Brothers and two women. Let me guess. The tall skinny redhead is yours."

"No," Cal said. "Refills all around for them, Scotch for me."

Shanna looked past him again. "You're with the little blonde in the blue? She looks vacant to me."

"Misleading," Cal said. "But no, not her, either. She's Roger's."

"Then where—" Shanna began.

"Hi," Min said from behind him, and he turned, smiling automatically. "I completely understand your need to flirt with the bartender, but Tony sent me to remind you to hurry."

Shanna leaned over the bar and stuck her hand out to Min. "Hi, I'm Shanna, Cal's next-door neighbor."

Min looked surprised but took it. "I'm Min." She hesitated, and then she leaned over the bar. "Can I ask you something personal?"

"Oh, please do," Shanna said, looking deep into her eyes.

"Excuse me?" Cal said, not sure whether he was annoyed or turned on that Shanna was hitting on Min in front of him.

"You have the most beautiful hair," Min said, ignoring him. "How do you keep it from frizzing?"

"I don't wash it," Shanna said. "Just rinse and condition it. It'll never frizz on you again."

"You're kidding," Min said. "I'm going to try that. I'm so sick of pinning my hair up that I'll try anything."

"Well, come back in when you let it down," Shanna said. "I want to see it."

Me, too, Cal thought.

"I will do that," Min said. "Thank you." She turned back to Cal. "Do you need help carrying the drinks?"

"Yes," Cal said before Shanna could say "No" and hand him a tray.

"I'll be right back then," Min said, and went over to the jukebox.

Cal leaned on the bar as he watched her cross the room. "Get those drinks, babe."

"Tell me she's bi," Shanna said, watching Min, too. "The things she could do with that mouth . . ."

"The things I could do with that mouth," Cal said. *The things I have done with that mouth.* He felt a little dizzy again. Well, it was warm in the bar.

"I'll get those drinks," Shanna said and left while Cal watched Min flip cards on the jukebox. He focused on the gorgeous curve of her neck as she read the song titles. She looked juicy, bitable there, and that set off a whole new train of thought that he told himself was all right as long as he didn't *do* anything about it.

When Shanna came back with six glasses and mugs on a tray, she said, "So how long have you been seeing her?"

"I met her a week ago, but we're not—"

"Early yet." Shanna nodded. "She's got another month, probably two before you wander off. Tell her nice things about me so I can lay a foundation."

"For what?" Cal said.

"She's going to need comforting when you tell her to have a nice life. I will be that comfort. Are you sleeping with her yet?"

"I'm not even dating her," Cal said as Min fed some coins into the jukebox and punched in some numbers. "Give me my Scotch. I think we're going to be listening to Elvis Presley and I will need it."

"Not dating her, huh? Good news for me." Shanna slid his glass across to him.

Cal shook his head. "No. She does not play for your team. And you're still grief-stricken, remember?"

"I'm feeling much better," Shanna said, as "The Devil in Disguise" boomed out of the jukebox. "How do you know she doesn't play for my team?"

"I kissed her. She plays for mine. Although not for me."

"Not for you, huh?" Shanna took two fives from her pocket and slapped them on the bar. "I got ten bucks says you can't kiss her again right here."

"No kidding." Cal laughed at the thought of the damage Min would do to him if he tried. "Also no bet."

Shanna tilted her head. "Okay. I got ten bucks says you *can* kiss her right here."

"I've explained this to you," Cal said. "You have to figure the odds and then take the side that's probable. You don't just flip a coin."

Shanna tapped her finger on the two fives. "Ten says you can do it."

"What's with you?" Cal said. "When did you turn into somebody who likes to watch?"

"I'm just—" Shanna began.

"Hey," Min said, from behind Cal, startling them both. "I thought you weren't going to bet on me anymore."

Cal looked down at her exasperated face. Her lush lower lip stuck out a little, not enough for a pout but enough to remind him of why he'd been staying away from her. "I never said that. Besides, what makes you think I'm—"

"You're both staring at me and there's money on the bar," Min said. "We've been here before." Her eyes were dark, crackling with heat now as she scowled at him, and he began to breathe a little faster, remembering.

"He didn't make the bet," Shanna said. "I did. In fact, he—"

Cal took a ten out of his pocket and slapped it on the bar over Shanna's two fives. "You're on," he said, and leaned down to Min.

Chapter Seven

"Oh, yeah, he's innocent," Min said and then stopped as Cal leaned closer, giving her plenty of time to back away.

Her eyes widened and her lips parted, and she said, "Uh," and then he kissed her, gently, wanting to remember every second this time, the way she felt and tasted, soft and sweet, and he felt her suck in her breath, and then she kissed him back, giving him everything again, and the voice in his head said, *THIS ONE*, and he forgot his good intentions and cradled her face in his hand and lost himself in her.

When he broke the kiss, her eyes were half-closed and her cheeks were flushed. "Did you win?" she said, breathless, and he said, "Yes," and kissed her again, harder this time, feeling her hand clutch his shirt, and then something smacked him on the back of the head and knocked him into her, and she jerked away and said, "Ouch. Ouch."

"*Damn it,*" he said, swinging around to face Liza. "*Stop doing that.*"

"I will if you will," she said.

"No, really," Min said, sounding dazed. "It was okay. It was just another bet."

"Scum," Liza said.

"Look," Cal said, trying to catch his breath. "Min can take care of herself."

Liza stepped closer. "Yeah, tell me you know her. Tell me you care about her. Tell me you're going to love her until the end of time."

"What *is it* with you?" Cal said. "I kissed her. It happens."

Shanna picked up the twenty bucks on the bar. "And I, for one, am very grateful you did. Thank you very much,"

"I thought you won," Min said to Cal. Her eyes were hot, and she was breathing faster, too.

"I did," Cal said, falling back into her. "I just lost the bet."

"Come on, Stats," Liza said, pulling on her arm.

"Right," Min said, shaking her head a little as if to clear it. "Did anybody see that?"

"The entire bar was holding up numbers," Liza said. "It was like the Olympics."

"How'd we do?" Cal said, putting an edge on his voice as he cooled off.

"The Russian judge thought you needed work," Liza said. "There was hooting."

"Well, the Russians are tough," Cal said. "Could you let go of her, please?"

"I don't think so," Liza said and tugged Min's arm again.

"I should go back," Min said to Cal. "You know. Because of the plan."

"What plan?" Cal said.

"Not dating. Taking a break. Remember? Both of us?"

"Right," Cal said, thinking, *Why did I think that was a good idea?* "The plan. Waiting for Elvis. Great." He picked up his Scotch again. "Here's to the plan."

"Yeah, well, have a nice life." Min picked up the tray of drinks and followed Liza back to the table.

"So the tall redhead hates you," Shanna said.

"Liza," Cal said. "I have never done a thing to that woman."

"I think it's what you want to do to her friend," Shanna said. "Still, it does seem like an overreaction. Is there something you're not telling me?"

"Like what?" Cal said. "I am innocent on this one." *No, I'm not.*

"No, you're not," Shanna said. "I saw that kiss. And you're right. She plays for your team."

"Not anymore," Cal said, feeling the back of his head. "We agreed on a plan. Not dating." He gestured with his glass. "I'm going to drink this and then go home for aspirin."

"That's not going to help," Shanna said. "Try a cold shower, too."

"Good to see you've got your sense of humor back," Cal said, and went home to find some peace and painkillers.

That week, Min began screening her calls to duck David, who had developed a pressing need to talk to her, but she didn't need to screen for Cal, who remained annoyingly silent. It was really frustrating avoiding the calls of somebody who didn't have the decency to pick up a phone. Even the If Dinner turned annoying when Liza told them about meeting Cal's ex-girlfriend.

"Cynthie says he's a great guy," Liza said. "He's just caught up in some kind of pathology where he has to make women love him and then leave him. He got conditional love as a child and now he's desperate for it."

Min frowned. "He does not strike me as desperate."

Bonnie shook her head. "Me, either. The ex sounds sort of over the top."

"Well, she's a psychologist," Liza said. "You know how they are. But it does explain why he'd leave such a string of broken hearts behind him and still be the guy we know. I'm suspicious of him but I don't think he's cruel. He wouldn't enjoy dumping them." She looked back at Min. "Cynthie said one of the things he'd do would be to find things you needed and give them to you. I told her about your snow globes, and she said you should brace yourself for incoming."

"He brought me a cat," Min said, and Liza put down her fork.

"A cat?" Liza said. "He must be losing his touch. That should have been a snow globe. Where is this cat?"

"Bedroom," Min said and Liza got up and went to look. When she came back she said, "It's the cat from hell. What was he thinking?"

Min shrugged, not wanting to argue. "He brought me takeout from Emilio's and it followed him in. And then he saw the snow globes."

"And?" Liza said.

"And he told me I collect couples," Min said. "Which I had never seen before, but he's right."

Liza opened her mouth to object and then got up and went to the mantel. "I'll be damned," she said after a moment. "They're all couples except mine, unless Captain Hook is dating Maleficent on the sly. How'd I miss this?"

"Better question is how'd he get it?" Bonnie said.

Min shook her head. "I think he's just really, really, *really* good with people. Empathetic." She hesitated and then said to Bonnie, "After you said he was dyslexic, I researched it on the net. There are all kinds of barriers—"

"Do not feel sorry for him," Liza said.

"I don't," Min said. "Are you kidding? Look at him, he has it all. But he's had to work for it. Anyway, one of the aspects of dyslexics is that they're often very empathetic. That's Cal. He spends all his time looking outward, making sure he understands other people. I don't think he has much self-knowledge, but he makes sure he knows the people in his world. He knows me."

Liza put the villains down with a clunk and came back to the table. "No, he doesn't. He's trying—"

"No," Min said, losing patience with her. "We talked about my weight. He said I dress like I hate my body."

"Good for him," Liza said. "I mean, he's a beast, but he's right on that one. What did he say exactly?"

Min pushed her plate away. "Lots of things, but the gist was that I had a sexy body and I should dress like I'm proud of it."

"Then he asked you to bed," Liza said.

"No, then he said we should eat," Min said. "Oh, and he told me what I was doing wrong on the chicken marsala, so I'm going to try it again."

"He brought you food, understood your snow globes, taught you to cook, said you had a sexy body, and left without making a pass," Bonnie said.

Min nodded.

Bonnie looked at Liza. "He *is* a beast."

"No, this is what Cynthie was talking about," Liza said. "He will fulfill her every need until she falls for him and *then he'll leave.*"

Min bit her lip. "Look, I'm not falling for him, although I swear every time he kisses me, I hear voices and see stars. If nothing else, there's that bet. Which I asked him about and which he lied about, so it's over. Really."

"Uh huh," Liza said, clearly not convinced.

Neither was Min, so on Friday afternoon while she was at work, she very sensibly decided not to go to The Long Shot that night and called her sister instead. "I want to go shopping."

"Shopping?" Di said.

"Somebody told me that I dress like I hate my body."

"You do," Di said. "You want to change? *Yes.*"

"Just a little," Min said, hastily. "I—"

"I know where we'll go," Diana said. "We're going to *transform* you!"

"No," Min said. "Soften a little, maybe, but not—"

"I'll be waiting out front at five," Di said. "This is going to be *so much fun.*"

"Well," Min said, but Di had already hung up. "Oh. Well. All right."

She hung up and decided not to worry about transformation until she was actually in Diana's clutches. She went back to finishing up her work week, and then, as she was putting on her jacket to go meet Di, the phone rang. When she answered, a woman said, "My name is Elizabeth Morrisey, and I'm looking for a Min Dobbs who met my son Harrison at Cherry Hill Park a week ago."

"Bink?" Min said, dumbfounded.

"Yes," the woman said. "Oh, good. I'm so sorry to bother you at work, but I couldn't find a home listing. Just a moment." Min heard the phone clunk a little, and then Harry came on. "Min?" he said, breathing hard into the phone.

"Yes," she said, grinning. "How are you, Harry?"

"I'm fine. Are you coming to the park tomorrow?"

"Well, I wasn't—"

"Because you could come to my game," Harry said, showing an ability to focus that was much like his uncle's. "It's at ten o'clock. In the morning. And we could have a doughnut."

"Well," Min said, taken aback.

Harry breathed into the phone again. He sounded like Darth Vader, only smaller.

"Sure," she said. "Why not? I'll get the doughnuts—"

"My mom'll get them," Harry said. "I told her what kind."

"Well, good," Min said, regrouping. "Thank you for—"

Harry dropped the phone, and Min heard Bink say, "Say good-bye politely, Harry," and Harry came back on and said, "Good-bye," and dropped the phone again.

"Hello?" Bink said when she'd picked it up.

"Hello," Min said, trying not to laugh.

"We're still working on our phone skills," Bink said.

"He did pretty good," Min said. "Except for the breathing."

"I appreciate this," Bink said. "Harry has spoken of you often this week."

"He has?" Min said, surprised.

"And your shoes," Bink said.

"He's a lot like his uncle," Min said.

"We can only hope," Bink said. "Tomorrow at ten, then?"

"Tomorrow at ten," Min said and sat for a moment after Bink hung up.

That hadn't been Cal's idea. If he'd wanted her there, he'd have called her. He probably didn't even know she was coming. She finished putting on her jacket and thought about surprising him the next day. It would be good to take *him* off guard for a change, catch *him* flatfooted.

She picked up her purse and went down to meet Diana, suddenly interested in being transformed.

The next morning, Cal was watching a particularly hopeless outfielder named Bentley try to throw a ball when two cool hands covered his eyes from behind. He smelled lavender and cinnamon and felt a rush of pleasure so intense, he almost sighed. "This is not like you, Minnie," he said, and then he turned and saw Cynthie, like a cold shower, pulling her hands back. "Cyn?"

"Hi," Cynthie said.

"Sorry," Cal said, taking a step back. "You wear the same perfume as a friend of mine. Except she doesn't wear perfume, come to think of it." *Nor does she come to these damn games*, he thought, mad at himself for making such a stupid mistake.

"Perfume," Cynthie said, looking poleaxed.

"So," Cal said, taking another step back. "How've you been?" A ball rolled past his feet and he bent to pick it up. "You should get back to the other side of the fence. These kids have no control."

"Right," Cynthie said, swallowing. "I just wanted to say, 'Hi!' "

"Hi," Cal said. Something in the bleachers caught his eye and he looked past her to see Harry climbing up to the top. "Where the hell is he—" Cal began and then he looked past Harry and saw Min, sitting at the top, her hair cut short in loose curls that glinted in the sun. She was wearing a filmy, flowing white shirt, and her face lit up when she saw Harry so that she looked positively angelic, and he lost his breath for a moment. "She cut her hair," he said out loud, and Cynthie said, "What?" and followed his eyes.

Cal nodded to the bleachers, recovering. "Go up there and send Harry back down here, will you? He's supposed to be playing ball, not flirting with older women."

"Right," Cynthie said, in that brittle tone that Cal knew meant "I'm very upset, but I'm going to be an adult about it."

"You okay?" he said to her.

"Just fine," Cynthie said, even more brittle, and went around the fence to climb the bleachers.

What's her problem? Cal thought and then forgot her to look back at Min again, glowing in the sunlight while Harry wiped his nose on his arm and adored her. *I am not interested in Minerva Dobbs*, he told himself. *She's too high maintenance. She's never peaceful. And, oh yeah, she hates me.* Then Min smiled at Harry, and Cal thought, *Damn, she's pretty*, and kept staring.

When Min got to the park, the kids were warming up, and she saw Harry out on the field, smaller than the other kids and grubby as usual, and felt a twinge for him. Then he saw her and smiled the Morrisey smile at her, and she thought, *Oh, he's going to be fine,* and smiled back. She climbed up to the top of the bleachers and felt the wind ruffle her newly short curls and the fluttery sleeves of her organdy blouse as she sat down. She tried to watch Harry, but it was hard because Cal was there, and her eyes kept going to him. *It's purely physical,* she told herself, but it wasn't; she loved the way he was with the kids. He hated coaching, but he was doing it right. That was Cal.

Oh, stop it, she thought. *You don't even know him.*

A slender brunette walked up behind Cal and put her hands over his eyes, and Min thought, *Of course,* and felt all her ludicrous happiness deflate. It didn't matter that he was good with kids, since she didn't want any. But it did matter that he was a beast with women, so—

Someone sat down beside her and said, "Hello," in a beautifully modulated voice, and Min turned and saw a pale-haired, paper-thin woman smiling faintly at her. She had a heart-shaped face and huge gray eyes, her platinum hair was razor cut close to her finely boned head, and she couldn't have weighed more than ninety pounds. "I'm Bink," she said.

"Right," Min said. "Hi. I'm Min."

"It's so sweet of you to come for Harry," Bink said. "I do appreciate it."

"Well, Harry's a sweet kid," Min said, looking back to find him, only to discover that he'd escaped from the field and was climbing the bleachers toward them, looking even grubbier as he came closer.

"Most people don't notice that," Bink said, looking at him with love.

"Hi, Min," Harry said when he was one row down. He was beaming at her and she smiled back because anybody would.

"Hey, Harry," she said. "How's it going?"

"I have to play baseball," Harry said. "Otherwise, pretty good."

"Well, live through this and we'll celebrate with a doughnut afterward," Min said.

"Cool," Harry said, bobbing his head.

"You're looking good down there on the field," Min lied.

"Thanks," Harry said, still bobbing.

"You can really throw that ball," Min said, guessing.

"Not really," Harry said, but he didn't seem depressed by that.

He sniffed and kept nodding, and Bink said, "I think Uncle Cal wants you, Harry," and he turned around and saw Cal and the brunette watching him.

"Yeah," he said and sighed.

"Just keep thinking about that doughnut," Min said.

"Cool," Harry said again, beaming at her.

Min smiled back.

"I gotta go," Harry said, not going anywhere.

"Good luck," Min said.

"Yeah," Harry said, nodding for another minute or so. Then his smile faded and he trailed down the bleachers, avoiding his uncle's gaze.

"That was nice of you," Bink said, and Min looked at her, surprised.

"No, it wasn't," she said. "I like Harry."

The wind picked up before Bink could answer, and Min half expected her to blow away. *I'm so glad she's sitting beside me*, she thought bitterly. *Because I didn't look hefty enough sitting up here by myself.* Then she kicked herself. Bink might turn out to be nice, she was certainly polite, and Cal had warned her about hating her body. *Okay*, she thought. *I'm one of those heavy cream wedding invitations, the kind you have to touch because it's so beautiful, and she's the expensive tissue paper that's wrapped around me.*

"Are you all right?" Bink said.

"Yes," Min said. "Why?"

"You were frowning," Bink said.

"I have to work on my metaphors," Min said. "So Harry plays baseball."

"Unfortunately," Bink said, and Min thought, *She's not one of the people who shanghaied Cal and Harry. I wonder—*

"Hi!" somebody said brightly from Min's other side, and this time when she turned she saw the brunette who'd been flirting with Cal. She had a heart-shaped face and big gray eyes, and her dark hair was thick and silky.

Kill me now, Min thought as the paragon sat down beside her. *I've been bookended by the thin and rich.*

"How *are* you, Bink?" the woman said, and Bink smiled at her faintly—Bink evidently did everything faintly—and said, "Hello, Cynthie."

Cynthie. Min turned back to the brunette with renewed horror. Cal's ex. Wearing, Min now noticed, a black halter top that wasn't appropriate for a kids' baseball game. Except that Cynthie was wearing it with no self-consciousness at all, probably because her breasts were those perfect perky kind men were always going on about. *Bite me,* Min thought and looked down on the field to see Cal staring up at the three of them with a very strange expression on his face. Probably realizing with horror that he'd been kissing a woman who was never going to wear a size eight. That hurt a lot more than it should have.

"There's Cal," Bink said.

"What's wrong with him?" Min said. "Besides the fact that he hates this."

"He doesn't hate this," Cynthie said. "He agreed with me that this was great for Harry."

"Oh," Min said. "This was your idea?"

"Yes," Cynthie said, smiling.

Min turned to Bink. "Cynthie got Harry into baseball."

"Yes," Bink said. "Cynthie discussed it with Harry's grandmother and they agreed it would be good for him. Harry's grandmother can be very forceful."

"Oh," Min said, and turned back to the field to see a batter hit a wobbly shot into left field where a kid on Harry's team bobbled the ball. Cal missed all of it, staring up into the bleachers at them.

Then Cal began to turn away, and the kid in the outfield picked up the ball and threw it with desperation and an impossible force for an eight-year-old. It smacked Cal on the back of the head, knocking him off balance so that he fell to his knees and then to the ground.

"*No,*" Min said and zapped down the bleachers and around the chain link fence. "Cal?" she said, going down on her knees beside him as he tried to sit up. "Cal?"

He looked dazed, so she stared into his eyes, trying to see if the pupils were different sizes. They weren't, his eyes were the same hot, dark depths they always were, and she fell into them again, growing breathless, as music swelled behind her, Elvis Costello singing his heart out on "She," and the voice in her head said, *THIS ONE.*

Then she heard Tony say, "Turn that damn thing off," and when she looked up, she saw two girls with a radio next to the fence and Cynthie coming around it to kneel beside Cal, too.

"Sorry," one of the girls said, and the other said, "Is he dead?"

"Go away," Min said and they left, taking the music with them.

"Cal, are you all right?" Cynthie said, and Min looked down at him again to see him still staring at her.

"Cal?" she said.

The assassin from the outfield came running up. "Did you see that, Mr. Capa? I really threw it."

"Yeah, you did, Bentley," Tony said, looking down at Cal. "You okay, there, buddy?"

"I knew I could do it," Bentley said. "I saw Wyman getting close to third base, and something just *told me* I could do it, and I really *threw* that sucker, boy."

"Cal, *say something*," Cynthie said, panic in her voice.

"Boy, I really *threw that sucker*," Bentley said.

"Yeah," Tony said. "Too bad you missed third base by a mile and took out Mr. Morrisey." He crouched down next to Cal. "Say something or Min takes you to the ER now."

"Did you hear music?" Cal asked, still staring into Min's eyes.

"I really *threw* that sucker," Bentley said.

Tony handed Min his car keys. "Go. The Cherry Hill ER is up the road a mile."

"I know the way," Cynthie said, standing. "I have a car."

Min helped Cal to his feet, trying to steady him as he lurched, and Tony took his other side.

"I'll take him," Cynthie said. "My car is just—"

"No," Cal said as he righted himself. "If I'm going to throw up, it'll be in Tony's clunker."

"Drive fast," Tony said to Min, and helped them both to the car.

Cal lay on the table in the ER, trying to remember what had happened. He'd been staring at Min, watching the breeze flutter the ends of her blouse and tousle her curls, and he'd been telling himself that she was a pain in the ass and that he didn't want anything to do with her, and then that ball had come out of nowhere and—

"Cal?" Min said, leaning over him. The fluorescent light above back-lit her hair and she looked like an angel again.

"Hi," he said.

"The doctor said you're going to be all right," she said, trying to look cheerful. "I just filled your prescription." She held up an amber plastic pill bottle. "For the pain. In case you have headaches. Do you have a headache?"

His head felt like a vise. "Yes."

She opened the bottle and dumped out two pills into her palm. "Here," she said, handing them to him. "I'll get water."

Cal thought about telling her that he'd already had a pain pill and then decided that since the damn thing wasn't working, two more would be good.

"You *scared* me," she said, when she came back with the water. "You got hit in the head. People get killed that way. I don't know how many a year. I haven't had time to look it up."

Cal propped himself up to take the pills. "Bentley," he said bitterly.

"I'm sure he'll be sorry," Min said. "When he gets over how hard he threw the ball."

"Little bastard," Cal said without heat. "Was there music? I could swear I heard—"

"—Elvis Costello singing 'She.' " Min nodded. "You did. Some kids had it on a radio. Which is weird because I don't think it gets a lot of airplay. My sister's using it in her wedding." She sounded as if she were babbling, which was so unlike Min that Cal chalked it up to his general dizziness. "I called Bink on her cell and told her you were okay and I was taking you home."

"Your sister likes Elvis Costello?" Cal said.

"No," Min said. "My sister likes music from Julia Roberts movies."

"Oh," Cal said and focused on her. "You cut your hair."

"Diana took me to her stylist," Min said. "To go with the new clothes. I did what you said."

"I didn't tell you to cut your hair." His eyes dropped to her blouse, looking through the thin fabric to the equally thin camisole underneath, and he almost fell off the table.

"Easy," Min said, breathless as she tried to prop up his weight, and he looked down the open neck of her blouse and saw pink lace under the camisole.

"Pink," he said.

"Oh, good, you're feeling better," Min said, relief in her voice. "Come on. I'll take you home."

"Okay," Cal said. "I like your hair."

Half an hour later, Min pulled up in front of Cal's apartment, having followed his increasingly groggy directions. "Let's go," she said, and opened the car door for him.

"I can get up there myself," Cal said, weaving a little as he got out. "Take the car—"

"You're not going up there alone." Min pulled his arm across her shoulders. It felt good there, if heavy. "My mother raised me better than that."

"Well, then you're going up first so you can't look at my butt."

"There's an elevator, Charm Boy," Min said, kicking the door shut behind them. "Move it."

"Wait a minute," he said, and she stopped so he could get his bearings, but he put his hand on her curls again, patting them. "Springy."

"Right," Min said and herded him upstairs to a white, slightly battered apartment that looked like something he would have lived in during college. She steered him through a living room furnished with

Danish modern furniture that would have made all of Denmark cringe, into an even bleaker, uglier bedroom. "How are you feeling?" she said as she guided him toward his headboardless bed.

"Better," he said, sounding groggy. "The drugs kicked in and I'm not coaching baseball."

"There you go," she said, "Always a bright side." She shouldered him toward the bed, and he bounced when he sat down.

"You're a lot more aggressive than I thought you'd be." He fell back onto the pillows, but his feet still hung off the side.

"You're a lot heavier than I thought you'd be," Min said, and realized that was probably because he moved so well when he was conscious. Semiconscious, he moved like a lurching glacier. She pulled off his Nikes, and her heart skipped a beat. "You're an eleven-D."

"Yes," Cal said, sleepily. "Tell me that proves I'm a beast. You haven't said anything lousy to me all day."

"Elvis wore an eleven-D," Min said, and Cal mumbled, "Good for him."

She picked up his feet and threw them on the bed, and then realized that he was way too close to the edge; if he rolled off in his sleep, he'd hit his head on the battered bedside table. She shoved at him to get him to the center of the bed.

"What are you doing?" he said, half asleep as she tried to rock him over.

"Trying to keep you safe," she said between her teeth as she put one knee on the bed and shoved again. "Roll over, will you?"

He rolled just as she shoved and knocked them both off balance. She grabbed at him to save herself, and he pulled her down with him.

"I should be awake in about eight hours," he yawned into her hair. "Stick around."

"Fine," she said into his chest. "Fall on the floor. Get a concussion. See if I care." He didn't say anything, so she shoved at him again, but it was like shoving at a wall. She stopped to consider the situation. There was something very protective in the way he held onto her. Thoughtful.

He began to snore.

Instinctive.

"Okay," she said, and squirmed around until she got one foot on the floor and shoved off, toppling him over onto his back in the middle of the bed, which stopped his snoring. Then she stood up and looked at him, sprawled out on an ugly, generic bedspread in a plain, cheap bedroom with lousy, awkward lighting. He looked like a god.

"It is *so* unfair," she said to him. "Couldn't you at least drool or something?"

He began to snore again.

"Thank you." She opened his closet door and found a blanket folded on the top shelf, over a tasteful collection of expensive suits. "You are so weird," she said to him as she snapped the blanket over him. "This place does not look like you at all."

He breathed deeper, and she looked down at the beautiful strong bones of his face, his lashes like smudges on his cheeks as he slept, and thought, *I could love you.*

Then she straightened and returned to reality. Every woman in the city thought that when she looked at him so it wasn't as if . . . *Oh, the hell with it*, she thought, and put his shoes where he wouldn't trip over them, got him a glass of water for his bedside table, made sure his pills were within reach, and pulled the blanket up so he wouldn't get chilled. Then, at a loss as to what to do next, she patted his shoulder and left.

On Monday, David picked up the phone and heard Cynthie say, "I talked to Cal. He thinks she smells like lavender. He noticed she cut her hair. His nephew loves her. *There was a copulatory gaze in the park.*"

"Isn't that illegal?"

"Don't make *fun*, David. This isn't *amusing*. We could *lose them*." He heard her take a deep breath over the phone. "The best thing for you to do right now is to ask her to lunch. Evoke joy. Did you even call her?"

"She's not returning my calls," David said, trying not to sound annoyed.

"How do you feel about that?" Cynthie said. "A little angry?"

"A little," David said. "But—"

"And you're angry that she never let you pay for dinner, too. She was rejecting your sexual advances, just as she's now rejecting your phone calls. So now—"

"This is ridiculous," David said, moving beyond annoyed.

"Your problem is that you're angry with her and she can sense that, so you're going to have to get over it. *Now*."

"I'm not angry, damn it," David snapped.

"Ask her to lunch and insist on paying. You'll feel much better, the anger will go away, she'll see you as a potential mate, and then you can make your move."

"This is such crap," David said.

"I don't care," Cynthie said. "*Do it*. Or she's going to end up with Cal."

Cal. Cal was going to win that damn bet. He always won, the bastard. "I'll call her," David said. "We'll have lunch. I'll play it by ear."

"Don't screw this up, David," Cynthie said. "My life is riding on it. My *career* is riding on it. *I need that wedding picture on my book cover*."

"You know—" David began, but Cynthie had already hung up. "Wonderful," he said, and began to dial Min.

Min was sitting at her desk, trying to be sensible, when the phone rang. *Cal*, she thought, and then kicked herself. They had a good sensible plan that would prevent either one of them from getting hurt, they were logical, rational people, so that certainly wasn't him calling. The phone rang again, and she picked it up and said, "Minerva Dobbs," and waited for Cal to say, "Hi, Minnie, how's the cat?"

"Min," David said. "Have lunch with me. We need to talk."

"No, we don't," Min said, trying hard not to be disappointed. "But I do need lunch. We can go Dutch."

"No, *I'll pay*," David said. "I mean, I'd like to pay."

"Sure, fine," Min said, confused.

"I'll meet you at Serafino's at noon then?" David said.

"Is that the place where the chef is trying to make a statement with food?"

"It's the hottest place in town," David said.

"This should be good," Min said and hung up, chalking the whole thing up to the general weirdness of her life lately.

When she got to the restaurant, David was waiting. He stood and smiled when he saw her, and then he stared. Min looked down and realized he was focusing on the blue gauze top beneath her gray-checked jacket.

"You look wonderful," he said.

"I'm evolving," Min said, sitting down at the inlaid table. "I'm also starving. What's good here?" She looked around at the silver and blue. "Besides the decorating."

"I already ordered," David said. "I didn't want you to have to wait."

"Thoughtful of you." Min called the waiter back and changed her order to salad and chicken marsala. Might as well see what Emilio's competition was doing.

"I think I made a mistake," David said, when the waiter had placed his bowl of chilled chestnut watercress soup in front of him.

"I think so, too," Min said, looking at the beautifully garnished sludge in his bowl. "You're going to hate that soup. There's a hot dog vendor outside. Maybe we should—"

"Not the order." David took a deep breath and smiled. "Min, I want you back."

Min stopped fishing overly artistic vegetable flourishes out of her salad. "What?"

"I was hasty," David said, and went on while Min thought, *The bet. That damn bet. You're afraid you're going to lose the bet.*

She sat back and considered the situation as David rambled on. Somehow, David had gotten the idea she was going to sleep with Cal. Now where would that have come from? The thought that it might be Cal gloating to him made her ill for a moment, but then common sense came back. Cal wasn't a gloater. Also, he wasn't dumb, and it would take somebody really dumb to tip off an opponent that he was about to lose. And anyway, Cal wouldn't.

"Are you listening to me?" David said.

"No," Min said. "Why are you doing this?"

"That's what I was just telling you—"

"No," Min said, "you were telling me about you. You were hasty, you were thoughtless, you were stupid—"

"I didn't say stupid," David said, sounding testy.

"Where am I in all of this?" Min said.

"In my life, I hope," David said, and he sounded so sincere, Min was taken aback. "I asked you out in the beginning because I thought you'd make a good wife, and I still think that, but what I missed was how . . ." He stopped and took her hand and Min let him, just to see what would happen next. ". . . how *sweet* you are."

"No, I'm not," Min said, trying to take her hand back.

"And how . . ." He looked at her gauze blouse. ". . . *sexy* you are. You've changed."

Min yanked her hand back. "David, this is buyer's remorse, or the opposite of buyer's remorse. If you got me back, you'd dump me again. Go date one of those skinny women you like to look at."

David started to say something but stopped as the waiter brought his veal whatever and her chicken marsala. Min sliced into the chicken and tasted it. "Bacon. And *tomato*. What kind of fool puts bacon and tomato in chicken marsala?"

"Min . . ."

"You can even see the bacon pieces in the sauce. Emilio would spit."

"You're not taking me seriously," David said.

"I know," Min said, putting down her fork. "Honest to God, what were they *thinking*?"

"What I'm trying to tell you," David said, "is that I think we should date again."

"No, you don't," Min said. "You're panicking because I'm dating somebody else. Taste your soup."

"I'm not—"

"The soup," Min said.

David tasted the soup and made a face. "What the hell?"

"I told you." Min pushed her plate away. "Never go anyplace the chef is trying to talk with food. You'll end up paying for his ego. Sort of like dating." She picked up her purse. "I'm sorry, David, but we have no future. We're not even going to finish this lunch, although I do appreciate you paying for it. Thank you."

"Where are you going?" David said, outraged as she stood up.

"To get a hot dog," Min said. "I think that vendor had brats."

Emilio called Cal on Tuesday night at six. "Min ordered takeout again," he said. "You taking it to her?"

"Yes," Cal said automatically and then remembered they weren't seeing each other. "No." Which didn't mean they couldn't be friends. "Yes." Which was a huge rationalization. "No."

"Uh huh," Emilio said. "So that's a no?"

On the other hand, he had to eat. And he should thank her for taking care of him on Saturday. And he wanted to see her. "No," Cal said. "That's a yes. I'll take it to her."

Chapter Eight

Min answered the door in her godawful sweats again, no makeup and her curly hair going every which way. She looked wonderful. "Hi," she said, sounding surprised, and then she grinned. "Emilio shanghaied you, huh?"

"He said you were starving," Cal said, smiling back in spite of himself. "You took me to the ER. You put a glass of water by my bed. I owe you."

"That's lame," she said, but she stood back and he walked in, glad to see her ugly cat staring one-eyed at him from the back of her ugly couch.

"I can't believe you still have that cat," Cal said, unpacking the bag onto the table. "What did you name it?"

"I can't believe you brought me that cat," Min said, heading for her kitchen alcove. "And I haven't named it anything yet. We're still trying to decide if we want to make a commitment. Although he does come home every night and sleep with me."

"Smart cat," Cal said.

"I was thinking about trying to make him an indoor cat because cats live longer if they're kept indoors, but he's a guy, so I'm assuming he'd hate being tied down."

"Depends on what you tied him to," Cal said, thinking of her brass bed.

Min brought plates to the table. "You know, if you'd brought me a snow globe I could understand, but a cat?"

"You said you didn't want a snow globe."

"I don't," Min said. "Well, I want my grandma's Mickey and Minnie globe back. Bring my grandma's back to me, and I'll love you until the end of time. Bring me another cat, I'm going to rethink the whole chicken marsala thing."

"Speaking of which," Cal said, "what happened this time?"

Min groaned and went back to the alcove and Cal followed her, feeling right at home. "It doesn't look bad," he said when he saw her latest effort. "It just doesn't look like chicken marsala."

"I was trying to avoid the olive oil and butter," Min said, and then held up her hand before he could speak. "I know, I know, I'm learning my lesson. I used chicken broth instead. It smells good but it doesn't look right."

"That would be because olive oil and chicken broth are not the same thing," Cal said. "You're all right. Just make a roux to thicken the broth and serve it over fettuccine."

"A roux," Min said.

"Melted butter and flour," Cal said. "I don't suppose there's a chance in hell you have butter."

"Bonnie might," Min said. "I don't have fettuccine or flour, either. I'll go borrow them from her."

"Do you have a big pot for the noodles and a colander?" Cal said, looking around the spare alcove. *She's got to find a better place.*

"In the basement," Min said.

"That's convenient. Where's the lid?"

"Lid?" Min said.

"Something that will keep the cat from going headfirst into this pan while we're down in the basement?"

"We're going down to the basement?"

"Do you want to learn to cook, Minnie?" he said with more affection than he'd intended.

Min blinked. "Yes. Yes, I do."

"Then you'll need pots and pans," Cal said.

They went to the basement, and Cal picked out one of the half-dozen unmarked boxes at random and opened it with his pocketknife. Min unwrapped the first package in the box: her grandmother's green colander. "This is the box," she said as she dropped the colander back in the box. "You went right to it. You're good."

"Hell, yes." Cal grinned at her and picked up the box. "Move it, Minnie, and don't forget to stop for butter, flour, and pasta."

Teaching Min how to make a roux should have been pretty innocuous, but the kitchenette was tiny, and she was close, and her curls smelled like lavender, and there wasn't anything about her that wasn't round, and there was that brass bed with a satin comforter just a room away, so after he'd explained the basics of roux, Cal retreated to unpack the box.

The cat was sitting in it. "Out," he said, and it switched eyes on him, lolling among the lumpy packages. He reached in and picked it up and put it on the floor, and it rubbed up against his leg, purring. "Very affectionate cat," he told Min.

"I know, I love the damn thing," Min said. "He curls up beside me every night and purrs along to Elvis. He's smart, too. He's learned how to hit the stereo button so he can play Elvis without me."

Cal pulled out the first package and unwrapped a thick, clear glass, angular bowl that looked as though it might have a specific function. "What's this?"

Min looked back. "It's an egg-beater bowl. There should be a metal lid for it with a beater in it."

Cal dug around the box until he found it. The lid sat on the bowl with the crank for the beaters above it, and the beaters below. "That's pretty neat," he said, and picked up the next wrapped package, a heavy one which turned out to be nested mixing bowls, thick white china with a blue stripe.

"Oh," Min said, "I *remember* those, my grandma used to make cookies in the big one. That was back when I ate cookies."

"The good old days." Cal picked up the next package. It was heavy and round and as he unwrapped it, he began to realize what it was. When he pulled the last of the paper away, he wasn't that surprised to see a snow globe with Mickey inside, dipping Minnie in her pink dress. But he was appalled.

"So, how long does this cook?" Min said. "I mean, before the flour loses the raw flavor? Cal?" She looked back at him. "What's wrong?"

He held up the snow globe, and she froze over the chicken pan.

It was heavy in his hand, heavier than a snow globe should be. He tipped it and saw the key on the bottom. "Music box?" he said to her and she nodded. "What's it play?"

" 'It Had to Be You,' " she said, faintly.

"Of course." Cal looked at Mickey and Minnie, trapped forever in the globe. *Bring my grandma's snow globe back to me and I'll love you until the end of time.*

"I've been looking for that for fifteen years," Min said, her voice flat. "And then you go right to it. How do you do that?"

"It's not me." Cal put it down on the counter.

"You didn't make a deal with the devil, did you?" Min said, staring at it. "What?"

"You know, some kind of bargain where everything you did would be perfect so that every woman you met would be unable to resist you, only you forgot to mention that should work only with women you wanted, and now we're stuck in this loop with each other?"

Cal took a deep breath. "Okay, leaving aside the fact that you think the devil exists and is making deals, I'm a little upset that you think I'd be hanging out with him."

"Well, hell, Cal, you're practically his first cousin," Min said. "You're tall, you're dark, you're handsome, you're charming, you wear suits, you never sweat, and you always show up with whatever I'm needing at the moment. That snow globe has been lost for *fifteen years*. I keep getting this feeling that if I say yes to you, I'll go straight to hell."

Cal nodded. *Why did I come back here?* "Okay. You know, I'm not hungry anymore. I think I'll be going."

"That might be good," Min said, staring at the snow globe.

He picked up his jacket and headed for the door and then paused as he opened it. "Have a—" he started to say and then stopped.

"Nice life?" Min said, still staring at the globe.

He shook his head. "It just doesn't have the same ring to it," he said, and went down the stairs.

When he was gone, Min walked over to the snow globe and wound it. It began to tinkle the first bars of "It Had to Be You," and she looked into it, and tried to get her breath back. The dome was heavy and perfect, sitting atop a black art deco base, and inside silver glitter and tiny silver stars swirled as Minnie beamed out at her, happy to be in Mickey's arms, and Mickey beamed at Minnie.

Maybe that's what I loved, she thought. *That she was so happy and he thought she was wonderful.* Plus there was that swirling pink dress Minnie was wearing and the great pink shoes to match. Well, the shoes were a little plain. Min tipped the globe to see, and the glitter and stars swirled again as the song slowed down and ran out.

It's not me, Cal had said, but it was him. She'd been going along, perfectly happy, and then he'd walked into the bar and shaken up her life and suddenly it was all glitter and stars everywhere. And every time things calmed down, every time she got things back to normal, he came back and shook—

Something furry nudged her leg and she jumped. The cat meowed at her and she picked him up and thought about the situation logically. Of course it wasn't him. Coincidences happened all the time. That was life. As long as nothing else happened . . .

"We'll just stay away from him," she told the cat. "We won't go to The Long Shot unless we know he won't be there, and this will all pass and we'll be normal again. No more goddamn glitter."

The cat switched eyes again, and Min realized that talking to an animal using "we" was probably not normal, either. "Chicken?" she said to the cat, and gave up on logic to eat dinner.

On Wednesday, Liza was at the bar trying to signal Shanna when Cynthie sat down next to her and smiled at her. "Hi. Where's your friend?"

"She said she had to stay home with her cat," Liza said, "but I think she's avoiding Cal."

"That's a good idea," Cynthie said. "The best way to resist him is to stay away from him." She looked around the bar. "Do you see him?"

"No," Liza said. "Tony said he's working late. Why?"

"Because if she's not here, he should be working on you."

"Me?" Liza said, appalled. "She's gone so he's going to pick me up?"

"No," Cynthie said. "It's important to the health of a relationship that her friends and family approve of him. I'm surprised he hasn't tried to charm you yet."

"He's not dumb," Liza said. "And we're not buddies."

"Well, your friend is doing the right thing by avoiding him," Cynthie said. "I don't think he's going to get to her at all."

"He got to you, though, huh?" Liza said.

Cynthie lifted her chin. "I . . ."

Liza waited.

"Yes," Cynthie said. "He got to me."

"Rat bastard," Liza said.

"No, he's not," Cynthie said. "He just—"

"Needs approval from women because of Mommie Dearest," Liza said. "You know, with all you know about him, you could write a book."

Cynthie sipped her drink.

"Ah," Liza said. "You are writing a book."

"Yes," Cynthie said. "But not about . . . well, not entirely about . . ."

"Boy," Liza said. "So when he left, you lost a lover and a research subject. I don't understand this. You're an expert in this relationship stuff and he still got to you?"

Cynthie bit her lip. "What you know logically doesn't help if you're feeling something emotionally."

The pain on her face was real, and Liza put her hand on Cynthie's arm. "I'm sorry."

"You know," Cynthie said, sticking her chin out, "it's not a problem. There are people with much worse problems than mine."

"Doesn't make yours any more fun to bear," Liza said.

"No," Cynthie said. "But it does help with the self-pity." She shoved her glass away. "If I've made Cal seem like a bad guy—"

"You haven't," Liza said. "In fact, I think you have a pretty rosy view of him."

"No," Cynthie said. "He's a good—"

"I don't care. I just want him to stay away from Min."

"Me, too," Cynthie said.

She finished her drink and left, and Shanna came down the bar and said, "Refill?"

Liza smiled. "Tell me about Cal Morrisey."

"Why?" Shanna said, warily.

"Because he's been kissing my best friend, and I've heard he has a commitment problem."

Shanna shrugged. "Him and half the male population."

"Half of the male population isn't kissing Min," Liza said. "He's not serious about her, is he?"

Shanna bit her lip. "He's the best guy I know. If I was ever in trouble, I'd call Cal, and he would come and get me out, I know that in my soul."

"And yet, not an answer to my question," Liza said.

Shanna was quiet for a moment and then she said, "Tell your friend not to get invested. He doesn't stay."

"Thank you," Liza said.

"But he's a really good guy," Shanna said.

"I keep hearing that," Liza said, getting up. "I'm just having trouble believing it."

At seven, Cal decided that one more minute of looking at the seminar packet would make him beat his head against the desk and he'd had enough cranial injury for the month. On the other hand, looking at Min at The Long Shot would only lead to being called the devil again. Or, if she was having a good day, a beast. He stood up and stretched, and then set out for home, slowing down as he passed the Gryphon Theater. They were doing the last week of the John Carpenter revival, and there was a short line out in front for *Big Trouble in Little China*.

Kurt Russell beats the bad guys, he thought. *Haven't seen that since I was a kid.* The last person left the box office, and he went up and bought a ticket. Better than spending the night alone, concentrating on not thinking about . . . anyone.

As he walked in, the previews were running for an Elvis Presley series, and he thought of Min. *Forget her*, he told himself, and found a place a few rows down and a few seats over, surrounded by empty seats. But as the movie began and Kurt started talking trash in his truck, a family of five came in and asked him to move down. The person to the right of his new seat was quiet, so he slouched down and lost himself in the movie, peaceful for the first time since the night before.

When the lights came up, he stood up to go at the same time as the woman on his right. Medium height, short curly brown hair tipped with gold, turning now to get her gray-checked jacket . . .

They stared at each other for a long, dumbstruck moment, and then she walked out of the theater and he followed. When they were outside she turned and looked at him.

"What are the odds?" Cal said.

"I don't even know how to calculate the odds," Min said, and started walking, and he fell into pace beside her because she shouldn't walk home alone in the dark in the city.

Coincidence, Cal told himself. *Happens all the time. No big deal. Means nothing.*

When they got to her apartment, she climbed the steps without any arguing about who was going first, and for once he was too stunned to think about her rear end. At her door she turned and said, "Thank you for walking me home," and he said, "You're welcome." They looked at each other for one long moment, and Cal felt breathless, falling into her eyes, and he thought, *Oh, Christ*, no, *not you*. Then she shook her head and went inside and closed the door, and he turned and walked down fifty-eight steps to the street, not sure whether to be relieved or not.

He paused and looked up at the dormer that was her bedroom window. The cat sat there, silhouetted against the light from her lamp, staring down at him, probably shutting one eye in the darkness. He imagined Min sitting down on that satin comforter, lying back on embroidered pillows that smelled of lavender, her gold-tipped curls against the blue satin, and he put himself there, beside her, pulling her to him, her arms around him, all her warm roundness against him, soft and yielding, imagined taking her lush mouth, feeling the swell of her breast under his hand, the rise of her hips to his, imagined pushing into all that softness, shuddering into the hot wetness of her, hearing her moan and sigh as he moved, and he realized that he wanted her more than he could ever have imagined wanting anything or anyone.

The light went out in her bedroom and broke the spell, and he closed his eyes against the darkness and the cold shock of reality. Then he turned and started back to the main street, to light and noise and safety.

On Thursday, when Liza showed up at Min's apartment for the If Dinner, Bonnie answered the door looking cautious. When Liza lifted her eyebrows to ask *What?*, Bonnie shook her head and stood back to let her in.

"Hi," Min said, a little too quietly, and Liza thought, *That rat bastard Cal.*

"What did he do?"

"Nothing," Min said. "Sit down. I made a huge Cobb salad and I'm starving. Let's eat."

Liza turned back to the couch and saw a one-eyed animal looking at her. "You still have the cat."

"I love that cat," Min said. "He's always there for me, he pats me with his paw when I'm depressed, he keeps me warm at night, and he has a beautiful voice. I've decided he's the reincarnation of Elvis."

"The long wait is over," Liza said. *He gave her something she didn't even know she needed. The bastard.*

After ten minutes of bread, salad, and stilted conversation about the cat, Liza had had enough. "I talked to Cynthie last night. She said Cal would try to—"

"I like him," Bonnie said.

Liza sat back in her chair. "What?"

"I like him," Bonnie said.

"That doesn't mean you should encourage—"

"It doesn't matter," Min said, and they both turned to look at her. "I'm trying to get away from him, but it's not working. Remember that snow globe I lost? He found it. He came over on Tuesday and went straight down to the basement and picked out the one box there that the snow globe was in."

"Dumb luck," Liza said.

"And then last night, I decided to go to the movies," Min said. "And when the lights came up, guess who was sitting beside me?"

"Now *that's* creepy," Liza said, going cold. "He's stalking you."

"No," Min said. "I picked up the paper, and the movie page fell out, and I saw *Big Trouble in Little China* was at the revival theater, and I thought, 'Oh, good, Kurt Russell beats the bad guys' and I went on an impulse. I didn't tell anybody. I didn't even mention it to the *cat*. And there he was. It's like he's magic."

"It's like he's the devil," Liza said.

"It's like he's the prince," Bonnie said.

Liza and Min looked at her.

"In the fairy tale," Bonnie said. "He has to go on quests to get you. And the snow globe was one."

"Bonnie, honey," Min said, jarred out of her numbness. "Let's do the Ifs instead. If I were a sane person, I wouldn't be so freaked out by this. So I'm going to be a sane person and not be freaked out. Liza? What's your If?"

"If I find out Cal Morrisey is stalking you, I'm going to tear him limb from limb," Liza said. "Bonnie?"

"If you two get any dumber, I'm going to have to find new friends," Bonnie scowled at Min. "Cal's winning you. Just like in the fairy tale. You said his kiss woke you up."

"I said his kiss turned me on," Min said. "Not the same thing." She leaned forward a little. "I was fine with using the fairy tale as a sort of metaphor, Bon, but this is real life. No prince, no stepmother, no poisoned apple."

"And no happy ending if you think like that," Bonnie said. "True love is beating you over the head to get your attention, and you're rejecting it because you don't want to believe. You have the fairy tale *right in front of you*—"

"*Wait* a minute," Liza said, trying to head off disaster.

"And you're *worse*," Bonnie said, turning on her. "Min doesn't believe in love for her, but you don't believe in it for anybody. You're a love nihilist."

"A love nihilist." Liza thought about it. "I kind of like that."

"Well, I don't," Min said. "I believe in love. I think. I just don't believe in fairy tales."

"I have known my whole life that sooner or later my prince would come," Bonnie said to Min. "How many times have you told me that everybody gets lucky breaks in business but not everybody is ready for them? Well, it's true about love, too. I've been planning my marriage my whole life because I'm smart enough to know that's the most important decision I'll ever make, and now Roger's here, and I'm ready to go. And you two are going to miss it when it comes for you because you don't want to believe because if it isn't true, you'll be disappointed."

Liza rolled her eyes. "Oh, come *on*—"

"You're *planning* on being disappointed, you'd be disappointed if you weren't disappointed, your whole world view depends on men disappointing you." Bonnie picked up her plate. "Well, that's just cowardly. Especially *you*," she said, scowling at Min. "You've got Cal right in front of you, loving you so much he can't see straight, you've got fate sending you so many signals even I can see them, and you're holding on to that bet like a shield. You haven't even asked him about the bet, have you?"

"What's he going to say?" Min said. " 'Yeah, but I'm really your prince and I love you truly, come to bed'?"

"You're not usually this slow," Bonnie said, "so it must be just chicken-hearted fear. What if this is real? What if this is the happily ever after and he truly loves you so much that it's forever? Then what are you going to do?" She shook her head. "You don't know. You never prepared for that. You've thought about everything in your life, but you never thought about that. You're hopeless." She took her plate out to the kitchen and came back to shove her chair under the table. "I'll see you tomorrow at The Long Shot. I'm going to go see Roger and remember why I believe."

"Bon, wait," Min said, getting up, but Bonnie was already at the door.

When she slammed it behind her, Min sat down across from Liza.

"Well, at least we're sane," Min said.

"Yeah," Liza said. "How's that working out for you?"

"Not that well," Min said. "Did you bring dessert?"

"Cherry Dove Bars," Liza said.

"Give me one," Min said. "I'll be sensible tomorrow."

On Friday, Cal was settling in to stay home for a change on the theory that if he didn't leave the apartment, nothing weird would happen to him, when he heard "She" go on next door.

"Oh, for crying out loud," he said and then stopped because that was what Min always said. "No," he told himself and went next door to distract himself with Shanna. "You got dumped again?" he said when she opened the door.

"No," she said, serious, but not tear-stained. "I'm trying to figure out my life. Come on in."

"Figure out your life?" Cal said, following her.

"I keep thinking if I listen to this song, there'll be a clue," Shanna said, getting out her bottle of Glenlivet.

"If you're planning your life based on a popular song, you need that Scotch more than I do," Cal said.

"It's not that." Shanna poured his drink. "I've always gone on the theory that one day the right woman would show up and I'd know."

"You've pretty much disproved that one," Cal said, taking the glass she handed him.

"So I thought since Elvis Costello had already made a list of things the perfect woman would have, I'd start there, and sort of figure out what kind of person I'd want to spend the rest of my life with. And then if I met somebody who didn't fit the list . . ."

"That's very organized of you." Cal sat down on the couch and thought, *That's very Min of her.*

"But the thing is," Shanna was saying, "Elvis is not saying she's perfect. So I'm thinking maybe I just need a few key things. Like she should be kind."

"Yes," Cal said, remembering Min with Harry.

"And smart," Shanna said. "Somebody I don't have to explain everything to."

"Maybe," Cal said, thinking about explaining chicken marsala to Min. "It's no crime not to know everything. I'd make that somebody who was open to new ideas, willing to learn. And who had things to teach you."

"See, this is good," Shanna said, sitting down on her coffee table trunk. "And I thought a sense of humor would be important."

"Right," Cal said. "If you can't laugh at the screwups, what's the point?" He thought of Min saying, "Good thing this isn't a date," when they'd confused their Elvises, and—

"And because I'm superficial, I put down physically attractive," Shanna said.

"Me, too," Cal said, trying not to think of Min in all her hot glory. "And great shoes."

"What?" Shanna said.

"Nothing. What else?"

"That was it," Shanna said. "I didn't want to make too long a list. Kind, smart, funny, attractive. How's that?"

"Damn good if you can find it," Cal said.

"Didn't you?" Shanna said. "Min? She seemed—"

"Not dating her," Cal said. "Barely know her."

"Uh huh," Shanna said. "And why is that? She's pretty, she's kind, she's smart, she makes you smile, and you get all dazed when you kiss her. What is it that she doesn't have?"

"Well," Cal began and stopped. "She bitches at me a lot."

"Chicken," Shanna said. "You could walk away from all the other ones because they weren't right. This is the real thing, so you're running."

"This from a woman who just made a shopping list for love." Cal stood up and handed the Scotch back to her. "I'm going now. Best of luck with that list."

Shanna clucked at him as he went out the door, and he went home to ignore her. Once there, he realized that he hadn't had dinner, and he wasn't going out because if he did, he'd fall over Min.

"Not a problem," he told himself and went out to the kitchen. He had bread and peanut butter and not much else, so he plugged in the toaster and put the bread in and then he leaned against the refrigerator and waited for the toast to pop.

His kitchen was ugly, he realized as he looked around. And through the archway, his living room was worse. Maybe if he fixed the place up a little, he'd want to stay home more. He was getting too damn old to be hanging out in bars anyway. The phone rang and he grabbed it, grateful to have a distraction.

"Calvin?" he heard his mother say, but even she was better than the silence.

"Mother," he said. "How are you?" His toast popped, and he cradled the phone between his shoulder and his ear as he opened the peanut butter.

"I'm calling about dinner on Sunday," she said.

"I will be there, Mother," Cal said, thinking, *I'm there the third Sunday of every month, Mother.* Definitely in a rut.

"I'd like you to pick up our guest."

"Guest?" Cal said, as he got out a table knife to spread the peanut butter.

"Minerva Dobbs," his mother said.

"What?" Cal said and dropped the knife.

"I called her because Harrison has been speaking of her often, and it occurred to me that it would be nice for him to have her there."

Cal sighed. "What did she say when you called?"

"She seemed surprised," his mother said. "But when I explained that Harrison would be so pleased if she came—"

"She said yes," Cal said, reaching for his toast. "However, I cannot bring her because I will not be seeing her ever aga—" His fingers brushed the metal top of the toaster and he burned himself and dropped the phone. "*Damn it,*" he said and put his scorched fingertips in his mouth.

"Calvin?" his mother said from the phone.

He picked up the receiver. "I burned myself on the toaster. Sorry." Cal turned on the cold water and stuck his fingers underneath the stream. "Anyway, I will not be seeing Minerva Dobbs again." He stepped away from the sink onto something hard and his foot slipped out from under him and smacked into the cabinets. "Ouch."

"Calvin?" his mother said.

"I stepped on a knife." Cal bent to pick up the peanut butter knife and smacked his head into the counter. "*Hell.*"

"Did you cut yourself?" his mother asked.

"No. I . . ." He put the knife in the sink. "I'll call you tomorrow, Mother."

"Calvin?" his mother said, and he hung up on her and considered the situation.

He was sabotaging himself, that had to be it. He was distracted, he was tired, he was hungry, he was careless. He picked up the phone again and called Tony's cell.

"Hello?" Tony yelled over the noise of the bar.

"Is Min there with you?" Cal said.

"Wait a minute," Tony said, and came back on a minute later without the background noise. "Sorry. What?"

"Is Min with you? I'm trying to make sure that wherever I go next, she won't be." He frowned. "She's driving me to incoherence."

"She's stalking you?" Tony said, sounding skeptical.

"No, she doesn't want it, either," Cal said. "It's like we're stuck inside a box. We try to go our separate ways and then we end up with each other anyway. You're not going to Emilio's, are you?"

"Chaos theory," Tony said. "Min's a strange attractor."

"This is true," Cal said. "Are you going to Emilio's tonight, or can I go eat in the kitchen there?"

"You can go," Tony said. "Seriously, the box you're talking about is the field of your attraction. You and Min try to get away and you hit the sides of the box at random because you're unstable, never repeating, but making a pattern."

"Good for us," Cal said. "Just keep Min away from Emilio's, will you? I'm starving."

"I think she and Liza are going someplace," Tony said. "They've been talking all night about some job Min wants Liza to take, and I think Min's going to drag her there to show it to her. Unless Emilio's been advertising for help, it's not there."

"He hasn't," Cal said. "He's full up on nephews. Thanks, Tony. I'll see you tomorrow."

He hung up, changed out of his work clothes, and started for Emilio's, trying not to think about Min. That didn't work, so he switched over to chaos theory, of which he had only vague memories. The Butterfly Effect, he remembered that, the idea that a butterfly flapping its wings in Hong Kong could cause a hurricane ten years later in Florida or prevent a tornado ten years later in Texas, take your pick because it was unpredictable. That was Min; she'd looked harmless that first night, and then she flapped her wings two weeks ago and now he was a mess. She was a goddamn stealth butterfly.

He looked down the block at the front of the Gryphon Theater, half expecting to see Min standing there since it was the first night of the Elvis revival week. Nope. Which made sense, since events did not repeat in chaos theory. Somehow, the idea that it was science made the whole thing a lot less worrisome. He wasn't insane, fate wasn't stalking him, he was just standing on the edge of chaos. Much better.

He turned down the street to Emilio's, trying to remember what "the edge of chaos" meant. It was something about flipping a coin, something about the edge being the moment when the coin was in the air. The point at which the system was pure potential, about to choose a path. Or something about a pile of sand, adding sand a grain at a time, and the edge of chaos being the point at which the critical grain landed and the pile either shifted or turned into an avalanche . . . Cal slowed as he remembered a grad assistant in a baggy blue sweater, his hair standing on end from his complete earnestness about the subject, saying that the edge of chaos was a time of turbulence, mental chaos if the system was a human being, but also the time of greatest potential, possibly the place where life starts. "The place," the grad student had said, "where the system cascades into a new order and moves from being to becoming."

Cal shook the grad student out of his head, and pulled open the door to Emilio's. When he got inside, he heard Roger say, "Cal!" and he stopped, frozen, knowing before he turned that Min would be there, strange attractor, effective butterfly, locus of fate. He turned and saw her, sitting at a table with everybody else, looking like a startled cherub, her beautiful lips open in surprise, her dark eyes wide, and he felt his breath go again, felt his blood heat, his entire system rushing about insanely, bouncing off the inside of his skin, his future impossible to predict, everything riding on his next lurch through chaos.

Min bit her lip and smiled at him ruefully, and without another thought, he walked across the room to her, feeling almost relieved as the avalanche began.

Chapter
Nine

Cal pulled a chair from another table, and Min scooted over to let him in. She was wearing another soft shirt, this one in panels of different colored sheer prints, and she looked pretty and warm and more desirable than he could have imagined.

Beyond her, Tony shrugged and looked apologetic.

"Tony said you'd told him you were going to work late tonight," Min said as he sat down.

"I lied."

Min shifted a little more to give him room, and he caught the faint scent of lavender and felt dizzy again. "Well, at least you're honest about your dishonesty."

" 'I was raised to be charming, not sincere,' " Cal said, and relaxed as she smiled at him.

"You know *Into the Woods?*" Min said, "That's my favorite Sondheim."

"Mine, too," Cal said, watching her face. "Tony likes *Sweeney Todd*, and Roger's is *Sunday in the Park with George*, but—"

"You're kidding me," Min said, blinking those dark eyes at him. "You're all Sondheim fans?"

"We roomed with a drama minor in college." *God, you look good.*

"There was a fourth roommate?" Min said, and then she closed her eyes. "Of course there was. Emilio. It was his restaurant you worked in when you were in college."

"No," Cal said. "It was his grandpa's restaurant. He went out on his own about two years ago."

"And he's not setting the world on fire." Min nodded. "That's why I brought Liza here. It took me all night to talk her into it, but I think she likes the place."

"Good," Cal said, not following and not caring. It felt too damn good to be sitting next to her again to insist on clarity, too.

"Liza's a fixer," Min said. "She finds businesses that need help and then she . . . helps them."

"So, she advertises that she can fix things," Cal said, not caring.

"No," Min said. "She chooses. There are a lot of places that need a kick in the butt to get going, and Liza gets a job and provides the kick. She's not good for the long term, once things are good she leaves, but for the year she stays, magic happens." She grinned at him. "Sort of like you and women."

"Hey," Cal said, but then he caught sight of Emilio, gesturing to him from the kitchen door. "Be right back."

Emilio dragged him through the door when he got there. "There's a woman out there," Emilio said. "The redhead with Tony. She just told me she's thinking about working here. Is she delusional?"

"Not even a little bit," Cal said. "Tony knows her better than I do, but if you're asking, I vote you hire her. It can't hurt, and Min says she's a genius at what she does."

"What does she do?" Emilio said.

"I'm not sure," Cal said, looking through the round window on the door to see Min. "I'm just going on what Min says."

"Min." Emilio nodded. "Min I trust."

"Me, too," Cal said and followed Emilio back to the table in time to hear Min say, "So here's something I just found out. These guys are Sondheim freaks."

"What?" Liza said, turning to Tony in amazement.

"What?" Tony said back. "I can't have facets?"

"Because of Emilio," Min said. "Which I bring up because I want to hear his voice."

"Uh," Emilio said.

"Don't fight it," Cal said, sitting down next to Min again. "She gets what she wants, too."

"I like the 'Moments' song," Min said, grinning at Emilio. "Or 'Into the Woods.' That's peppy."

"Nah," Tony said. "'Sweeney Todd.'" He sang the first line of "Sweeney Todd" in a surprisingly true bass, and Roger joined in on the next line, and they sang until Emilio gave up and helped them finish on "the demon barber of Fleet . . . *Street*," while Cal watched Min smile and thought, *Kiss me.*

"Probably not the best thing to sing in a restaurant," Cal said when Min was done clapping, and Emilio winced.

"You don't sing?" Min said to Cal.

"Only in the shower," Cal said, and imagined Min in the shower.

"Wuss," Tony said, breaking the moment. "He can sing, he's just a coward."

"But you are not," Liza said, turning back to Tony. "You are multi-talented. Who would have guessed it?"

"What else does he do?" Bonnie said, and Tony grinned at her.

"He has skills we'll discuss later," Liza said. "This is excellent pasta, Emilio. This place should be packed every night."

"Which is your job," Min said to her. "Save Emilio. I love him."

"I think so," Liza said. "Let me check out the kitchen first."

She got up, walked past Emilio, and pushed her way through the swinging doors.

"Is she—" he said to Min.

"She's the best waitress you'll ever have," Min said. "And she will get you business. She's checking out your kitchen now. If you pass muster, you've got her."

Emilio went to protect his kitchen from Liza, and Cal poured more wine into Min's glass. "Drink this. I'm about to try to talk you into something, and I need you juiced."

"I kind of miss the charm," Min said, picking up her glass. "Listen, I was thinking about the snow globe and the movies and everything, and I apologize for calling you the devil. They were all coincidences."

"Yeah," Cal said. "Tony thinks it's chaos theory."

"Bonnie thinks it's the fairy tale," Min said, and sipped her wine.

"Fairy tale?" Cal said, lost again.

"You know, you're a prince, it's meant to be, we'll live happily ever after. It's okay, she's sane on everything else." Min smiled at him. The point is, we'll be fine as long as we stick to the plan."

"Right," Cal said. "The plan." Her lips were soft and full, curved in that comforting smile, and he started to get dizzy again. *Kiss me.* "I think we should start dating. Want to go to the movies?"

Min blinked at him and put down her glass. "Did you hear anything I said?"

"Everything was a coincidence, we should stick to the plan," Cal said. "That's not going to work for me."

Min folded her arms. "Why not?"

"Because if we don't date, the universe is going to maim me."

"*What?*"

"The universe, fate, chaos theory, fairy tales, the spirit of Elvis, I don't know what it is, but I'm not fighting it anymore." Cal leaned closer and caught the faint scent of lavender again as Min looked at him as if he were insane. "You hate me, you're high maintenance, you're pathological about food, and your best friend will kill me someday, but it doesn't matter. I'm going to give this a shot. Does your mother still want to check me out at dinner? I'll go."

"Why, if I'm that awful?" Min said, looking annoyed.

He smiled down into her beautiful face. "Because you're smart and kind and funny, and my nephew is crazy about you, and you wear great shoes, and you look like a depraved angel." *Because I'm going to go crazy if I don't touch you.*

"Uh huh." Min nodded. "And because of that, you're going to dinner at my parents' house tomorrow night so my mother can see you're harmless?"

"Tomorrow?" He nodded, trying not to look appalled. "Good. We'll get that out of the way fast. Tomorrow night it is. So about tonight—"

"On the dating thing? No, so you're off the hook with my mother, you do not need to go to dinner. But if you want to do a friends-night-out thing, we could go to the movies. *Blue Hawaii* is playing at ten o'clock."

"*Blue Hawaii,*" Cal said. "I don't suppose that's porn."

"It's part of the Elvis revival," Min said. "You don't have to go."

Cal sighed. "Yes, I do. And I'm going to your parents' tomorrow, too."

"I'm not understanding this at all," Min said, and he took her hand, happy to be touching her again, and said, "Come with me, Minnie. I will explain."

He pulled her out of her chair and across the restaurant to the front door, and when they were out on the darkened street, he leaned down, his heart pounding, and he kissed her with no reservation at all. The familiar rush was fast and hot as always, hotter because he wasn't fighting it, but there was comfort there, too, she felt so right under his hands, against his mouth, and when she slipped her arms around his neck, he kissed her harder, falling into her helplessly, not even trying to save himself. He felt her move closer, and her perfect mouth opened as her lush body pressed against him, and years passed, and he saw paradise, and the voice in his head whispered, *THIS ONE, YOU IDIOT.* Then something smacked him hard on the arm and jarred them both out of the kiss.

"What the—" he began, still holding on to her, and then saw Liza, standing on the sidewalk with her purse. "You know, if Bonnie is right, a leprechaun will be by any minute to kneecap you."

"*Liza,*" Min said, stepping away from him a little, and he felt cold where she'd been touching him and held on to her.

"I didn't hit him on the head," Liza said.

Cal looked at Min. "Forget her. You want to know why? This is why. It really is bigger than the both of us, and I, for one, am not fighting it anymore." She opened her mouth to say something and he said, "And you want this, too."

Liza scowled at him. "Oh, tell me you know her. Tell me—"

"Yes, I do know her, although not as well as I'm going to," Cal said, facing her down. "And yes, I care about her. A lot. And I don't know the rest, but I'm going to find out. Is that all right with you?"

Liza looked at him for a moment. "Yes. But I'm watching you."

"All right then," Cal said, feeling relieved in general. The just-friends bit wasn't good, but that was okay, he was good at courting women. *We're playing my game now*, he thought and looked down at Min with great affection.

"Don't look at me like that," Min said and turned to Liza. "We're going to the ten o'clock movie, just as friends. Want to come?"

"Yes. Tony?" Liza said as Tony came out of the bar to find her. "We're going to the movies at ten."

"It's *Blue Hawaii*," Cal said to Tony.

"I don't suppose that's porn," Tony said.

"It's Elvis," Cal said.

"Why?" Tony said.

"Because it's time to make my move," Cal said, looking down at Min.

"Hey," Min said.

"Oh, well, hell, then," Tony said. "Let's go."

Min had started her Saturday by calling her mother to tell her that Cal would, in fact, be dining with them that night.

"We'll see what kind of man he is," Nanette said, her tone boding no good for Cal.

"You're going to love him," Min said. "He's gorgeous and successful."

Nanette sniffed. "Probably the kind who thinks he's an eight and you're a four. Men are shallow and treacherous. Wear something slimming."

"He's a ten, Mother," Min said. "And I'm not slim."

After that, baseball seemed an improvement, at least until she got to the park.

"You're sticking with me," she told Liza. "Bonnie always wanders off with Roger, but you are staying so you can jab me if I start to act goofy around Cal."

"There's not that much jab in the world," Liza said, but she followed Min to the bleachers anyway.

"*Min,*" Harry yelled when he saw her, and she stopped to smile at him as he came running up.

"Hey, you," she said as he skidded to a halt in front of her. "How's it going?"

"Good," he said, nodding his head. "Thanks for coming." Then he looked down and said, "Whoa. Cool shoes."

"Thank you," Min said as Harry bent closer to see the blue plastic fish that overlapped across the toes of her sandals. "You know, you're a lot like your uncle."

"Harrison, your instincts are right," Cal said from behind them, and Min jumped. "Women are more important than baseball, but get your butt back to the outfield anyway." Then she turned and he grinned at her, his face softening, and her heart rate bumped up again. "Minnie, you're getting freckles on your nose."

"I know." Min rubbed the bridge of her nose, trying not to care about the affection in his voice. "It's these Saturday mornings. I never go out in the sun so I keep forgetting to get sunscreen."

"I like them," Cal said, and Min felt her heart bump again.

"Me, too," Harry said from below.

"I don't," Min said, trying to keep a grip. "But I'm stuck with them because I keep forgetting—"

Cal took off his cap and put it on her head. "Problem solved." His grin widened. "Very cute. You can play for my team any time."

"Stop that," Min said, and tried to adjust the hat so it wouldn't squash her curls. It felt warm from him, and she kept her hand on it a minute longer just to feel it. *You're worthless,* she told herself.

"Harry!" somebody called, and Min turned and saw Cynthie walking toward them in a fluttery pink dress, smiling beautifully at Harry. "How are you, buddy?"

Harry scowled. "Hi."

"Hi, Cynthie," Min said, trying not to hate her, and turned back to Harry. "We're going to go get good seats. Knock 'em dead, kid." She looked past Cal's ear, avoiding eye contact. "Thanks for the hat. I'm sure it makes me look like hell."

"Nah." Cal tapped it on the brim. "It makes you look like a butch angel. Shanna should be here."

Min smiled at him in spite of herself, warm all over, and then Tony yelled, "Hey, we're playing *baseball* here," and Cal dragged Harry onto the field.

"How'd I do?" she said to Liza.

"As well as could be expected under the circumstances," Liza said.

"Do at what?" Cynthie said.

"I'm practicing my cool," Min said.

"Oh," Cynthie said. "Well, good job."

Min followed Liza and Cynthie over to where Bonnie was sitting and watched Harry's team get killed in the first three innings, trying not to watch Cal. When he looked up and caught her looking at him, he grinned, and she thought, *Oh, for heaven's sake, Minerva,* and turned to Liza to distract herself. "You'd think Tony would be apoplectic by now," Min said to Liza.

"No," Liza said. "He just wants them to have a good time. He yells at them so they'll get better, but he doesn't care if they win. He says all their games are practice for the future."

"Really?" Min said. "He does have layers."

"Only about three," Liza said. "I was wrong about him being dumb, though, he's actually quite bright. He's a nice guy."

"That's all?" Min said.

"Yes," Liza said. "That's all. He is not The One. Speaking of which, nice ball cap you got there, Stats." She tapped the brim. "Maybe he'll buy you a soda after the game."

Min shook her head. "We're just—"

"It's the fairy tale," Bonnie said. "He's winning you."

"What?" Cynthie said. "Fairy tale?"

"Yes," Bonnie said. "Min and Cal, they're a fairy tale. She's the girl who doesn't have the life she deserves, so her fairy godmother got her a prince to rescue her."

"Fairy godmother?" Min said.

"Liza," Bonnie said. "She picked Cal out for you."

"*Wait a minute*," Liza said. "I am *not* accepting responsibility for Calvin Morrisey."

Min started to laugh. "You did pick him out. You sent me over there to meet him. Now, *that's* funny."

"A fairy tale," Cynthie said, sounding as if she wasn't sure they were serious.

Bonnie nodded. "Cal gave her the ball cap because it's part of his quest."

"No, he gave her the ball cap because he's courting," Cynthie said, a little sharply. "It's part of the attraction stage."

"Attraction stage," Liza said.

"He is not attracted—" Min began.

"There are four stages to mature love," Cynthie said. "Assumption, attraction, infatuation, and attachment."

"Now, see, I would have called the way he looks at her infatuation," Liza said.

"Excuse me?" Min said, looking at her best friend, the betrayer.

"It's the fairy tale," Bonnie said.

"It's attraction," Cynthie said flatly.

"It's love, a random reaction," Liza said. "Chaos theory."

"Hey," Min said, and they looked at her. "It's a kind act by a friend because I don't want freckles. Not everything is a theory."

"The fairy tale is not a theory," Bonnie said. "Even if you won't believe it's happening to you, it's happening to me." She smiled at them all, too happy to be smug.

"So how's Roger?" Min said, more than willing to have somebody else be the topic at hand.

"He is The One," Bonnie said. "He's going to propose in a couple of weeks and I'll say yes. I told my mama to plan the wedding for August."

"He told you he's going to propose?" Cynthie said, and when Bonnie looked at her, surprised, she said, "I'm writing a book on this. It's none of my business, but I am interested."

"Oh," Bonnie said. "Well, no, he hasn't told me. I just know."

Min tried to look supportive, but the silence that settled over them must have reeked of skepticism because Bonnie turned back to the field and called Roger's name. When he came trotting over to them, she said, "Honey, are you going to ask me to marry you?"

"Yes," he said. "I didn't want to rush you, so I thought I'd wait till our one-month anniversary. It's only eleven days."

"Very sensible," Bonnie said. "Just so you know, I'm going to say yes."

Roger sighed. "That takes a lot of the worry out of it." He leaned over and kissed her and went back to the field.

"That was either really sweet or really annoying," Liza said.

"It was sweet," Min said, trying to imagine Cal saying any of that. *Stop thinking about him.* "And annoying."

"I told you," Bonnie said. "It's the fairy tale. You have to believe."

"Positive thinking," Cynthie said, nodding. "There's good evidence for that. Could I interview you? For my book. Because this is fascinating. You've moved into the infatuation phase very quickly."

"Sure," Bonnie said. "But it's not infatuation. This is True Love. Like Cal and Min."

"Will you stop that?" Min said.

"Of course," Cynthie said to Bonnie with no conviction whatsoever, and they began to talk.

Min took a deep breath and turned back to Liza. "Cynthie seems nice," she said quietly, hoping for a conversation that didn't have Cal in it.

"She is," Liza said. "But I think she wants Cal back."

Min gave up and stared out at the field where Cal was talking to somebody on third base. His face was serious again, and the kid nodded, hanging on his every word. *What a darling*, she thought and then remembered, *No, beast*, but that wasn't working anymore. Well, it had never worked, really.

"Are you going out tonight?" Liza asked.

"Yes, but just as friends," Min said. "He's doing me a favor. We're going to my mother's so she can stop worrying about him being a vile seducer."

Liza shook her head, looking doubtful. "I don't think meeting Cal is going to reassure your mother."

"Why not? Elvis likes him. And Elvis has very good instincts."

"Elvis?" Liza said, sounding alarmed.

"The cat. I named him Elvis," Min said.

Liza sighed. "Thank God. I thought you'd finally cracked."

"Hey, I'm not the one who believes in the fairy tale," Min said. "Or in chaos theory, for that matter."

"Or the four-step program to love," Liza said, jerking her head toward Cynthie, who was listening to Bonnie finish up the theory of fairy tale love.

"Right," Min said. "That's all garbage. You don't need a theory, you just have to be practical, figure out what it is you want in a man, and then find one who has those things. Make a plan. Stick to it." Her eyes went to Cal. "Don't get distracted."

Liza rolled her eyes. "Or you could just fall the fuck in love."

"Oh, *right*," Min said, looking away from Cal. "That's like saying you could just fall off a building. Because it won't hurt until you *land*."

Liza drew back. "I just meant—"

"*No*," Min said as several people turned to look at her. "You have to be sensible. It's not silly love songs and sloppy kisses, it's dangerous. People die for it. People die *from* it. Wars are fought. *Empires fall.*"

"Uh, Min . . ."

"It can *ruin your life*," Min said, shutting her eyes so she wouldn't look for Cal. "Which is why I'm staying friends with Cal, nothing more. I'd have to be insane to think there could be anything permanent. Masochistic. Suicidal. Delusional."

"Uh huh," Liza said.

"So that's my plan," Min said. "And I'm sticking to it."

"Right," Liza said.

When the game was over, Harry came up and said, "Uncle Cal said we can go to lunch if you'll come," and Min said, "Well . . ." and thought *Calvin, you nephew-exploiting bastard.* Still, lunch wouldn't kill her. It was okay to have lunch with a friend. And his nephew. Like a chaperone.

"Uh huh," Liza said, even though Min hadn't spoken.

She made him take them to a retro diner where she and Harry played Elvis all the way through lunch, a new experience for Harry, who'd been raised on Chopin. Cal didn't seem to mind. When they dropped her off, Harry said, "I'll see you tomorrow, Min," and she said, "Yes, you will. Dinner at Grandma's." Harry looked a little confused, and Cal said, "Harrison, I will pay you fifty bucks if you'll call your grandmother that tomorrow." "I don't think so," Harry said, and Min got out of the car feeling that tomorrow was going to explain a lot about Calvin Morrisey, assuming he lived through dinner that night with her parents.

"Keep the cap, Minnie," Cal said when she tried to hand it back to him through the window. "You look good in it. I'll pick you up at eight." Then he drove off and left her feeling ridiculously happy, which couldn't be good.

"You're a mess," she told herself, and went to get ready for dinner with her mother.

That evening, Cal picked up Min in his ancient Mercedes. She was sitting on the bottom step when he got there, dressed in a plain black dress that she'd pulled over her knees. She looked like a cranky nun.

"What are you doing down here?" he said when he got out of the car.

"You have to put up with my parents," she said, standing up. "It didn't seem fair to make you do those steps, too."

"I don't mind climbing as long as you're at the top." Cal looked down at her feet. She was wearing plain black flats, no toes showing at all. "Why the awful shoes?"

"They're not awful," Min said. "They're classic. Like your car, which is very nice and yet somehow not what I'd pictured you in."

"Graduation present." Cal opened the door for her. "Never look a gift car in the mouth. Get in, Minnie, we do not want to be late."

When he was in the driver's seat, Min said, "For the MBA?"

"What?" Cal said as he started the car.

"The car. A graduation present for the MBA? I got a briefcase, so I'm trying to put things into perspective here."

"High school," Cal said and pulled out into the street.

"High school," Min said, nodding. "What did they get you for the MBA? A yacht?"

"A place in my dad's firm."

"But—"

"I declined the gift," Cal said. "How's Elvis?"

"Really healthy," Min said, sounding mystified. "I took him to the vet and he says he's in great condition. Just weird."

"Like so much of my life lately," Cal said. "Speaking of which, is there anything I should know about your family before I get there?"

"You don't have to do this," Min said.

"Minerva, I am going. Prep me for your parents, please."

"There's nothing, really," Min said. "My mother is always polite, and my father is not talkative unless you hit a nerve. Don't hit a nerve."

"Right," Cal said. "Could I have a list of nerves?"

"Insurance fraud, younger men who want his job, music after 1970, and sex with his daughters."

"Sex with his daughters," Cal said.

Min nodded. "My father will assume you're trying to debauch me."

"Your father is a keen judge of character," Cal said. "How about your mother?"

"Well, normally, she'd be scoping you out for son-in-law potential. There would be a quiz by dessert."

"Written or oral?"

"Oral."

"Good. Oral I'm good at." The silence stretched out until he said, "I didn't mean that the way it came out."

Min stared straight ahead. "Perfectly all right. There won't be a quiz. My mother has other things on her mind at the moment."

"Does she have any other issues I should know about?"

"Yes, but they're all about me."

Cal shook his head. "I don't care. Give me that list, too."

"Eating carbs, wearing white cotton underwear, not losing weight, failing to hold onto my ex-boyfriend whom she loved," Min said. "I don't think any of those are going to come up in your conversation with her."

"My mother likes my ex, too," Cal said. "I think it's laziness. She just doesn't want to learn a new name. Who else is going to be there?"

"My sister, Diana. You're safe with her. She's nuts right now because she's getting married in a week, but she's great just the same. If things get too awful, you can sit and look at Di. She's beautiful."

"Good to know," Cal said. "Mom, Dad, Diana, you, me. Cozy group."

"And Greg," Min said, trying to keep her voice from going flat. "My sister's fiancé."

"Right. Greg of the faulty memory. How's that going?"

"Something's wrong," Min said. "I don't know what it is but he's not helping. The thing is, he's not a bad guy, except for dumping Wet which he had every right to do, and he adores Diana, so I can't figure it out." She looked over at Cal. "See what you think of him."

"Me?" Cal said, surprised.

"You're a good judge of character," Min said. "Intuitive. Intuit Greg for me."

"The chances of me figuring out what's wrong over dinner are slim," Cal said as Min's cell phone rang.

When she pulled it out of her purse, he said, "A plain black cell phone. You lied to me that first night, Minnie."

"Which you knew," Min said, and answered the phone. "Hello. What?" She listened for a minute and then said, "Oh, for crying out loud." She listened again and said, "Di, it's Saturday evening. I don't know where . . . Wait a minute." She turned to Cal. "Greg promised to get the wine for dinner."

"Let me guess," Cal said.

"You wouldn't have a bottle or two at your apartment, would you?" Min said.

"Emilio's," Cal said, and made a U-turn.

Min turned back to the phone. "Cal's going to fix it." There was a note of pride in the way she said it, and Cal grinned. Then she turned off her phone and said, "You are a prince."

"Thank you," Cal said. "Say something bitchy to me, will you? You're confusing me."

He stopped and got the wine, and when he was back in the car, Min looked at the labels on the bottles. "These were expensive, weren't they?"

"Not really," Cal said. "About forty bucks each."

Min started to laugh. "Serves Greg right, the dumbass."

Ten minutes later, Cal had followed Min's directions and parked in front of a fairly large, fairly new house. Min said, "You know, you can still get out of this. Drop me off and I'll tell—"

"Nope." Cal opened his car door. "Stay there."

"Stay where?" Min said, reaching for her door handle.

Cal came around the car and caught the door for as she opened it. "You cannot leap out of cars without assistance." He caught her hand and pulled her to her feet as she got out, and she ended up closer to him than he'd planned, which was fine by him. "It makes me look weak and powerless when you get out without me," he said, watching the breeze ruffle her curls.

"Yeah, weak and powerless," she said. "I bet you get that a lot." She detoured around him as he shut the car door, and he caught sight of someone vanishing from a window. "Well, the good news is, you just made points with my mother. She was scoping you out from the window."

"Great," Cal said, taking her elbow. "Now all we have to do is survive dinner."

Min's father met them in the hall, a lumbering man with a shock of blond hair and heavy white eyebrows who should have been hearty and welcoming but instead had the vaguely paranoid look of a sheepdog whose sheep were plotting against him.

"Dad, this is Calvin Morrisey," Min said. "Cal, this is my father, George Dobbs."

"Pleased to meet you, Calvin." George's gruff voice was firm as if to belie any indication that he wasn't pleased, but his eyes telegraphed, *What are you up to?*

"Pleased to be here, sir," Cal lied, and Min patted him on the back, which was more comforting than he could have imagined.

"You're late," George said to Min. "We've already had cocktails."

"Sorry, sir," Cal said, and Min said, "No, you're not. It was my fault, Dad, we had to go back for something."

"Well, come in now," George said, and Min sighed and went into the dining room, and Cal followed and met Min's dragon of a mother.

The house was a showplace, clearly done by a decorator, and Min's mother, standing in her perfect living room, matched it: Both were designer creations with no warmth whatsoever. The house at least had some color, but Min's mother was small, thin, dark-haired, dressed in black, and groomed to within an inch of her life, the exact opposite of Min. "This is my mother, Nanette," Min said, practically chirping. "Mother, this is Calvin Morrisey," and Nanette Dobbs said, "Welcome, Calvin," in a voice that could have flash-frozen fish.

"Did I do something?" Cal whispered when she'd turned to speak to George.

"You frenched me in the park on a picnic table," Min whispered back.

"How do they know that?" Cal said.

"Greg ratted us out," Min said. "He also mentioned your hit-and-run past."

"And I got him wine," Cal said.

"And here he is," Min said. She lifted her voice and said, "Greg! This is Cal Morrisey."

Greg was young and smooth, clearly polished by prep schools and buffed in the gym until his surface gleamed. He smiled at Cal and then realized who he was shaking hands with. "Oh," Greg said.

Cal waited for something more, but that was it. "Yep," he said and leaned forward. "The wine is in the front seat of my car."

Greg exhaled in relief. "Thanks, man," he said, clasping Cal on the arm. "Be right back," he said in a voice that was a fraction too loud. "Left the wine in the car."

"And this is my sister, Diana," Min said, her voice softening, and Cal looked up to see a younger, sweeter version of the dragon. Diana was slender, dark, and lovely, and clearly the princess in the family. She beamed when she saw Min, and welcomed Cal with more warmth than everyone else in the room put together, and asked about his baseball team.

"Nice kid," he told Min when Diana had gone to find the amnesiac she was marrying.

"Kid?" Min said.

"Cute," Cal said. "But she's not you."

"You're not the first to have noticed," Min said. "Listen, don't let the 'rents get you down. They're just . . ." Her voice faded away as she tried to think of something to call them.

"Fine," Cal said, and then Nanette called Min away as Greg showed up with the wine.

When Min came back a few minutes later, all her curls were pulled back in combs, and they went in to dinner.

"What's with the hair?" Cal said in her ear when they were seated.

"It's not flattering to my round face when it's left loose," Min said. "I knew better."

"I liked it," Cal said, and Min said, "I did, too," and then dinner started.

"So what is it you do for a living, Calvin?" George asked when the soup had been dispatched with small talk and the prime rib had been served.

"Training seminars," Cal said, keeping a wary eye on Nanette, who had been staring at him throughout the soup course. He couldn't call it a frown since her forehead wasn't furrowed, but it was not warm.

"So you're a teacher," George said. "There much money in that?"

"Dad," Min said.

"There's enough," Cal said, distracted because Min had discreetly begun to pat his back again. He was grateful to her for the support, but it felt way too good to be something he should be enjoying in front of her father.

"What firm are you with?" George said.

"Morrisey, Packard, Capa." Cal smiled at Min's mother. "This beef is excellent, Mrs. Dobbs."

"Thank you." Nanette Dobbs did not look appeased.

"Morrissey," George said. "So you work for the old man. Not too hard getting that job, huh?"

"Uh, no," Cal said. "I'm the old man. It's my company."

Min stopped patting and glared at George. "I wonder what the statistics are on the number of daughters who return home to visit after their guests *are harassed by their fathers.*"

"You inherited it?" George said.

"I started it," Cal said.

"I'm guessing they're *pretty low,*" Min said.

"But your old man bankrolled you," George said.

"No, he didn't," Cal said. "He wanted me to go into his business, so I went outside the family for capital."

"For crying out loud, Dad, that's enough," Min said, taking her hand away from Cal's back. "Let's talk about something else. I got a cat."

"So it's a start-up," George said. "Thirty-three percent of start-ups fail in the first four years."

"It's sort of a *mutant* cat," Min said.

"It was a start-up ten years ago," Cal said to George. "It's up."

"It annoys all my friends," Min said. "*I'm thinking of calling it George.*"

"*Minerva,*" Nanette said. "Not your loud voice."

"Bread?" Min said, shoving the basket under Cal's nose.

"Yes, thank you." Cal took a roll and handed her the basket back. She took one, too, and her mother spoke again.

"Min."

"Right," Min said and put the roll back.

"So you own your own business," George said, skepticism heavy in his voice.

"Yes." Cal frowned down at Min. "Why can't you have a roll?"

"I told you, I have this dress I have to fit into," Min said. "It's all right. I can eat bread again in July."

"Min is Diana's maid of honor next weekend," Nanette said. "We don't want her to get too big for the dress."

"I'm already too big for the dress," Min said.

"You should come," Diana said to Cal, leaning across the table. She hadn't touched the bread, the butter, or her beef, Cal noticed. Her water glass was getting quite a workout, though. "To the wedding. And the rehearsal dinner. Min needs a date."

Before Cal could answer, George said, "Who are some of your clients?," and Nanette said, "How long have you and Min been dating?," and Min tugged on his sleeve. When he looked down at her, she said, "Do you have family?"

"Yes," Cal said, trying to sound noncommittal about it.

"Are they this awful?" Min said.

"*Minerva,*" Nanette said, warning in her voice.

"Well, they do let me eat bread," Cal said, keeping an eye on Nanette. "Other than that, pretty much."

"I beg your pardon?" George said.

"Look, I don't mind you grilling me about what I do for a living," Cal said. "Your daughter's brought me home and that has some significance. And I don't mind your wife asking about my personal life for the same reason. But Min is an amazing woman, and so far during this meal, you've either ignored her or hassled her about some dumb dress. For the record, she is not too big for the dress. The dress is too small for her. She's perfect." Cal buttered a roll and passed it over to Min. "Eat."

Min blinked at him and took the roll.

Cal looked past her to her mother. "I've never been married. I've never been engaged. My last relationship ended about two months ago. I met your daughter three weeks ago." He turned back to Min's father. "The business is in the black and has been for some time. I can give you references if you'd like to check. Should things between Min and me ever grow serious, I can support her."

"Hey, I can support me," Min said, still holding her roll.

"I know," Cal said. "Your dad wants to know that I can. Eat." Min bit into the roll, and he looked around the table. "Anything else anybody wants to know?"

Diana held up her hand.

"Yes?" Cal said.

"Are you Min's date for the wedding?"

Min tried to swallow the bite she'd just taken.

"She hasn't asked me." Cal looked down at Min. "Want to go to your sister's wedding with me?"

Min choked on her roll and he pounded her on the back.

"Of course she wants to go with you," Nanette said, smiling for the first time. "We'd be delighted to have you. The rehearsal dinner, too."

"Good," Cal said, feeling progress had been made as Min gasped for air.

"This wine is excellent," George said to him.

"Thank—uh, thanks to Greg," Cal said. "Knows his wine."

"Uh huh," George said, looking at Greg, who smiled back at him feebly.

"You have a *cat?*" Nanette said to Min, and the evening rolled on while she harangued Min about cat diseases, and George asked questions about the seminar business, and Greg glowered, and Diana smiled, and Cal's head pounded. He'd had worse evenings, but not many.

Then Min smiled up at him and said, "I'm sorry" so softly he almost missed it. He said, "For what? I'm having a great time," and felt better about everything.

After dessert, which only the men ate, Min dragged Diana into the hall. "Are you out of your mind," she whispered. "Why in the name of God did you ask that man to the wedding?"

"Why not?" Diana said. "You needed a date. He's darling. I don't see a problem."

"That's because you don't know our history," Min said.

"Well, at least you have a date now," Diana said. "I think it was a pretty good idea."

Min stabbed her finger at her. "Don't do anything like that again. Ever. *Ever.*"

"Okay," Diana said. "But you've still got a really hot date."

Her really hot date came out in the hall, said a pleasant good-bye to her parents, walked her down the front steps, handed her into his car, got in the driver's side, reached over and pulled the combs out of her hair.

"These are ugly, Minnie," he said, and threw them out his car window into the street.

"I know," she said, trying not to feel rescued. "Thank you."

The next day, Min dressed very carefully for her dinner with the Morriseys, pulling out her plain black dress again, polishing her black flats, and trying to make her hair lie down. Things didn't get better when Nanette called.

"Darling, your Calvin is lovely," Nanette said.

"Thank you, Mother," Min said, bracing herself for whatever was coming next.

"And Daddy checked his financials and he's very solvent," Nanette went on.

"He checked on a Saturday night?" Min said. "How?"

"You know your father," Nanette said in a tone that said she wished she didn't. "And your Calvin seems very taken with you. That was very sweet, the thing with the bread and butter. You won't eat it again, of course, but still . . ."

"A man who will feed you is a good thing," Min agreed.

"So don't ruin this one," Nanette said. "I was upset about you losing David, but that's all right now. Just don't lose Calvin, too."

"Mother, I don't want him," Min lied.

"Of course you want him," Nanette said. "You'll have beautiful children."

"I don't want those, either," Min said. "New subject. I'm thinking about quitting my job to become a cook."

"Don't be ridiculous, dear," Nanette said. "You around food? You'd blow up like a balloon."

"Thank you, Mother," Min said. "I'm going to go now."

"Go where?"

"I'm having dinner with Cal's parents."

"That's nice. Who are they?"

"Jefferson and Lynne Morrisey. I don't know—"

"You're having dinner with Lynne Morrisey?"

"Yes," Min said. "Because she gave birth to my date, otherwise, I wouldn't be."

"Min," her mother said, her voice dropping in respect. "Lynne Morrisey is *huge* in the Urban League."

"I'm so sorry," Min said, thinking that was the first time she'd ever heard Nanette say "huge" with approval.

"No carbs, darling," Nanette said. "And tell me *everything* when you get home."

"Oh, dear Lord," Min said and hung up to go back to her hair problem.

When Cal knocked on her door, she and Elvis were contemplating a headband without much confidence.

"Do you think a headband?" she said to Cal when she opened the door.

"Christ, no," he said, reaching down to pet the cat, who had come to purr at his feet. "Look at you, you're in mourning again."

"Don't even try to talk me out of this dress," she said.

He looked down. "At least give me your feet. How about the shoes with the black bows, the ones you wore the first night?"

"Cal," Min said.

"It's not a lot to ask," he said, leaning in the doorway grinning at her. "Go change your shoes, Minnie, and then we'll face the dragons together."

She smiled back in spite of herself. "That charm stuff doesn't work on me," she told him and went to change her shoes.

Chapter Ten

W hen they were in the car, she said, "Okay, give me the cheat sheet for your parents."

"There is none," Cal said. "They will be very polite but not warm. We don't have to chill the wine at home, the atmosphere does it for us."

"Oh, good," Min said, "this is exactly the time I want to hear jokes."

But when they arrived at his parents' home, she realized he wasn't being funny. The house was large, one of the Prairie mansions that always looked to Min like ranch houses on steroids; the maid at the paneled door was polite, the paneled hall was cool, and when they went into what Min doubted they called the living room, Cal's parents were downright frigid.

"We're so pleased to have you," Lynne Morrisey said to Min, taking her hand. She didn't look pleased; she didn't look anything but darkly, stunningly, expensively beautiful, as did her husband, Jefferson, and her son, Reynolds, possibly the only man on the planet who made Cal look a little plain.

"*Min!*" Harry said from behind her, and she turned and saw him towing Bink into the room.

"Hey, you," she said, bending down to him. "Thanks for the dinner invitation. I was *starving*."

Harry nodded and then leaned forward and whispered, "I like your shoes. The bows are neat." He nodded at her, grinning maniacally.

"Thank you," Min whispered back, and stole a glance at Cal. His face was expressionless, and she realized he hadn't said a word since they'd arrived. *O-kay*, she thought. *Welcome to hell.*

She did her best to make politely chilly conversation until they were all seated and served with a series of plates beautifully presented with syrup swirls. Then she gave up and just ate.

"What is it that you do, Minerva?" Jefferson said when they'd reached the filet-and-piped-potatoes course.

Min swallowed and prayed she didn't have anything in her teeth. "I'm an actuary."

"I see," he said, not impressed but not scornful, either. "Who's your employer?"

"Alliance," Min said, and went back to her rare beef. The food was both beautiful and excellent, she had to give the Morriseys credit for that, but it wasn't Emilio's. They needed a few comic ethnic photos on the wall to liven things up. Not that they'd ever admit to being ethnic. She glanced around the table. Irish, she'd bet, and not just because of the name. Dark and beautiful, all of them, in that austere, tragic way. She looked down at her lavishly presented plate. Although the potato famine was clearly behind them.

"Dobbs," Cal's father said, and Min realized he'd been silent for a while. "George Dobbs is a vice president there."

"That's my father," Min said.

Jefferson Morrisey smiled at her. "You went to work for your father's firm."

"Well, it's not as if he owns it," Min said, positive there was a land mine somewhere in the conversation. "But he was a help in getting me the job."

"You didn't need any help," Cal said, his voice flat. "You're an actuary. You must have had forty offers."

"There were a lot," Min said, wondering what the hell was going on. "But there weren't a lot of great offers. My dad helped."

"That was very wise of you," Lynne Morrisey said.

Min turned to meet her cold dark eyes and thought, *I don't want you approving of me, lady.*

"To take the help your father offered," Lynne went on. "Very wise."

"Well." Min put down her fork. "It came with no strings attached, so there wasn't a down side."

Across the table, Reynolds smiled and became even better looking. *I don't like you, either,* Min thought. Bink sat frozen, not in terror so much as in watchfulness, and between them, Harry clutched his fork and plowed his way through his piped potatoes, keeping an eye on everybody.

"And many benefits, no doubt," Jefferson was saying. "I'm sure your father helped you along the way."

"She made it on her own," Cal said, his voice still flat. "Insurance companies are not sentimental. She holds the record for promotions within her company and nobody's saying it's because of her father. She's smart, she's hardworking, and she's excellent at what she does."

There was something bleak and awful in his voice, out of proportion to the tension in the conversation, and Min discreetly put her hand on his back. Even through his suit coat, his muscles were so rigid that it was like patting cement. She felt him tense even tighter for a moment at her touch, and then his shoulders went down a little.

"Of course she is," Jefferson was saying, but he was looking at his wife, a half smile on his face. "We think it's admirable of her that she followed in her father's footsteps."

"My father's not an actuary," Min said.

"Of course not, dear," Lynne said, a little edge to her voice. "We admire you for making the right choice and staying in your father's business." She smiled past Min to Cal. "Don't you think so, Cal?"

"I don't think Min ever makes a mistake," Cal said. "This filet is excellent."

"Cal didn't go into the family business," Reynolds said, smiling at

Min, pseudo-pals, and Min thought, *And you are dumb as a rock to be the one who says that out loud.*

"Well, for heaven's sake, why would he?" Min said brightly. She took her hand away from Cal's back, thought, *I'm never going to see these people again so screw 'em all.*

"Why would he go into the family business?" Lynne echoed, raising one eyebrow, which annoyed Min because she was pretty sure she couldn't do it. "Because it's his legacy."

"No," Min said, and across from her Bink's eyes widened even farther. "It would be completely wrong for him. He's clearly doing what he should be doing." She turned to smile at Cal and found him staring straight ahead, at the space between Bink and Harry. *Okay, he's gone,* she thought, and looked at Harry. He was still clutching his fork, checking faces. No wonder the kid threw up all the time.

Jefferson cleared his throat. "Wrong for him to go into a well-respected and established law firm? Nonsense. It's the Morrisey tradition."

Min blinked. "You went into your father's business? I thought you and your partner started the firm."

Across the table, Bink did the impossible and made her little owl face even more impassive.

"They did," Reynolds said from across the table, indignation in his voice. "They began the tradition."

"I don't think you can call two generations a tradition," Min said, trying to make her voice speculative, as if she were considering it. She looked at Harry. "You want to be a lawyer, Harry?"

Harry blinked at her. "No. I want to be an ichthyologist."

Min blinked back. "Fish?"

"Yeah." Harry lifted his chin and grinned.

"Good for you," Min said.

"Harrison is a child," Lynne said. "Next week, he'll want to be a fireman." She smiled at Harry, almost with warmth.

"No, next week, I'll want to be an ichthyologist," Harry said, and finished his potatoes.

I love you, kid, Min thought.

"Harrison," Lynne said to him. "Why don't you have your dessert in the kitchen with Sarah?"

"Okay." Harry scooted back his chair. "May I be excused?"

"Yes, dear," Lynne said, and Min watched him trot out of the room, thinking, *Harry, you lucky dog.*

"Now," Lynne said, turning back to the table with her lizard smile. "I apologize for interrupting you, Minerva. What were you saying?" She looked at Min as if to say, *You have a chance to back down; take it.*

Min smiled back at her. *Bite me, lady.* "I was saying that if you analyze the situation, you'll see it was always impossible that Cal would go into the firm."

Jefferson put down his fork.

Min picked up her wineglass. "To begin with, he's the younger child. Older children tend to follow in the family footsteps because they're pleasers." She smiled across the table at Reynolds. "That's why they're so often successful." She took a sip of excellent wine, while they all watched her with varying degrees of frigidity. "Also, they tend to get the lion's share of attention and respect so their success is a kind of self-fulfilling prophecy. But youngest children learn that they have to be more demanding to get attention, so they become rule breakers."

"I suspect your psychology is less than professional," Jefferson said, smiling at her with no warmth whatsoever.

"No, it's pretty much a given," Min said. "The colloquial evidence is even there. All the way back to myth and legend. After all, it's always the youngest son who goes out to seek his fortune in fairy tales."

"Fairy tales," Reynolds said, chuckling like a fathead, while Bink continued her imitation of a frozen owl.

Min turned back to Jefferson. "Then consider Cal's personality. His friends tell me that he rarely makes a bet he doesn't win. The knee-jerk reaction to that is that he's a gambler, but he's not. If he were a gambler, he'd lose half the time. Instead, he calculates the odds, and only takes the risks he knows he can capitalize on." She looked across the table at Reynolds. "As the younger son in the family firm, he'd never make it to the top. That's such a bad risk, I doubt he ever considered joining the firm."

"He'd have made partner," Jefferson said, all pretense of light conversation gone.

"Third partner, maybe, after he'd followed you and Reynolds around," Min said. "Plus there'd be your partner and his children to contend with. Within the family, he's always going to be the baby. He had to get out. And then, of course, there's the dyslexia."

The silence that settled over the table that time was so complete that Min was amazed there wasn't hoarfrost on all of them. She picked up her knife and fork and cut into her filet again, wishing she could ask for a Styrofoam box and go home.

"We prefer not to discuss Cal's handicap," Lynne said with finality.

Min took her time with the filet, but when she'd swallowed, she said, "Why? It's part of who he is, it helped shape him. It's not shameful. Over ten percent of the population is dyslexic, so it's not rare. And it's a large part of why he started his own firm. Ninety-two percent of dyslexics go into business for themselves. They need to control the environment in which they work because the regular working environment isn't sympathetic to their needs. And they generally do very well because they are generally intelligent, empathetic people." She picked up her water glass. "You have a son who's smart, hardworking, successful, popular, healthy, charming, and extremely pleasant to look at. I'm surprised you're not passing his picture around to all your friends, bragging about him." She turned to smile up at Cal and found him watching her, his face wooden. "I'd brag about him if he were mine and I had a picture."

"We are, of course, quite proud of Calvin," Lynne said, her voice bleak.

"Oh, good," Min said, going back to her plate. "He's right about the filet, too. It's fabulous."

"Thank you," Lynne said, and then she turned to Reynolds and asked him about work. Fifteen minutes later, dessert was served; Reynolds, Lynne, and Jefferson were discussing the firm; Cal was still silent; Bink had eaten three slivers of carrot and sucked down all her wine; and Min had had enough.

She put her napkin down by her plate, and said, "You know, I'm really Harry's date, so if you'll excuse me, I'll join him." Then she got up and went out to the hall to find the kitchen.

When she got there, Harry was finishing off his ice cream under the watchful eyes of the woman who'd served dinner.

"Hey, fish guy," she said. "Is there any more of that?"

Harry nodded at the woman. "She's the one, Sarah."

"Huh," Sarah said, surveying Min from head to toe. "What would you like on your ice cream?"

"Chocolate," Min said, sitting down across from Harry. "Chocolate is always good."

Harry scraped the bottom of his bowl with his spoon, and then sat silently looking at Min, as owlish as his mother, until Sarah put Min's ice cream in front of her. There was a lot of it.

"Thank you," Min said, taken aback. "I'm Min, by the way." She held out her hand to the maid.

"Sarah," the woman said, shaking it. "Eat it before it melts."

Min nodded and scooped up a spoonful. The ice cream was heavenly, superfatted and smooth, and the chocolate exquisitely light and bittersweet. She had to hand it to Lynne Morrisey: The woman provided excellent food.

Sarah leaned back against the sink. "So you talked back to the Snow Queen?"

Min thought about pretending she didn't understand and then shrugged. "I disagreed with her."

Sarah nodded. "You won't be back."

"Lord, no," Min said.

Harry put down his spoon, alarmed. "Are you still coming to the park?"

"Yes," Min said. "Although I'm not sure your uncle Cal is still speaking to me."

"He seems like a nice guy," Sarah said. "Quiet. We don't see him much."

"I can imagine," Min said, and then Cal came into the kitchen. "Hi, there," she said, waving her spoon at him. "Turns our your mom has great taste in ice cream, too." Which figured, come to think of it.

Cal nodded, expressionless. "You ready to go?"

Min looked at her full bowl of premium sugar and fat, and sighed. "Yes," she said obediently and put her spoon down. If she were Cal, she'd be screaming to get out of here, too.

Cal went out into the hall and Harry said, "Can I have your ice cream?"

"Will you barf?" Min said.

Harry shook his head. "Not ice cream."

Min pushed the bowl across to him. "Knock yourself out." She stood up. "It was very nice meeting you, Sarah."

"Yeah," Sarah said. "Good luck."

She met Cal in the hall, and he opened the door for her without speaking. They'd almost made it to the steps when Bink appeared in the doorway. "Well?" she said to Cal.

Cal shook his head at her, and she smiled at Min and said, "It was so nice to see you again," sounding as if she meant it. Cal turned and walked down the steps as Bink slipped away again, and Min followed him, fairly sure they were about to fight.

Well, she had no regrets. She slid into the front seat of Cal's car and settled into the leather seat. Okay, she'd miss the car. And the food, although she could still go to Emilio's without him. And—

Cal got in the car and slammed the door and then sat there for a moment, and Min looked at his rigid profile and thought, *And you. I'm going to miss you.*

"What did Bink want?" she said, trying to stave off whatever was coming.

Cal turned to her, and when he spoke, his voice was so strained it almost broke. "I am so sorry about that."

"What?" Min said, taken aback.

"My family." He closed his eyes, and then said viciously, "They usually behave *very well* in front of strangers."

"I don't think I was their type," Min said, keeping her voice light. "And then I was rude. But the good news is, I got great food and I never have to see them again. Do you know what kind of ice cream that was? Because it was phenomenal, although I'm guessing it wasn't nonfat."

"You don't care?" Cal said.

"That your mother is a witch and your father is a bastard and your brother is a supercilious moron?" Min said. "No. Why should I? They're not my family. Who are looking pretty damn good right about now, so I owe you for that. Now about the ice cream—"

He leaned forward and kissed her, hard, and she put her hand on his cheek and kissed him back, falling into that same hot, glittery rush she got every time, so glad to be touching him, to have his hand laced through her curls, to be *with him*. When he broke the kiss, she stayed close to him, not ready to let him go. "Was that because I insulted your mother?" she said, a little dazed. "Because I have lots of other horrible things to say about her."

Cal grinned, and she relaxed because he looked like Cal again. "Nah, I just like kissing you."

"Oh, good," Min said, recovering. "Except, stop that because we're not doing that. I was just relieved because I thought you were never going to want to see me again. I'm positive your family doesn't want to."

Cal put the key in the ignition and started the car. "Oh, some of them do."

"Harry." Min leaned back in her seat, and tried to think about something else besides kissing him. "That's just because I gave him my ice cream."

Cal slowed the car. "He had yours and his?"

"Yes," Min said. "He said he didn't throw up ice cream."

"He lied." Cal stopped the car. "It's sugar in general that makes him sick."

"Do we have to go back?" Min said, alarmed.

"Christ, no." Cal pulled out his cell phone. When he'd warned Bink about the imminent vomiting, he started the car again.

"Great, I poisoned her kid," Min said. "Now she hates me, too."

"No. She knows Harry and the cons he pulls for sugar. She likes you."

"She didn't look like it."

"No, she really likes you," Cal said as he pulled out into the street. "She offered me a hundred thousand dollars to marry you."

"What?" Min laughed. "I didn't think she had a sense of humor."

"She does, but she wasn't joking. She can afford it." Cal picked up speed as they left his parents' street and sighed. "Thank *God*, we're out of there."

"Wait a minute," Min said, not laughing. "She honestly offered you—"

"She's been going to dinner there every Sunday for ten years," Cal said. "That was the first one she enjoyed. When you figure that my parents are in their fifties and likely to be around for at least another thirty years, she's looking at a minimum of sixteen hundred more miserable Sundays. That's her estimate. Add in holiday dinners, and she says a hundred K would come out to about sixty dollars a dinner, which is a real bargain in her book." He thought about it. "Actually, that's a bargain in my book, too, although nothing on this earth could get me there every Sunday."

"My Lord," Min said.

"Plus Harry's been singing 'Hunka hunka burning love' since we went to lunch yesterday. She said the expressions on my parents' faces alone were worth a hundred grand."

There was a smile in his voice now, and Min said, "Well, that's a mind-boggler."

"It wasn't the only one this afternoon." They drove on for a while and then he said, "How did you know I was dyslexic?"

"Roger told Bonnie so I looked it up on the net. And then you wouldn't write the recipe for chicken marsala down when I asked. You never say no to me, so I knew it had to be something you couldn't do." Min rolled her head on the back of her seat to look at him. "Are you upset?"

"No," Cal said. "Is that true, about dyslexics starting their own businesses?"

"Yes," Min said. "Everything I told them was true. How'd you know about my promotions?"

"Bonnie told Roger," Cal said, and turned into a parking lot.

Min squinted at the storefront. It looked expensive and snotty. "Be right back," he said, and went inside. Fifteen minutes later he came back with a glossy shopping bag embossed in gold, which he tossed in her lap as he got in the car.

"What?" she said, catching it. It was heavy, so she peered inside at the square white cartons sealed with gold labels.

"The ice cream my mother serves," he said as he pulled out of the lot. "Eight flavors. I'll send flowers, but you deserved this now."

"Oh." Min clutched the bag tighter. He really wasn't mad. Relief swept over her, and she realized just exactly how much she didn't want him out of her life. It was not a good realization.

"Everything okay?" Cal said, and she forced a smile at him.

"Well, no," she said, trying to sound exasperated. "Where's the spoon?"

Without taking his eyes from the road, he took a plastic spoon from his suit pocket and handed it to her.

"I'm crazy about you," she said without thinking.

"Good," he said. "I'm crazy about you, too."

"In a friendly kind of way," she said, hastily.

"Right," Cal said, shaking his head.

"Just so you know," Min said, and opened the first carton.

"He calls her Minnie," Cynthie said when David picked up the phone that evening. "He gave her his ball cap."

"Well, if he gives her his class ring, let me know," David said. "Could I have one Sunday in peace?"

"I don't know, David," Cynthie said, her voice dangerous. "You want any of them in the future to be with Min?"

"Yes," David said. "But she hated lunch, and she won't return my calls. Look, Cal always dumps his girlfriends after a couple of months. It seems to me the smartest thing to do is wait until he dumps her and then comfort her."

"And it doesn't bother you that he's going to be fucking her blind for those two months?" Cynthie said.

"Hey." David sat up. "That's—"

"You have no idea what that man can do to a woman in bed,"

Cynthie said. "What makes you think you're going to be able to please her once she's slept with him?"

"I do just fine in bed," David said, outraged.

"Cal does more than fine," Cynthie said. "If I were you, I wouldn't wait until she finds out how much more."

"Cynthie, this is distasteful."

"Fine," Cynthie said. "Let him win."

Her voice was like a fingernail down a blackboard. "It's not about winning," David said and thought, *The bastard's going to win.*

And he'd lose Min. It was all her fault, really. She was the kind of woman who just asked to be taken for granted, and now that Cal Morrisey was showering attention on her to win a bet, she was flattered. He thought about how grateful Min would be if he went back to her and paid attention. She was such a simple woman. Which was why Cal could get to her. Which meant it was his duty to stop Cal. And save her.

"David?" Cynthie said, prompting him. "You do want her back, don't you?"

"Yes," David said.

"Then go over to her apartment and dazzle her," Cynthie said. "Tell her how important she is. Take her a gift, she likes snow globes, take her a snow globe. Give her joy, damn it."

"Snow globe," David said, recalling there had been some on Min's mantel.

"And if she resists, leave something there so you can go back and get it and try again the next day," Cynthie said. "Your tie or something."

"Why would I take off my tie?" David said.

There was a short silence, and then Cynthie said, "Just *do it*, David. I don't have time for remedial seduction lessons."

"All right," David said. "I'll go over after work. I'll surprise her. We'll talk about marriage."

"*Talk?*" Cynthie said, exasperated. "For once in your life, could you do more than talk?"

"Well, I'm not going act like a caveman with her," David said.

"Ever tried that?" Cynthie said.

"No, of course not."

"Then how do you know it doesn't work?"

"Well," David said. "Oh, hell, all right. I'll kiss her. She's a good kisser."

"Good to know," Cynthie said. "Don't screw this up, David."

"I won't," David said, but she'd already hung up. "God, you're a witch," he said to the dial tone, and then he hung up, too.

On Monday morning, Nanette called Min to find out how dinner at the Morriseys had gone. "Tell me everything," she said.

"Mother, I'm at work," Min said.

"Yes, but your father would never fire you," Nanette said. "He'd never betray *you*."

"Mom?" Min said.

"What was their house like?" Nanette said. "Did his mother like you?"

"It was very beautiful," Min said, "and his mother hated me."

"Min, if she's going to be your mother-in-law—"

"She's not going to be my mother-in-law."

"—you're going to need her. For when you hit the bad times. Not that your grandmother ever helped me in the slightest—"

"When did you ever need help with Daddy?" Min said.

"Well, *now*," Nanette said, goaded.

"Well, she's dead now," Min said. "She can't help. What's wrong?"

There was a long silence, and then Nanette said, very dramatically, "He's having an affair."

"Oh, he is not," Min said. "Honestly, Mom, when would he? You know where he is every moment of the day."

"It's those lunches," Nanette said darkly.

"He has lunch with Beverly," Min said. "Beverly who adores her husband and would really like not to work through lunch. He is not having an affair with her."

"You're so naïve, Min," Nanette said.

"You're so paranoid, Mother," Min said. "What's going on that makes you think he's cheating?"

"It's not the same. We never talk anymore."

"All you ever talk about is clothes and the wedding and my weight," Min said. "He's not interested. Take up golf. You'll be chattering away in no time."

"I should have known you wouldn't understand," Nanette said. "You have your Calvin, after all."

"I do not have a Calvin," Min said, fishing in her drawer for a paper clip. "I'm not seeing—ouch." She pulled her hand out to see a staple stuck in the end of her finger.

"You don't have time to think about your mother," Nanette said.

"Oh, for crying out loud," Min said. "Go back to worrying about the wedding and do not do anything dumb like leaving Dad, because there is nothing going on. As God is my witness, the man is innocent."

"The daughters are always the last to know," Nanette said, and hung up.

"Nuts," Min said, and hung up the phone to blot her fingertip on a piece of scrap paper.

The phone rang again, almost right away, and she answered it to hear Diana say, "Hi," in a wavery little voice.

"What's wrong?" Min said, blotting more blood on the scrap paper.

"I'm just a little . . . down," Diana said. "Could we do something together?"

"Absolutely," Min said. "How about tonight?"

"I can't," Di said. "I have to go to Greg's parents' house for dinner. How was it at Cal's parents?"

"Very bad," Min said. "How about tomorrow night?"

"I can't," Di said. "Susie and Karen are throwing a sex toy shower for me."

"Sorry I'm going to miss that," Min lied, trying not to think about Worse with a vibrator in her hand.

"How about Wednesday?" Diana said. "I know you go out with Sweet and Tart that night, but can I come along?"

"Yes," Min said, trying not to laugh. "Especially if you promise to call them Sweet and Tart."

"Liza would *kill* me," Diana said, but her voice sounded lighter.

"Come here first," Min said. "And then we'll go out and you can come back and spend the night. It'll be like old times. Except we'll be folding your cake boxes because they have to be assembled, I've just found out."

"Okay," Di said. "Okay. I feel better. It's just pre-wedding jitters."

"Right," Min said. "You haven't talked to Mom recently, have you?"

"Well, yes," Diana said. "I live with her."

"No, I mean *talk*. Because she just called to tell me Dad's cheating on her."

"Oh," Diana said, sounding taken aback. "No, she hasn't mentioned that."

"Well, good," Min said, and reassured Diana that their father was not sleeping with his secretary—"It would mean he'd have to skip lunch, Di, and do you really see that happening?"—and hung up with a renewed promise that they would have a wonderful time on Wednesday.

Then she sat and looked at the phone and waited for it to ring again. She'd told Cal not to call her, that she wanted Monday to herself, but he was not good at taking directions, so maybe . . .

By five that evening, it had become clear that the bastard had learned to take directions. Min went home and heard Elvis playing on the stereo before she opened the door. She went in and saw the cat splayed out on the back of her couch, his ears close to the speakers. "Turned it on again, did you?" she said, and went over and cuddled him to make up for leaving him all day, something that didn't seem to bother him much at all. Then she made spaghetti and began the pleasant evening she'd planned with her cat, keeping one ear cocked for a knock at the door, just in case. When it came, she felt equal parts exasperated and happy. Okay, Cal wasn't good at listening, that was bad, but she was still glad he was there.

Then she opened the door and he wasn't, it was David, and her feelings simplified down to just exasperated.

"What are you doing here?" she said.

"I need to talk to you." He walked in and stopped dead, staring at the end of her couch. "My God, what is that?"

"That's Elvis," Min said closing the door behind him. "My cat. I love him. Insult him and you're history."

David sat down on the couch, as far away from Elvis as he could get. "I've been thinking about us," he began as he loosened his tie.

"There is no us," Min said. "There never was an us. The best thing you ever did for me was dump me. I'd be grateful but I'm still mad at you for it."

"I know, I know, I deserve it." David pulled the knot out of his tie, looking more undone than Min could ever remember seeing him. "It was the dumbest thing I ever did." He patted the couch beside him. "Come here and let me talk to you."

Min went over and sat down on the couch. "Make this fast," she told him. "Elvis and I have a big evening ahead of us." At the sound of his name, Elvis crept forward on the back of the couch and sat beside her, growling softly, and she put her hand up and rubbed him behind the ears. "Easy, tiger," she told him. "He's leaving."

David leaned closer, keeping one eye on the cat. "I want to marry you, Min."

Elvis reached out a claw and buried it in David's sleeve.

"*Hell,*" David said, scooting back on the couch. "What was that for?"

"Elvis doesn't want to get married," Min said. "I think Priscilla broke his heart. He always loved her, you know."

"It's not funny," David said.

"Who's laughing?"

"Look, I'm serious." David reached in his coat pocket and handed her a package. "This is how serious I am."

"That's not a ring, is it?" Min said with horror.

"No," David said, so she unwrapped the box. Inside was an expensive, three-inch snow globe with the Eiffel Tower inside.

"The Eiffel Tower?" Min said. *This guy doesn't know me at all.*

"That's where we'll honeymoon," David said, edging closer. "In Paris. We'll have a wonderful life, Min. And I don't mind starting a family right away, we can—"

"I don't want kids," Min said, peering into the snow globe. "David, this isn't my kind of—"

"Of course you want kids," David said. "You were born to be a mother."

Min put the snow globe on the end table and looked at the cat. "There are two men, Elvis. One calls you a depraved angel and the other calls you a natural born mother. Which one do *you* pick?"

"Well, you're more than that, of course," David said. "But—" He stopped when the cat jumped down from the back of the sofa, brushing against him and leaving a smudge of rusty cat hair on his sleeve. "Your cat just got cat hair on me."

"It's only fair," Min said. "Your suit just got expensive suit lint on him."

"Min, I know you're seeing Cal Morrisey," David said.

"You do?" Min said, thinking, *You miserable son of a bitch, you're still trying to win that bet.* It was enough to make her sleep with Cal just to get even with David. The thought was much more exciting than it should have been.

"You shouldn't see Cal," David said seriously. "Ever again."

The cat jumped up on the end table and nosed the snow globe off with enough force that it landed on the stone hearth in front of the fireplace and smashed, water running everywhere.

"Elvis!" Min shoved herself off the couch to shoo him away. "Stay away from there. There's broken glass."

"He did that on purpose," David said, outraged.

"Yes, David, the cat is plotting against you." Min fished the base out of the water and glass shards and put it on the table. Then she went to get her wastebasket and began to put the glass pieces in it.

"That cat—" David said.

"Yes?" Min said as she picked up the biggest piece.

"Never mind," David said. "You don't know what Cal Morrisey's up to."

"Sure, I do," Min said, picking up another piece. "He's trying to get me into bed."

"Well, yes," David said. "But it's more than that."

"I know." Min picked up the third and last large piece and then looked at the rest. "Give me that magazine on the table, will you?"

David passed the magazine over and she tore off the cover while he said, "You don't know. He's capable of anything."

"That was the impression I got." Min slid the cover under the glass while using the rest of the magazine as a broom. She dumped the glass in the basket and then saw one more large piece, a little beyond her sweeping area. "Look, David, you don't have to worry about me. I am not in love with Cal Mor—*ow!*" She pulled back her hand as the blood welled up. "What the hell?" She picked up the last piece and dropped it in the basket and then went out to the kitchen to wash off the blood.

"Are you listening to me?" David said.

"No," Min said over the running water. "I'm injured. Go away. I don't want to marry you." She turned off the water, wrapped a paper towel around her finger, and went back to get rid of him.

"Min," David said, standing up. "You're not taking me seriously."

"Lord, no," Min said, opening her front door. "You're a nice man, David. Well, not really. Go—"

"No, Min, I'm staying," he said, his voice deep and serious.

Then he grabbed her and kissed her hard.

Chapter
Eleven

David was holding Min's head in his hands too tightly for her to pull away, so she drew back her hand to slap him, only to have him yank away and scream before she could complete the smack.

At his feet, Elvis snarled, his front claws planted in David's shin.

Min wiped her mouth off as David kicked Elvis off his leg. "Well, that was *gross*. As I was saying, go find some woman who meets your criteria for a good mate and marry her. I have an attack cat, and I'm accessing my inner bitch all the time now, so you'll never survive here."

"I'm sorry," David said. "I just want you so much."

"Yeah," Min said. "Do that again and I'll Mace you. Now get out."

"Promise me you won't see Cal Morrisey again," David said, and Elvis lowered his head on the back of the couch and growled.

"No, David, I will not promise you anything." Min pointed to the door. "Out or I get a restraining order."

"At least think about it," David said.

"No," Min said and pushed him out the door. When she had it shut behind him, she looked at Elvis, now stretched out on the back of the couch, his head close to the stereo he loved. He batted the stereo with his paw until he connected with the ON button, and "Heartbreak Hotel" boomed out of the speakers.

"Turn that down," Min said and then remembered she was talking to a cat. She went over and moved the volume lever down. "That was weird, Elvis."

Elvis patted the UP button over and over again until "Love Me Tender" came on.

"Well, it could be worse," Min said, looking at him sprawled on the back of her couch. "You could like music from Julia Roberts movies."

Elvis's tail began to twitch to the music, and Min gave up and went to get a Band-Aid.

Cal didn't call Tuesday either, and Min was congratulating herself that night that she was finally free of him and feeling lousy about it when somebody knocked on her door. She stirred her chicken marsala one more time and went to answer it, picking up her Mace on the way. After forty-eight hours and no phone call, she was hoping it was a mugger so she could release some tension. But when she opened the door, Cal was leaning in the doorway, holding the usual sack from Emilio's and another, smaller shopping bag, looking more tired than she'd ever seen him. His shirt collar was open, his tie ends hanging down, his shirtsleeves were rolled up, and he was rumpled and sloppy and the sexiest thing she'd ever seen, and her heart lurched sideways just because she was so damn glad he was there.

He said, "Hi," and saw the Mace. "You can just say no," he said, and she opened the door wider, and he came in and kissed her on the forehead. She leaned into him because he looked so solid and because she was so glad to see him and then, on an impulse, she stretched up and kissed him gently, a hello-how-are-you kiss that felt like exactly the right thing to do.

When she pulled back, Cal looked stunned.

"What?" she said. "That was a friendly kiss."

He shook his head and closed the door behind him with his shoulder.

"That was . . . nice. Here." He handed her the small shopping bag. "I'm courting. You get gifts."

Min took the bag and felt deflated. "Bad kiss? Did I do it wrong?"

"No." He grinned tiredly at her. "You couldn't possibly do it wrong." Then his smile faded. "That's just the first time."

"Oh, please," Min said. "We've been kissing for days."

"I've been kissing you for days," Cal said, tossing his jacket on the armchair as he went to put Emilio's bag on the table. "That's the first time you've kissed me. What smells so good?"

"Chicken marsala," Min said. "I think I got it. What do you mean, that's the first time? I . . ." Her voice trailed off as she thought about it. He was right. He always kissed her.

"Don't worry about it," Cal said as he came back to her. "So—"

Min dropped the shopping bag and went up on her toes and kissed him again, this time giving it everything she had. The rush made her dizzy, and she grabbed his shirt to steady herself, and he held her, kissing her back until she was hot and trembling.

"That's two," Cal said, breathlessly. "Not that I'm counting."

"There should have been more," Min said, trying to get her breath back. "I mean, we're not doing this anymore, but I shouldn't have made you do all the work."

"I didn't mind," Cal said, pulling her closer, and she knew she should pull back but she didn't want to because he felt so damn good against her. "Although I'm liking this."

"I just didn't want you to get the wrong idea," Min said, putting her forehead against his chest.

"Which would be what?"

She felt him kiss the top of her head again, and smiled. "That I wanted, you know, more."

"Right," Cal said. "Just friends. You bet. Kiss me again."

Min grinned and lifted her head. "It doesn't count if you tell me to."

"It always counts," Cal said and kissed her, and she let herself fall into him until she lost track of time and everything but the way he felt wrapped around her. Then he came up for air and said, "I may be getting the wrong idea."

"No," Min said, backing away. "Don't do that. Forget any of that happened." She held up the Mace can. "I have Mace."

"Right," he said and let go of her to collapse onto the couch. "Elvis, old buddy, how are you doing?" He reached up to scratch Elvis behind the ears and Min almost said, "Don't," remembering what had happened to David. But Elvis flattened his head so Cal could get closer and purred his appreciation. "You know, this is a nice cat."

"I know." Min tried to calm her pounding heart as Elvis rolled to his feet. "I don't know how I ever lived without him." She picked up the bag she'd dropped and went to sit next to Cal on the couch. "So. I've heard about this," she said, pulling open the bag. "You're going to give me something I didn't even know I needed."

"What do you mean, you heard?" Cal said, but Min was pulling out a shoe box and ignored him.

"I have very specific tastes in shoes," she said, shaking her head. "The possibilities for disaster here are huge."

"I live on the edge," Cal said.

Min opened the box. Inside were mules with her favorite French heel, but they were covered in white fur. "What the hell?" she said but when she pulled them out, she saw the bunny faces on the furry insteps. "You got me *bunny slippers?*" she said, holding them up. The bunnies looked back her, dopey and sweet. "*Open-toed bunny slippers?* These are *incredible.*"

"I know," Cal said, scratching Elvis's stomach now. "There's music in there, too."

"Let me guess," Min said, reaching in the bag again. "Elvis Costello." She pulled out the CD and read the title: "Elvis Presley, Fifty Greatest Love Songs." She looked at Cal. "You got me Elvis *Presley.*"

"It's what you like," Cal said, as the cat rolled away from him. "Why would I get you what I like?"

"Boy, you *are* good at this," Min said, looking back at the bunnies. "I *love* these shoes."

"Every woman needs bunny slippers," Cal said, taking one of them. "Especially women with toes like yours." He reached down and picked up her foot and stripped her sweat sock off, and Min wiggled her suddenly cool, pink-tipped toes at him. "Very hot toes, Minnie," he said, rubbing his thumb along the bottom of her foot.

"Ticklish," Min said, trying to pull her foot back, but he slipped the shoe on before she could move, and she closed her eyes and sighed at how good the fur lining felt on her skin. "Oh, lovely," she said and then looked down at her foot again, and wiggled her toes under the bunny's mouth. "These are perfect."

"I know," Cal said, and let go of her foot.

Min stripped her other sock off and slid into the other bunny slipper. "You're a genius at this. I'll wait to play the CD when you're gone so you don't have to suffer."

"I like Elvis," Cal began, but Elvis the cat had crept his way down the chair arm, and now he pushed something off the sewing machine table at the end of the couch.

"Hey." Cal leaned out to retrieve it. "Careful, cat, you'll—" He stopped as he picked it up. "Why do you have a statue of the Eiffel Tower?"

"Somebody brought me an Eiffel Tower snow globe last night," Min said, watching her toes wiggle under the bunnies' chins. "Elvis broke it."

"Good for Elvis." Cal handed her the tower and she dropped it in the wastebasket and went back to looking at her bunnies. "So who was clueless enough to give you a snow globe without people in it? Greg?"

"No," Min said cheerfully as she saw trouble loom. "You know what? I think I made the chicken right." She stood up. The slippers felt wonderful. "These fit *perfectly*."

"Minerva," Cal said. "You're keeping something from me."

"Many things," Min said, and went out to the kitchen, concentrating on the way the slippers tapped on her hardwood floor. "I may never take these shoes off again."

Behind her, "Love Me Tender" began to play, and Cal said from the couch, "The cat knows how to turn on the stereo?"

"He knows the power button," she called back. "And replay, unfortunately. I heard 'Love Me Tender' four times last night before I took the CD out." She stirred the chicken one more time, tasted it, and thought, *I really think this is it.* She smiled to herself and tasted it again to make sure before she called back, "I think you should taste this."

"I will," Cal said from behind her. "First tell me who this belongs to."

She turned and saw him holding up David's tie.

"Where'd you get that?" she said.

"Elvis was playing with it," Cal said.

She took it from him and dropped it in the kitchen trash. "It's none of your business who that belongs to."

"I know," Cal said.

"You can't be jealous," Min said.

"And yet, much to my own disgust, I am," he said, folding his arms. "All right, I have no business asking."

"This is true," Min said.

"So who was it?"

She leaned against the stove and realized she was glad he was jealous. *You're a mess*, she told herself.

"Minnie," Cal said.

"My ex-boyfriend. He dropped by and proposed."

"He did?" Cal said calmly, but his jaw tightened.

"Yes, he did," Min said, enjoying herself. "He brought the paperweight because we were going to honeymoon in Paris."

"Thoughtful of him," Cal said, biting off the words.

"Not really." Min straightened. "I don't want to honeymoon in Paris."

"Did you tell him that?"

"No," Min said, her patience at an end. "I told him I didn't want to get married, and then I kicked him out."

"Uh huh," Cal said.

"That's it," Min said. "He's gone."

"No, he's not," Cal said.

"I assure you—"

"He left his tie, Min."

"So?"

"So he left it so he could come back for it."

"That's . . ." Min thought about it. ". . . entirely possible."

"Give me the tie," Cal said.

"Why?" Min said, exasperated.

"So I can messenger it back to the son of a bitch tomorrow," Cal said. "Who is he?"

"Have you lost your only mind?"

Cal closed his eyes. "Yes."

"There we go," Min said. "The first step in solving your problem is admitting you have one."

"Don't see him anymore," Cal said, making it a request, not an order.

"I won't," Min said. "I don't even like him much."

"Can I return the tie, please?" Cal said, holding out his hand.

Min fished it out of the trash. "Here. His name is David Fisk. He runs a soft—" She stopped at the look on Cal's face. "What?"

"Your ex is David Fisk?" Cal said, and Min remembered the bet.

"Yes," she said. "Do you know him?"

"Yes," Cal said. "He's —" He stopped and she waited. "He's a client."

"Oh," Min said, and thought, *The bet, he's not going to tell me about the bet. Damn it.*

Cal crumpled up the tie. "I'll send it back to him. How's the chicken?"

"I think it's excellent," Min said, feeling depressed as Elvis sang about true love.

"It looks great." Cal picked up a spoon from the dish drainer and scooped up some sauce. He tasted it and Min waited, caring way too much about what he thought. "Damn, that's good," he said, looking at her with surprise. "I think that's better than Emilio's. Did you do something different?"

"Yes," Min said. "But that's my secret. You have secrets, I have secrets."

"I don't have secrets," Cal said.

"Dinner," Min said and went to set the table as "Love Me Tender" began again.

They talked through dinner and the dishes, and Min tried not to enjoy it, tried to remember the bet, but it was so comfortable being with him that she kept forgetting. Somehow he'd slipped into her life and under her skin, and she was happy about that even though she knew that was his plan. *I don't have a plan*, she thought, and that was so good that she gave up and smiled at him and when he left, she kissed him good night without reservation, and he leaned in the doorway and said, "Minnie, about this friends thing," and she pushed him out gently and closed the door to keep from saying, "I hate that, forget that, make love to me."

Because that, she told herself as she went back to Elvis, would be bad.

At seven Wednesday night, David was in his shirtsleeves, trying to find two shipments that had gone astray and thinking about how to get to Min, who'd once brought him a Caesar salad (no croutons), when his office door banged open and Cynthie stood here in another tailored suit, this one pink.

"Oh good, it's you," he said flatly.

"They're still dating." Cynthie came in and closed the door. "You were supposed to make your move."

"I did," David said. "She said no. And I left the tie but Cal messengered it back to me so that didn't work. But she also said she wasn't going to sleep with him, so I'm thinking if we wait—"

"Well, wait for this. He took her home to meet his mother."

David sat up straighter as the cold hit his spine. "What?"

"He took her home to meet his mother," Cynthie said again. "It took me seven months to get Cal to take me home to his parents. She did it in *three weeks.* David, *I'm losing him.*"

"His mother," David said, and thought, *The bastard. He'll do anything to win that bet. "Fuck."* He looked up, startled that he'd said it out loud. "Sorry."

"No," Cynthie said, stopping in front of him. "You are not sorry. You are *mad.*"

"Yeah, I am." David thought about Cal Morrisey and got madder. Somebody should stop guys like him. He stood up. "So what am I supposed to do about it?"

"Fight for her," Cynthie said. "She's your girlfriend. Get her back."

"I tried," David said, losing some steam. "She likes Cal."

"You are the most *passive* son of a bitch," Cynthie said. "No wonder she never slept with you. You probably never asked her."

"Thank you," David said. "That's great coming from somebody who got turned down after putting out for nine months. Don't see that being aggressive worked for you, sweetheart. Maybe you're the one with the heat problem."

"Listen, you," Cynthie said. "I have a perfect body and I am *great* in bed."

"You know, I doubt it," David said, coming around his desk. "Don't bother to open your jacket again. I already saw that commercial."

Cynthie gaped at him. "You *bastard.*"

"Well, hell, Cynthie, what do you expect? You come in here screaming at me and calling me names because your ex took the woman I love home to meet his mother. If you want to stop it, go get him. Unbutton your jacket at *him*." David stopped and closed his eyes. "Look, I'm tired, I'm miserable, and I haven't had sex in three months. Take your perfect body back to the guy who was having perfect sex with you. I have work to do."

When she didn't say anything, he opened his eyes. She was frowning at him.

"They're not sleeping together," Cynthie said.

"I know," David said. "So nobody's getting any. Great. Go away."

"You can tell by the way they act together," she said, and he stopped. "I was just at The Long Shot. Min was there with Cal. I watched them. They haven't done it. You can tell, people touch differently when they've had sex, they relax, they . . ." Cynthie took a step closer. "They haven't done it. We can still get them back. And I know a great aphrodisiac."

"Right," David said. "You unbutton your jacket."

"No," Cynthie said, so close now she was almost touching him. "Pain. If joy doesn't work, try pain. Like jealousy. It's a physiological cue, a very powerful one. They're going to Emilio's now, I heard them say so. We're going to go."

David stepped back and bumped into his desk. "Cynthie, I don't—"

"But first," Cynthie said. "We're going to have sex."

David froze.

"It's been three months for me, too," Cynthie said. "So we are going to have incredible, athletic, sweaty sex right here, and then we're going to go to dinner. And Cal will know. People look different when they've just had sex."

David swallowed. "Well, thank you, but I don't think it's going to—"

Cynthie unbuttoned her jacket, revealing a shiny pink bra that was so sheer it was probably illegal in several states.

"—accomplish anything beyond making us both feel foolish—"

She dropped her jacket to the floor and unzipped her skirt.

"—after the shallow physical thrill—"

Her skirt slid down her remarkable legs, and David was left looking at the most perfect body he'd ever seen in the flesh.

"—subsides," he finished lamely.

She walked up to him. "You're not going to say no to me."

"I guess not," David said and let her drag him to the floor.

It was odd having Diana with her, Min realized when they were in The Long Shot. Like two different worlds colliding. Di looked around at everything with new eyes, smiled her delight at Shanna, laughed at everything Tony said, watched Cal with approval, and asked where Liza was, as if she wanted the complete cast of Min's life there.

"Working," Tony said. "She's decided that she's going to revamp Emilio's night shift first and save lunch for later. I haven't seen her since she started."

"We should go to Emilio's," Roger said. "That way you could see Liza."

"I don't want—" Tony said, but Min said, "You know, that's a good idea. I'm hungry and Di's never been there," and they migrated the two blocks to Emilio's.

"These guys are so great," Di whispered to her. "I didn't know you had such a great group."

"Well, I don't know that I have a group," Min said and then realized that Di was right, that she was as relaxed with Tony as she was with Cal and that she'd long ago accepted Roger as the honorary brother-in-law that Bonnie was about to make him.

Liza met them at the door, in a little black dress that looked like a million dollars but probably cost her ten in a thrift store somewhere. "Welcome to Emilio's," she said, winking at Di. "You're going to love it here."

"I don't know," Cal said, sotto voce from behind Min and Di. "I heard the service was Tart."

Di elbowed Min, and said, "You weren't supposed to tell anybody," and then Cal grinned at her and she laughed.

"Charm Boy," Min said.

Brian showed up, impeccably dressed, as Liza led them to the table by the window. "Hello," he said. "I'm Brian, and I'll be your server tonight."

"*Brian?*" Cal said.

"Mr. Morrisey," Brian said, glaring at him.

"Don't let the consumers get you down, Brian," Liza said, putting her hand on his arm. "Remember, you're better than they are."

"Yes, Liza," Brian said, adoration oozing from his pores.

"Oh, God," Cal said.

"You have my permission to be rude to Mr. Morrisey," Liza told Brian.

"Good," Brian said, and slapped Cal on the back of the head with the menu, making Di laugh again.

"What is this place?" she said, looking around.

"Home," Cal said, and Min nodded, seeing her life through Di's eyes. It was a damn good life but somehow it had gotten tangled up in Cal's. *What am I going to do when he leaves?* The thought chilled her, that she'd let things get this far, that she was in this much danger, and she stayed silent through most of dinner, listening to Diana chatter on with everybody else, watching Cal, his tie loosened and his sleeves rolled up, completely at home and smiling at her. He looked solid sitting there, not like David's fashionable leanness or Greg's gym-toned obviousness, but broad and strong and real and infinitely desirable. *I could say yes to him before he goes,* she thought and felt a wave of heat roll over her, and even though she knew she'd never do it, she let herself have one brief fantasy of falling back with his solid weight on top of her, his hands hot on her again, her arms wrapped around the broad bulk of him, one visceral moment that made her half close her eyes and bite her lip, and when she shook it off, he was watching her, not smiling anymore.

"Come here and tell me what you're thinking, Minerva," he said, leaning toward her.

"I don't think so, Calvin," she said, regrouping.

"*Hel*-lo," Tony said, and the rest of the table looked where he was looking.

David and Cynthie had come in, looking flushed. Brian gestured them to a table like a pro, and David put his hand on Cynthie's lower back as they followed. Cynthie didn't seem to mind.

"Why don't they just wear T-shirts that say, 'We did it'?" Tony said.

"Shhh," Cal said. "Don't ruin this beautiful moment."

Min looked at him. "You don't mind?"

"Why would I?" Cal said.

"Well, she . . ." Min let the word trail off.

"Is history," Cal said.

"Okay," Min said, trying very hard not to feel glad about that.

"How about David?" Cal said.

"Not even history," Min said. "The man brought me an Eiffel Tower snow globe, for heaven's sake."

"We should send them a nice bottle of wine," Cal said.

"Why?" Tony said.

"So they'll get drunk and go back to bed," Cal said. He caught Liza frowning down at him and said, "What now?"

"Nothing," Liza said. "I'm just thinking."

"Well, think about somebody else," Cal said. "Think about Tony."

"I have Tony figured out," Liza said. "You, however, are a mystery."

"I'm a mystery," Tony said, wounded.

"Want to have sex tonight?" Liza said.

"Yes," Tony said.

"No mystery," Liza said, and turned back to Cal. "Do you have any weaknesses?"

"Min," Cal said, smiling at Min.

Liza closed her eyes in disgust. "I'm trying to think if I've ever seen you caught off guard."

"Well, there was the time Bentley hit me with the ball," Cal said.

"I know." Liza straightened behind Cal's chair. "Singing. You're not shy but you won't sing. Why is that?"

"Lousy voice," Cal said.

Liza looked at Tony. "True?"

"Nope," Tony said. "Quit hassling him."

"You take care of your friends, I'll take care of mine," Liza said to him and turned back to Cal. "So why not?"

"Stage fright," Cal said. "I can't perform in public. Too self-conscious."

"You?" Liza said. "I would never have guessed it." She folded her arms. "So what would it take to get you to sing?"

"A gun pointed at my head," Cal said.

"*Liza*," Min said, seeing a light in Liza's eyes that boded no good for anyone. "Why are you pushing this?"

"Here's the deal," Liza said, leaning over Cal's shoulder, her mouth close to his ear. "You sing right now, here, in front of everybody—"

"No," Cal said.

"—and I will never say or do another thing to keep you away from Min."

Cal sat very still for a minute, and then he said to Min, "Does she keep her deals?"

"Of course she does," Min said. "Which doesn't mean—"

Cal looked up at Liza. "What do you want to hear?"

"Oh, I'll let you pick," Liza said, straightening. "That should be interesting all by itself."

"Why are you doing this?" Min said to Liza, exasperated.

"Because up until now, he's had it easy," Liza said, still watching Cal. "I want to see if he'll break a sweat for you."

"It hasn't been all that easy," Cal said.

"You don't have to do this," Min said to Cal. "I mean it."

"Why?" Cal said. "Men have been singing to women for centuries. It's right up there with giving them jewelry."

"Buy me a nice keychain," Min said.

He put his hand on the back of her chair and leaned forward. "Pay attention, Minnie, because you'll never hear me do this again."

"Cal," she said, but then he began to sing "Love Me Tender," his snarky grin in place as he oversold the song, deepening his voice in a not-bad Elvis impression.

"Not *Elvis*," Tony groaned, and Roger shook his head and laughed at the ceiling, but Min lost her breath because Cal's voice was beautiful and because, after the first verse, his grin faded, and he began to sing it for real. All other sound stopped, and it was just the two of them as he looked into her eyes and asked her to love him, and she felt dizzy because he meant it, whatever else was going on, whatever else was happening between them, this was real. Even if it was just for this moment, *and it's just for this moment*, it was real, and he loved her, and it was better than anything she could have dreamed of, and she felt her heart ache, felt it clench in her chest because she loved him so much she couldn't stand it. *Don't do this to me*, she thought as he sang, *don't break my heart, I don't deserve this, please don't*, and when he finished, perfectly on key with "I love you, and I always will," the silence around them was deafening. *Oh, God*, Min thought, and looked in his eyes and saw the same surprise there, and regret and confusion, and she thought, *It wasn't him, it's this* thing *that's haunting us, he didn't mean it.*

Then Diana said, "Wow," and Liza said, "All right, I am impressed," and Min grabbed her purse and walked out of the restaurant.

 Chapter
Twelve

M in let the restaurant door bang behind her and crossed the sidewalk, blind with the need to save herself. She stepped off the curb and a horn blared and somebody yanked her back from the street, and she turned and barged into Cal.

"I'm sorry," he said, holding on to her. "Whatever it was that I did—"

"You're going to hurt me," she said, breathless.

"What?" he said, looking appalled. "*No.* I'd never—"

"You're going to break my heart," Min said, taking a breath like a sob. "I'm going to love you, and you're going to leave, you always do, it's what you do, and I don't think I can get over you, if I ever let go and love you, I think it'll be forever because it's so deep, it already hurts just the little bit I let myself—"

"Min, I'd *never* hurt you," Cal said.

"Not on purpose," Min said. "But you have the right to leave. You've never promised me you'd stay. That's the way it always is. You're wonderful, you know us, and we love you, and you leave. I can't do that. I could tell myself that David was an idiot who didn't know me, but you know *me.*"

"Min, wait," Cal said, trying to put his arms around her.

"*No,*" Min said, slipping away. "Nobody in my life has ever known me the way you do. Nobody in my life has ever made me feel as good as you do. You know me, you know everything about me, and when you leave me, you're going to be leaving the real me, the me nobody else has ever seen, that's who you're going to be rejecting."

"What makes you so sure I'm going to leave you?" Cal said, his voice sharp.

"Because that's *what you do.* You *always leave.* Are you going to promise me right now that you'll stay forever?"

"I've known you three weeks," Cal said. "That'd be a little impulsive, don't you think?"

"*Yes,*" Min said. "So why the full court press? Why the perfect shoes and the perfect song and . . ." She shook her head, helpless. "I *told you* we should start as friends, *I told you*—"

"You want more than friends," Cal said flatly. "That's the dumbest line you ever pulled on me."

"Look, I'm not *ready* for you," Min said. "I'm not *prepared.* I don't have any defenses when you're around. I make these plans and I mean it, I really do, and then I kiss you because I'm crazy about you which would be fine if I didn't fall in love with you but there that is, just standing there, and you know it, you know you've got me." She stopped because she was sounding hysterical.

"All right," Cal said, setting his jaw. "Maybe we—"

"I need to go home," Min said.

"All right," Cal said again. "We can—"

"*No,*" Min said. "Diana will be out to find me in a minute and she'll walk me. We'll walk each other."

"Min," Cal said.

"I just wasn't expecting that song," Min said. "Not the way you sang it."

"Neither was I," Cal said grimly.

"I know," Min said. "I could see it in your eyes. You didn't mean it."

"Of course I meant it," Cal snapped, as Diana came out into the street. "I just didn't know I meant it until I sang it. Fucking Elvis and his love songs."

"Well, that's the thing about Elvis," Min said, finally losing her temper. "You make all the fun you want of the fried bananas and the sequined jumpsuits, but he never lied when he sang, he always meant it. There weren't any damn secrets—"

"*What* secrets?" Cal said.

"—and there weren't any damn lies. So the next time you want to snow somebody, *don't channel Elvis.*"

Min turned away and started off down the street, making her heels click on the pavement like a backbeat.

"You know, all I wanted was a little *peace and quiet,*" Cal yelled after her. "But no, I had to get *you.*"

Diana hurried behind her to catch up.

"Why are you upset?" Diana said when she was beside her. She looked back over her shoulder at Cal. "That was the most romantic thing I've ever heard."

"I know," Min said and walked faster.

"What's *wrong?*" Diana said.

Min stopped. "I'll tell you if you tell me what's wrong with you and Greg."

Diana bit her lip. "You first."

"The first night Cal picked me up?" Min said.

Di nodded.

"He did it because David bet him ten bucks he couldn't get me into bed in a month," Min said.

"No, he didn't," Diana said, positive. "He wouldn't do that."

"I heard him, Di," Min said. "He did it. And I know there's more there now, but I've only known him three weeks, and I'm already lost whenever he's around, and it's just too big a gamble. He's just . . . he leaves women all the time. Greg was right about that. I don't want to be in a place where I'll die if he leaves me because he's going to leave me." She felt tears start and blinked them back. "And then the son of a bitch sings to me like that, and I just . . . He's just too . . ."

"Dangerous," Di said. "That's why I picked Greg. I knew he'd never be dangerous."

"What happened?" Min said.

"I don't think he wants to get married anymore," Di said, and Min heard the tears in her voice. "I asked him, I told him if he wasn't ready we could postpone it, but he keeps saying he's ready, he wants to, and I think it's just because he can't stand disappointing everybody but he's—"

"What are you guys doing?" Tony said, coming up out of the dark and scaring them both into shrieks. "Standing around waiting to get mugged?"

"And now our wait is over?" Min said, trying to get her breath back.

"Cal sent me," Tony said. "He doesn't like you walking home alone. So you get me."

"You don't have to," Min said.

"Are you kidding? I'm with two hot women in the dark," Tony said. "By the time I'm finished retelling this in my head, it's going to be phenomenal."

"Is he joking?" Di said to Min.

"I don't think so," Min said. "Could you picture me about twenty pounds lighter in this fantasy?"

"No," Tony said. "I'm picturing you just the way you are, babe. Don't tell Cal or he'll break my teeth."

"Your teeth are safe," Min said, and began to walk again.

"So what would we be doing in this fantasy?" Di said to Tony as they fell into step beside Min.

"Well, first we'd read a good book because I know that classy women like you go for guys who read," Tony said.

Min took his arm. "Thank you for walking us home."

"Anything for you, kid," Tony said, patting her hand, and then he went on with his fantasy, and Min held on to him and tried not to think about what she was walking away from.

Back in the restaurant, David looked at Cynthie triumphantly and said, "We did that."

"No," Cynthie said, her face white. "That wasn't us."

"Min was jealous," David said, feeling better than he had in weeks. "And then Cal made a fool of himself with that stupid song and embarrassed her. You were right about us . . ." He waved his hand and added silently, . . . *having the best sex in the history of the world. God, I'm good.*

"I wish that were true," Cynthie said, still staring at the door.

"You know they're out there fighting," David said. "Why aren't you happy?"

"There's a certain kind of fight that is . . . a relationship adjustment," Cynthie said, her voice dull. "You fight, and then reconcile and move closer together. And then fight again, and reconcile. Each time there's a compromise. Each time you grow closer."

"Fighting is good?" David said. "That's nonsense."

"What's the best kind of sex there is, David?" Cynthie said. "Make-up sex. It's because you've come back even closer. If it's the right kind of fight. You're going to have to move fast if she truly is upset with him."

"I'll call her tomorrow," David promised. "She's emotional right now. Better to let her calm down."

Cynthie looked back at the door. "All right. Be careful."

"Stop it," David said, covering her hand with his. "We won."

Cynthie shook her head. "Nobody won tonight."

Later that night, after Min and Diana had folded two hundred cake boxes and talked about the wedding but not Greg or Cal, Diana went to bed, and Min sat alone on the couch with Elvis in her lap, and tried to figure out where she'd gone wrong. Maybe if she hadn't said yes to that picnic in the park, if she hadn't kissed him back, if he hadn't kissed her at all, if she hadn't met Harry. Definitely before she met Harry. Maybe if she hadn't thought she was so damn smart that she could play David and Cal in the beginning. Maybe if she'd had enough sense not to cross the damn bar in the first place, if she'd looked at him and known nothing good could come of him and had never overheard that damn bet. It was hard to pinpoint exactly where she'd moved past reckless and into insanity, but she kept thinking if she could just figure out where she'd gone wrong, she'd understand what happened, and then she'd be done with it—

Somebody knocked on the door, and when Min opened it, Bonnie was standing there in her chenille robe holding a teapot. "I made cocoa," she said, and Min felt the tears start. "Oh, baby," Bonnie said and came in, putting her arm around Min, balancing the cocoa pot in her other hand. "Come on. We just need to talk about it."

"I thought I was so smart," Min said, fighting to keep her voice steady. She took a shuddery breath. "I kept thinking I had it all under control."

"I thought you did pretty well," Bonnie said, putting the cocoa pot down on the sewing machine table. She took a cup out of each pocket, and Min laughed at her through her tears.

"Where's Roger?" Min said. "I don't—"

"He's asleep downstairs," Bonnie said, picking up the pot. "He's worried about you, but it gets to be midnight and he clonks right out for a solid eight hours."

Min laughed again and then sniffed. "If I'd had any brains, I'd have grabbed Roger that first night."

"Roger would bore you to tears," Bonnie said, handing her a filled cup. "Just like I'd have shoved Cal under a bus by now."

"You would have?" Min sniffed again.

"Oh, please, that master of the universe act?" Bonnie said. "That's one scared man you've got there. I don't have the time for that. I want kids, I don't want to marry one."

"He's a good guy, Bon." Min sipped her cocoa and began to feel better.

"I know," Bonnie said. "And some day he'll grow up and be a good man. In the meantime, he broke your heart so I'm mad at him."

"No, he didn't," Min said. "He tried not to be with me."

"No, he didn't." Bonnie sat down next to her on the couch with her own cup. "He had every opportunity in the world to get away from you and he passed up every one of them to be with you."

"That's because he couldn't charm me," Min said. "It wasn't—"

"Oh, stop being such a baby," Bonnie said, and Min jerked her head up and startled Elvis. "Well, listen to yourself. You're miserable, but it's not his fault and it's not your fault. Well, screw that."

"*Bonnie,*" Min said, scandalized.

"What do you want, Min?" Bonnie said. "If life were a fairy tale, if there truly was a happy ending, what would you want?"

"I'd want Cal," Min said, feeling ashamed even as she said it. "I know that's—"

"Don't," Bonnie said, holding up her hand. "Why do you want him?"

"Oh, because he was *fun*," Min said, smiling as she blinked the tears away because she was so shallow. "He was so much fun, Bonnie. And he made me feel wonderful. I was never fat when I was with Cal."

"You're never fat when you're with Liza and me," Bonnie said.

"I know," Min said. "He was almost like you except I couldn't trust him and he really turned me on."

"Maybe that's why he turned you on," Bonnie said. "Somebody you couldn't handle."

"Yeah." Min let her head drop back against the couch. "He was exciting. I never knew what was coming next. And neither did he. We fed off each other. What dummies we were."

"I wouldn't rush to use the past tense," Bonnie said. "So back to the fairy tale. Tell me your happily ever after."

"I don't have one," Min said. "Which is why I'll never get one."

"Mine," Bonnie said, "is that I marry Roger, and we have four kids. We live in a nice house in one of the suburbs with good schools, but not one where everybody wears plaid."

"Makes sense," Min said, and sipped her cocoa again.

"I'm a stay-at-home mom," Bonnie said, "but I do keep a few clients, my favorite clients, and I watch their portfolios like a hawk so I don't lose my edge. And word gets out, and as the kids get older, I add to my client list because there are so many people who are dying to get me."

"That's not a fairy tale," Min said, putting her cocoa cup down. "That can all happen."

"And our house," Bonnie said, as if she hadn't heard, "becomes the place everybody comes home to, for the holidays and everybody's birthdays, everybody comes to us. And we have these big dinners and everybody sits around the table and we're family by choice. And you and Liza and Cal and Tony are all godparents to our kids, and every time there's a big school thing, you all come out and cheer our kids on—"

"I'll be there," Min said, trying not cry.

"—and none of us will ever be alone because we'll have each other," Bonnie said. "You're going to like my grandchildren, Min. We're going to take them shoe shopping."

"Oh, *Bonnie*," Min said and put her head down on the couch cushion and howled, while Bonnie stroked her hair and drank her chocolate.

When Min had subsided to a few gasping, shuddering sobs, Bonnie said calmly, "Now you."

"I *can't*," Min said.

"Well, you're gonna," Bonnie said. "It starts with Cal, right?"

"Why?" Min sat up and wiped her face with the back of her hand. "Why does it always have to start with some guy?"

"Because it's a fairy tale," Bonnie said. "It all starts with the prince. Or if you're Shanna, with the princess, but still. It starts with the big risk. You're all alone sitting on a tuffet, on in your case, an Aeron, and this guy rides up and there it is, your whole future right there before you—"

"What if he's the wrong one?" Min said. "Accepting for the moment, which I don't, that the whole thing starts with the prince, how do you tell the prince from—"

"The beast?" Bonnie said. "Honey, they're all beasts."

"Roger isn't," Min said.

"Oh, please," Bonnie said. "He's down there snoring like a bear now," and Min laughed in spite of her tears. "You really think Cal's a mistake?"

Min swallowed. "Well, logically—"

"Do not make me dump my cocoa on you," Bonnie said.

"I don't have anything else to go on," Min said. "How am I supposed to know?"

"Tell me your fairy tale," Bonnie said. "It's just between you and me, nobody else will ever know. If you could have anything you wanted, no explanations, no logic, just anything you—"

"Cal," Min said. "I know that's stup—"

"Stop it," Bonnie said. "God, you can't even dream without qualifiers. Tell me your fairy tale."

Min felt the tears start again, and she gathered Elvis up and petted him to distract herself. "It's Cal. And he loves me, so much that he can't stand it, as much as I love him. And, uh," she gulped back tears, "we, uh, we find this great house, here in the city, maybe on this street, one of the old bungalows like the one my grandma used to live in. I'd like that. With a yard so Elvis could stalk things. And maybe a dog, because I like dogs."

Bonnie nodded, and Min sniffed again.

"And I keep working because I like my work, and so does Cal because he loves what he does." She sighed. "And sometimes he calls me up and says, 'Minnie, I've been thinking about you, meet me at home in twenty minutes' and I do and we make love and it's wonderful, right in the middle of the day. . . ." She stopped to sniff and Bonnie nodded.

"And sometimes we go to Emilio's, we meet all you guys at Emilio's, like every Wednesday, we all meet, and we laugh and catch up on what's happening, and when you and Roger have your kids, Emilio adds more tables, and he and his wife and kids eat, too, and Brian serves us, and sometimes we go out to your house . . ."

Bonnie smiled and nodded.

". . . and the guys watch the game and hoot and moan, and you and I and Liza and Emilio's wife sit out in the kitchen and eat chocolate and talk about all the things we've done and they've done and laugh. . . ." Min took another deep breath and realized she was still crying.

"And then Cal and I go home," she said, her voice breaking, "and it's just the two of us, and we laugh some more and hold each other and eat and make love and watch dumb movies and just . . . be with each other. We just feel good because we're with each other." She wiped her eyes again. "That's all I'd need. The two of us, talking and cooking and laughing. It's so simple."

She took a deep shuddering breath and met Bonnie's eyes. "I can have that, can't I?"

"Yes," Bonnie said.

"But only if Cal is who I need him to be," Min said.

Bonnie nodded.

"So I just have to trust that he's who I think he is and not who he thinks he is," Min said.

"Big gamble," Bonnie said.

"Do you ever wonder what happened after the happily ever after?" Min said. "After the wedding was over and the townspeople went home, and they finished opening all the stuff that was monogrammed with a gold crown? Because the story's over then. All the questing and the courting and the trauma. From then on it's just sitting around the castle, polishing all the toasters they got for wedding gifts."

"That would pretty much depend on the prince," Bonnie said. "I can see David polishing a lot of toasters."

Min laughed in spite of herself.

"But Tony would hot wire them all together and calibrate them so they'd shoot toast at varying intervals," Bonnie said and Min laughed harder.

"And Cal would bet on it," Min said, smiling and crying at the same time now, "but only after he'd seen Tony shoot the toasters a thousand times and calculated the odds."

"And Roger would put out stakes and yellow tape so that nobody got hit by flying bread," Bonnie said with affection.

"And Liza would figure out how to make the whole thing pay," Min said. "And you'd make sure Tony bought the bread at cost and invested the profits wisely."

"And you'd look at the whole thing and gauge the risk and tell us what we'd missed," Bonnie said.

"You know this toaster thing might be worth looking into," Min said. "Tony's nuts, but his ideas are always good."

Bonnie nodded.

Min bit her lip and swallowed more tears. "I want the fairy tale."

"Okay," Bonnie said. "Now all you have to do is figure out how."

"Yeah," Min said. "I can do that. I just have to think it out." She looked at Bonnie. "Are you going to dump cocoa on me?"

"No," Bonnie said. "The only illogical thing you have to do is believe. After that, you need brains."

"Oh, good," Min said. "Brains, I got. Leap of faith, taken. Plan, still in the works."

Bonnie nodded again. "Can you sleep now?"

"Uh huh," Min said, tearing up again. "Why can't I stop crying?"

"When was the last time you cried?" Bonnie said.

"I can't remember," Min said.

"When was the last time you cared enough to cry?" Bonnie said.

"I can't remember that, either," Min said, appalled.

"So you've got some catching up to do," Bonnie said, standing up. "I have to go downstairs and sleep with a bear."

Min gave her a watery grin. "Do not expect me to feel sorry for you because you've got Roger."

"I don't," Bonnie said airily. "I expect you to envy me beyond measure."

"I do," Min said, thinking of the man she'd left enraged in the moonlight. "But I want Cal."

Cal didn't call, and that was all right, Min told herself, because she'd see him at the rehearsal dinner since he hadn't called to cancel, plus she didn't have time to think about him with the wedding only four days away, especially since she found herself fielding a dozen calls a day from her increasingly frantic sister, and anyway she was better off without him as a distraction.

She missed him.

Sunday, she kept telling herself, *on Sunday this will all be over, Diana will be married, and I can fix my own life then.* The only part she wasn't sure about was the "Diana will be married," but since Diana was insistent that her romance was a fairy tale, there wasn't much Min could do besides hold her hand, make supportive noises, and listen. So she propped Diana up, went to the If Dinner on Thursday night and brought the rest of the hand-packed quarts of ice cream that Cal had given her, told Liza there was no need to apologize for making Cal sing since their fight had been inevitable, and tried to figure out a way to make things right without actually talking to him or seeing him.

But on Saturday morning, she had to go to baseball for Harry, so she put on her newest sandals—clear plastic mules with French heels and cherries on the toes—and got to the park a couple of minutes after the game started. She found a seat to one side, trying to stay inconspicuous and wave to Harry at the same time, but Bink saw her and motioned her up. Min smiled at her and then realized that the man sitting next to her wasn't just a miscellaneous father, he was Reynolds. Cynthie was on Bink's other side, wedged in next to another parent, which meant Min was going to be stuck sitting beside Reynolds. *This has to be payback for something*, she thought, and climbed to the top and sat down.

"So how we doing?" she asked him.

"These kids can't play," Reynolds said, shaking his head. "No discipline."

"Well, you know, they're *eight*," Min said.

"Discipline starts young," Reynolds said, looking at her with contempt, and Min thought, *There goes our chance at bonding.*

Down on the field, Bentley bobbled a catch and the ball rolled over to Harry, who picked it up and threw it in the general direction of a base he thought might be appropriate.

"Oh, God, *Harry*," Reynolds said loudly.

Min saw Cal off to one side of the field and felt her stomach lurch. *Ridiculous*, she told herself and swallowed hard. He spread his arms out at Harry as if to say, *What?* and Harry shrugged and crouched down again. Cal shook his head but Min could tell from the set of his shoulders that he wasn't mad. When he turned around he was grinning, and then he caught sight of her and his grin vanished, and she felt the rejection in the pit of her stomach.

Oh, ouch, she thought and looked away to the dugout where Tony was eating a hot dog and shaking his head, and Liza was sitting next to him with her chin on her hand. Down at the bottom of the bleachers, Bonnie was keeping some kind of tally for Roger who would use it to explain to the kids later the importance of something or other. *Lucky kids*, she thought and wished she were down there with Bonnie, or with Liza, or better yet, shoe shopping somewhere. Anywhere but here, looking at what she couldn't have. Or didn't have the guts to go after. Same thing, really.

Throughout the rest of the game, Reynolds continued to express his disgust at the general ineptness of the team in general, winning no friends among the parents in the bleachers, and making an already jittery Min long to hit him with something. Bink grew more and more owl-like, and Min wondered why she put up with him. *I'd have left his ass a long time ago.*

Down on the field, Harry came up to bat. He looked up at them, and Min waved to him, smiling. He pounded his bat on the ground a couple of times and then put it on his shoulder, dead serious. And when the pitch came, he missed it by a mile.

"Come on, Harry," Reynolds yelled. "You can do better than that. You're not trying."

Shut up, Reynolds, Min thought.

Down on the field, Harry's shoulders hunched a little, and up in the bleachers, Bink grew even stiller.

Harry fanned the next one, too, and Reynolds yelled, "Concentrate, Harrison! You can't swing at anything like a *dummy. Think,*" and Min saw Cal look up at his brother, his face set.

Might want to ease back on that, Reynolds, Min thought, and then Harry stiffened up and swung at a pitch that was so bad it didn't even cross the plate, and Reynolds stood up and yelled, "Harry, that was *stupid,* damn it, can't you do anything right?," and Harry froze, his little shoulders rigid, and Cal left the field, coming straight for his brother, murder in his eyes.

"No, no," Min said, panicking as Cal hit the bleachers. She stood up and stepped in front of Reynolds and hit him hard on the arm with her fist.

"Hey!" Reynolds said, grabbing his arm.

"You miserable excuse for a parent," she said to him under her breath. "You do *not* humiliate your kid like that." She raised her voice and yelled, "Harry is really smart, he's always smart," and then she whispered, "But you are the dumbest son of a bitch I have ever seen in my life."

"I beg your pardon," Reynolds said, outraged.

"It's not my pardon you need, you miserable butthead," Min whispered, leaning closer. "It's your kid's, the one you just humiliated in front of all his friends, and if you think that made you look good to anybody here, your head really is up your butt."

"You're out of line," Reynolds said, but he looked wary now, darting a glance at the other parents, who were clearly not amused. He shook his head, trying for bluster. "Who the hell do you think you are?"

"Well, for starters, she's the woman who just saved your ass," Cal said from behind her. "Because I was going to throw it off the bleachers until she got in my way."

"You," Reynolds said, looking past Min. "Like you could do anything about it. You can't even coach these kids—"

"Oh, give it up," Min said. "You know you screwed up, and the best you can do is blame your brother?"

"Listen," Reynolds said, raising a finger. "You are not—"

"You know, Reynolds," Cal said. "When you get home, you're going to figure out that you just gave your kid the same kind of flashback you and I have been having all our lives. And while you are a butthead, you're not a mean butthead, so that should give you some good nightmares about your parenting skills. In the meantime, you're picking a fight with somebody who takes no prisoners. I'd back away slowly if I were you."

"We're going home," Bink said.

"I don't see why—" Reynolds began and then Bink looked at him, her gray eyes steely cold.

"We," she said, "are going home where we will discuss this. Min, will you and Cal see that Harry gets home safely?"

"Yes," Cal said from behind her, and Min nodded, shaking now that the first adrenalin rush had passed. She stepped sideways, back to her own seat, feeling incredibly rash, not to mention rude, and when she turned and sat down, Cal had already started back down the bleachers, Reynolds and Bink following him.

Out on the field, Harry had his back to them, but Tony was talking to him, so that was all right. Of course, Tony was probably telling him that his father was a jerk, but as far as Min was concerned, that was all right, too.

She glanced over at Cynthie, who looked thoughtful. "Hi," Min said, taking a deep breath. "Enjoy the show?"

"I wouldn't have done it," Cynthie said, "but good for you anyway. You have more guts than I have."

"It wasn't guts," Min said. "I probably overreacted."

"No," Cynthie said. "Cal overreacted, but he couldn't help it. Reynolds played that family script and it makes Cal insane. He can't stand being called stupid."

"They get that a lot when they were kids?" Min said.

"I think they both had lousier childhoods than we can imagine," Cynthie said. "That doesn't mean you get to hit your brother in front of your nephew."

"He probably wouldn't have," Min said.

"I don't know," Cynthie said. "But now you're the bad guy for the family, not him. So you did him a favor there."

"I was already the bad guy," Min said. "His parents hated me."

"I don't think they like anybody much," Cynthie said. "They're very self-absorbed people. Not cruel. They just don't pay attention."

"So," Min said. "You're the psychologist, right? What do we do for Harry?"

"Cal will take care of it," Cynthie said, nodding down at the field, where Harry and Cal were now sitting in the dugout. She tilted her head at Min. "It was doubly bad because you were here, you know. Harry has such a crush on you that to be embarrassed like that . . ." She shook her head and sighed. "You're right. Reynolds is a butthead."

"Is that the clinical term?" Min said.

"In Reynolds's case, yes," Cynthie said.

Down in the dugout, Tony sat down next to Liza and said, "You know, I used to think that if I was ever in a bar fight, I'd want you backing me up, but I think Min just moved ahead of you in the ranking."

"I wouldn't cross her," Lisa said. "That man is a complete loss."

"Yeah," Tony said, his eyes on the field. "But Harry'll be okay. He has Cal and Bink and Min on his side. I'd take that team any day. Christ, look at that." He raised his voice. "Hey, Soames, look where you're throwing the ball." He shook his head but kept watching Soames anyway, ready to help.

That was Tony all over, Liza thought. He acted like a big lug but if anybody needed him, he was there.

She was really going to miss him.

"Tony," she said as he bit into his hot dog, waiting until he was eating on the theory that it would soften the blow. "We are not going to work out."

"What was your first clue?" Tony said around his hot dog, his eyes still on the field.

Liza let out her breath in relief. "It's not that you're not a great guy—"

"I know." Tony swallowed and bit into his sandwich again. Out on the field, a kid bobbled a catch, and he closed his eyes. *"Jesus."*

"We just got caught up in that threesome thing," Liza said, and Tony stopped chewing and looked at her. "I mean, the three of us, the three of you. You know."

"Right." Tony resumed chewing and watching the field.

"Bonnie and Roger," Liza said, "that's a little spooky, but Bonnie doesn't make mistakes."

Tony swallowed. "Neither does Roger. They'll be okay."

Liza nodded. "And Min and Cal . . . well, I don't know, but he's not taking her for a ride, so I'm butting out of that one."

"Good." Tony took another bite, squinting at the field.

"But you and I are toast," Liza finished.

"Yep." Tony shook his head at the field. "That kid has no arm."

"I'm glad to see you're taking this so well," Liza said, annoyed.

Tony shrugged. "I like you, but you're always charging someplace, creating disturbance, and I like my stability."

"Chaos theory," Liza said.

"Yep," Tony said. "Disturbed systems move to a higher order or disintegrate. We disintegrated. Also, you hate sports. Big deal. Nobody's mad. What's not to take?"

"Then why didn't *you* end it?" Liza said, annoyed.

"I liked the sex. Oh, hell." Tony scowled at the field where a hapless child had just missed a grounder. "You know, some kids should not play baseball."

"Actually, I liked the sex, too," Liza said, thinking about it.

"Anytime," Tony said. "Now *that's* an arm." He lifted his chin and shouted, "Nice one, Jessica!"

Jessica waved back at him and then forgot Tony and crouched down, waiting for whatever came next.

Jessica is no dummy, Liza thought. "I do like you," she told Tony, and he looked at her and grinned.

"I like you, too, babe," he said. "If you ever need a guy beat up, call me."

"Thank you," Liza said, touched. "If you ever need a woman slapped, you have my number."

"Really?" Tony perked up a little. "Can I watch?"

"And this is why we're no longer having sex," Liza said. "So you're okay?"

"Yes," Tony said, and then yelled, "No, no, no," at the field.

Liza stood up and kissed him on the top of the head. "Don't be mean to these kids," she told him before she left him. "They're going to grow up to own the companies you'll be working for."

A few minutes before the game ended, Min went down to the fence where Cal was leaning on the dugout. She stood there for a minute, not sure what to do, and then she cleared her throat.

"That was good, what you said to Reynolds," she said, hooking her fingers in the chain link. "Really good."

Cal looked out at the field.

Look at me, damn it, Min thought, and searched for something that would get his attention. "And . . . really hot," she lied, and swallowed hard. "I was very turned on. If there hadn't been so many people here, I'd have done you in the dugout."

Cal stood very still and then turned to her, his face still wooden.

Uh oh, she thought.

"Give me five minutes," he said. "I'll clear the place."

Min exhaled in relief. "You had me worried."

"Sorry." Cal walked over to her and leaned on the fence to talk to her, looping his fingers through the chain link so they touched hers. "That was a bad flashback."

"Your dad." Min crossed her fingers over his because touching him again felt so right. "I got that. Is Harry okay?"

"No," Cal said. "But he'll live."

"I don't know if Reynolds will," Min said. "Bink looked like the Angel of Death."

"His ass is grass," Cal said. "Doesn't help Harry much."

"Why did she marry him?" Min blurted. "I'm sorry, but—"

"He blinded her with charm." Cal smiled at her tightly. "He met her in college and took one look at her money and threw everything he had at her. She never had a chance."

Min thought of Bink, probably a frightened little owl in college, running into the glamorous and gorgeous Reynolds. "Why does she stay?"

"Because he loves her now," Cal said. "Harry's birth changed him. He's a lot better than he used to be."

"Damn," Min said. "What was he before?"

"A charming bastard," Cal said, his face grim again as he looked down at her. "Just like all the Morriseys."

"That's not you," Min said.

"Oh, honey, it is sometimes," Cal said miserably. "More than you know."

"I've never seen it," Min said.

"That's because I wasn't a bastard with you," Cal said. "You beat that out of me early."

Min grinned. "Well, you asked for it, Charm Boy."

"Thanks for coming down here," he said softly, and then Tony called him and he went back to the field.

Min went to sit beside Bonnie, and it wasn't until Bonnie reached over and covered Min's hands with hers that she realized she was shaking.

"How's it going there?" Bonnie said.

"This fairy tale thing," Min said. "It's not for kids."

Min went out to the parking lot after the game and found Harry in the backseat of Cal's car, and Cal leaning against the passenger door, waiting for her. *Don't lunge for him*, she told herself. *Harry will notice.*

"How are we doing?" she said.

"We're going to have lunch," Cal said, straightening. "And hear a lot of Elvis because thanks to you, that's now Harry's favorite music." He opened the car door for her.

"That's because Harry has great taste," Min said, sticking her chin out. She got in the car and said, "Hey, fish guy, I hear we're going to the diner for lunch. All Elvis, all the time."

Harry nodded.

"If I were you, I'd ask for processed meats," Min said. "In fact, ask for a brat. Milk this sucker for everything you can get."

Harry looked surprised and then he nodded.

"Ready, Harry?" Cal said as he got in.

Harry nodded at him, soberly. "May I have a brat for lunch?"

"What?" Cal said and turned to look at him.

Harry peered back, woebegone.

"Minerva," Cal said, looking straight into her eyes. "You're corrupting my nephew."

"Me?" Min lost her breath and smiled at him. "No, no. It's just that Americans eat twenty billion hot dogs a year and I think Harry should have one of them."

"Yeah," Harry said from the backseat.

"Twenty billion," Cal said and started to laugh, and Min relaxed a little.

When they were on the road, Min looked over the seat at Harry. "So what's new in the world of fish?"

"Are you wearing those fish shoes?" Harry said.

"No," Min said. "I found another shoe sale. I am wearing glass slippers with cherries on the toes."

Cal looked down at her feet. "They're okay," he said after a moment. "But they're not fish."

Harry nodded.

"So explain to me about ichthyology," Min said, and for the next two hours, Harry did, while Min tried to be fascinated but mostly thought about ways to get Cal to touch her. Anywhere. She'd take a pat on the head. To start with. But even with the distraction of Cal, by the time they were finished with lunch, Min knew more about fish than she thought possible.

"I may never eat seafood again," Cal said, as he held the car door for her.

"Yes, but if there's any money in fish, Harry will support you in your old age," Min said, trying to ignore how close he was, and got in.

When Cal was in the car, too, Min said, "So, Harry, how you doing back there?"

"Can I have a doughnut?" Harry said, looking woebegone again.

"Harrison," Cal said. "You are pushing it."

"Drive to Krispy Kreme," Min told Cal, who rolled his eyes and drove.

When they got there, the "Hot" sign was on, and Harry turned his owl eyes on Min. "Can I have two?"

"Harry," Cal said.

"Yes," Min said. "Today you can have two."

"This is a mistake," Cal said, but he went inside with them and they drank milk and ate warm chocolate-iced glazed doughnuts and talked about fish, and Min remembered the picnic table and tried not to breathe faster. By the time Harry was done with his second doughnut, he didn't look woebegone anymore.

When they got back to the car, Cal said to Min, "You're in the back-seat."

"Okay," Min said, and got in the backseat, not sure why she'd been banished. Maybe Cal had seen the lust in her eyes and was trying to protect himself.

Harry looked happy as a clam riding shotgun for about five minutes. Then he turned green.

"Yep," Cal said and pulled over.

Harry opened the door and lost two doughnuts and a pint of milk into the gutter.

"Oh, honey," Min said, wincing with guilt. "I'm sorry."

"It was worth it," Harry said, wiping his mouth. "And I kept the brat."

Cal passed him a bottle of Evian. "Rinse and spit. At least twice."

"Where'd you get that?" Min said while Harry rinsed and spat.

"I bought it when I paid for the doughnuts," Cal said. "I've been here before."

Harry sat back in his seat. "It's pretty gross out there. Should I pour the rest of the water on it?"

"Sure," Cal said, and met Min's eyes in the rearview mirror. "We Morriseys always wash out gutters with Evian."

"You people are pure class," Min said.

When they pulled into Harry's driveway, which was a clone of

Cal's parents' drive, Harry turned to Cal and said, "Thank you very much."

"You're welcome, Harry," Cal said.

Then Harry leaned between the seats and whispered, "Thank you for the doughnuts."

"My pleasure," Min whispered back, and then she leaned closer and whispered in his ear, "I love you, Harry."

He grinned at her, and then shot a superior look at his uncle.

"Harrison, if you're making time with my girl, you're in big trouble," Cal said.

Harry grinned wider and got out of the car. "See ya," he said and slammed the door.

"He's a little young for you, don't you think?" Cal said, meeting her eyes in the rearview.

Min swallowed. "Yes, but he's a Morrisey. You can't resist that charm."

"Yeah, I thought it was particularly charming the way he barfed in the gutter," Cal said. "You going to move back up here with me?"

"I kind of like it back here," Min said, faking unconcern. "Home, Morrisey."

"Get your butt up here, Dobbs," Cal said, and Min laughed and got out of the car.

When she was in the front seat and Cal had pulled out of the driveway, she said, "Is he okay?"

"Sure," Cal said. "Harry's used to throwing up."

"I mean about the game."

"Yeah," Cal said. "It'll come back to haunt him at odd moments from now on but he'll handle it. He got rescued. The people around him told him he was fine. And Bink will handle it for him at home. It's just tough when it's your dad telling you that you're stupid."

"Yeah," Min said, hating Jefferson Morrisey with a passion. "How are you doing?"

"Me? I'm fine."

"Good," Min said, and took a deep breath. She'd been on simmer for way too long. She had him alone, it was time for a plan. The smart thing to do would be to get everything out in the open, beginning with telling him she knew about the bet, discuss it like adults, and then maybe she could jump him—

"What?" Cal said into the silence.

"What?" Min said, jerking back in guilt.

"You went quiet," Cal said. "Spill it."

"Oh." Maybe a full frontal approach wasn't the way to go. "Well," Min said. "I was thinking . . ."

"Uh huh," Cal said.

". . . that we have some issues to, uh, settle. I think. I would like to settle them."

"Yes," Cal said, sounding as if he didn't have a clue what she was talking about but was willing to play along anyway.

"Because I think . . . maybe . . . we could . . . you know . . . give this a shot," she said. "If we talked."

Cal's hands tightened on the wheel, but he kept his eyes on the road. "All right."

You're not helping, Min thought. "Did you know that seventy-eight percent of couples keep secrets from each other?"

"I wouldn't be surprised," Cal said.

Min nodded.

"You made that up, didn't you?"

"Yes," Min said. "Although I bet it's close. Is there something you're not telling me? Something from . . ." She shrugged. ". . . oh, before you met me?"

Cal didn't say anything, and when she looked over he had that *Oh, hell* look on his face. "You already know," he said, "or you wouldn't ask."

"Well, yes," Min said, every muscle she had tensing. *Why'd you have to ask? All those people who say, "Just talk about it," they're idiots.*

"Min, it was years ago. My life was hell, and she was so great, and Reynolds was treating her like dirt—"

What? Min thought, her stomach plummeting.

Cal shook his head. "She's a good person. I fell pretty hard."

"Oh," Min said, and told herself, *Next time be more specific about the confession you want, you dumbass.*

"Nothing happened, Min," Cal said, glancing at her as he drove. "Bink isn't a cheater, and as much as I want to smack my brother every time I see him, I wouldn't do that to him. We just talked. A lot."

"Uh huh," Min said, trying to sound bright and encouraging.

"It was years ago," Cal said. "She said I was the only person who didn't care about her money. You've met her. You know what she's like. She's wonderful."

"Uh huh," Min said. *I'm going to kill myself now.*

"Are you okay?"

Min turned to look at him and blurted, "Did you love her?"

Cal slowed the car and Min thought, *Oh, just hell, when will I learn not to ask what I don't want to know?*

He pulled over and shut off the ignition and turned to her. "Yes."

"Oh." Min nodded. "Okay. From now on, when I ask you something, just refuse to answer, okay?"

"All right," he said.

"Do you still love her?" Min said.

"Yes," Cal said.

"You don't *listen*," Min said.

"Min, it's not like that. I haven't been in love with her for a long time. I think we both saw where it was going and neither of us wanted that nightmare, and Reynolds starting paying attention to her again, and I dated other women, and over time, it went away."

"Not really," Min said. "There's something nice between you. More than in-law affection."

Cal nodded. "Yes, she's special. But it's not . . . romantic. That was over a long time ago. Years and years ago."

"Uh huh," Min said, still coping.

Cal stared out the window. "Cynthie," he began, and Min thought, *Oh, kill me now.* "She never caught that. She's the psychologist, we were together for nine months, and she never saw that I'd felt like that about Bink. How did you?"

"I'm very acute," Min lied.

Cal slid a little way down in his seat and stared out the windshield, and Min watched the ease in his broad body and wanted him more than she thought was possible. "You know, Cyn spent months trying to figure out why I was a serial dater."

"A what?" Min said, trying to find her way back from lust and misery.

"That's what she called it. The hit and run thing you keep busting me on. She decided it was because I was trying to make up for my mother, that I was trying to get love from all these women, and then when they gave it to me, I'd leave them to try to earn it from somebody else."

"That Cynthie, a theory for every occasion," Min said, feeling bitter and wanting somebody to take it out on. Cynthie seemed good.

"I wasn't looking for my mother," Cal said. "I was looking for Bink." He turned and Min smiled at him so he wouldn't see she was about to open the car door and throw up in the gutter. "I wanted somebody I could talk to, somebody I didn't have to charm and please, somebody it just felt good to be with." He shook his head. "I just didn't realize it until now."

"Well, good luck on that," Min said brightly.

"Pay attention, Minnie," he said. "I was dead in the water the minute you sat down on my picnic table."

Suddenly Min realized there was no air anywhere. That would account for the dizziness.

"It took me a while to figure it out," he said. "I wasn't used to anybody like you. Because there isn't anybody else like you."

Keep breathing, Min thought.

"And then you ripped up at me in the street in front of Emilio's, and I thought, *Well, the hell with you*. For about five minutes. Then I just wanted you back. You're the only woman I've ever wanted back. And I've been trying to figure out a way to get you back ever since."

Min sucked in some air before she passed out.

"I love you," Cal said. "I know it's insane, we've only known each other a few weeks, we need more time, I get all of that, but I love you and it's not going to change."

Min took another deep breath. You needed air to talk.

"For God's sake, Min, *say something*," Cal said.

"I love you," Min said on a breath. "I've loved you forever."

"That'll do it," Cal said and reached for her.

Chapter Thirteen

Min wrapped her arms around his neck, so grateful to be back in his warmth that she dragged him over the stick shift to get him closer to her.

"Ouch," Cal said.

"Sorry," Min said, trying to pull back.

"Not a problem," Cal said, holding on. "God I've missed you." He kissed her and the glittering heat flared low just like always, except that this time she wasn't fighting it and it went everywhere. She clutched at him, amazed that he was kissing her again, breaking the kiss to kiss him again, over and over until he stopped to breathe.

"Listen," she said. "About my heart. Don't break it."

"Right. Me, too." Cal pulled her back, and she fell into him and lost herself, drunk on the knowledge that she could have him, would have him, that everything was going to be wonderful. She felt his hand slide under her shirt and touch her breast, and she shuddered against him and bit his lip, and his hand tightened on her, and then her cell phone rang.

He pulled back, breathing hard, his eyes dark for her, and she held on to him.

"Ignore it," she said, gasping, "it's Diana, she calls twelve times a day, *come back here and love me,*" and he shook his head.

"Answer it," he said, between breaths. "We have to stop. We're parked on a public road."

"I *don't care,*" she said, reaching for him again.

He put the car in gear. "Your place or mine, Minnie, *not* in a car."

"Whatever's *closer,*" Min said, and answered the phone to stop the ringing as Cal pulled out into traffic.

"*Min,*" Diana said, her voice tight. "Oh, *Min,* we're in *trouble.*"

"Okay," Min said, trying not to sound dizzy with lust. "What?"

"The *rehearsal dinner,*" Di said. "Greg was going to get the caterers because he could get us this deal."

"Oh." Min looked at Cal, who was much too far away. "Greg was going to get the caterers for the rehearsal dinner. In four hours."

"I hate Greg," Cal said.

Diana sounded as breathless as Min felt. "Mom's going to *crucify* Greg and he's already *a nervous wreck. This is my perfect wedding.*"

"Okay," Min said. "Let me think." *Cal, naked, in my bed, in me.* No, not that thought.

"What are we going to do? There's *nothing,*" Di said.

"I'm trying to think," Min said and met Cal's eyes for a long moment, until the car drifted and hit the edge of the pavement and Cal yanked it back.

"Where is this dinner?" he said, keeping his eyes on the road.

"At some bed and breakfast near the chapel," Min said. "Down by the river. Why?"

"How many people?" Cal said.

"Fourteen, I think," Min said and spoke into the phone. "Dinner for fourteen, right?"

"*Yes,*" Diana said.

"We can do it," Cal said. "Tell her it's okay."

"We can?" Min said. "We who?"

"Tony and Roger and I worked in a restaurant, remember? We'll get supplies from Emilio's, you make chicken marsala, and they'll plate it and serve it. Your parents don't know Tony and Roger so they'll buy them as servers. It'll work."

"I'm making chicken marsala?" Min said, and then thought, *What the hell.* "Okay, I'm making chicken marsala." She spoke into the phone. "We've got it covered. Relax. Your job is to give Mom a story if Cal and I are late and to make sure the back door to that kitchen is open. We'll do everything else."

"Oh, thank God," Di said. "I didn't interrupt anything, did I?"

"Yes," Min said. "But it's okay. We have a couple of hours before we have to cook. You can do a lot in a couple of—"

"*No, you don't,*" Diana said. "*Are you crazy?* You've got the *last fitting right now.* We thought *you were on your way.* We're here *now.* We're *waiting for you.* You can't miss *the fitting.* Mom will *kill you.* I *need you.* You *can't*—"

"Right. Now," Min said. "I forgot."

"Don't tell me," Cal said as he slowed the car.

"Fitting," she said to him. "I have a fitting right now. I have to—"

"Not a problem," Cal said, taking a deep breath. "I'll drop you off at the fitting, I'll get the food for the dinner, we'll cook, we'll go to the dinner, and *then*—"

"I have to spend the night with my sister," Min said, closing her eyes. "I hate it, but it's the night before her wedding, I promised—"

"Fine," Cal said. "Not a problem."

"*Maybe not for you,*" Min said, and thought, *Loud voice, loud voice.* She took a deep breath. "I want you *now.* I want—"

"Oh, *Christ,*" Cal said. "I'm trying to be—"

"Min?" Diana said from the other end of the phone.

"I'll be there," Min told her and hung up.

"Where's the fitting?" Cal said, his voice resigned.

"Bridal department at Finocharo's," Min said bitterly. "Why couldn't Greg have been in charge of the dresses?"

Cal drove to the store, kissed her several times, and then drove off to get the dinner supplies, and it wasn't until he was gone that she realized that he still hadn't mentioned the bet.

We didn't have time, she thought. *There's a good reason, I didn't give him a chance, and even if there's not a good reason,* I don't care, *nothing is going to screw this up for me.*

Then she went to face her mother and that damn corset.

"You're late again," her mother said as she came through the door.

"Hi, Mom," Min said, prepared to savage her if she said anything nasty.

"Eat this," Nanette said and handed her an apple.

"Why?" Min said.

"Because God knows what those caterers that Greg got will make. He is completely unreliable. And you know he didn't tell them not to use butter. So fill up on that."

"On this." Min looked at the apple, shook her head, and put it down to go jam herself into the corset. Half an hour later, the fitter left Min's dressing room, and Min stared at herself in the mirror, all heat gone, and thought, *I'd kill myself, but this is not the last thing I want to see before I go.*

She was once again in the blue skirt that zipped up only when she sucked in all the air in the room, the lavender chiffon blouse that still pulled across the bust, and the new blue corset that only laced shut when Min gave up breathing and the fitter used the force of ten. And she wasn't going to be taking any deep breaths now that the damn thing was on: one good heave and she'd pop out the top of it.

Why would Cal want to sleep with somebody who looks like this?

Min came out of the dressing room, and Nanette said, "It still doesn't fit," in a tone that did not bode well for her fat daughter.

"As God is my witness, I have followed that diet," Min said to her, feeling depressed. "Mostly."

"You've had a year," her mother said bitterly. "And now you're going to ruin Diana's beautiful wedding."

"Here's an idea." Min tried to tug the corset up. "Why don't I sprain an ankle and Karen can be the maid of honor? That way the entire wedding party will be beautiful and thin, and—"

"*No*," Diana said from the doorway, and they both turned to her.

"Not your loud voice, dear," Nanette said.

Di pointed at Min. "You're *my sister* and you're going to be my *maid of honor* and you're going to look *beautiful* because that lavender is *just your color* and it's all going to be *perfect*." She had the same maniacal look in her eye that Nanette did, so Min shut up.

"Well, there's nothing we can do about it now." Nanette stood up, disgusted. "You were late, and we have a million things to do. The dinner's in three hours, for heaven's sake. You'll have to try on the rehearsal dinner dress without us."

"Rehearsal dinner dress?" Min said. "Why—"

"I found something for you that will be slimming." Nanette shook her head at her eldest daughter, the disappointment. "Make sure the hem is in the right place. If it cuts you at the knees, your legs will look like fence posts."

"Thank you, Mother," Min said, figuring this was a fight she didn't care about. She just felt tired.

Her mother stopped and met her eyes. "I know you think I'm awful. But I know how the world works. And it's not kind to fat people, Min. It's especially not kind to fat women. I want to see you happy and safe, married to a good man, and it's not going to happen if you don't lose that weight."

"She's *not fat*," Diana said from behind her. "*She is NOT FAT.*"

"Not your loud voice," Nanette said, and Diana glared at her.

"*Screw* my loud voice, stop telling her she's *fat*." Diana stopped, looking as surprised as Nanette and Min that she'd said it. She went on, in a calmer voice. "Leave her alone."

Nanette shook her head and leaned forward to grip Min by the upper arms. "I just want you to be happy," she said, and then stopped and squeezed Min's arms again. "Have you been lifting weights the way I told you to? Because if your arms aren't toned, those chiffon sleeves—"

"We have to go now," Diana said, pushing her mother toward the door. "We'll be late as it is." She turned back at the door and said, "You look *great*," before she left, too.

"Yeah," Min said and turned back to look at herself in the mirror. The chiffon blouse wasn't too bad, but her breasts were just obnoxious.

"Oh, Lord," she said, and tried to sit down but the skirt was too tight.

"Wait a minute, wait a minute," the fitter said and scurried around behind her to unzip the skirt before it split.

"I hate this," Min said as she stepped out of the skirt.

"The color is wonderful on you," the fitter said, and Min looked back into the mirror and thought, *She's right. Diana has a perfect eye for that kind of thing.* "You're lucky you didn't get the green one," the fitter went on as she unlaced the corset and Min began to breathe again. "The colors are going to look lovely going down the aisle, green and blue and your blue-violet, but the little blonde who has to wear the green is so unhappy about it."

Wet, Min thought. Well, that's what you get for dating the groom.

"Now, I'll bring you the dinner dress, and we'll get you all fixed up."

"Yeah," Min said. She took the blouse off and stood looking at herself in the mirror. Full breasts, full hips, full thighs . . . She tried to remember what Cal had said but her mother's voice was louder.

"Here we go," the fitter said, coming back. "We'll just slip this over your head . . ."

Min looked at herself in the mirror as the dresser zipped her up. Her mother had chosen black, of course, a sheath dress with a vertical white insert down the front that made her look vaguely like a penguin. V-shaped inserts at the waist were supposed to give the illusion of a waistline but instead made her look like a penguin whose bow tie was riding low.

"It's very slimming," the fitter said.

"Right," Min said, and picked up her mother's apple. "Slimming."

From behind her Cal said, "*God*, that's an ugly dress," and she turned to see him leaning in the doorway, holding a bottle of wine and two glasses.

Min's heart gave a leap. "Oh, good, it's you."

"What were you thinking, Minnie?" Cal said, coming into the room, his eyes on hers. "Take that thing off. It's an insult to your body."

"Only one of many today," Min said. "My mother picked this out. She has excellent taste."

"I don't think so." Cal put everything on the low table by the couch. "I could pick out a better dress than that."

"You're on," Min said. "I'll give you five minutes while I eat this apple, and then we're hemming this thing so my legs don't look like fence posts. Did you bring a corkscrew? I could use the wine, too."

Cal took the apple out of her hand. "Apples and wine? I don't think so." He tossed the apple in the small gold wastebasket beside the table and pulled a corkscrew out of his pocket. "Your legs are great. Take that dress off. There must be a better one someplace."

"Downstairs," the fitter said eagerly, looking at Cal as if he were the best thing she'd ever seen.

Min looked at Cal and remembered he was gorgeous.

"Hi." Cal smiled at the fitter. "I'm Cal."

"Hi," she said back, smiling wider. "I'm Janet."

Oh, for crying out loud, Min thought.

"Janet, you look like you have exceptional taste," Cal said to her. "I know you didn't pick that thing out."

"No, no," Janet said, disavowing all knowledge.

"I bet you could find her the perfect dress," Cal said, looking right into her eyes, sincerity made flesh. "Maybe something bright red."

"Blue," Janet said. "She looks wonderful in blue or violet."

"So she does. Go find a great blue dress and we'll celebrate with a drink."

Janet hesitated. "Mrs. Dobbs was very clear . . ."

"I'll take care of Mrs. Dobbs," Cal said. "You take care of the dress."

When Janet was gone, Cal screwed the corkscrew into the cork and yanked it, and the cork popped out without a fight. Then he poured her a glass. "Here. You're tense."

"My mother was here," Min said, taking the glass and wishing he was touching her. Except she was fat.

"That explains why Janet looked like a deer caught in headlights." Cal looked over his shoulder. "She's not here and you haven't kissed me in an hour, Minerva. Come here."

Min stepped down off the platform and went to him, loving the way his arms went around her, trying not to think about how fat she must feel under his hands, and then he kissed her hard, and she sighed against him, grateful to have him even if she didn't know why he wanted her.

The bet.

Nope, never, that was not it, she believed in him.

"What's wrong?" he said.

Min shook her head. "Rough fitting."

"Let me guess," he said. "Your mother. Ignore her. Think about me."

She smiled in spite of herself, and he kissed her again, his mouth gentle on hers, and she felt the tension in her body begin to ease.

"There you go," he said, patting her back. "Now drink your wine. I'm going to get you drunk and then have my way with you under the table at the rehearsal dinner."

"Oh, if only," Min said and sipped her wine.

Half a glass of wine and several kisses later, Min was feeling much better, and Janet came back with a hanger full of something dark purple and slinky.

"You're kidding me," Min said. "This is for *me*, remember?"

"No, this one's for me," Cal said, looking at it on the hanger. "I'm taking you to this thing and I'm not going to look at a butt-ugly dress all night."

"Leave," Min said. "I'm not undressing in front of you." *Yet.* She thought of Nanette grabbing her arm and squeezing. *Maybe never.*

"Well, a guy can hope," Cal said, and took his wine out the door with him.

When he was gone, Janet said, "*That's* your boyfriend?"

"Yes," Min said, surprised to realize he was.

"My God, he's *beautiful*," Janet said.

"He's nice, too," Min said. "But about this dress—"

"No, it'll be good," Janet said, shaking the dress out as she held it up. "Your boyfriend likes it. Does he know anything about women's clothes?"

"I think he's removed a lot of them," Min said, stripping off the penguin dress.

"He could remove mine," Janet said and then froze. "Sorry. I didn't mean—"

"Not a problem," Min said, handing her the penguin dress. "I'm used to it. How does this one go on?"

"You pull it over your head," Janet said, giving her the purple dress. "It's a draped surplice top."

"I don't know." Min held the dress up.

"Try it on," Janet said. "*He* likes it."

"And he brought me wine," Min said. "Where's my glass?" She tossed back the rest of her glass and then, with a sigh, pulled the dress over her head and looked in the mirror.

There were many things right with the dress. The surplice neck made her look thinner and the way it draped over her breasts was downright sexy as long as she didn't slump. And the drape made her hips look voluptuous instead of buslike. But still, this was the kind of dress that thin women wore, this was—

"The handkerchief hem is genius," Janet said. "He's right, you do have good legs. They're just . . . curvy."

"Thank you," Min said. "The rest of me is curvy, too."

"You look really sexy in this," Janet said. "I'll go get him so he can see."

"I'll have some more wine," Min said, but the dresser was already gone, Cal-hunting. Min poured a second glass and sipped it while she stared into the mirror. The dress was a vast improvement over the penguin dress. Plus her mother would be annoyed, which served her right. Even better, she wouldn't be able to say anything because Min could tell her that Cal liked it. "So, okay," Min said, toasting her reflection, and knocked back the entire glass. The warmth of the wine spread through her, melding nicely with the warmth from Cal's kisses, and she sighed.

She was bending over the table to get a third glass of wine when Cal came back.

"I hear you look—" he began and stopped.

"What?" Min said, looking up from the wine.

"Uh," he said and she followed his eyes to her cleavage, most of which was displayed because the surplice was gaping. "You look good," Cal said with enough tension in his voice to make it an understatement.

"It's not a fat dress," Min said, turning back to the mirror. "It doesn't hide anything."

"Haven't we talked about this?" Cal said, coming to stand behind her.

"Yes, but my mother has talked since then," Min said. "Also, there's this mirror which tells me I don't have much of a waistline."

"You have a waistline." Cal put his hands on her hips. "It's right here." He slid his hands across her stomach and she shivered, watching him touch her in the mirror. With Cal's hands on her, she looked different, good, and when he pulled her back against his chest, she relaxed into him and let her head fall back on his shoulder. "Very sexy dress," he whispered into her ear, and then kissed her neck. She drew in her breath and he whispered, "Very sexy woman," and moved his hand up to her neckline, drawing his finger down the edge of the silky fabric, making her shudder as the heat spread and she began to feel liquid everywhere.

"I have to stop drinking wine when I'm with you," she whispered to him in the mirror. "I start believing all this garbage you tell me."

He grinned at her, his reflection warming her as much as his body against her back.

She bit her lip. "It feels so good to be alone with you. And I can't because we have to go to this rehearsal dinner, we have to *make* this rehearsal dinner, and then tomorrow I've got to go to this wedding in a ridiculous dress and I'm feeling fat again."

"That's because you're not paying attention," Cal said in her ear. "Look at yourself."

"I am," she said, and he said, "Not the way I look at you." His hand moved up her side and he whispered, "Look at the beautiful curve of you, how full you are," and as his voice in her ear made her dizzy, his hand moved up around her breast.

She turned her head and said, "Hey!" and brought her hand up to move his, and he stopped her breath with his mouth, kissing her hard, catching her hand to press her open palm against the warm heaviness of her breast, and she thought, *That feels so good*, and let the heat wash over her.

"Look how *beautiful* you are," he whispered in her ear as he laced his fingers in her other hand. "There's not a man alive who could see you like this and not want to touch you." He rolled her other hand so her palm was against her stomach and slid it up to her breast. "You're a fantasy, Min. You're my fantasy."

He pressed both her palms against her breasts and she felt the fullness there and shuddered under his hands and believed him. She turned in his arms and kissed him with everything she had, pressing herself against him with no other thought than to get close, loving how hard his body felt against hers, the way her body yielded to him, the heat of his hands on her as they slid down and pulled her to him. She arched her hips against him, bit his lip and licked his mouth, felt him shaking as she whispered, "*I want you*," and heard his breath shudder as he kissed her on the neck and then softly bit the place he'd kissed.

"Whoops," Janet said from behind them, and Min pulled back, dizzy and breathless.

"We'll take the dress," Cal said, without looking around, his voice husky.

"This is a very dangerous dress," Min said, trying to catch her breath.

"That's why we're taking it," Cal said, and kissed her again before he let her go.

When they got to the bed and breakfast, Diana had left the back door unlocked as promised. "It's a decent kitchen," Cal said when they'd unloaded the car. "We can work here."

"It's a great kitchen," Min said with envy. She turned to Cal and said, "I think—" and he kissed her while she smiled against his mouth and moved closer to him. "What was that for?"

"Because I can," Cal said and pulled her closer. Her cell phone rang, and he leaned back. "What did Greg forget now?"

Min clicked her phone on. "Hi."

"Where are you? We're at the B and B. Mom's fussing over my dress," Diana said, all in frantic whisper. "She wants to know where you are."

"We're downstairs getting ready to cook," Min said, as Cal kissed her on the neck. She stifled a giggle and said, "Stall her."

"She's going to be mad at you," Di said.

"And this is news," Min said. "She'd have been mad when she saw my dress anyway. Cal picked it out. I look like a ho." She felt Cal laugh against her hair.

"Really?" Di said. "What color is it?"

"*Di—*"

"I'll stall Mom," Di said. "*Thank you!*"

"You don't look like a ho," Cal said when Min clicked off her phone. "You look like an expensive call girl." He slid his hand down to her rear end. "And I have money."

"Try to think of cooking as foreplay," Min said, and Cal sighed and started to unpack the food.

Fifteen minutes later, Min had the bottoms of four frying pans covered in hot olive oil, Cal had pounded sixteen chicken breasts flat as flounders and was washing mushrooms, and Diana had stuck her head in to say, "No butter. And thank you, thank you, thank you."

"Where am I, by the way?" Min said as she began to dredge the chicken breasts.

"Cal's car broke down and you're somewhere on 275," Di said.

"My car did *not* break down," Cal said, stopping in mid-mushroom. "I keep that car in—"

"Thank you, that'll work," Min said, and Diana left. "I know, but can you park your male pride for the night?"

"What's in it for me?" Cal said.

"My eternal gratitude," Min said and leaned over the table and kissed him on the mouth, loving the way his mouth fit hers.

"How much gratitude?" Cal said, leaning to follow her as she pulled away.

"More than I can express in a single night," Min said. "Slice some of those, will you? We need some for the salad." She held the first chicken piece over the hot oil and stopped.

"Problem?" Cal said.

"No," Min said and put down the chicken. She rummaged in one of the bags and pulled out a pound of butter. "You know," she said as she opened the box, "you really can't cook without a *little* butter."

"Yep," Cal said and grinned at her.

Min dropped a healthy pat into each of the four pans and inhaled the sweet smell. Then she smiled and dropped the chicken breasts in.

"They'll never know anyway," Cal said.

"My mother can smell butter on me three days after I've eaten it," Min said. "She'll know. I just don't care. Tear up the romaine next, will you? I've got to steam beans."

Half an hour later, Tony and Roger showed up in white shirts and black bow ties with Bonnie behind them.

"What?" Min said, trying not to laugh at the ties.

"Yeah, you snicker now, but you're going to be impressed later," Tony said, and did water goblets faster than she could have imagined, as Roger slung fourteen plates in a row and squirted raspberry sauce on them in a pattern and then plated salads that looked like they'd come from the Ritz.

"I'm impressed," Min said.

"So am I," Bonnie said from her stool at the end of the table where she was cutting scallions into strips, and Roger beamed at her as Tony carried the glasses out.

When Tony came back, he said, "They're all out in the parlor, being polite. Di looks bored. Well, she did until she saw me in this tie."

"Must be hell," Min said over the steaming pan of beans. "I'd much rather be in here with you guys. From now on, I'm catering all my mother's dinners."

"Not once she tastes the butter," Cal said, and helped Tony lay out another fourteen plates for the entrée.

Ten minutes later, the plates were ready for the chicken, the chicken looked like heaven simmering in its dark wine sauce, the green beans were tossed with the almonds and tied into bundles with the scallion strips, and Min was talking to herself.

"Salad, done," she said to herself. "Meat, beans, done. Emilio's corn relish, ready to plate. Rolls out of oven and in baskets. What have I missed? Oh, damn. Dessert."

"I got dessert." Cal picked up the last bag and pulled out two boxes that said KRISPY KREME.

"*Doughnuts,*" Min said, appalled.

"Get me a cake plate," Cal said, and Bonnie rummaged in the cupboard and found one. Then while they watched, he made a ring of seven chocolate-iced cake doughnuts with one in the middle topped by a ring of five chocolate cake doughnuts, topped by a ring of three vanilla-iced glazed, topped by one beautiful chocolate-iced Kreme on top, all stuck together with the white glaze icing that Bonnie had dribbled between the layers.

Min's mouth began to water.

"I read about this," Bonnie said, standing back. "It was in *People* magazine. People do this all the time."

Cal picked up a box he'd set to one side, ripped it open, and dumped out a very small bride and groom under a plastic arch. It looked like hell until he shoved it into the top doughnut, and then it looked funky.

"This is the cake I want at my wedding," Min said. "Of course, my mother is going to go into cardiac arrest."

Cal grinned at her, and she laughed as she took off her apron. "You're a genius, Calvin. I need one moment in the closet to put on my dress, and then it's showtime."

She changed as fast as she could, and when she came back she heard Tony say to Cal, "Okay, we got it. You can go—" He stopped when he saw her, and then Roger turned to follow his eyes and stopped, too, and Bonnie peered out from behind Roger.

"Oh, Min," she said. "You look *wonderful*."

"*Very* hot," Tony said, staring at her, and Cal clipped him on the back of the head. "I'm just *saying*," Tony said.

Cal handed the cake to Roger. "You guys can handle everything now?"

"Piece of cake," Tony said, and Min stopped, startled. "What?" he said.

"Nothing." Min shook her head and then checked her face in the mirror by the door to make sure she wasn't wearing flour as foundation. The heat from the kitchen had flushed her skin and kinked her hair and she looked . . .

"You look beautiful," Cal said, and Min turned and saw Roger and Tony with him, and realized that a month before, she hadn't known any of these guys, and now they'd all come together to bail her sister out of trouble.

"This is so *great* of you," she said to them. "This is so above and beyond the call of friendship."

"Anything for you, babe," Tony said. He bent down and kissed her cheek, and Min blushed, and Cal said, "Enough with the flirting with other men, Minerva," and took her hand, and Roger patted her shoulder as Cal pulled her out the back door.

"Those are the best people," she said to him, as they hit the gravel path around to the front of the house.

"Yes," Cal said. "And now we get to have dinner with your family."

"Oh, hell," Min said.

Looking back on the rehearsal dinner later, Min was hard put to choose the low point of the evening.

There was the moment when Nanette spotted them coming through the door and was so caught off guard by Min's purple dress that she stopped after "You're late . . ." and just glared while Min braced herself.

But then Cal patted her on the back and Greg's best man said, "Whoa," and nodded at her.

"Thank you," Min said.

"I told you so," Cal said in her ear. "Stay away from him."

Or there was the moment when Min saw Greg, who had decided to have his hair cut in a Caesar cut the day before his wedding, and looked, if possible, dumber than ever.

"Don't ever do that," Min whispered to Cal and Cal said, "No, I don't think so."

Or the moment when Roger and Tony were serving the salads, and Di grinned and said, "Gee, such *cute* waiters," and Roger almost dropped Greg's salad in his lap.

"Watch it," Greg said sharply, and Di lost her smile.

"*Very* cute," Min said, and frowned at Greg, who blinked back at her.

Or the moment when Greg's mother said, "This chicken is delicious. Who did you say catered this?" and all eyes turned to Greg. Min let him flounder for a couple of seconds and then said, "Emilio's, wasn't it?", throwing him a rope that he grabbed onto so gratefully she almost felt sorry for him.

That was followed by the moment when Nanette said, "There's *butter* in this."

"Yep," Min said and kept eating while Cal patted her back.

But the low point probably came toward the end of the meal when Min's cell phone rang. She looked over at Diana, startled, since Diana was the only one who would be calling her, and then remembered the trio in the kitchen. "I'll be right back," she said, and slipped outside to answer it. "Hello?"

"Min," David said. "I've been trying to get you all day."

"Why?" Min said. "Never mind, I don't care. This is my sister's rehearsal dinner, David. Go away."

"It's about Cal," David said, and Min grew still. "I still care for you, Min, and you need to know something about Cal Morrisey."

"Do I," Min said flatly.

"That night he picked you up?" David said. "He did it because he made a bet that he could get you into bed in a month."

"He did," Min said, thinking, *What a waste you are.*

"The bet's up next Wednesday, Min," David said, sincerity oozing through the phone. "And Cal Morrisey does not lose. He'll do anything to win that bet. I thought you should know. I don't want you to get hurt."

"Gee, thanks," Min said.

"You don't sound upset," David said.

"Boys will be boys," Min said.

"I thought you'd be shocked," David said, sounding shocked himself.

"David, I knew," Min said. "I overheard you. Which is why I also know that Cal didn't make the bet, you did. It was your idea, which makes you the chief slimeball in this."

"No," David said hastily, "no, I was upset because we'd broken up—"

"David, *you* dumped *me*," Min said. "What the hell were you upset about?"

"—I've regretted that bet a thousand times since, but Cal won't call it off."

"Asked him to, have you?" Min said, not believing him.

"Over and over," David said.

"David?" Min said.

"Yes?" David said.

"Rot in hell," Min said, and clicked off the phone.

She stood on the porch of the bed and breakfast and looked out over the river beyond. It was very pretty. "Damn," she said. She believed in Cal, she really did, but that bet . . .

I'll ask him after the wedding, she told herself. When she was out of that awful corset, when they were alone, when they could talk it out without Diana tugging on her arm for help, she'd ask him then.

Tomorrow night, she told herself and went back inside in time to catch what was definitely the high point of the evening, Nanette's face when she saw the Krispy Kreme cake.

"Hey," David said when Cynthie picked up the phone on Sunday afternoon. "I haven't heard from you. What's—"

"It's over," Cynthie said, and she sounded as if she been crying. "They're in infatuation. It could be years before he comes to his senses. We lost, David."

"No, we didn't," David said. "I don't lose."

"Cal loves her. He's being honest with her. There's nothing—"

"No, he isn't," David said, fed up with hearing about Cal. "He's chasing her to win that damn bet."

"What?" Cynthie said.

"Uh," David said, trying to find a way to explain that without looking like slime.

"Tell me," Cynthie said, her voice brooking no nonsense.

"That first night," David said. "I was mad. And hurt. And—"

"David, *I don't care about you,*" Cynthie said. "Tell me about the bet."

"I bet Cal that he couldn't get Min into bed in a month," David said.

"Cal would not make that bet," Cynthie said, her voice sure.

"Oh, because he's too noble."

"He distracted you with something else."

"He bet me he could take her to dinner."

"She left with him because *you made a bet?*" Cynthie said, fury in her voice.

"It wasn't my fault," David said.

"It doesn't matter now anyway." Cynthie's voice dropped back into misery. "Even if you told her about the bet, she'd check with Cal."

"She already knew," David said, resentfully. "I called her and told her last night. She said she'd overheard us."

Cynthie didn't say anything.

"I think she went to dinner with him to make me mad," David said. "He sounded like she was pretty snippy, so she must have made him pay, too." The silence stretched on until David said, "Cynthie?"

"Does he know?" Cynthie said, her voice tight. "Does he know that she went out with him to make him pay?"

"I don't think so," David said. "He hasn't called me to tell me the bet's off, and once he knows that she knows, it's off."

More silence.

"Cynthie?"

"Do you know where Cal is now?" Cynthie said.

"No, but he'll be at Diana's wedding tonight," David said. "What diff—"

"I know how to break them up," Cynthie said, her voice like lead.

"How?" David said.

"Take me to the wedding. If she hasn't slept with him yet, he's frustrated to the breaking point. I'll watch them, and if something makes him tense, if she turns him down again, if something goes wrong . . ." Cynthie paused again, and then he heard her take a deep breath. "I'll tell you, and you go tell him that Min's been making a fool of him all along. Tell him that everybody thinks he's stupid."

"That's enough to break them up?" David said.

"That's enough to give Cal nightmares for years," Cynthie said, her voice miserable. "It's illogical, but it's been his trigger since he was a kid. Push that button and he explodes. If he does it in front of her family and friends—"

"Wow," David said, impressed with her once again.

"What time is the wedding?" Cynthie said.

"Seven," David said. "Diana wanted it at twilight. Some fairy tale garbage."

"Pick me up at six," Cynthie said, and hung up.

Min had spent the night with Diana, who'd been so manic that she'd still been up, fixing bows on cake boxes, when Min gave up and went to bed, too tired even to miss Cal. But the next day, Di was quiet, still tense but not manic with energy anymore.

"I just didn't get enough sleep," she told Min.

When they got to the chapel dressing room, Wet, Worse, and Nanette were waiting, and Min ducked Nanette and her hair combs ("Min, you look awful with your hair like that"), took the cake boxes to the reception hall next door, and then went into the bathroom at the chapel to put her dress on. She was not going to struggle into the damn thing while Nanette made comments and Worse smirked.

Something was very wrong, she thought as she tried to get the corset tied around her. Something besides her insane mother and the idiot wet and weeping bridesmaid in green, something beyond the cake Bonnie was now trying to decorate in orchids and pearls, something, she was pretty sure, much like the groom. *I've got to talk to Di*, Min thought, but what was she going to say? "You're miserable and your groom is a moron and I think we should eat the cake and go home"?

"Oh, hell," she said and left the bathroom to go back to her sister.

"You're late," Worse said, patting her ornate chignon as Min came into the room.

"Bite me," Min said, and went to stand beside Di. "Hey, baby, what's up?"

"Nothing," Di said. "I'm just . . . glad you're here."

"Yes, I am in all my glory," Min said, holding her arms out to show off her gaping corset.

"That corset's not tight enough," Nanette said, and turned her around. "Honestly, Min." She untied the bow at Min's neckline and then began to tighten the laces, working up from the bottom.

"Uh," Min said, as her lungs constricted. "Mother." She put her hand on the back of Di's chair to stabilize herself as Nanette yanked on the ribbons. "I have to be able to . . . breathe . . . during . . . the ceremony."

Nanette gave the ribbons a final excruciating pull at the top, tied them with a knot that would have had Boy Scouts staring in awe, and stood back to consider her work.

"Well, it's the best I can do," Nanette said, and Min thought, *That pretty much sums up our entire relationship*, and turned away from her, her hand on her side, trying to breathe and see Diana at the same time.

"Di?" Min said, and when Di didn't say anything, she leaned over to see her sister's face, constricting her lungs even more.

Di was staring into the mirror, her eyes huge, the line of her beautiful jaw rigid, and Min forgot she couldn't breathe.

"Di? Are you all right?"

"Fine," Di said faintly, not taking her eyes off the mirror.

"You look beautiful," Min said. On Di, even the corset looked right. "Swanlike," Min added, hoping to get a flicker.

"She's just got pre-wedding jitters," Wet said as she settled her wreath of ivy and white baby orchids on her smooth, blond hair. She looked miserable.

Worse nudged Min aside. "Go put your wreath on straight." Her own wreath of cornflowers and orchids was perfectly centered on her head, balanced in back on her chignon.

"Oh, *Min*," Nanette said. "Your *wreath*."

Min picked up her wreath of lavender and orchids and slapped it on her head. At least it smelled good. She jammed a couple of hairpins in to hold it, watching Diana in the mirror the whole time.

Di met her eyes and sat up straighter. "Go away."

"Okay," Min said.

"Not you," Di said. "Everybody but you."

"What?" Worse said, stopping with her hands in midair, reaching for Diana's wreath.

"*Diana*," Nanette said, shocked.

Min took a look at Di's frozen face. "Sister time. We'll see you all outside in a minute."

"Hey," Worse said. "I'm a *bridesmaid*—" Then she saw Diana's face and stopped.

"Out," Min said, jerking her thumb toward the door.

"Well, I'm not going," Nanette said. "This is my daughter's wedding."

"So go to it," Min said. "Weren't the pews all supposed to have flowers?"

"Honestly, Min," Nanette said and stopped. "Of course they're all supposed to have flowers."

"Better check," Min said, and Nanette took off for the chapel.

Wet picked up her bouquet of orchids, leaned over, and kissed Di's cheek. "You look wonderful," she whispered. "You look like a size two!" She handed Worse's bouquet to her and pushed her toward the door, and Worse looked back, not so cocky anymore.

Then Min and Di were alone.

Min leaned against the counter and tried to work her fingers under the edge of the corset to gain a millimeter more of air so she could say what need to be said. "Okay," she said. "This is it. You tell me what's wrong now, or I'm stopping this wedding."

"I want a Krispy Kreme doughnut," Di said, the threat of a sob under the words.

"I'll get you one," Min said, regrouping. "I'll go out and—"

"I can't have one," Di said. "There are twelve grams of fat in every Krispy Kreme."

"Well, yes," Min said, "but I'm thinking since it's your wedding day—"

"Everything is perfect," Di said.

"Not even close," Min said. "Listen, if you want out of this wedding, I'll get the car keys from Cal, and you and I can go back to the apartment and drink champagne and eat many Krispy Kremes."

"Want out?" Di straightened. "No. No."

"Okay," Min said. "But if you change your mind, I'm not kidding about the car keys and the doughnuts."

"I won't change my mind," Di said. "This is my fairy tale wedding."

"Then it's time to go," Min said, hoping action might jog something loose in Di's brain.

Di stood up and Min held out her arms again to show her the corset. "So what do you think?"

"This was a dumb idea," Di said, her voice unsteady as she looked at Min. "Why would I put you in a corset?"

"So I'd have a waistline," Min said.

"You have a waistline," Di said. "It's not a small waistline, but there's nothing wrong with it." She stood looking into Min's eyes, breathtakingly beautiful, cold as ice.

"Okay," Min said, taking her hand. "You *have* to tell me what's wrong."

"Nothing is wrong," Di said. "Everything is perfect."

Worse knocked on the door and poked her head in. "Are you ready?" she asked, sounding more tentative than Min had ever heard her. "Because we're supposed to be lining up."

Di ignored her, and Min said, "We'll be right out."

Worse opened the door farther. "You look wonderful, Di."

Di picked up her bouquet.

"Wreath," Min said, and Di reached down for the wreath of white orchids and roses and slapped it on her head, the fingertip-length veil askew. "Oh. Okay. I can just pin—"

But Diana was already crossing the room.

"I'll fix it," Worse said, giving Min her usual "you're impossible" stare.

"I don't think you can," Min said, and picked up her bouquet and followed Diana out.

Chapter
Fourteen

The setting sun flooded the vestibule, but Di's face was pale and cold under her now perfect wreath and veil. George stood beside her, uncomfortable in his morning suit, darting anxious glances at her. He frowned a question at Min, and she shrugged. She felt for him, but he was low on her list of people to save at the moment.

Wet stood in front of them beside the arch, and then the processional started, and she gave her bustle one final twitch, sniffed, broke into a rigid smile, took a step forward, and turned into the chapel.

Worse moved forward, stood counting until it was her turn, blew a kiss to Di, took a step, smiled a broad cheerleader smile, and turned into the chapel.

Min looked back at Di. "You are my sister, and I am with you no matter what. If you want out of this, *I will get you out.*"

"Min?" her father said, startled, and Di shook her head.

"Okay." Min picked up the count from the music, plastered a smile on her face, took a step, and turned into the chapel.

Something caught at her bustle and left her stuck, leaning into the archway in midstep. She looked behind her and saw Di's hand clutching the lavender chiffon ruffles on her butt.

"Diana?" her father said, bewilderment in his voice.

Min stepped back. "Daddy, go smile in the archway so they know everything's all right." She pried Di's hand off her ruffles and towed her out onto the church steps into the waning light. "Talk."

Di's bouquet trembled in her hands. "Greg slept with my brides-maid."

"*Susie?*" Min said, not surprised but sick just the same. "I knew she—"

"Worse," Di said.

"How could it be worse?" Min said and then the other shoe dropped. "*Karen?*"

Di nodded.

"Oh," Min said, trying to think of what to say as her rage rose. "Oh, *honey*." She put her arm around Di. "Tell me this was before he pro-posed to you and not—"

"Last night," Di whispered, and Min took a deep breath, corset or not.

"*Son of a fucking bitch.*"

"Thank you," Di said, and sniffed.

"That *whore*, I swear I'll rip out *every hair on her goddamn head*." Min held Di tighter. "I'll nail her fucking chignon *to the church door*, the mis-erable *bitch*. And Dad will take Greg apart. He's been wanting to for months."

Di sniffed back a sob.

"We'll take care of you," Min said. "You are *not alone*. Liza and Bonnie—" She broke off, realizing that flaunting her friends wasn't the best move now, trying to imagine how she'd feel if either of one them betrayed her, if Liza slept with Cal, and it was incomprehensible, it couldn't happen, they'd never—

"I watched you and Cal last night," Di said, tears blurring her eyes, "and you were so perfect for each other, you were just you, laughing and whispering together, you didn't have to be anybody else, thin or any-thing, he loves you just for being you, and I wanted to talk to Greg, I wanted to be that with him, too, so when you fell asleep, I drove over to his apartment, and they were in the bedroom." Her face crumpled. *"They weren't even on the bed."*

Min put both arms around her and held her close. "And Karen's blowing you kisses today. The skanky *whore*."

"They don't know I know," Di said into her shoulder. "They didn't see me. I backed out."

"That was very mature," Min said, gritting her teeth. "I would have put blood on the walls. Okay, I'll go stop the wedding—"

"No," Di said, straightening fast. Her pearl-studded corset rose and fell as she sucked in air. "No, no. No."

"What?" Min said.

"No," Diana said. "I'm ready to go."

"Okay, I admire how you've handled this," Min said, trying to sound calm, "but I think actually *marrying* the son of a bitch may be carrying maturity *too far*."

"I have to," Di said, breathless. "It's all planned. There are presents. Bonnie put pearls on a cake."

"I'll eat the cake," Min said. "I'll send the presents back. I'll even maim the groom for you."

"No," Di said. "It wasn't . . . He wasn't . . . It was just pre-wedding jitters. We'll be fine."

"Di." Min took as deep a breath as possible and tried to sound calm. "Pre-wedding jitters means he panics at the bachelor party. *It doesn't mean he fucks your best friend.*"

Di shook her head. "No, no. Not everybody finds a Cal. Greg is a good man. He just . . . panicked. I'm getting married." She swallowed. "I just had to tell somebody. It's a relief to tell somebody."

"Oh." Min felt sick. "Okay. But if you change your mind *at any time*, in the middle of the ceremony, in the middle of your honeymoon, in the middle of the *birth of your first child*, I will be there to help you leave. You say the word and we're *gone*. You are *not alone*." She tried to take another breath and her corset fought back. "Listen, are you sure? Because I—"

Di nodded. "I just had to tell somebody. I'm okay."

"Wonderful," Min said, "I'm not." She waited another beat for her to back down, but Di walked past her into the vestibule, leaving her nothing to do but follow.

Min smiled at her father, who looked crazed, took her place in the arch, and started down the aisle, vaguely aware that David and Cynthie were in a pew together looking tense, that Bonnie and Liza were in the third pew from the altar sending her "What the hell?" looks, that Cal was in the second row staring fascinated at her neckline, and that Greg-the-bastard was up at the front looking annoyed. *Die, you treacherous scum-sucking pig*, she thought, and that was so inadequate she began to think of other things, not realizing she was scowling until she saw Cal's eyes widen and Greg take a step back.

She smoothed out her face. Okay, there was that "show just cause or hold your peace" moment for stopping weddings, the escape clause. She could say something there. But if she did, she'd ruin Di's wedding, and she had a feeling the wedding was more important to her sister than the marriage. And even if it wasn't, it was Di's choice. She was not going to be her mother, running Di's life for her.

She took her place beside Worse at the front of the church and thought about smacking her in the face with her bouquet. Maybe she could say she'd slipped. A couple of times.

Worse sighed and shook her head at Min, pointing at her own wreath.

Bitch whore, Min thought, and straightened her wreath.

The wedding march kicked in, and Min turned and watched as Diana started down the aisle, a Hollywood vision with the sun shining behind her like a blessing.

Her face was lost, and Min's heart broke for her.

Min turned away and saw Cal frowning at her. He mouthed "What?" at her and she shook her head, almost in tears. Not even he could fix this one.

Di reached the front of the church, the ceremony began, and after a while people began to stir in their seats. *They know something's wrong*, Min thought. They weren't getting that happiness buzz people were supposed to get at weddings. Even Di's bustle looked tragic.

Then the minister said, "If any man can show just cause why they may not lawfully be joined together, let him now speak," and Min took a step closer to her sister.

Di turned to look at her, and Min met her eyes. "Do it."

After a moment, the minister nodded, and began the vows.

Di reached out and clutched Min's arm and whispered, "I do," and Min sighed in relief.

"Not yet, dear," the minister whispered back.

"*No,*" Min said to him. "That's not what she means." She nodded at Diana again. "*Do it.*"

Di swallowed. "I object," she said, but her voice was so faint that the minister leaned forward.

"She *objects,*" Min said loudly.

"To *what?*" Greg said.

"To *you,* you *traitorous son of a bitch,*" Min said, and heard a gasp from the front pews. *Loud voice, loud voice,* she told herself. *Not your loud voice.* Then she looked at Greg again, and thought, *Hell, yes, my loud voice.*

"I object," Di said, her voice up to room temperature again. She turned so she was facing the pews. "I object to the groom sleeping with my bridesmaid last night. I object to the groom being a—" Her voice broke.

"*Cheating, scum-sucking pig,*" Min said to Greg behind Di's back, definitely in her loud voice.

"*Yes,*" Di said, and walked down the steps, her bouquet quivering.

"Also, your hair is *stupid,*" Min said to Greg, and started down the chapel steps after her sister. Greg caught her arm, and said, "*Wait a minute—*" and she swung back to let him have it, and then Cal was between them, shouldering Greg aside. Behind them Wet said to Worse, "You slept with *Greg?,*" and then somebody tapped Greg on the shoulder just as Wet lunged for Worse, and Greg turned around and met George's fist as Wet yanked hard on Worse's chignon, and Worse went ass over elbow into the front pew.

Cal caught Greg by the shoulders just before he hit the ground, and they both looked up to see Nanette, coming at them, exquisite in pearl gray.

"You're a *horrible* man," she said to Greg, and kicked him in the ribs with her pointed Manolo Blahniks.

"*Mother,*" Min said.

Nanette said, "*Thirty-seven goddamn years,*" kicking him on every word, until Min pulled her away. She staggered sideways and ended up facing George, who was trying to get past Cal to hit Greg again. "*And you, too,*" Nanette said and smacked him in the head with her purse.

George put his hands up to ward her off and said, "*What did I do?*" and she stormed down the aisle, her head held high.

Behind George's back, Wet said, "You *bastard,*" to Greg and began to hit him in the face with her bouquet while Worse tried to crawl out of the pew.

"I have to go to Di," Min said to Cal. "Step on his head, will you?"

"Go," Cal said, and the last thing she saw as she turned for the door was Cal dropping Greg on the carpet to block George from hitting him again while Wet whaled on him with her orchids.

Cal found Min at the reception, since Di had insisted on going to meet anybody who might show up. They were sitting in the mostly deserted ballroom with Liza, Bonnie, and an entirely too cheerful Wet, while Roger ferried champagne back and forth and Nanette consoled Di with the news that all men were cheating scum.

"*Mother,*" Min said, and Cal took her hand and pulled her out into the hall with him.

"My mother is *insane,*" Min said to him.

"You just noticed?" Cal said, trying not to be distracted by her bulging neckline. "That looks like it hurts."

"It does," Min said. "I've spent the entire day in bondage." She peered back through the archway. "Look at Wet. She's in there *giggling.* To think that I ever felt sorry for that wench. Did you need me for something?"

"Yes," Cal said, getting a little dizzy as her cleavage rose and fell. "Especially now that you brought up bondage. When can you take that off?"

"I think I could lose it now, except the knots are so tight I can't get them undone." She ran her finger around the top of the corset, and Cal thought, *Let me do that.* "It's killing me."

"Wait," Cal said, and fished in his pocket for his pocketknife.

He slipped the knife under the bow and sliced through the ribbon, and Min took a deep breath as the rest of the corset began to unlace itself from the pressure. "Oh, Lord, that feels good."

Cal watched the rise and fall of her loosened corset. "Looks good, too." Even though he knew better, he drew his finger down the slope of her breast and felt the need for her that had been simmering for weeks flare up again.

If he didn't have her soon, he was going to lose his mind.

She said, "Hey," and caught his hand.

"Not my fault," he said, close to her mouth. "You were flaunting."

Her mouth melted under his, warm with familiarity, and her breath came faster as his hand curled around the firmness of her breast. "Oh," she said, and he kissed his way down the smooth curve of her neck and felt her sigh under his hand. "Oh, that feels so good. But I have to—"

"I know," he said, holding on to her. "I shouldn't have—" He kissed her again, wanting her so much that he couldn't let go.

"Yes, you should have," Min said, against his mouth. "But Di—"

"Right," Cal said, remembering his mission. "That's what I came to tell you. One of the ushers has Greg out in the car. Does Diana want to see him before he goes? He wants to apologize."

"Hell, *no*," Min said, pulling away from him. "What can he possibly say?"

" 'I'm the biggest cliché in bad wedding stories'?" Cal said, missing her warmth. "If it helps, the ushers are disgusted with him, too."

"I hate him," Min said, looking back into the ballroom.

"How is she?" Cal said, following her eyes to her sister, feeling guilty that he was having carnal thoughts while Di was in misery.

"I think she's almost relieved," Min said, watching her. "Not happy, and she's going to cry, but I think she knew she wanted the wedding and not Greg."

"Very sensible of her," Cal said. "Who would want Greg?"

Min stretched up and kissed him. "I'm staying with her tonight."

"I figured," Cal said, hating it anyway. He wrapped his arms around her and hugged her close. "I want you, Minerva."

"I'm free tomorrow night," she said, smiling up at him. "Go get rid of that jerk and come back for champagne."

"Be right back," Cal said, and kissed her again, surprised all over again that it was so easy, that everything with her had become so easy. *That can't be right,* he thought, but he grinned anyway as he went to tell the ushers they could remove Greg.

On his way back from the car, Cal ran into David.

"I think the reception's over, David," Cal said, trying not to snarl. "You can go home now."

"I can't," David said, looking noble. "There's something you should know."

Oh, hell, Cal thought and said, "What?"

"That bet we made," David said, "the one where you could get Min into bed in a month."

"What?" Cal looked at him, confused. "What bet? We didn't make that bet. That was you, being drunk and reckless."

"Min knows," David said, and Cal felt a chill. "She overheard it that night, that's why she went out with you, to pay us both back and to get a date to this fiasco. They all knew, Liza, Bonnie, her sister, she told everybody. They've all been laughing at us."

The hallway suddenly seemed too narrow, not enough air, and it was much too cold for June.

"I had to tell you because if she knows about it, the bet's off. You never had a chance to win. She's been playing you the whole time."

"No," Cal said, his throat tight. "She wouldn't." The familiar slug of shame and self-loathing hit him—*how stupid can you be*—even while common sense told him this was David making trouble, that Min wouldn't do that—

"Face it," David said, clapping him on the shoulder. "She made fools of us. Well, you more than me because I wasn't trying to get her into bed, but I feel pretty stupid, too."

Cal looked at him with loathing. "At last, some self-knowledge." *She knew. She thinks I'm stupid.*

"Hey." David held his hands up. "Don't turn on me. *I'm* not the one who's been making you look *stupid* for a month."

Cal flinched and then turned and walked away, back into the reception hall. It wasn't true, Min wasn't like that, she wouldn't do that, except that suddenly a lot of things that had been inexplicable now made sense.

He walked across the almost-deserted reception hall to where Min was trying to shield Diana from Nanette. "Could I talk to you for a minute?" he said.

Min looked up from Diana and said, "Now isn't—"

"*Now*," Cal said, and Min's eyes widened and she nodded. "I'll be right back, baby," she said to Diana, and let him draw her out into the hall, casting anxious looks back to her sister as she went.

"Is it Greg?" she said when they were in the hall where she could still keep an eye on Diana. "Did he—"

"Why did you go to dinner with me that first night?" Cal said.

"*What?*" Min said, so surprised she stopped looking at Di.

"Tell me the truth."

Min straightened. "I went . . ." She looked away from him and shook her head. "I went because you made a bet with David you could get me into bed in a month, and I needed a date for this wedding. And then we went out and you were so slick I knew I couldn't stand that for three weeks and I thanked you for dinner and went home. And why we have to talk about this now is beyond me."

"Why in hell would you keep going out with me if you thought I'd do that?" Cal said, a month's worth of frustration morphing into anger. "For the *sport?* Was it *funny?*"

"*No,*" Min said, sounding annoyed. "That's why I kept turning you down. Could we discuss this la—"

"So," Cal said. "You turned me down to make a fool of me, and you and Bonnie and Liza sat around and laughed about it."

"No," Min said, exasperated. "We thought you were slime. It wasn't funny at all."

"Ah," Cal said, nodding at her. "*This* is why Liza kept hitting me."

"Yes. But I don't *care*." She spat the last word from between her teeth. "It doesn't *matter*."

"You care," Cal said, grimly. "You're mad as hell. That's why you've been playing me, making me crazy for you, making me look like—"

"Hey," Min said, pointing her finger at him. "I have been completely honest with you."

"You never asked me about the bet," Cal said.

"Yeah, I did," Min said, folding her arms. "And you ducked it every time I asked."

"No, you didn't ask." Cal folded his arms. "And you know how I know? Because I'd have told you I didn't make that bet."

"I was *standing right there*," Min said.

"Then *you didn't listen very well*," Cal said. *"I told him no."*

"You said, 'Piece of cake,'" Min snapped.

"I have never said 'Piece of cake' in my life," Cal said. "It's a *stupid* thing to say." He took a deep breath and thought, *Fuck it.* "How *stupid* do you think *I am?*" he said savagely, and Min froze. "How *stupid* does *everybody* think I am?"

"Not stupid," she said, watching him warily now. "What's going on?"

"They all thought I'd made that bet with a *sleaze* like David." Cal shook his head at the breadth of her betrayal. "Because *you told* them I made that bet. And they watched you play me, and like a fool I fell for it."

"You did make it," Min said, but she sounded uncertain. "Look, I didn't think you were stupid, I thought you were . . . awful. But then you weren't awful so I . . . Where is this coming from? You know how I feel about you. I love you. The bet doesn't matter—"

"It doesn't matter?" Cal said. "How *stupid are you?*"

"Hey," Min said, her face darkening. "Okay, look, I know this is pushing all your buttons, but get a grip. I love you, you know I love you, but I don't have time to baby-sit you right now—"

"Baby-sit me?" Cal clenched his jaw to keep from screaming at her, because she'd betrayed him and because he still wanted her, desperately. *Get out of this*, he thought, and said, "Well, you'll never have to baby-sit me again."

"What?" Then she started to nod, her face twisted in anger. "Oh. I get it. *Of course.* You're running. *You bastard.* You got what you wanted, I said 'I love you,' the game is over, and now you're out the door. I knew you'd do this. *I knew you'd do this.*"

"This is not about me," Cal said, not meeting her eyes.

"Oh, *please*," Min snapped. "This is all about you. One hundred percent of your relationships end with you running away. This is you grabbing any excuse to get—"

"*Hey*," Tony said, and they both turned to see him standing in the doorway, looking madder than Cal had ever seen him. "I don't know what the fuck you're doing, but whatever it is, it's not as important as what that kid in there is going through. You've got the rest of your lives to fight, she needs you now."

"Tell Min I didn't make that damn bet with David to have sex with her," Cal said.

Tony looked at Min, exasperated. "He didn't make that bet."

"I heard him make the bet," Min said. "David said that he'd have to get the gray-checked suit into bed in a month and he said, 'Piece of . . . cake.' " She looked from Tony to Cal. "Oh."

"I said 'Piece of cake,' " Tony said. "I was wrong. I don't care. Fight about it later. Right now, get your ass back in there and help your sister. Your mother took her champagne away because it has too many calories, and that damn bridesmaid in the green dress keeps laughing."

"You're right," Min said, stepping toward the door. "But we won't be fighting about it later because *Calvin* has decided it's time to *go*."

"You're kidding me," Tony said, looking at them both with contempt. "You two are the biggest babies I've ever seen."

"What?" Min said, stopping.

"Here's the short version," Tony said to Min. "You're a man-hating bitch and he's a woman-fearing coward." He looked at Cal. "Get over that, will you?"

"*The hell with both of you*," Min said and went back to her sister, as Cal turned on Tony.

"They're all like that," Nanette was saying to Di when Min got back to them, seething. "You can't trust any of them." She gestured with the champagne glass she was holding. "They tell you they love you and then—"

Min grabbed the glass out of her hand. *"Here,"* she said, handing it to Di. "We're drinking about twelve bottles of this tonight, so get started."

"Do you know how many calories—" Nanette began.

"Listen, you," Min said to her. "You're going home and throwing out every damn fashion magazine in the house. You're going cold turkey, it's the only thing that's going to save you."

Nanette straightened. "Just because you won't lose the weight, doesn't mean Diana has to be fat."

"I'm not *fat,* Mother," Min said. "But while we're on the subject, I don't see where not eating for fifty-five years has made *you* particularly happy. Go home and eat something, for Christ's sake." She looked around. "Where are those goddamn cake boxes?"

"I'll get them," Roger said, and went fast.

"I think that's very sensible," Wet said, beaming at Min.

"And *you,*" Min said. "Go someplace else and gloat. In fact, go find Greg. You deserve each other. He's a selfish bastard and you love to be beat."

"That's not fair," Wet said, back to her familiar whine.

"Hit the road, Wet," Liza said. "You've been laughing ever since you stopped hitting Worse. If you're not going to be a comfort, have the decency to be an empty space."

"Well, at least I'm not *Tart,*" Wet said and stalked off.

"Did she just call me a tart?" Liza said to Bonnie.

Min sat down next to Diana in Wet's vacated chair.

"Here's what we're going to do," she said, taking her hand. "We're going to get those cake boxes and a case of the champagne, and we're going back to my place."

"Okay," Diana said, her voice breaking again.

"And we're going to eat cake and get drunk," Min said.

"Oh, *Min,*" Nanette said. "It'll take you weeks to work off those calories."

Min looked at her mother for a moment and thought, *This is what Diana lives with every damn day.* "And then," she said to Diana, "since you have the week off for your honeymoon, I'm going to take the week off, too, and we're going to go house-hunting."

Diana stopped crying. "House-hunting?"

"Yes," Min said. "I'm going to buy a great two bedroom Arts and Crafts bungalow. And you're going to move in with me."

"I am?" Diana said, sitting up a little.

"Yes," Min said. "You've lived with the calorie police for too long."

"That's ridiculous," Nanette said. "She is not going to move."

"But there are some rules," Min said, and Diana swallowed and nodded. "There will always be butter in the refrigerator. There will be no sound tracks from Julia Roberts movies. And from now on," she said, looking toward the door where Cal was glaring at Tony, "we only date ugly men."

Diana was nodding at Min. "And I'll get out of the way on Thursday nights."

"Why?" Min said, mystified.

"So you guys can have your If Dinner," she said, and Min realized that the worst thing that had happened to Di wasn't that she'd lost Greg, it was that she'd lost her best friends. She thought again of what it would be like if Bonnie and Liza had betrayed her, and she lost her breath at how far beyond horrible that would be.

As bad as losing Cal.

"You'll come, too," Bonnie said, putting her arm around Di.

"Hell, yes," Liza said, as Roger came back with a tray of cake boxes and the cake topper. She ripped the bride and groom off the cake top and put it in front of Diana and said, "Pay attention, Little Stats, we're about to have a moment." Diana looked up and Liza stomped on the head of the groom, shattering it into dust. "Now," she said. "He is officially history. And if there's a God, he has a splitting headache."

"I think you can count on that," Roger said. "He got hit a lot."

"Good," Liza said. "Now we're going back to Min's and get drunk."

Diana looked at Min through her tears. "Can I wear your bunny slippers?"

"You can *have* my bunny slippers," Min said, thinking of Cal in furious misery.

She looked toward the door and saw him standing there, watching her, and then Tony was in her way, spreading out his hands, saying to

Liza, "Nice job on the cake topper, ace. I suppose you had to kill the groom," and Liza said, "Defend him and die," and Tony said, "No, he was an asshole even without the haircut," and Diana laughed and then cried again.

Out in the hall, Cal turned and Min saw Cynthie standing behind him. He stopped for a moment, and then he left, and Cynthie went with him.

Right. You wouldn't stay to help because it's not about you, is it, buddy? Min thought and then shoved him out of her mind and turned back to Diana.

"I'm a coward?" Cal had said to Tony when Min had gone, pleased to be fighting with somebody he could hit.

"I can't believe you're running away from this one," Tony said. "Hell, Cal, you're thirty-five, aren't you tired of that shit by now?"

"You're thirty-five, too," Cal said grimly.

"And I have never in my life looked at a woman the way you look at Min," Tony said. "I'd be pissed at her, that all-men-are-pigs bit is a pain in the ass, but I'd *tell* her that, I wouldn't walk away from her. What's wrong with you?"

"This is not about me," Cal said.

"Jesus," Tony said and turned back to the ballroom.

"Where are you going?" Cal said.

Tony shook his head. "Back to where there's real trouble. We're all in there. Why aren't you?"

Then he walked away and Cal looked past him to where Min had her arms around Diana, and Bonnie was leaning close to them, and Roger was holding a tray of cake in one hand and patting Diana on the back with the other, and Liza was smashing something with her foot, and as Tony got closer, he spread his hands out, and Diana looked up and gave him a watery smile and Cal knew he was clowning again, doing his bit. *Fuck*, he thought. *I should be in there.* Then Min looked up and saw him, her face set and stormy, and he flinched and thought, *The hell with you*, and turned, furious and miserable to see Cynthie, looking lovelier than ever.

"Are you all right?" she said.

"No," Cal said.

She smiled at him. "I know a place we can get a drink."

"Where's that?" Cal said.

"My place," Cynthie said.

"Let's go," Cal said, and left, knowing Min was watching.

Cal spent most of Monday fuming about what a bitch Min had been, and Tuesday wasn't much better. It didn't help that in the same two days, Cynthie had called twice to talk him into the drink he'd turned down when he'd dropped her off at her place, every client had become intensely stupid, and his partners kept looking at him as if he'd been drowning puppies. Worst of all, he missed Min so much, wanted her so much, that it was making him sick. The crowning touch to his day was his mother, calling him at work to find out if he was seeing Cynthie again.

"No," he said. "I'm never going to see her again, so *get off my ass about her*."

"*Calvin*," his mother said, in a voice that would have stopped him cold any other day.

"In *fact*," he said, "since I'm such an *overwhelming disappointment* to you, I'm never going to see *you* again, either."

"Calvin?" his mother said, a new note in her voice.

"*Forget it*," Cal said, and hung up.

Tony came over and unplugged his phone. "You get this back when you call her," he said. "Until then, you don't talk to people."

"I'm never calling her again," Cal said. "She's been a bitch my whole life and I'm done with her."

"Not your mother, you dumbass," Tony said. "Min."

"She's been a bitch for a month and I'm done with her, too," Cal said. "The hell with both of them."

"That's very mature," Tony said, sounding just like Min.

Roger shook his head and went back to work, and Cal ignored them both to savagely edit a seminar packet.

When he got home, he threw his suit coat on the couch, picked up his Glenlivet and then stopped as Elvis began to sing "She" next door.

"Jesus fucking Christ," he said and slammed the Glenlivet down.

When he pounded on Shanna's door, a strange woman answered, brown-haired, a little below medium height. "Oh," he said. "I thought . . . Shanna . . ."

"Oh, she's here." The woman smiled at him, a sweet smile that reminded him of Min, her eyes huge in her round face as she stepped back. "Shanna?"

Cal looked past her to Shanna, carrying two ruby goblets out of the kitchen.

"Cal!" she said, smiling. "This is Linda. Linda, this is my next-door neighbor, Cal." Her smile widened and she jerked her head toward the stereo. "First date music."

"Oh," Cal said, taking a step back. "Hell, I'm sorry . . ."

"Don't you just love Elvis?" Linda said.

"Yeah," Cal said. "Good for you, Shan. I'll see you later."

"Stay for a drink," Shanna said, with a look that telegraphed, *Get lost*.

"Can't stay," Cal said. "I have to . . ." He jerked his head toward his apartment, at a loss for what he might have to do over there besides fume.

"Is Min there?" Shanna said, putting the glasses down on the break-fast bar. "Maybe later we could—"

"No," Cal said, his rage back on the surface again. "Min is not there."

Shanna stopped, reading his face. "Oh, no. What did you do?"

"Strangely enough, *nothing*," Cal said. "Why do you assume—"

"I don't care," Shanna said. "Get her back."

"It's *done*," Cal said.

"No, it is not," Shanna said. "You really lost something this time."

"This is not about me," Cal said.

"Yes, it is," Shanna said. "This time it is. What happened?"

Cal shook his head. "Nope. Not interesting." He nodded at Linda. "Very nice to meet you." He turned to go but Shanna grabbed the back of his shirt in her fist and yanked.

"Sit down and tell me everything," she said. "Or I will track you back to your apartment and bitch at you until you tell me there."

Fifteen minutes later she said, "Well, it's a toss-up as to which of the two of you is dumber."

"*Hey,*" Cal said.

"You're desperately in love with each other and you're playing footsie with it. Do you know how rare what you have is?"

"Christ, I hope so," Cal said. "I'd hate to think there was an epidemic of this garbage."

"Stop it," Shanna said. "You want her back."

"*Why* would I—"

"*Stop it!*" Shanna said. "You want her back."

Cal sat back on the couch and the memory of Min he'd been fighting for two days came back. He put his head in his hands. "Oh, Christ, I want her back. Which shows you how stupid I really am."

"Oh, for heaven's sake, *call her,*" Shanna said. "Tell her you're sorry."

Cal jerked his head up. "Hey, *I'm the injured party here.*"

"Yeah," Shanna said. "That been keeping you warm at night, has it? Call her. Tell her you want to talk to her tomorrow night. Take a nice bottle of wine, tell her you love her, work out this non-problem, and live happily ever after."

"Why tomorrow?" Cal said, confused. "If I'm going to apologize for something I *did not do,* I could go over there now—"

"Because by then you'll have lost the bet," Shanna said.

"*I didn't make the bet,*" Cal said.

Linda moved a little farther away from him on the couch.

"Stop yelling," Shanna said. "It doesn't matter. You hit her where it hurts."

"What—"

"She's not beautiful," Shanna said over him. "She's not thin. She knows that everybody who sees you with her wonders how she got you."

"That's not true," Cal said. "She's amazing."

"Right," Shanna said. "We see that, but there are many people who don't. Including, I believe, her ex-boyfriend who dumped her and then tried to make that bet with you."

"*Ouch,*" Linda said.

"And then you come along, gorgeous and perfect, and you convince her you love her—"

"I do love her, damn it," Cal said.

"—only it turns out you made a bet—"

Cal stood up. *"I did not make that bet—"*

"—that you could take her to dinner," Shanna went on.

Cal sat down.

"And she thought you were trying to get her into bed for a bet, and then in the end, when things got tense, instead of standing by her, you walk out with your gorgeous ex-girlfriend."

"Not good," Linda said.

"Oh, hell." Cal put his head in his hands again. "I can't believe I fell for this. I can't believe I let that asshole David Fisk do this. I *am* stupid."

"Only this once," Shanna said. "It's going to be okay. All you have to do is throw the bet. Big deal, you lose a little pride and ten bucks."

"Ten thousand bucks," Cal said.

"Whoa," Linda said, straightening. "This is like cable."

"You bet David ten thousand dollars you could get Min into bed?" Shanna said, incredulous.

Cal looked at the ceiling. "Does *anybody* here listen to me?"

"He didn't make the bet," Linda told Shanna.

"Thank you," Cal said.

"Everybody knows about the bet," Shanna says. "It exists in everybody's minds and if you sleep with her before . . . when is the bet up?"

"Tomorrow at nine, nine-thirty, I don't know," Cal said, trying to remember when they'd made the damn thing. *Hadn't* made the damn thing. Christ, even he was doing it.

"Is she worth losing ten thousand dollars?"

"Hell, yes," Cal said.

"Well, there you are. Go call her and tell her you'll see her after you lose the bet." Shanna folded her arms, implacable. "Don't make me come over there and do it for you."

"Do it," Linda said to Cal. "It's romantic in a perverse sort of way."

"Thank you," Cal said to her. "On that note, I'm going home." He got up and left, ignoring Shanna's *"Cal."*

Shanna was *wrong*, he told himself as he poured himself another Scotch, but the thought didn't have much conviction. He closed his eyes and thought of Min and tried to remind himself that it was all treachery, but he kept hearing her say, "I love you," and he knew it was true.

"Oh *fuck*," he said and when the doorbell rang, he yanked it open, prepared to deck Shanna if she was going to yap about Min anymore.

It was Cyn, looking hot as hell in her blue halter top and short black skirt. She tilted her head up at him and her glossy black hair swung back. "I know you're upset," she said, softly. "I don't want you to be alone."

"I'm all right," he said, as she stepped closer.

"No, you're not," she said. "She hit you hard." She held up a bottle of Glenlivet. "Come on, talk about it. You'll feel better."

She'll do anything I ask, Cal thought. *And the world is full of women like her. Why do I need Min?*

Cynthie smiled up at him, lovely and warm. "Do I get to come in?"

"No," Cal said. "I have to make a phone call."

 *Chapter Fifteen*

Cynthie said, "I can wait," and he remembered Min saying, "You get to know the real us and then you leave us." Cynthie smiled up at him, her heart in her eyes, and he thought, *Oh, hell.*

He shook his head at her. "I'm sorry. Somebody explained to me what I've done to you. I'm sorry. I never meant to hurt you, I never meant to hurt anybody, but I never meant to marry you, either."

Cynthie took a deep breath and nodded. "That's all right, I can wait—"

"There's somebody else," Cal said, as gently as he could. "I'm sorry, but I'm in love with somebody else."

She flinched. "No. You love me."

"I never said that. You know that."

"Yes, but you do." Her hands gripped the bottle tighter. "You don't realize it, but you do. We're perfect for each other."

He closed his eyes so he wouldn't see how desperate she was.

"It's Min," Cynthie said. "I know it's Min. Look, she's a nice woman, but she's not me."

"I know," Cal said. "That's the problem." Cynthie's face twisted, and he said, "I'm sorry, Cyn."

He shut the door in her face and leaned against the door for a moment, trying not to think about how much damage he'd done to her, not even wanting to think about anybody else.

Except Min.

Fix this, he told himself and sat down to figure out a way.

At about the same time Shanna was reading Cal the riot act, Min was listening to Liza say, "This is really good," as she speared the last marsala-soaked mushroom at Min's dining room table. Then Liza said, "Tell me again why we're doing this."

"Because we always had chicken marsala on Tuesday nights," Min said, stabbing her chicken with no enthusiasm as Elvis prowled about her ankles, impatient for leftovers. "I'm trying to cloud the association."

"Very practical," Lisa said. "Except you're miserable, so there's not enough cloud in the world, babe."

"May I have the butter, please?" Diana said, picking up another piece of bread from Emilio's.

Bonnie pushed the butter dish her way. "Have you heard from him?" she asked Min.

"Of course not," Min said, revving up her anger again so she wouldn't have to think about how she'd been waiting for a phone call for two days. "He's *mad at me*. Can you believe it? *He's* mad at *me*. Did I make a bet? Noooo. But *he's*—"

"Oh, *please*, no more of this," Liza said. "You've bitched about him for two days. Face it, the man has a point."

Min put down her fork, and Diana stopped buttering her bread.

"He does not have a point," Min snapped. "This whole mess is because he does not have a point and now you're turning on me? It's not enough that Bonnie sandbagged me with that fairy tale garbage, now you—"

"It's not garbage," Bonnie said. "You got the fairy tale. You got the handsome prince who loved you. It worked."

"It did not work," Min said, slamming her hand down on the table. "He went into a snit and *left*. Just my luck, I get a *snitty prince*. Which is why he wasn't *a prince*. Which is why I don't believe *that garbage. I do not believe in the fairy tale, okay?*"

"I don't think it matters," Bonnie said, mild as ever. "The fairy tale believes in you."

Min turned to Liza. *"Tell her."*

Liza leaned her elbow on the table. "She's right."

Min flopped back in her chair. "Oh, for crying out loud. If this wasn't my apartment, I'd leave."

"Well, look at it from his point of view," Liza said. "He didn't make the bet. He tried not to date you, but he had to keep coming back because he was nuts about you, and you kept kissing him and then turning him down. He was patient, he charmed your parents, he was good to your friends, he found your snow globe, he taught you to cook, he got you a *cat*, for Christ's sake, and then it turns out that while he was knocking himself out for you, you were playing him for a fool."

"No, I wasn't," Min said, but her anger cooled considerably.

"He really is a sweetie," Diana said, licking butter off her lip.

"Liza's right," Bonnie said. "You know how awful school was for all three of these boys. They're all sensitive about being dumb. You hit Cal right on his sore spot, in front of his friends, in front of Cynthie, in front of David."

"Ouch," Min said faintly. She tried to summon up her old outrage over the bet, but after two days of venting, she'd been running out of steam anyway.

"I know you needed to be mad to deal with the pain," Liza said. "I do that, too. But if you want him back, get over it. Because if there wasn't a bet—"

"There wasn't," Min said miserably. "I believe him on that."

"Then he's given you everything and you haven't given him a damn thing."

"That's pretty harsh," Bonnie said to Liza.

"Why didn't you just ask him about the bet?" Liza said.

"I did," Min said.

"You said, 'Did you make a bet with David that you could sleep with me in a month?'"

"No," Min said, not meeting her eyes. "I asked him if there was anything he wasn't telling me."

Bonnie nodded. "And what did he say?"

Min sat back. "He kept confessing to things that weren't the bet."

"That must have been fun for everyone," Liza said. "Why didn't you flat out ask him?"

Min put her head in her hands. "I was afraid, okay? You know how all those people say, 'If they just *talked* about their problems, they'd all go away'? Well, I bet none of those people talk about *their* problems. I mean, it *sounds* good, but it's a terrible gamble." She looked up at Liza. "I knew he made that bet. I *heard him*. And I . . ." She stopped and swallowed. "I knew I only had a month and I wanted that month with him." She shook her head. "Not everybody faces life head-on the way that you do."

"Well, they should," Liza said. "You screwed up. So now you're going to have to grovel."

"What?" Bonnie said, while Min gaped at Liza, and Diana watched them all, fascinated.

Liza got up from the table, picked up Min's phone, and brought it over to her. "Call him. Tell him you were wrong, he was right, and you'll do anything to make it up to him."

Min swallowed. "*You* want me to grovel?"

"Yes," Liza said. "I'm not going to watch you lose him because of your dumb pride. Call and offer him anything he wants if he'll take you back."

Min looked at Bonnie, who nodded.

Min looked at the phone. If she called Cal, she'd at least get to hear his voice. How pathetic was that? "Pathetic," she said out loud.

"Only if you let this go," Liza said. "For once in your life, do the irrational, reckless thing. Call him."

Min sat there, frozen in fear. Then she took a deep breath and picked up the phone.

Cal was rehearsing his "How about a late dinner tomorrow?" speech when the phone rang, but when he picked it up and heard Min's tentative "Hi?" he forgot it all.

"Hi," he said and sat down hard on the couch.

"Don't say anything," she said, her words coming out in a rush. "Let me get this out. I was wrong not to tell you I knew about the bet. I was wrong not to trust you. Everything you said at the wedding was right. It's my fault. I want you back. I want us back. I love you and I need you—"

Relief made Cal dizzy.

"And I want you to see you now," she went on, and Cal thought, *Christ, yes,* and then the other shoe dropped. "Now?" he said and looked at the clock. Twenty-six hours before the bet was up. *Just tell her yes,* he thought, *she doesn't care about the bet anymore, she said so,* and then he remembered how she'd sounded when she'd said it at the wedding.

"It's been driving me crazy saying no to you all these weeks," Min was babbling, "but if you're not ready for that, that's okay, I just want to see you. I haven't seen you for two days, and I miss you so much. Can I come over right now? Just to talk? Or, you know, we could do other things. I can think of several. If you want more than talk. More would be good with me. Or not. Whatever."

More would be great with me, Cal thought and shook his head to clear it.

"I'm on my knees here," Min said, her voice straining to be chipper. "And not in a good way. Can I come over?"

"No," Cal said. "I'll come to you. Later." He swallowed. "Tomorrow. Nine-thirty. Tomorrow night, nine-thirty."

"Not *now?*" Min said, her voice cracking.

"*No,*" Cal said. "No. Nine-thirty. Tomorrow. I'll bring dinner."

"I can cook now," Min said. "I can make dinner. I can make it now."

"I'll bring dinner tomorrow," Cal said, thinking, *Christ, I've been stupid.*

"Fine, whatever." Min waited for a moment and then added, "I'm kind of hungry now, though."

"Tomorrow, nine-thirty, your place," Cal said, gritting his teeth.

"Okay," Min said. "All right. Tomorrow night it is." He was about to say good-bye when she said, "Are you seeing Cynthie?"

"Christ, no," Cal said, casting a guilty look at the door.

"Because you left with her. And David said you were. Or I wouldn't have asked. I mean, it's none of my business."

"It's your business," Cal said. "And David is an idiot. Stop talking to him."

"I'm trying," Min said.

Cal felt all his tension morph into a much more convenient anger. "What does that mean, you're trying?"

"He calls. For some reason, this whole mess has convinced him that he and I should get married."

"He's wrong," Cal snapped.

"I *know that*," Min said, her voice not placating anymore.

"You've got caller ID. Stop picking up the phone."

"Look, I'm not completely stupid."

"You're not stupid at all," Cal said, "your past month's performance notwithstanding." He winced. *Stupid. Stupid.*

"Hey, you made the bet."

"*I did not—*"

"The second one. The take-me-to-dinner one. I screwed up but I'm not going to pay for it for the rest of my life. You're culpable here, too. You made that dinner bet."

There you go, Cal thought. Shanna was right, damn it.

"Not that I'm assuming you're going to be around for the rest of my life," Min said, tentative again.

"*Tomorrow night,*" Cal said and hung up, before either one of them said something even dumber, pretty sure he'd done the right thing. *Christ, I'm in a Doris Day movie,* he thought, and went to tell Shanna that he'd done what she said.

"I love you," Min said forlornly to the dial tone.

"What happened?" Liza said. "What was all that stuff about Cynthie and David? I told you to grovel, not fight."

Min put the phone down and picked up Elvis for comfort. "He doesn't want to see me until tomorrow."

"That's strange," Liza said. "If I'd promised Tony sex like that, he'd have been here before I hung up the phone."

"I didn't actually promise him sex," Min said.

"Oh, please," Liza and Bonnie said together, and even Diana nodded and said, "Yes, you did."

"Could I keep some shred of dignity here?" Min said. "He just said no to sex, the bastard."

"No, he didn't," Bonnie said, patting her hand. "He just said, not until tomorrow." She frowned. "I don't get him."

"Tell us what he said," Liza said.

"He said he'd come over here tomorrow at nine-thirty, and he'd bring dinner. Like I want to eat." Min sniffed. "I hate this. This is dumb."

"What's so special about nine-thirty tomorrow night?" Liza said. "What's tomorrow? It's just Wednesday."

"It's Roger's and my anniversary," Bonnie said. "He's ordering champagne, and then he's going to pick me up at the bar the way he did four weeks ago, and then he's going to propose."

"Cute," Min said.

"That's it," Liza said, straightening. "Tomorrow night it's four weeks since David made the bet."

"But Cal didn't take the bet," Min snapped. "I'm tired of this conversation. He didn't—"

"But everybody knows about it," Liza said. "So if you give in before the time's up, he wins. And he loves to win. He always wins. He lives to win."

"Not seeing your point," Min said.

"He's throwing the bet," Liza said.

"Why?" Min stood up and Elvis leaped for the floor. "Why in the name of *God*—"

"It's sort of gallant," Bonnie said.

"If you ask me, it's a control thing, too," Liza said, disdain in her voice. "He gets to call the shots. What happened at nine-thirty?"

Min shrugged, confused. "We got to the restaurant a little before ten so we were probably leaving the bar about then."

Liza nodded. "He's giving himself some leeway." She frowned.

"Although more than he needs if he's bringing dinner. Then there'll be foreplay. It's going to take some time to get you—"

"He can have me when he walks in the door," Min said.

Diana picked up her bread again. "I'll go to the movies tomorrow night. You're going to need this place to yourself, and I'm not going back home. Mom's still mad I moved in here. She's convinced I'm eating carbs." She bit into the bread, and Min laughed in spite of herself and then began to consider the situation.

So what if Cal lost the bet? Ten bucks. He could afford it. "No," she said. "I'm not going to be the bet he lost, that's not how I want us to start. He's going to win that bet tomorrow night, and he's going to be *very* happy doing it."

"Why tomorrow?" Liza said.

"Because I'm going to need a really hot nightgown," Min said. "And a lot more courage than I have right now. And a plan."

"Explain," Liza said, and Min leaned in and they began to talk.

"What the hell is going on?" David said the next evening when he called Cynthie. "I thought you said that fight at the wedding would end it."

"We lost," Cynthie said, her voice sounding tired. "He loves her so much, he's forgiven her."

"I just talked to Min," David said, reliving the experience in vivid detail. "She told me she's going to make sure he wins so I should get my checkbook out. She sounded mad *at me*."

"David, it's done," Cynthie said. "The only thing we can do is wait and hope infatuation wears itself out and they come to their senses."

"Six months to three years? I'm not waiting on Calvin Morrisey." David thought of Cal with loathing. He had Min so snowed she believed he'd actually throw that bet. He'd probably set it up so she'd insist on his winning. He'd probably . . . David sat back. "Wait a minute. What if Min found out *he* was playing *her*? What if he tricked her into sleeping with him so he could win the bet?"

"He's not," Cynthie said, tiredly. "It's *done*, David."

"No, it's not," David said. "Not if the bet's for midnight. What if her family and friends found out he made that bet?"

"*It's done, David,*" Cynthie said.

"I'm not done," David said. "I'm going to win."

At eight, Cal had a bottle of wine and a box of Krispy Kremes ready to take to Min's apartment, and an hour and a half of rabid sexual frustration to kill when the phone rang.

"*Cal,*" Diana said when he answered. "You have to *get over here.* Min's *in trouble.*"

"What—" Cal said, and then all he heard was a dial tone. "Okay," he said, and headed over to Min's apartment, deeply suspicious.

When he knocked on the door, Diana opened it. "Thank God you're here," she said, and hauled him inside. Then she slipped out the door and left, slamming it behind her.

"What is this?" Cal turned around and saw Min, dressed in a short black trench coat, her back against the door, that glint in her eyes. "Oh, funny," he said, trying to sound mad. "Did you ever hear the story about the actuary who cried 'Wolf'?"

"Yes," Min said. "The wolf ate her." She grinned at him, and his pulse kicked up. "I have news for you, Charm Boy. You are not going to throw this bet."

"Oh, yes, I am," Cal said, retreating around her couch while Elvis watched with contempt. "If we sleep together now, there will come a day when we're arguing about the electric bill, and you'll say, 'You only dated me for the bet.' I'm not paying for this for the rest of my life when all I have to do is wait an hour and a half." He looked at the clock on the mantel. "Eighty minutes."

"The rest of your life, huh?" Min said.

"Yes, Minerva, the rest of my life. You think I'd go through the hell this month has been just for the sex?"

Min blinked. "Well, yes."

Cal thought about it. "Okay, you have a point."

"Did I mention I'm not wearing underwear." Min slid around the couch and he backed around to the other side.

"You do this to torture me, don't you?" Cal said.

"No, I'm doing it to get you into bed," Min said. "The torture is just a perk."

"Min," Cal said.

"No," Min said. "I don't want to spend the rest of my life as the bet you lost. Plus I'm tired of hearing about how I'm not a risk-taker. So I'm taking a risk on you." She pulled a ten-dollar bill out of her trench coat pocket. "I've got ten bucks says I'm going to have you naked and inside me before nine-thirty."

Cal went dizzy for a moment and when he'd shaken his head to clear it, she'd slapped the ten on the table by the couch.

"There it is, sport," Min said. "You going to be a wimp, or are you going to play?"

She was smiling at him, heat and love in her eyes, and he started to laugh. "Min, it's eighty minutes, not a month. You really think I can't hold out that long?"

"Yep," Min said, her hands on her hips.

He got out his wallet, took out a ten, walked over to the table, and slapped it on top of her ten. "You're on," he said, keeping the table between them. "Let's see what you've got, Minnie."

She unbuckled her trench coat, dropped the belt onto the couch, and took off the coat. She was wearing a strapless black lace nightgown, and as far as Cal could see, there was nothing holding it up. "I know it would have been better if I'd been naked," she said, rocking on her heels so that everything bounced. "I'm just not that confident yet."

"Actually," Cal said, staring at her, "now I'm going to think about ripping that off you for the next eighty minutes, so this may be the way to go." He looked at the top of the nightgown where the lace cut into her flesh. "It doesn't look that hard to get off."

Min put her finger inside the top of the lace and snapped it. "Elastic. One good tug and—"

"Not for eighty minutes." He looked at the clock. "Seventy-seven minutes. But I want to make it clear that when the time's up, you're mine."

"Oh, yeah," Min said, nodding.

"Well, then," Cal said. "Read any good books lately?"

"No," Min said, beginning to move around the table. "I can't read because all I can think about is you."

Cal moved away from her, toward the other end of the couch. "That must be boring."

"No, you're always doing the most amazing things to me," Min said, moving closer.

Cal moved around to the front of the couch. "You know, I'm not that good in bed."

Min reversed direction and surprised him, grabbing his shirt. "That's all right. I'm fantastic."

She pushed him onto the couch and straddled him, her soft weight pinning him down, and Cal thought, *I should do something about this*, but even as he thought it, his hands were on her, feeling her heat through the scratch of the lace. "I've been told my mouth is a miracle," she whispered, leaning into him, and he closed his eyes as her breasts pushed softly against his chest.

She kissed him, and her mouth was hot and sweet, and he tightened his hands on her and pulled her close. "Christ, I've missed you," he said against her mouth.

"I missed you, too," she said, not playing anymore. "I don't ever want to be without you again."

"You never will," Cal said. "I'm not walking away from you again. Ever."

"Thank you." Min sat back and took a deep breath and Cal watched, heat rising. "Listen, there's something I have to tell you."

His hands cupped her rear end and pulled her tighter. She really wasn't wearing underwear. "Talk slow." He bent his head to kiss her neck and bit it softly instead.

Min shivered. "Remember, I said, 'Don't break my heart'? Well, I changed my mind. You can break it."

"Hey," Cal said, his hands tightening on her. "I'm not—"

"It doesn't matter, I'll love you anyway," Min said, "I loved you when I thought you'd made that bet, I loved you when I thought you were playing me, I loved you while I was screaming at you in the street, I loved you when you left the wedding with Cynthie, you rat bastard—"

"I took her home and left," Cal said, alarmed. "I swear to God, I—"

"It doesn't matter," Min said. "That's what I'm trying to tell you, it doesn't matter what you do or say. I'm going to love you till the end of time."

Cal looked at her, stunned.

"I know," Min said. "It's really un-PC. I just thought you should know that you can't screw this up."

"I can't?" Cal said, wanting to believe her.

"No," Min said. "Which doesn't mean I'm not going to yell if you make me mad again. I will shout and slam doors. I just won't be on the other side of the door when I slam it. You've got me for life."

He lost his breath and put his forehead against her shoulder. "God, I love you."

Min sighed. "That's good because there's something else I have to tell you."

Cal nodded, still dazed.

Min swallowed. "The thing is, I'm going to spread. Hips, thighs—"

"Not till nine-thirty," Cal said, trying not to picture her.

"—waist," Min said, and then stopped. "What? Nine-thirty? Not till my *forties*, probably, I think I can fight it off that long, but then—"

"What?" Cal said.

"I'm going to get fat," Min said, and he blinked. "Er. I'm going to get fatter." She frowned at him. "What did you think I meant?"

"For future reference," he said, starting to laugh. "If you're sitting half naked on my lap and you tell me you're going to spread—"

"*No*," Min said and tried to push him away, and he toppled her so she landed, lush and hot beneath him. "I would never say that," she said, looking up at him as her arms slid around his neck. "That would be crude."

"I liked it," Cal said and kissed her.

"What I'm trying to tell you," Min said when she came up for air, "is that I'm going to grow up to be one of those chubby old ladies. It's in my genes. Like self-rising flour. I'm going to pouf."

"That's going to work out well for me," Cal said. "Because I'm going to grow up to be one of those horny old men who chases chubby old ladies around the couch."

"I'm *serious*," Min said, but she was smiling, her soft lips open for him.

"So am I," Cal said. "You think I care what you weigh? Hell, woman, you've called me a beast, a wolf, the devil, and a vile seducer. Plus your best friend has beaten me up three times—"

"You hit me in the eye," Min said.

"—and you yelled at me in public, and I'm still here. If you think you getting softer is going to get rid of me—"

"Men are visual," Min said.

"Yeah." Cal slid his finger under the elastic edge of her nightgown. "That's why I like this thing you're not wearing. But I still want a chance to rip your sweats off you, too." He stopped smiling, trying to give her what she'd given him. "It's just you, Minnie. That's all I want. I just want to spend the rest of my life with you."

"Oh." Min reached up for him, and he remembered the bet and sat up, hating to let her go.

"Starting at nine-thirty." He looked at the clock. "Which is in seventy minutes. What do you want to do for seventy minutes, Minnie? Got a Scrabble board?"

"I'll use dirty words," Min said.

"Yeah, like 'spread,'" Cal said, and laughed.

Min looked at the ceiling. "See, this is one of those things that doesn't matter, I love you anyway."

"I love that part," Cal said. "So what's new with you?"

"That would be saying 'yes, you can have me any way you want me' to you." She sat up and pulled him to her again, and he shifted on the couch to make room for her and felt something dig into his hip. Min kissed his neck, and he shivered as he reached behind him and pulled out her coat belt, buckle first. Then she bit him, and he said, "Ouch," and she leaned back and smiled at him.

"You're going to win the bet with David and lose the bet to me, hot-shot," she said. "Think of it as breaking even."

He looked at her and thought, *she's right*, and then looked at the belt in his hand. "Just for the record, no matter what I do, you'll love me?"

"Yes," she said.

"Good." He tipped her back onto the couch and stretched her wrists over her head. "I like being in control, Minnie."

"I know." Min smiled up at him. "I can work with that."

He kissed her again, and while she was distracted, he wrapped the belt around her wrists.

"Hey," she said, breaking the kiss, but he'd already wrapped the ends of the belt around the arm of the couch.

She stretched up to see her wrists as he tied the knot. "This is a little kinky, Calvin."

"Not really," Cal said, getting up. "You know, I had a dozen doughnuts to bring over here, and then you cried wolf, and now we don't have them. But I forgive you because that's the kind of relationship we have." He moved to the kitchen alcove. "So what do you want to talk about for . . ." He stretched to see the clock. ". . . sixty-seven minutes."

"*Cal*," Min said.

There was a familiar green and white sack on the kitchen counter. "Krispy Kremes," he said. "Great minds think alike." He brought the sack back into the living room. "You know, Minnie, you tortured me for a month, looking so good I lost my mind every time I saw you. I wanted you so much I was insane from it." He looked down at her, tied to the couch. "Still am, evidently."

"Okay, I'm sorry about that," Min said, tugging on the belt.

"So now it's your turn." He sat down across from her. "Now I'm going to torture you."

Min stopped tugging. "This could be good. What are you going to do?"

He took a Krispy Kreme out of the bag.

"I'm going to eat this in front of you," Cal said, and bit into the doughnut.

David went down to the street to the pay phone on the corner because damn near everybody had caller ID these days. He dialed Min's parents' number, and when the phone stopped ringing, he said, "You should know this," only to be overrun by their answering machine. Well, that was all right, they never stayed out longer than nine anyway. Plenty of time. When he heard the beep, he said, "You should know this. Calvin Morrisey is seducing your daughter to win a bet. They're at her apartment right now." Then he hung up and considered what he had just done. As far as he could see, it was flawless.

Feeling pretty good about himself, he began to look through the directory wired to the pay phone for the Morriseys' number.

Min scowled at Cal, but all the bastard did was grin back, looking desirable as all hell while he finished his second doughnut. Slowly.

"And you wonder why I wouldn't sleep with you," Min said. "It was because I sensed the sadist in you." She shifted to get more comfortable and watched his jaw tense. *Hello*, she thought, and shifted again.

"I haven't see Elvis for a while," he said, watching her. "He must have gone out the window again. What are the statistics on outdoor cats?"

"You know," Min said, trying a new strategy. "This is scaring me. There's a strange man in my apartment, and I'm tied to my couch. I'm *terrified*." She tried to put some fear into her voice, but it was hard since it was soaked with lust.

"Funny, you just look pissed off." Cal picked up the remote. "TV?"

Min gritted her teeth. "Men get arrested for this."

"Only if they get caught. I usually check CNN about this time." Cal looked down at her. "Of course, I usually don't have something better to look at. You have a great body."

"Oh, please," Min said. "I know you want to get laid but—"

"Guys buy magazines to look at breasts like yours," Cal said, "and here I am with a pair tied to a couch." He tossed the remote back on the coffee table. "CNN has lost its appeal."

"If I ever get off this couch," Min said through her teeth, "you're never seeing these breasts again. Now untie me."

"You didn't think that through," Cal said. "Try again."

"*Calvin*—"

"Do you have any idea," he said conversationally, "how hard it is for me to keep my hands off you?"

"So untie me and let's go," Min said, starting to feel cheerful again.

"Forty-five minutes," Cal said. "What do you want to talk about?"

Okay, Min told herself. *You're not thinking. You have the upper hand here, aside from being tied to the couch. He wants you. He can have you. He just needs jump-started.* "I've wanted you, too," she said, relaxing back against the pillows.

"Right," Cal said, picking up another doughnut. "That's why you kept walking away."

"That was the bet," Min said. "Remember that picnic in the park? I wanted to knock you down and rip off your shirt and bite into you."

Cal stopped with the doughnut halfway to his mouth.

"I used to close my eyes and imagine you naked against me, all the things you'd do to me." He drew back a little and she said, "Especially my breasts. I have really sensitive breasts, did I mention that? I could almost come just imagining your mouth on my—"

"You don't play fair," Cal said.

"*I* don't?" Min said, trying to rise up. "I'm *tied to the couch.* How is that fair?"

"It's not," Cal said. "One of the many reasons I like it."

She exhaled in frustration, and he watched her, and then he got up and moved around the table to sit beside her. He scooped some chocolate icing off the doughnut with his finger. "Do you know how many fantasies I've had about your body?" He drew his finger around the slope of her breast, smearing the chocolate under the lace, and Min sucked in her breath. "This wasn't one of them," he said, marking her other breast the same way. "But it should have been."

"Sticky," Min said, complete sentences escaping her for the moment.

"Not a problem," Cal said, bending over her. "It's coming right off."

"Pervert," Min said, closing her eyes as she felt his tongue on her.

"Yep," he said, moving the lace lower. "But you like it."

"Ha," Min said.

Cal straightened enough to look into her eyes. "Want me to stop?"

he said, and Min felt his hand under her breast, felt his thumb move across the heat there to the edge of the lace.

"I want everything you've got," Min said and watched his eyes darken as his hand tightened on her. "Untie me."

"Nope," Cal said.

Min arched against him and he pushed her back, his breath coming faster, and bent down to her again, and this time he pulled down the lace, and when she felt his mouth on her, she arched as every nerve she had flared in relief.

He pulled back as she jerked and looked down at her, breathing hard, and just as she realized he was staring at her naked breast, he stripped the rest of the nightgown down so she was naked to the waist. "Hey," she said and moved instinctively to cover herself and remembered she was tied.

"God, you're beautiful," he said, still staring at her breasts.

Min tugged at the belt, torn between embarrassment and lust, and then he slid his hands up to cup her breasts, and lust won. She closed her eyes and felt the heat of his mouth on her again, felt herself tighten and shudder, and pressed against him, praying he wouldn't stop.

The Morriseys weren't in the book, so David called Cynthie. "I need the number for Cal's parents."

"Why?" Cynthie said flatly.

"It doesn't matter why," David said. "What matters is that Cal would be furious if he found out that you told me how to start that fight on Sunday. Give me the number or I tell him."

There was a long silence, and then Cynthie put down the phone. When she came back, she gave him the number.

"Thank you," David said, and hung up and dialed the number. When the ringing stopped, he said, "You should know this," only to be overridden by the Morriseys' answering machine. "This is ridiculous," he said, but when the beep sounded, he said, "You should know this. Your son is seducing a woman right now to win a bet. Her name is Min

Dobbs and she is litigious and vindictive." Then he gave her apartment address and hung up.

"Not bad," he told himself and picked up the phone again, feeling pretty good about himself in general.

Because he was going to win.

Fifteen minutes later, Cal picked up the rest of the third doughnut, and Min tried to remember her name.

"What are you *doing?*" she said.

"Pacing myself," Cal said, sounding ragged. He bit into the doughnut. "I figure," he said after he'd swallowed, "that as long as I have this in my mouth, I won't put you there." He looked at the clock. "We've got half an hour. I don't think you bought enough doughnuts."

"Could you at least pull my nightgown up?" Min said, feeling a blush start as the heat receded.

"Nope." Cal finished the doughnut. "I'm thinking you should always go topless."

"That'll perk things up at work," Min said, and then remembered that there was nothing perky about her. "I meant—"

"Not in public, dummy," Cal said. "Just at home. We'll put it in the wedding vows. You can promise to love, honor, cherish, and be naked from the waist up every night."

"Married?" Min said, trying to sit up.

"Well, of course, married," Cal said, watching her with interest. "You think I'd tie up somebody I wasn't serious about?"

"You haven't *asked*," Min said, yanking on the belt.

"Will you marry me?" Cal said, still watching her breasts.

"*No,*" Min said, torn between love and murder.

"Right," Cal said. "Because years from now when Harry asks how I proposed, you don't want to say, 'Well, he tied me to the couch and ripped off my nightgown and ate doughnuts off my breasts and then he asked me.'" He bit into the doughnut again.

"All I want is to make love so we can put this dumb bet behind us and start a real relationship, although maybe not after this." She yanked on the belt again. "This could set us back some."

"Nope," Cal said, insufferably calm. "We agreed that nothing could hurt this relationship now. It's a little bent, but I like that about us."

"You're a little bent," Min said. "I am completely normal. Now untie me and fuck my brains out."

Cal caught his breath for a minute, and Min thought, *Take me*, and then he bit into the doughnut again, and she exhaled through her teeth in frustration.

"Maybe I'm filling the wrong mouth," he said, and tore off a piece of the doughnut. "Open up."

"Look, I don't—" Min said, and Cal slipped the pastry into her mouth, and the sugar flooded everywhere. "Oh," she said and let the chocolate melt into her senses.

"My goal in life is to put that look on your face without chocolate," Cal said.

Min swallowed. "You do. You're just never looking at me when it's on there."

"Really." Cal cupped her breast and began to stroke her with his thumb, and Min felt herself tighten under him again, but this time, when she opened her eyes, he was staring at her, watching her, and she blushed, from embarrassment and from heat and from wanting him. "Damn, you're right," he said and bent to kiss her, and Min forgot to be embarrassed and rose to taste him as he caressed her, sighing against his mouth.

"Untie me," she whispered, and he looked over her head.

"Nope, we still have half an hour to kill." He slid his hand down her calf. "I think I'll start with the toes this time. It's never been toes for me before, so this will be new."

"You're going to suck my toes for half an hour?" Min said in disbelief.

"I'm going to start at your toes," Cal said. "And work up."

"Up?" Min said.

"And in about fifteen minutes, you're going lose the rest of this nightgown."

"With the lights on?" Min said, outraged, and he laughed and bent to her toes.

David dialed Diana's cell phone on the theory that after what had happened to her on Sunday, Diana would be ripe to maim any man in her path, especially one hurting her sister. When the ringing stopped, he said, "You should know this," only to be overridden by Diana's voice mail. "Don't any of you people stay home on Wednesdays?" he snapped, but when the beep sounded, he said, "You should know this. Calvin Morrisey is seducing your sister right now to win a bet." Then he hung up and thought about the last call he had to make. The scary one.

It's anonymous, he told himself. *She'll never know.*

He went back up to his apartment to have a drink first anyway.

At quarter after nine, having been touched everywhere she could imagine and a couple of places she hadn't thought of, Min felt Cal untie her.

She sat up and slugged him on the arm. "Don't *ever* do that again."

"Ouch?" Cal said, and she pushed him back and climbed onto his lap and kissed him hard, wrapping herself around him as tightly as she could.

When she came up for air, she slapped him on the shoulder again. "I *mean it*, never again," she said, and then went for his mouth again, hungry for it. A minute later she broke the kiss, breathing heavily, slugged him again, and said, "*Never* ever again."

"Really?" he said, as breathless as she was, and she looked back at the arm of the couch, the belt still tangled around it, and shivered.

"Well, not in the living room," she said. "And not for so long, and not with all these lights—"

He dumped her back on the couch, pressing her against the pillows. "When we do it again," he told her, his hands hot on her, "it'll be where I want, when I want, with spotlights if I want."

"I don't think so," she said and he kissed her again and she thought, *Oh, hell, whatever you want,* and kissed him back.

"Whatever I want," he whispered in her ear.

"Okay," she whispered back. "But can I have you now?"

"Almost," Cal said into her neck. "Fifteen—"

"You know what my favorite fantasy is?" she whispered in his ear, and he groaned. "It's you, sliding hard inside me." His hand tightened on her, and she said, "I love that part of sex, the first part, the way it feels, and it's going to be the best with you because everything else with you has been the best I've ever had, the way I feel when you touch me, the way you kiss me, that's why I know the way you—"

He kissed her hard, pushing her back on the pillows, taking her voice and her breath away, and when he stopped, he said, "Shut up, we've got fifteen minutes yet," and began to lick his way down her body.

"Uh," Min said, as he set every nerve she had alight again. "What are you going to do for fifteen minutes?" and he bit into her thigh as he moved her legs apart with his hand.

"Oh, *God*," Min said, as he licked inside her. "*I'm going to lose ten dollars.*"

Liza's cell phone rang in the kitchen at Emilio's, and Tony got it out of her purse and handed it to her, never dropping the fork he had buried in his spaghetti.

"You sure we're not seeing each other?" Liza said as she took the phone. "Because you sure show up here at lot."

"I eat here," Tony said, twirling more spaghetti on his fork. "I pre-date you."

"Right," Liza said, clicked her phone on. "Hello?"

"Liza?" a man's voice said. "You should know this. Cal Morrisey is tricking Min into winning that bet."

"What?" Liza said. "Who is this?"

"The bet's over at midnight," the voice said, sounding smugly famil-iar. "And he wants to win."

"David?" Liza said.

The phone clicked off and Liza was left with a dial tone.

"David?" Tony said, looking up from his spaghetti.

"Hey, Emilio?" Liza yelled over the kitchen noise. "I'm taking a break."

"Oh, no," Tony said.

"Eat your pasta," Liza said, moving toward the door.

"Oh, hell," Tony said and dropped his fork to follow her.

Chapter Sixteen

When Min was wound so tight, she was shaking, Cal laced his fingers in her hair and turned her head to show her the mantel clock. "It's nine-thirty-five," he said, his voice husky. "I lost the bet to David. It's over."

"We wasted five minutes?" Min said wildly.

"You weren't complaining," Cal said, resting his head on her stomach.

"Take me to bed or do me on this couch," Min said, breathing hard. "I want you *now*."

"I'm definitely marrying you," Cal said, and pulled her up off the couch and toward the bedroom.

She tripped behind him and then gasped as he toppled her onto her satin comforter, her body sizzling against the cool fabric as he stripped and found a condom, and then he was beside her, pressed hotly against her, and she closed her eyes to savor him, bone and muscle hard against her. "*Don't wait*," she said, and felt his hands on her again, sliding over her, making every nerve she had scream, and when his fingers slipped inside her again, she opened to him, shaking under him, and when she felt his body between her thighs, she arched to meet him, desperate to feel him hard inside her. His eyes were hot on her and she stared back, caught, crazy for him, and then he kissed her and slipped his tongue in her mouth as he slid into her, slick and hot, and she gasped and clutched at him as the shock of him went everywhere.

He pulled back and then slid deeper, and she bit her lip, weak with pleasure as heat thickened in her, and then she began to move with him, catching his rhythm, dizzy with the rightness of him, of them together. He whispered in her ear as he moved against her, telling her that he loved her, that she was beautiful, that she was his, over and over and over, until she could feel him everywhere, his voice and his breath and his hands and his body, all loving her, making her drunk with love and lust. She licked her tongue across his lips and she told him she loved him, forever, forever, no end, forever, and she felt him build in her blood, felt him everywhere, in her fingertips, behind her eyes, and deep and low where they were locked together, where the heat and the pressure and the tension twisted and tightened, glitter and stars, fusing into brightness sharper than anything ever before. He rocked higher, sharper, and she dug her fingernails into him and cried his name as he rocked again and again and then she broke, arching under his hands as he held her down, spasming helplessly as his body surged against hers. And then, while she was still clutching him, still gasping from shattering ecstasy, he shuddered, too, and collapsed into her arms.

"Oh, *God*," Min said, when she could speak again.

"Good?" he said, breathless, and she shook her head.

"Very good. World class. Phenomenal." She took a deep breath to stop the gasping and he slid his hand up to her breast where it belonged. She put her hand over his and pressed it tighter to her, and drew in another deep breath. "God, I love you."

"Good," Cal said, looking exhausted. "I love you, too. Sorry we didn't have time to talk about what you wanted."

"I wanted that," Min said between breaths.

"You got it," Cal said, and rolled his head and caught sight of her clock. "Oh, Christ."

Min looked up at her curling brass headboard and drew in a deep sighing breath. "I think I might want to be tied to this headboard someday."

"Just for the record," Cal said, "I usually last more than seven minutes." He let his head fall back onto her pillow. "Of course, foreplay usually doesn't last a month." He took a deep breath. "Go ahead, tell me the statistics on how long foreplay usually lasts."

"Not long enough," Min said. "You're the exception. Maybe I'll tie you to this headboard. And *I'll* do the chocolate icing."

Cal closed his eyes. "Thank you. I'd like that. Make a list. We'll do it all. Probably not tonight, but eventually."

Min curled into him as her pulse began to slow. "I'm so happy. I'm so crazy about you, and I'm so happy."

He rolled closer to her and kissed her, and she settled into him, safe and warm and satisfied.

"I love you," he said, and she opened her mouth to tell him that she loved him, too, when someone began to pound on her door.

"What the hell is that?" Cal said.

"My door?" Min said.

"Did Diana forget her key?" Cal eased himself up into a sitting position. "Ouch. You're a very athletic woman, Minerva."

"Not really," Min said as the phone rang. "I got C's in gym."

"They were giving you the wrong assignments." Cal patted her on the hip and reached for his pants. "You get the phone. I'll get the door. I'll meet you back here. Stay naked."

Cal buttoned his shirt as he crossed Min's living room, reminding himself that yelling at his future sister-in-law would be bad. That made him almost glad when he yanked open the door and saw David instead. He could yell anything he wanted at that dickhead.

"Is Min here?" David said, looking smug.

"Yes, go away." Cal started to close the door and then remembered. "You won. I'll send you a check tomorrow. Now go away."

"I don't think so." David blocked the doorway. "I have to see Min."

"David?" Min said from behind them, and when they turned, Cal lost his breath.

She had her blue-violet comforter wound around her and Elvis twining around her ankles, but her shoulders were bare, and she looked disheveled and rumpled, her gold-tipped curls tousled, her baby-doll cheeks flushed, and her full lips bruised and rosy, and Cal thought, *I did that*, and wanted her again so much that he took a step toward her.

"God," David said, slackjawed.

"Mine," Cal said. "Go away."

"You won," David said, and shoved the check at him.

"What?" Cal frowned at him. "No."

"The bet was for midnight," David said, still staring at Min. "You've got more than two hours left." He smiled at Min. "Guess Calvin the Great is also Calvin the Fast."

"Oh, for crying out loud," Cal said as Elvis hissed at David and David took a step back.

"*It was for midnight?*" Min's voice was too high as she came closer to them, tripping over the comforter on the way.

Minerva, what are you up to? Cal thought, and watched her with interest and rebounding lust.

"Of course it was." David smiled triumphantly at Cal. "All bets end at midnight."

Min hauled the comforter up again. "Do you mean to tell me," she said, her voice breaking, "that Cal *won this bet?*"

"Oh, yes," David said, smugly.

"Well, gee, thanks," Min said in her normal voice as she took the check out of his hand. "I can always use ten bucks."

"What?" David said, losing his smug.

Min smiled cheerfully at David. "I know Cal won it," she said, "but we have this unwritten rule that I get all the money he wins on me. I'm picking up quite a bit of spare change that way, so this—" She looked at the check and almost dropped her comforter. "*Oh, my God.*"

"Not ten bucks," Cal said, yanking up the comforter before she lost it.

Min looked up at him, appalled. "You bet *ten thousand dollars* you could get me into bed?"

"No," Cal said. "I'm going to get a T-shirt made that says, 'I did not make that bet.'"

"Ten thousand dollars," Min said, looking at the check again. "If you'd told me about this the first night and offered to split it, I'd have slept with you then."

"Really?" Cal said.

"No," Min said.

"I didn't think so." Cal took the check out of her hand and pushed it at David. "You can go now."

"What is that?" David said, pointing to the couch.

Cal looked back and saw Min's belt still draped over the arm.

"He tied me to the couch," Min said helpfully. "Then he ripped off my nightgown and smeared chocolate icing on me and licked it off. It was a *nightmare*." She grinned. "If you leave, we can do it again." She looked at Cal. "We're not out of doughnuts, are we?"

"If we are, I will run out and get more," Cal said. "Run being the operative word."

David looked floored. "That's . . ."

Min waited.

". . . so not like you," he finished.

"Well, it wasn't," Min said. "It is now."

"But—" David began, and then Nanette and George pushed him out of the doorway to get into the room.

"Oh, great," Cal said, lust evaporating as George caught sight of him.

"That's what I came to tell you," Min said, clutching her comforter more tightly. "David called Di, who called to warn me that he'd probably called some others."

"*You*," George said, heading for Cal, and Min stepped between them.

"You're overreacting," Min said to George.

"I've never liked your apartment, dear," Nanette said, looking around. Then she saw the green and white bag on the table. *"Dough-nuts?"*

"You should have been feeding me cocaine," Min said to Cal. "I understand that's slimming."

George stuck to his guns. "Min, David says this man made a wager that he could—"

"No," Min said. "*David* tried to get him to make that bet but Cal said no. Go yell at David."

"Then what's this?" George ripped the check out of Cal's hand. "This is—" He caught sight of the amount. "—for ten thousand dollars." He looked at Cal. "You're not only immoral, you're reckless with money."

"I didn't make the bet," Cal said. "And no one will ever believe that."

"I believe it," Min said, smiling up at him.

"Then the hell with everybody else," Cal said, and moved closer to her.

George drew himself up. "Minerva, get your clothes on, you're coming home."

"Dad, I'm thirty-three," Min said. "No." She reached out and took the check out of his hand. "Go home now. Take Mother with—"

"Calvin," a voice like ice said from the doorway.

Cal looked around George to see his mother. "Oh. Wonderful." He looked down at Min. "This is pretty much my fantasy. I finally make love to the woman of my dreams, and my mother shows up for the afterglow."

"Well," Min said, trying to keep the comforter up. "It really isn't a party until somebody brings the ice."

"Excuse me," Nanette said, trying to push George out of the way. "You're Lynne Morrisey, aren't you?"

Lynne looked at Nanette as if she were part of the work force.

Nanette held out her hand. "I'm Min's mother, Nanette? So pleased to meet you."

"How do you do," Lynne said, without taking the hand, and turned back to Cal. "Calvin."

"Hello, Mother," Cal said. "This is the woman I'm going to spend the rest of my life with. If you don't approve, we'll spend the third Sunday of the month listening to Elvis at the diner. Your call."

Lynne looked at him for a long frozen moment, and then Cal saw Cynthie come through the doorway behind her, looking sheet white. "Cynthie?"

"I called her," Lynne said. "I felt that—"

"No," Cal said to them both.

"You cannot be serious—" Lynne began.

"Don't push him," Cynthie said, quietly. "That's what I came to tell you. This is infatuation. It'll pass. Give him time."

Cal shook his head and pulled Min toward the couch, away from the loons.

"I'll give him time," George said, still scowling. "I'll give the bastard—"

"Oh, *you'll give him time*," Nanette snapped. "Like you're not worse than he is."

"What?" George said.

Min curled up next to Cal on the couch and laced her fingers with his. "So I owe you ten dollars since you made me wait until after nine-thirty."

"Yep," Cal said, tightening his grip on her. "Except I won it on a bet on you, so you'll just take it away from me again."

"I *know what you're doing*," Nanette said to George, rage in her voice.

"I'm . . . yelling at the bastard who seduced my daughter," George said, knocked off stride.

"*I know what you're doing on your lunch hour,*" Nanette said, murder in her eye.

"I'm eating," George said, perplexed.

"Yes, *but who?*" Nanette yelled, and Min cringed and said, "Oh, God, *Mother*," and Lynne looked at Nanette in contempt, and Cynthie closed her eyes, and David looked frustrated and confused and mad as hell, and then Liza walked in with Tony behind her and stopped, scowling at all of them.

"What the hell is this?" she said.

"Tony," Cal said, an edge to his voice.

"For the record," Tony said to him, "I tried to stop her."

"Why didn't you lock the door so these people couldn't get in?" Liza said to Min.

"I did," Min said. "Cal opened it. Yell at him."

"Just hit me," Cal said. "Save us all some time."

"What did you mean by that?" George said to Nanette, his face red.

"Your *lunches*," Nanette said, her voice rising. "*You take your secretary to lunch every damn day.*"

"Loud voice," Min said, thinking of her neighbors. "Not your loud voice."

"They're *working lunches*," George said. "I need a secretary *to work.*"

"*You never take me to lunch,*" Nanette yelled.

"*You don't EAT,*" George yelled back.

Min craned her neck to see around them to Liza. "You know, that bet was for ten thousand dollars."

"You're kidding." Liza looked at Cal, surprised. "You bet ten thousand dollars on—"

"*No,*" Cal said. "Damn it, *look.*" He took the check out of Min's hand and tore it in two. "See? *No bet.*"

"We could have used that," Min said, but she didn't sound upset.

They all began to talk, and Cal looked at Min and thought, *all I want is to be alone with her for the rest of my life.*

"Hey!" he said, and they all looked at him with various degrees of contempt, despair, and rage. He picked up a doughnut and turned to Min. "Minerva Dobbs, I love you and I always will. Will you marry me?"

"This is so sudden," Min said, grinning at him.

"We got an audience, Minnie," Cal said. "You in or not?"

"I'm in," Min said, and he took her left hand, spread her fingers out, and slipped the doughnut over her ring finger, knowing with a certainty he'd never felt before that this was exactly the right thing to do.

"I'll get you a better ring later," he said, looking into her dark, dark eyes. "I'll do this better, too. This is just to get these people off our backs."

"Well, when you do this better, I'm going to say yes again," Min said.

"Thank you," Cal said and kissed her, falling into her heat all over again. "God, I love you," he whispered in her ear. "I can't believe how much I love you."

"Okay," Liza said. "Show's over." She looked at Lynne. "You have to be the mother. Don't mess with Min. If Cal has to choose—"

"Elvis," Lynne said, her voice flat. She turned and walked out of the apartment.

"*Lovely* woman," Liza said, and turned to Nanette. "Now you. Your husband is not cheating on you. I know men and he's not the type." She looked at George. "Stop working through lunch and take your wife out to eat instead." She turned back to Nanette. "And you. Eat."

Nanette's face crumpled, and George put his arm around her. "I'm not cheating," he said. "I don't have the time."

"*Dad,*" Min said, but Nanette sniffed and said, "Really?"

"I didn't think I'd find you here," Liza said to Cynthie, not unkindly. "It's the book, isn't it?"

"No," Cynthie said, staring hopelessly at the doughnut squashed between Min's fingers. "No."

"Listen," Liza told her, "nobody wants to hear an incredibly beautiful woman tell about how she landed an incredibly beautiful man. That's just smug. Write a book about how you lost the love of your life and recovered. People could *use* that."

"I—"

"It's over, Cynthie," Liza said. "He's gone. Forever."

Cynthie's face fell, and Liza turned to David.

"And you are a worthless piece of garbage," she said. "So do something decent and take Cynthie home."

"This is a mistake," David told Min. "Do you know what this man is?"

"Yep," Min said, pulling a piece of chocolate icing off her engagement ring. "It's okay. We're going to evolve together."

"*Out,*" Liza said to him, and Cynthie left. Liza glared at David. "Well, go *after her,* you vicious dork. Do something nice for a change instead of anonymous phone calls."

David drew himself up. "I didn't—" he began, but Liza folded her arms, so he transferred his attention to Min. "He's a terrible user, Min."

"No, he's not," Min said. "He's a prince. And you're a toad who makes anonymous phone calls."

"You never did understand me," David said, and walked out.

"What a fathead," Liza said.

"You're going to marry this man?" George said to Min, sounding incredulous.

"Yes," Min said. "Don't be mean to him, or you'll lose us to Elvis, too."

George shot Cal a look that said, *I'm watching you, buddy,* and then turned on his heel and left.

"Well, you'll have beautiful children," Nanette said, cheering up.

"We're not having kids," Min said, and when her mother's eyes narrowed, she added, "because you know I'd never lose the weight afterward."

"That's true," Nanette said, and then George came back and dragged her out the door.

"All right then," Liza said, looking around the emptied apartment. "My work here is done."

"Who are you again?" Cal said. "Because you look like this woman who keeps hitting me, but you seem to be on my side. Do you have an evil twin?"

"I'm Min's fairy godmother, Charm Boy," Liza said, frowning down at him. "And if you don't give her a happily ever after, I'm going to come back and beat you to death with a snow globe."

"What happened to 'bibbity bobbity boo'?" Cal asked Min.

"That was Disney, honey," Min said. "It wasn't a documentary."

Liza went to the door and stopped when she saw Tony there, his arms folded. "Come on. You can yell at me on the way back to the restaurant."

"Nope," Tony said. "That was good what you did." He leaned closer. "Very hot."

"I'm not going to sleep with you," Liza said, and went out the door.

"Can't blame a guy for trying," Tony said and followed her out, closing the door behind them.

Silence settled over the apartment.

"I'll never forget my first time with you," Min said as she edged the doughnut off her finger. "The earth moved, and then my mother asked my father who he was going down on at lunch."

"Yes, there were some moments there," Cal said.

Min shook her head. "We're never going to be rid of those people."

"I know," Cal said.

"Thank God we have each other." Min looked up at him. "I love you."

"Thank you," Cal said and kissed her.

"So I'm buying a house," Min said when she came up for air. "How do you feel about an Arts and Crafts bungalow like my grandma used to live in?"

"Are you in it?" Cal said.

Min nodded.

"I'm there," Cal said. "Can we go back to bed now?"

"Yes," Min said. "Bring the doughnuts."

An hour and a half later, Min lay curled beside Cal with Elvis asleep at the foot of the bed, looking like rusty velvet on the lavender blue satin. Cal was breathing almost loudly enough to be called snoring, and she patted his shoulder. *A month ago, I didn't know him*, she thought dreamily. *And now he's the rest of my life.*

Then she pulled back a little. That sounded ridiculous. Completely irrational, in fact. *Screw rationality*, she thought, but the thought didn't go away. You'd have to be insane to pin the rest of your life on somebody you'd only known a month, especially somebody with a past like Cal's.

She slid out from under his arm, and picked up his shirt from the floor. When she put it on, it failed to meet in the middle over her chest. *That always works in the movies*, she thought, disgusted, and dropped it on the floor. Instead, she pulled the comforter off the bed, annoying Elvis but leaving Cal asleep under the sheet. It was June. He wasn't going to freeze.

Then she went out and sat on her grandmother's couch, wrapped in her comforter, and tried to make sense of everything. Elvis padded out to join her and curled up on the back of the couch, and she moved her head a little bit to rub against him and make him purr.

So, she thought, *essentially what we have here is that I'm looking at the biggest player in town and thinking he's True Love That Will Last Forever. What are the odds on that?* Across from her, the clock on the mantel clicked as the hands hit midnight.

"Hey," Cal said, and she looked up to see him in the doorway, stifling a yawn. "What are you doing?"

"It's midnight," she said, trying to sound cheerful. "I'm turning back into a pumpkin."

"That explains the couch," he said and came to sit beside her. He put his arm around her and pulled her close and kissed her on the forehead, and she closed her eyes and leaned into him, loving him so much she was weak with it. *I'm in big trouble here,* she thought.

"Something wrong?" he said. "I thought everything was pretty much perfect once the loons left."

"It is," she said. "I'm just trying to figure out what's next."

"Next." Cal nodded. "Okay. Well." He took her hand and yawned again. "Tomorrow, I'll call my mother so she doesn't put a curse on us, and we'll go have dinner with your parents and make sure they're not still nuts."

"There's a hope," Min said. The comforter slipped down over her shoulder, and Cal put his hand there, making lazy circles on her skin with his fingertips as he talked.

"And then we'll go looking for that house you were talking about, one with only six steps up from the street." He shifted a little to avoid a spring and added, "And we'll get a new couch."

Min felt herself start to smile, the happiness bubbling up in spite of the odds, and he held her tighter. "And then we'll get married, and we'll live happily ever after."

Min went cold as he brought her hand to his mouth and kissed her knuckles. "Yeah. That's the part I'm wondering about."

Cal's hand tightened on hers. "You think we're going to have problems?"

"I don't know," Min said, looking into his eyes. "I think we're going to love each other till the day we die, but I don't know if that's enough. Life is not a fairy tale."

"Okay," Cal said. "It's midnight, I've had a very full evening, and I'm a little slow here. What are you worried about?"

"The happily ever after," Min said, knowing she was sounding like an idiot. "All the stuff we just did, the romance part, the fairy tale stuff, I know how that works, I read the stories."

"Fairy tale stuff?"

"But they don't tell you about the happily ever after. And as far as I can see, that's where it all breaks down. Fifty percent of marriages end in divorce, and yes, I know those statistics are skewed by repeat divorcers—"

"It's midnight, and I'm listening to statistics," Cal said to the cat.

"—but I'm worried. There aren't any happily ever after stories. That's where it ends. Where the hard part starts."

"All right," Cal said. "So?"

"So," Min said, meeting his eyes. "What are we going to do?"

"You want me to be philosophic about the future now?" Cal said. "I'm not even sure where I left my pants."

Min looked at him for a moment, loving him in spite of the fact that he had bed hair and was making jokes and wasn't helping. *In spite of everything*, she thought and smiled at him. "No." She clutched the comforter around her. "I don't know what I was thinking. Let's go back to bed."

"We're going to take it one day at a time," Cal said, holding on to her. "I don't know anything about this, either, I didn't plan for this, but I think we just stick together. Take care of each other. Pat each other on the back when things get tight." When she still looked unsure, he smiled at her with so much love in his eyes that she went dizzy, and then he said, "Bet you ten bucks we make it."

What are the odds? she thought, and realized with sudden, blinding clarity that she wouldn't take the other side of that bet, that only a loser would bet against them. *This is really it*, she thought, amazed. *This is really forever. I believe in this.*

"Min?" he said, and she kissed him, putting all her heart into it.

"No bet," she said against his mouth. "Your odds are too good."

"*Our* odds are too good," he said, and took her back to bed.

Chapter

Seventeen

In case you were wondering . . .

David got over Min pretty quickly, although the fact that Cal won bothered him for years. Four months later, he met a woman who agreed with everything he said and slept with him on the third date. They were married six months later. She never cooks with butter.

Cyn took longer to get over Cal because she really did love him. She holed up in her apartment, subsisting on carrots and nonfat ranch dressing, until Liza dragged her out into the sun, made her write about her breakup, and called in a favor from one of her many former bosses to get the book to another editor. The editor, a guy with glasses who was two inches shorter than Cynthie and slightly overweight, made her rewrite it four times and then threw all the promotional power of his publishing house behind it. He married Cynthie the day before the book hit number one on the *NYT* list. They have a penthouse in New York and eat only in the very best restaurants.

Emilio let Liza tell him what to do and within the year Emilio's was the hottest restaurant in town. He offered her a partnership if she stayed, but things were running well and she was bored, so she introduced him to a friend of hers with an MBA in management and left to go save somebody else.

George stopped taking his overworked secretary to lunch, for which she was grateful even though she missed the expensive food. He now has lunch with Nanette three times a week. She eats.

Reynolds spends so much time with Min, Cal, and Bink on social occasions that, given their willingness to say, "Reynolds, you're being a butthead," he has stopped being a butthead when he's with them. At all other times, he continues being a butthead. Bink loves him anyway.

Shanna and Linda parted company after a year with no hard feelings. Shortly after that, Shanna went to work for Emilio, where she met the MBA who, it turned out, adored Elvis Costello. Four months later they moved into a lavish loft in the city, and a year later they went to China and adopted a little girl. Shanna is a stay-at-home mom except when Emilio gets swamped and needs the help. Her Betty Boop cookie jar always has Oreos.

Harry got a growth spurt at fourteen, shot up and filled out and became a carbon copy of his father and uncle, except that his hair still flops over his forehead and he still wears glasses. He became an ichthyologist, met a zaftig girl on a dive in the Bahamas, fell in love, and married her a month later. She has brown hair with gold highlights, a logical mind, and a penchant for shoes. He still can't eat more than one doughnut.

Roger and Bonnie got married, moved to the suburbs, and had four kids. Everybody goes to their house for the holidays.

Diana got engaged twice more and broke off both engagements, crying in Tony's arms each time. He told her she had lousy taste in men and to try picking a good one next time, so she proposed to him. He said no, appalled. Six weeks later they eloped to Kentucky because Tony had tickets for the Derby. They have three kids, all big-boned, beautiful girls who dominate whatever field or court they play on, probably because they eat carbs.

Liza continues to have an exciting, varied, constantly changing life that is much too complicated to synopsize here.

Cal bought Min an engagement ring made of six perfect diamonds set in a circle. It looks nothing like a Krispy Kreme, but Min knows. They got married and bought an Arts and Crafts bungalow one block from Min's apartment. It has thirty-seven steps up from the street. They also bought a mission couch like Bonnie's, and occasionally somebody gets tied to it. They go to the If Dinner at Emilio's every Thursday night with Roger and Bonnie and Tony and Diana and Liza and whomever Liza's seeing that week. His mother tolerates her. Her mother adores him. They don't have kids, but they did get a black lab mix puppy from the pound that they named The Beast. Elvis is coping.

They all lived happily ever after.

228